I0639237

EMBRACING
THE LIFE

RACHAEL C. DUNCAN

Embracing the Life
by Rachael C. Duncan

Copyright © 2023 Rachael C. Duncan

Paperback Edition

All rights reserved. No part of this book may be reproduced by any means without the prior written consent of the publisher, other than brief quotes for reviews.

This book is a work of fiction. Any references to historical events, real people or real places are used fictitiously. Other names, characters, places and events are products of the author's imagination, and any resemblance to actual events, places or persons, living or dead, is entirely coincidental.

Published in the United States by Wolfpack Publishing, Las Vegas

CKN Christian Publishing
An Imprint of Wolfpack Publishing
9850 S. Maryland Parkway, Suite A-5 #323
Las Vegas, Nevada 89183

cknchristianpublishing.com

Paperback ISBN: 978-1-63977-465-4
eBook ISBN: 978-1-63977-464-7
LCCN: 2023943572

NOTE FROM THE AUTHOR

When I began researching for my first novel, I was blown away by the vast array of resources available concerning anything and everything biblical! It was thrilling to discover such a wealth of information regarding topics that have always intrigued me.

Because I write Bible-based novels, please allow me to state this simple disclaimer: The novels I write are categorized as biblical fiction, which means I have taken some literary license in instances where the Bible story itself remains silent, unclear, or disputed. As you can imagine, there's a LOT of controversy and differing opinions regarding certain biblical characters, settings, dates, etc. As we dive into the book of Acts in the *Crowning Crescendo: A New Era*, exact dates pertaining to certain events remain unclear, disputed, or unknown. I've also encountered tricky questions such as, *How do we know if every story in Acts is listed in chronological order?* Especially as the narrative passes back and forth between multiple characters and settings, these questions tend to surface. So just a reminder, while based on the biblical narratives, this is indeed a work of fiction.

So as I tackled this exciting new project, I sought to honor the Word of God and then I asked the Lord to help me fill in the blanks in a way that will reach my readers, touch their hearts, draw them closer to Him, and bring these beautiful Bible stories to life, inspiring each reader to dive headfirst into the precious Word of God!

Thank you for purchasing this novel. I hope you are blessed page after page!

EMBRACING
THE LIFE

CHAPTER 1

Adorina

Circa A.D. 35, Sychar

Silver moonlight slanted across an ancient stone court framed by sturdy walls, now shining like a glistening celestial city, bathed in the ethereal light of a storybook moon. Sheltered beneath an impressive stone arch, a tall bronze gate cast an imposing shadow across the span of the modest outer court draped in vibrant canopies fluttering and flapping smartly in the brisk and balmy predawn breeze.

Gently washed in the moon's soft glow, the court adjoining an unassuming stone house located near Sychar's main—and *only*—large thoroughfare posed a rather picturesque display, with fresh spring flowers spilling over graceful Grecian urns, elegant trellises boasting cascading emerald vines studded with colorful blossoms, and festive garlands of rich greenery and fragrant blooms gracing the formidable stone walls. Set within an arched niche chiseled in the central wall was a large, pot-bellied stone jar appearing somewhat out of place, its surface marred and stained from years—possibly even decades—of daily use. The simple, retired vessel now boasted a lovely arrangement of fresh flowers, the delicate leaves and petals fluttering in the wind.

Nearly prostrate on the ground, a trim, simply dressed young woman knelt reverently, her smooth forehead pressed against the cool flagstones, her lips moving in fervent, silent prayer. With tears streaming down her face, the woman presented her persistent request before the Throne Room of Heaven.

In *spirit and truth, in spirit and truth,* was the constant refrain pounding through her troubled mind. Surely, her desperate plea had reached the Father in Heaven, for it no longer mattered if one worshiped upon the illustrious and noble Mount Gerizim—though once she would have sworn that was the only place fit for worship. Nor did it matter that she—a disreputable Samaritan—was not permitted entrance within the austere golden courts of the magnificent Temple in Jerusalem, proudly heralded as the *holy city.* No, she worshiped the Father in spirit and in truth. Her worship was sincere. Her heart was laid bare before Adonai. She sought the Almighty as He commanded: *In spirit and truth.*

She would continue to do so as long as the great God of Heaven supplied the breath of life.

Even should He remain silent the rest of her days.

I *will not relent,* she thought, rocking back and forth in silent anguish. *I will seek His presence as long as I live.*

"Adorina?"

Lifting her tear-streaked face, Adorina saw the

shadowy form of her husband emerging from the mouth of their darkened house.

"I'm fine, Ephraim."

"Adorina, what keeps you from our bed at this late hour, love?"

"I did not wish to disturb you."

"You thought it not disturbing for your husband to awaken to an empty bed, his wife nowhere to be found?"

Looking away, Adorina held her tongue—a lost art she had somehow managed to grasp in recent years. Not perfectly, of course. She was, after all, a work in progress.

Descending the three stone steps framing the central doorway, Ephraim crossed the outer court, kneeling thoughtfully before his distraught wife. Taking her arms, he steadied her, his dark eyes boring into hers. "What troubles you?"

"Our people are falling away, Ephraim."

"Not *all* of them," he reminded her. Settling upon the cool flagstones, the corner of Ephraim's firm mouth tipped ruefully. He'd best prepare himself for a lengthy discussion.

Who needed sleep, anyway?

"But *most* have lost faith," his wife pointed out, shaking her head in frustration. "How could they forget His instructions so soon?"

Ephraim did not respond. He hadn't the answers, either.

"We need *help*, Ephraim," Adorina declared with great conviction, her quiet voice floating upon the still night air, disrupting the lively dirge of chirping crickets. "We need good, solid teaching and instruction."

"We go to the synagogue every Sabbath. Sometimes even during the week."

"Yes, we go. But no one talks about *Him*."

"Does talking change anything?"

"Yes!" she declared, rising angrily to her feet.

Her husband rose along with her, reaching out to touch her arm. He saw that she was deeply troubled.

"At least if we *talked* about Him, we wouldn't so soon forget Him," Adorina insisted, pulling her pale blue shawl tightly about her shivering frame. "Ephraim, when He was here, this place was *changed*. You remember!"

"I do," Ephraim assured her, tucking a dark, wayward strand behind her ear.

"But so soon, we have fallen away from His teachings. In our apathy, we have slipped into a dangerous state of ignorance and sin."

"Is that why you sought refuge in the garden court tonight? To seek the Lord on behalf of our people?"

"Tonight, and every night," Adorina replied, her dark eyes flashing passionate fire. "Always, I beg the Lord to send help, instruction. How can we walk in the Way of life if we cannot remember Him, His face, His teachings?"

"We can hide His words in our heart," Ephraim reminded her gently.

"But the words we have are few," she sighed, reluctantly allowing her husband to gather her in his strong arms. "He only stayed with us for two days, Ephraim. How much can one truly learn in two brief days?"

"Much can transpire in two days," Ephraim teased her, gazing into her soulful eyes. "In two days, I knew I wanted you for my wife."

Smiling faintly, Adorina did not resist when Ephraim stooped to kiss her lingeringly.

"I am simply concerned, Ephraim," she sighed, pulling away. Her heart ached dully within her chest. "We know Jesus is no longer walking this earth. He returned to Heaven several years ago, and though I rejoice for Him, my heart breaks at His absence. Surely there is *someone* capable of leading us in the Way."

"Persist in your prayers, love." Ephraim smiled, gently cupping her face in his hand. "The Messiah has not abandoned us."

"But our people have abandoned Him."

"*You* haven't. *I* haven't. And there are still some faithful among us."

"Our people are falling away from the truth, confusing the way of righteousness with secular ideology and pagan philosophies."

"Be still, dear one," Ephraim soothed, smiling softly at the woman he loved. Gently lifting her chin, he gestured toward the simple water jug on display, tucked safely within its graceful stone niche. "The Messiah found you long before you knew we needed Him. Why, then, would He forsake us now?"

***

Mary

Jerusalem

It wasn't wise, traveling alone after dark.

Hastening her steps, Mary balanced a large basket, now empty, upon her forearm as she traveled a fashionably paved avenue lined with graceful stone colonnades and towering palms. By God's grace, she had navigated the confusing maze of cobbled streets in the less reputable precinct of Jerusalem's Lower City before darkness had fully settled. Now, as she crossed the final span of the prestigious Upper City housing Jerusalem's many elite, Mary thanked God for the smoldering torches mounted upon the colonnaded walls, faintly lighting her path.

She should have reached her opulent Upper City villa long before dark, having left much earlier that afternoon to deliver provisions to incarcerated believers housed in the wretched common prison. But the prison guards were making it increasingly difficult for well-meaning friends and relatives to meet the needs of their imprisoned loved ones—undoubtedly by order of the Great Sanhedrin.

Mary's sharp, slender brows drew together in displeasure. If the guards continued to impede the believers' ability to provide nourishment for their brethren, they would surely perish by starvation.

But that's the idea, isn't it? Mary thought, peeved. She resolved she wouldn't let that happen—even if she was forced to stand for hours in a stale, squalid chamber beneath the leering stares of boorish guards spouting crude obscenities. Eventually, she had been permitted to see her imprisoned brethren—after several uncomfortable hours of waiting. Undoubtedly, the guards had expected her to lose patience and abandon her mission.

Well, now they know better! Mary absolutely refused to be intimidated or cowed by wicked, self-serving men. Undoubtedly, their tormentors hoped a dangerous trek through the city, after dark, would deter her from another visit.

T*hey'd best think again!* Soon, she would be back—with armed reinforcement, if necessary. She knew any one of her well-trained guards would willingly accompany her to the foul prison.

Sighing in dismay, Mary's steps slowed just a bit as the grand, multi-storied villas of the most luxurious neighborhood in Jerusalem towered into view, washed in the soft golden glow of steadily burning torchlight. How many years had passed since she had traveled these elegantly paved streets, arm-in-arm with her departed husband, Mark? How she missed his quiet strength, his reassuring presence.

The prison guards wouldn't have dared to defy her beloved Mark, one of the wealthiest businessmen of Judea. She thanked God that Mark's diligence in life had provided financial stability and security for her and their son, John Mark, even after his sudden death. Now that she oversaw his operations, she, too, had become untouchable. Her previous informant, Alexander, had dubbed her unlikely position akin to something like diplomatic immunity.

Clearly, the religious leaders feared her power and influence, though they would never admit it. Not to mention the fact that Temple operations— the very lifeblood of the ancient city—depended upon her flourishing grove of Gethsemane for the production of ritual oil. True, the religious leaders could arrange for the guards to make her prison visits utterly miserable. They could do everything in their power to test her grit and try her patience. But they wouldn't dare deny her rights.

If only her fellow brethren were so highly regarded.

In recent weeks, the wave of persecution against them had only intensified, picking up speed and gaining momentum. The young Pharisee, Saul of Tarsus, raged against the church of God with bitter vengeance. Only last week, three more believers were arrested, "tried" before the Sanhedrin, condemned, and swiftly put to death. Their offense? Blasphemy against the Law of Moses and the Temple of God.

Shaking her head in dismay, Mary soothed her rising fury, dismissing the temptation to harbor thoughts of vengeance. Should she allow herself that luxury, she would simply fall into the same deceptive trap as her persecutors, kicking a door wide open for the enemy of her soul, granting him entrance into her life.

No, vengeance belonged to the Lord. The great day of fiery judgment would surely dawn. And in that fearsome moment, *every* knee would bow and *every* tongue confess that Jesus Christ *is* indeed Lord—even the capricious men comprising the Great Sanhedrin. Even the malefic high priest.

Even the raging, incorrigible Saul of Tarsus.

Lost in brooding thought, Mary was caught off guard when a dark, looming shadow slanted across her elegant form. Her heart pounded furiously in her chest as an unfamiliar man stepped out of the shadows, emerging from the wide, arched mouth of a nearby colonnade like a darkened corpse arising from its tomb.

"Pardon me," Mary said coolly, attempting to veer around the imposing stranger. She didn't wish to betray her mounting fear.

The young man planted sandaled feet firmly in

her path, blocking her way, his piercing gaze making a clear statement: *You're not going anywhere.*

Attempting to steady her galloping heart, Mary paused, allowing herself a brief perusal of this unexpected offender. He was young, with a fastidiously kept beard and serious dark eyes. The fact that he donned a billowing head covering and plain, inconspicuous garments told her he didn't wish to be recognized by others. Even so, despite their simplicity, the quality of his sandals, clothing, and neatly embroidered belt hinted at wealth and prestige.

"May I help you, sir?" Mary dared, raising her eyes in challenge.

"I am Agabus." The young man shifted a bit uncomfortably, indicating he was ill at ease. "I must have a word with you."

Though wary, Mary was intrigued. "Did you follow me from the common prison?"

"I have awaited the opportunity to speak with you privately."

Mary waited, noting his rigid posture and the way his dark eyes shifted nervously back and forth.

W*hy, this man is more afraid of me than I am of him!* she thought, appalled. Sensing an unexpected opportunity, Mary began to pray.

"You are a Pharisee," she observed.

"How did you know?" Agabus asked, blinking in surprise. "Have you seen me about the Temple or perhaps at the Synagogue of the Freedmen?"

"Not that I can recall," Mary responded honestly, though she doubted she would remember him even if she had. There was nothing remarkable about his appearance or persona, nothing to set him apart from the rest. "It was your proud stance and bearing

that gave you away. A Pharisee needn't don traditional robes to announce his position."

Agabus appeared to be processing that unwelcome bit of information when Mary spoke again.

"What is it you seek, Agabus? It must be urgent
to risk being spotted in conversation with me—a
heretic woman, in the eyes of your associates."

"I seek answers. The truth, if you will." The Pharisee shifted again, even more noticeably this time.

Mary waited, intrigued.

"I've been having dreams," Agabus admitted,
pressing his hands together nervously. "They began
the night your evangelist was stoned."

"Our beloved Stephanos," Mary supplied, a dull
ache grasping her heart. Though she rejoiced in his
victory, Stephanos' glaring absence remained a keen
reminder of the church's inexplicable loss. "Did you
know him?"

"Not well," Agabus admitted, his voice low. "I was
baffled by his teachings. His arguments could not be
refuted. That troubles me."

"I see."

"I met his widow the day he died," Agabus confessed, his eyes haunted.

"Tabitha?" Mary asked, surprised. Her former
maidservant hadn't mentioned this brooding Pharisee.

"She found me in the synagogue. She was so distraught, so desperate to save him. But it was too late,"
Agabus sighed, shaking his head in disillusionment.
"I daresay, that moment remains forever etched in
my mind."

"We lost a noble man that day," Mary said frankly. "But our blessed Lord and Savior, Jesus Christ,

ushered Stephanos into His kingdom with open arms. What more could we possibly ask for our dear brother?"

"Ah, yes. That," Agabus conceded, his dark eyes flickering in confusion...and fear. "*Look! I see the heavens opened and the Son of Man standing at the right hand of God,*" he quoted, deeply disturbed.

"You saw it? You were there?"

"I remained at the synagogue when they dragged him out, refusing to participate in his grisly death. But my colleagues told me about the evangelist's shocking proclamation—and the way the entire meeting hall resounded with a mighty wind—an invisible shock wave, of sorts—the moment he cried out."

"Surely your colleagues recognize they witnessed the power of God that day," Mary prodded, her gray eyes intense.

"Some do, but others question the entire experience—along with their sanity."

"And you?" Mary pressed.

"I'm...wrestling," he finally admitted.

"I see."

"My soul is inexplicably troubled," Agabus confessed, his darting eyes betraying his deep distress. "I am haunted by memories I long to forget—such as the night your Rabbi was tried before the Sanhedrin."

Mary's slender brows rose in surprise.

"I was there, you see," Agabus admitted, anxiously wringing his hands. "The high priest asked the Teacher, '*Are you the Christ, the Son of the Blessed?*' And Jesus said, '*I am. And you will see the Son of Man sitting at the right hand of the Power, and coming on the clouds of heaven."*

"That's right." Mary offered a firm nod, sensing the Pharisee's anxiety and deep inner struggle. "But why do such words trouble you?"

"Because your evangelist wasn't there the night your Man was tried. And yet..." Agabus' voice trailed off as he struggled to compose himself and organize his thoughts. "The evangelist—Stephanos, yes?—he really saw Him, didn't he?" Agabus' countenance betrayed deep hopelessness mingled with traces of awe. "He saw your crucified Rabbi—*alive*—and standing at the right hand of God. Just as your Christ predicted. Just as your Teacher prophesied would happen!"

"Yes," Mary affirmed. "He did."

"And this is why I cannot stand idly by while the followers of your Rabbi are hunted down like mere animals," Agabus confided, the sweat upon his brow betraying his gnawing fear. "To do so would place me in danger of judgment."

Mary's brows rose in surprise as the pieces began falling into place in her mind. "You are the one responsible for freeing Alexander from prison," she declared, stunned by the revelation. She studied the nervous young Pharisee with new respect.

"Should word get out, I may very well pay with my life." Agabus' eyes shifted nervously. "I do hope he found a safe respite."

Smiling faintly, Mary considered the fearless Alexander and his bold young wife, Mara. By God's grace, the couple had escaped to his native Tiberias, now actively engaged in reaching his five brothers with the truth of the gospel message.

Oh, how she longed for those early days, when

the believers had gathered together in peace and safety, delighting in the presence of God and the fellowship of each other! Now, few remained in the hostile city. Her dear Tabitha had recently departed with her young daughter, Laurel, on an important mission. Philip and Kelila were bound for Samaria. And Simon and Candace, along with their young boys, Rufus and Alexander, had boarded a ship for Cyrene, intending to present the gospel to their respective families.

At least Simon and Candace planned to return to Jerusalem after a brief stint in their homeland. Mary's heart ached at the absence of so many loved ones, especially her beloved maidservant, Tabitha. When would she see them again?

"I'm sure you can see why I hesitate to embrace this...this doctrine, this truth, that has endangered the lives of its adherents," Agabus was saying, drawing Mary's thoughts back to the present moment.

Lifting serious gray eyes, she met his anxious gaze, her own mesmerizing in the orange glow of flaming torchlight. "Why do you resist the truth, Agabus?"

The Pharisee threw up his hands in defeat. "Surely you know. How can I forfeit my family, my position, my colleagues, my reputation, possibly even my *life*? I have dedicated my entire existence to this calling. As you can see, I have much to lose."

"But so much more to gain." Eyes kindling with fervency, the intensity of Mary's gaze pinned the reluctant young Pharisee in place. "You have found the Way, Agabus. And after much seeking, you have indeed discovered the truth. And now I must beseech you—don't be afraid to embrace this new life, this new calling."

Agabus lowered his gaze, his sagging shoulders and defeated posture betraying the intensity of his struggle.

"You speak of temporal, earthly things," Mary reminded him, her tone gentling in sympathy. "But the truth is this, dear brother—at this decisive moment in history, you have everything to gain. And truly nothing—absolutely nothing—to lose. Nothing of lasting value, that is."

Slipping past Agabus without another word, Mary left the anxious Pharisee standing alone in the gathering darkness, wrestling against his mounting convictions.

CHAPTER 2

Tabitha

Joppa

Standing before an imposing set of ornamental double doors overlaid in shimmering gold, Tabitha repositioned her tired, two-year-old daughter on her hip, breathing a quiet prayer.

The journey to Joppa had proven rigorous and exhausting, especially with a petulant toddler in tow. During the lengthy trip from Jerusalem to Joppa, the shy child had eventually found her voice—to Tabitha's endless delight...and angst. The toddler's favorite word was *no*, which she exercised with maddening regularity.

Glancing over her shoulder, Tabitha saw two armed guards just beyond the outer court, watching her with flinty expressions. She was relieved they had permitted her past the elaborate iron gate, though she wondered if they had taken bets about whether she would be received within the opulent seaside manor.

Drawing a slow, steadying breath, Tabitha reached forth, gingerly grasping the heavy golden knocker and giving it several solid raps. Stepping back, she waited nervously, clinging to little Laurel for emotional support.

After a momentary pause, the doors were opened by a well-dressed servant sporting a bright turban, a tidy beard, and an impatient expression.

"Good afternoon," Tabitha managed cheerfully, her tone nearly as bright as the golden sunshine streaming down on them.

Observing her travel-worn garments and the protesting child on her hip, the servant appeared singularly unimpressed. "The master does not offer charity," he said tersely. "However, if you are in need of assistance, there is a synagogue located just down the—"

"Oh, I haven't come seeking charity," Tabitha hastily explained, instantly self-conscious. Why, she had just been mistaken for a hapless beggar woman! After many days of hard travel, she must look even worse than she suspected.

"No?" the servant replied, arching a brow in question.

"No," Tabitha insisted, bouncing Laurel on her hip when the little one began to whimper. "I seek an audience with your master, Joram."

"Oh?" the servant studied her, his expression less than encouraging. "And is he expecting you?"

"I do hope so." Tabitha chuckled brightly. "I sent word ahead of my arrival."

The servant blinked at her in surprise. "*You* are the master's niece?"

"Indeed," Tabitha affirmed, hoping she appeared far more confident than she felt.

"I see." Clearly attempting to mask his surprise, the servant turned on his heel. "One moment, please," he said curtly, promptly closing the door behind him.

Surprised, Tabitha stared at the impenetrable gilded doors. The servant hadn't even invited her to wait in the reception hall!

Oh, dear Lord, this doesn't seem to be going well.

Sensing her mother's steadily mounting angst, Laurel's quiet whimpering increased.

"Hush, little one," Tabitha soothed, stroking her daughter's back. "Everything will be just fine," she added, reminding herself as well as the child.

While awaiting the condescending servant's return, Tabitha allowed herself a moment to observe the grandiose surroundings, wondering about the aloof relative residing within this resplendent seaside mansion. The sprawling outer court in which she stood was truly an impressive affair, with exotic spring blossoms and curling ivy tendrils gracing the towering stone walls encircling the massive estate. Underfoot, smooth white stones shone in the early morning sunlight. The stonework was impeccable and complex, with intricate carvings framing the giant arch gracing the iron gate. Just beyond the massive, gated entrance, proud, graceful palms unlike any Tabitha had ever seen towered into a crystal blue sky, lining the broad thoroughfare on either side. Overhead, a snowy white sea gull swooped into view, releasing a gusty cry.

Within moments of her arrival, Tabitha had decided that Joppa, meaning *beauty*, was aptly named.

The quaint seaport town afforded a wealth of exotic sights, sounds, and smells, bursting with vibrant color and far exceeding her expectations. Hedged by verdant greenery and flowering gardens, the city appeared rather like the fanciful setting of a child's tale. Perched upon a towering cliff overlooking the vast, deep blue Mediterranean, Tabitha could only imagine the splendor of a golden sunrise splashed across the wide-open sky, its breathtaking reflection shimmering upon the boundless sea. Accustomed to the austere white marbled and red-roofed structures of Jerusalem, she was nearly mesmerized by the raw, natural beauty of her surroundings.

Breathing deeply of the salty air, Tabitha smiled faintly. Wouldn't Laurel love exploring the white sandy beaches of the magnificent Great Sea, stretching forth like an endless, glittering azure canopy just beyond the imposing city walls! Even at this distance, Tabitha was certain she could hear the churning waves beating against a rocky cliff face.

Suddenly, the double doors burst open with the force of a battering ram, shattering Tabitha's blissful reverie. Startled, Laurel burst into hysterical tears, clinging to her mother's garment like a lifeline.

Surprised, Tabitha found herself face to face with a scowling, gray-haired man wearing a fine crimson robe embroidered in gold, his silver brows drawn together in disdain, his glowering expression anything but welcoming.

Mustering her bravest smile, Tabitha extended her free hand even as she attempted to console her howling daughter. "*Shalom*, Uncle Joram," she managed, trembling inside at his fearsome, deepening scowl. "I am overjoyed to finally meet!"

"Ah, so now it's *Uncle* Joram, is it?" the older man hissed, his face contorting beneath a neatly shaved layer of gray scruff. Perhaps he had once sported an impressive beard, but Tabitha couldn't be certain. "I don't recall extending an invitation, *Niece*."

Though Tabitha's entire being went cold at Joram's callous response, she forced an understanding smile. "No, but I have long desired to meet with you. I sent word, announcing my departure from—"

"Ah, the letter. Yes, I received it." Her uncle's cold eyes narrowed in disdain as young Laurel wailed inconsolably, frightened by his glowering presence. "You failed to mention having a child."

"Her name is Laurel," Tabitha managed, desperately attempting to calm the wailing little girl.

"Does she always shriek like a devil from Hades?" her uncle inquired with a sardonic lift of his silver brow.

Whispering soothing words into her daughter's ear, Tabitha attempted to swallow her rising offense. After all, her uncle's soul was at stake.

"Some might call it rude and intrusive," Joram continued coldly, "showing up on one's doorstep, uninvited."

Tabitha stared at her uncle in surprise. She certainly hadn't expected this to be easy, but she hadn't anticipated facing blatant animosity, either. Laurel's terror was perfectly understandable, for Joram presented an imposing picture with his harsh manner, deep scowl, and flaming gaze.

"Well?" Joram demanded imperiously.

"I suppose you're right," Tabitha conceded, silently begging the Lord for guidance. "Some might consider this visit intrusive. But we're *family*, are we not?"

"Is that what we are?" Joram drawled, his lips twisting in a sarcastic sneer. "I find it ironic—you showing up here claiming to be *family* the moment your husband dies, leaving you a helpless widow without financial assistance."

Bristling, Tabitha drew upon the patience her Lord provided. "Before my husband passed, he wrote a letter urging me to reach out to our respective families," she explained, her insides churning with hot fury. "I have heeded his counsel, Uncle, because life is fleeting, and I don't wish to live with regrets. Though we are relatives, I know next to nothing about you, and I'd like to remedy that. As for financial support, my employer in Jerusalem compensated me very well. I am not looking for handouts."

"No?" her uncle drawled, leaning indolently against the doorframe. "So you're telling me a life of leisure within a magnificent seaside mansion doesn't appeal to you?"

"Your estate *is* lovely," Tabitha replied evenly. "But, no, a life of leisure has never suited me."

"It's a good thing, that," her uncle responded, his eyes flashing in indignation. "Because you certainly won't be living off *my* back on the estate I've built with my own two hands!" Slamming the door in her face, Joram retreated with a loud sneer.

Stunned to her very core, Tabitha stared, thunderstruck, at the closed double doors while poor Laurel screamed in fright. "Shhh," Tabitha soothed, sorely tempted to follow her daughter's example, bursting into tempestuous tears herself. "It's all right. We're all right."

Adjusting the heavy pack on her back bearing all her worldly possessions—at least, all she had deemed worthy of travel—Tabitha wondered what to do next. Her uncle's stout refusal had been so swift, so *final*. She seriously doubted he would experience a change of heart.

Have I traveled all this way just to be turned away at the door? Tabitha thought, anxious and disheartened. Hadn't the Lord led her here? Had she simply been misguided?

"That didn't go very well, did it?"

Spinning around in surprise, Tabitha followed the sound of a cheerful voice just beyond the iron gate.

From the quiet street beyond the outer court, a bright-eyed woman peered between the two guards still standing at stiff attention at the gate. Ignoring their knowing smirks, Tabitha slipped past them, relieved her daughter seemed to be quieting after their shocking encounter with Joram. Crossing the distance between herself and the pleasant-faced stranger, Tabitha met her on the broad, paved street, offering a weak smile. "You heard all that, then?"

"Most of it," the woman confessed. "Your uncle's an ornery one, he is."

"Do you know him?"

"As well as anyone else around here, I suppose," the woman admitted, her lips tipping in a knowing smile. "As I'm sure you've noticed, he doesn't let people get particularly close to him."

Not that they'd have any desire to do so, Tabitha thought rather snidely. The nasty man was completely incorrigible!

"Come," the kindly woman offered, leading

Tabitha off the main thoroughfare and up a stone ledge to a picturesque cobblestoned way hugging the street. Tendrils of ivy spilled over the high wall framing the narrow way. "You are Joram's niece?" she inquired, her eyes twinkling with interest.

"Yes," Tabitha replied, instantly drawn to the helpful, inquisitive woman. "My name is Tabitha, and this is my daughter, Laurel."

"What a beautiful child," the woman smiled, pinching Laurel's rosy cheek. Grinning shyly, the little girl buried her face in her mother's neck. "I am Tirzah."

"Tirzah," Tabitha repeated, warmed by the woman's unexpected kindness. "A lovely name."

"My mother always said I was named after the woman bold enough to persist after her inheritance and receive it," Tirzah replied with an airy smile, resuming their stroll along the cobbled way.

"Ah, the daughter of Zelophehad," Tabitha supplied. "Though their father died without a male heir, Moses heeded the Lord's command to grant his daughters an inheritance."

"That's the tale," Tirzah confirmed, strolling along in a breezy manner.

"So have you?" Tabitha dared with a mischievous smile.

Tirzah paused, lifting a dark brow in question. "Have I what?"

"Persisted after your inheritance and received it?" Tabitha grinned.

Tirzah smiled faintly, though her hazel-colored eyes flickered with a hint of sadness. "I have clothes on my back, a roof over my head, and food on my table. What more do I need?"

Tabitha smiled her understanding, admiring Tirzah's gratitude and inner strength. Hoisting her daughter a bit higher up on her hip, she was beginning to feel like a beast of burden beneath the weight of her heavy traveling pack—not to mention the two-year-old joined at her hip. She was glad Laurel's attention had been captured by the picturesque avenues bustling with various citizens, both Jews and Gentiles, rich and poor, slave and free—even occasional Roman soldiers sporting flowing crimson robes and impressively plumed helmets. Women toting water jugs chattered pleasantly in the breezy sunshine, mindful of the lumbering ox-drawn carts clattering down the stone-paved way, bearing all manner of heavy loads. Seagulls swooped majestically across the pale blue sky, while smaller, more delicate birds perched upon flowering branches, chirping blithe, sunny tunes.

Tabitha marveled at the beauty surrounding them. She was quite certain Laurel would love living here—that is, *if* her uncle permitted them to stay.

"You are a brave woman to face the meanest old miser in Joppa," Tirzah remarked, skillfully averting the conversation from her own plight. Pausing along the meandering way, she offered Tabitha a wry smile as they crested a gentle slope. "From whence have you come?"

"All the way from Jerusalem."

"Surely you didn't travel all that way alone?"

"I sojourned with friends, also going their respective ways," Tabitha explained, thankful her arduous trek upon the northwestern road from Jerusalem to Joppa had ended. "My brothers and sisters accompanied me as far as the city gates, and though they offered to escort me to Joram's estate—"

"You feared inciting his wrath by bringing a delegation to his doorstep," Tirzah chuckled in understanding.

"Exactly."

"How many siblings do you have?"

"None, actually. My parents died when I was very young."

"My deepest sympathies regarding your loss," Tirzah said sincerely. "Forgive me, but didn't you say your *brothers and sisters* wished to accompany you?"

"Ah, yes," Tabitha laughed, understanding Tirzah's confusion. "That's what fellow believers call themselves in Jerusalem."

"Fellow believers?" Tirzah repeated blankly. "Fellow believers in *what?*"

Tabitha realized she had a great deal of explaining to do. In Jerusalem, word about the rapidly growing church had spread like wildfire. But here in Joppa, where very few—if *any* at all—bore the banner of Christ, the gospel must be carefully, patiently presented. Suddenly feeling terribly inadequate, Tabitha wondered if she was qualified to explain the Good News in a place where Christ's mission remained largely unknown. She was still mulling over this shocking discovery when Tirzah interrupted her clouded thoughts, momentarily sparing her the daunting task of evangelism.

"Have you ever seen anything quite like it?"

Distracted, Tabitha followed Tirzah's gaze and instantly drew a sharp intake of breath, for before them stretched the most spectacular view she had ever seen—the dazzling Mediterranean Sea glittering in the morning sunlight, clearly visible above the towering stone walls. The clear blue waters appeared to encompass the very ends of the earth.

"What a sight!" Tabitha breathed, pointing toward the vast sea before them so Laurel, too, could delight in the breathtaking scene.

"The best," Tirzah agreed, smiling fondly. "I've lived here all my life and couldn't imagine putting down roots anywhere else."

Smiling her acknowledgment, Tabitha decided that Tirzah belonged in this idyllic setting. Despite her drab and simple dress, her face and form were arresting. Rich brown hair and side-swept bangs peeked out beneath her worn head covering, framing a feminine face with high cheekbones and a firm but lovely jawline. Large, hazel eyes conveyed her perception and intelligence, while a ready smile betrayed a hint of both amusement and dry humor. Though Tabitha could only guess at Tirzah's age, she presumed her to be in her mid-thirties, perhaps even a bit older. If so, she had aged gently, gracefully.

"You needn't fret, Tabitha," Tirzah was saying, shaking Tabitha from her silent speculation. "Your uncle's growl is far worse than his bite. I believe he will come around."

Tabitha's deep frown betrayed her skepticism. Even little Laurel stared at the woman with wide brown eyes, though Tabitha doubted the small child fully followed their conversation.

"I have known your uncle my entire life," Tirzah told her, smiling wanly as brisk sea breezes tugged at her threadbare shawl. "Not well, mind you. But well enough to know his pride won't allow him to turn away his own kin, sparking rumors throughout the village about how he refused to receive a poor, widowed niece."

"But the servant minding the door said Joram refuses to offer charity—"

"To beggars and the likes of such, yes," Tirzah replied knowingly. "But I have a feeling this will be different. As cold and heartless as that man seems, I believe his heart craves acceptance and companionship—though he'd die before admitting it, even to himself."

Tabitha studied the perceptive woman before her with deep respect. Somehow, her unlikely observation rang true.

"Simply allow your uncle time to brood and stew in that big, empty house of his," Tirzah suggested, a rueful smile teasing her lips. "See if my words prove true. And, in the meantime, I shall serve you and your daughter a meal. You must be famished, and my house isn't far from here."

"That would be absolutely wonderful." Blinking back tears, Tabitha was moved by Tirzah's undeserved kindness. "Thank you, my friend. You are an answer to prayer."

"I haven't much to offer by way of refreshments, and my little house is nothing like your uncle's seaside manor, I assure you," Tirzah grinned. "You may soon find yourself retracting that lofty statement!"

Fighting back warm tears of gratitude, Tabitha praised her merciful Father for His tender provision.

CHAPTER 3

Tabitha

Joppa

"So, this is home," Tirzah announced, pushing open a weathered front door that protested loudly upon ancient-looking hinges. "It's not much, but it's a roof over my head and provides relief from the elements."

"It reminds me very much of the house I shared with my husband in Jerusalem," Tabitha said warmly, depositing her heavy pack by the door and crossing the narrow threshold with a sleepy Laurel in tow. Despite the obvious age of the weathered stone dwelling, both the interior and exterior were immaculately clean and fastidiously organized. Tabitha decided Tirzah must be an impeccable housekeeper.

"Please, let me wash your feet, and your daughter's, as well," Tirzah offered, rolling up fitted sleeves and reaching for the cloth draped over a stone basin.

"Please, allow me," Tabitha insisted, unwilling to

ask her hostess to perform a slave's task. Tirzah had already done so much for them.

Removing her daughter's sandals and her own, Tabitha took the cloth, swished it about the basin, and gently wiped the road dust from her daughter's small feet. After quickly cleansing her own, Tabitha swished the cloth in the basin, wringing out the excess water in a separate bucket designated for dirty water.

After washing her own feet, Tirzah set about readying the house for guests.

Smiling, Tabitha watched as her cheerful hostess busily threw open shuttered windows, allowing the sunlight to spill into the small house and revealing a tidy cook space boasting a large stone kiln, neatly organized wooden shelves stacked with dry goods, and a low wooden table bearing baskets of fresh produce and a single oil lamp. A worn, faded curtain hung from a wooden rod at the far end of the house, sectioning off another small room, quite reminiscent of the simple, makeshift bedchamber Tabitha had shared with Stephanos. With a sharp little pang, she braced herself against the flood of poignant memories invoked by the familiar scene.

"Please, be seated," Tirzah offered graciously, gesturing toward the faded cushions scattered near the low table. "Make yourselves comfortable. You must be exhausted having traveled such a long way."

"Thank you, Tirzah," Tabitha said with great feeling. "Truly, your kindness is overwhelming."

"Nonsense," Tirzah declared stoutly, dismissing Tabitha's praise with a wave of her hand. "This is what neighbors do for one another."

If only my uncle had proven so hospitable! Tabitha

thought, bemused. Helping Laurel get situated on a comfortable cushion, her observant gaze swept the unfamiliar surroundings. Though sparsely furnished, the modest home was cozy and inviting. Tabitha was especially intrigued by the old potter's wheel set up in the far corner near an open window. Stone shelves hewn into the walls above the wheel boasted an impressive array of simple, handcrafted pottery, along with several empty rows for drying new pieces. A threadbare apron stained with clay hung upon a peg near the shelves above several stone jars, some filled with white sand, others brimming with fresh water.

"Ah, I see you've noticed my workstation," Tirzah observed wryly, arranging dried, salted fish on a clay platter. "My father was a potter. He died when I was about your daughter's age, but not before teaching my mother the tools of the trade. She, in turn, taught me the craft."

"This is the first I've heard of a lady potter," Tabitha breathed, her tone and expression revealing her admiration. "You must do fine work!"

"Well, fine enough to scratch out a living," Tirzah conceded dryly, adding several flat loaves of unleavened bread to the large platter before carrying it over to the low, wooden table. Ladling fresh water into several clay mugs, Tirzah placed one before each of her guests before joining them, settling onto a mat on the opposite side of the table.

Stomach rumbling at the welcome sight and tantalizing aroma of fresh food, Tabitha wondered if she should wait for her hostess to bless the meal or silently pray over it herself. Tabitha assumed that Tirzah was, indeed, a God-fearing Jewess, for upon entering the house, she had reverently touched the *mezuzah* fastened to her doorpost, afterward raising delicate fingertips to her lips in the customary manner.

Tabitha's heart sprang to her throat in sudden realization. Perhaps Tirzah would be receptive to the gospel, even if her uncle would not!

Her harried thoughts halted abruptly when Tirzah lifted a thin, round loaf of unleavened bread, offering the traditional Jewish prayer of thanksgiving and blessing over the meal. "Blessed are You, Lord our God, King of the Universe, who brings forth bread from the earth."

"Amen," Tabitha affirmed, accepting the barley bread her hostess offered her, relieved that Tirzah had joined her in thanksgiving for God's provision. Breaking the bread into smaller pieces, Tabitha somehow resisted her own gnawing hunger, offering the bite-sized pieces to her daughter before partaking of any herself.

"Are you religious, Tabitha?" Tirzah asked directly, catching Tabitha off guard.

"Actually, yes," she replied honestly, appreciative of her hostess's forthright manner. "In Jerusalem, I was raised in a devout Jewish home. When my father and mother died, a gracious Jewish couple from Cyprus took me in." Heart aching just a bit at the thought of her beloved mistress, Tabitha lowered her gaze. So much had changed since those early days when Jesus first returned to His Father in Heaven. She could hardly remember a time when the believers had gathered without fear of reprisal. Since then, so many—herself included—had departed the holy city, dutifully introducing the gospel to new lands. And though Tabitha knew the Lord's great commission was being carried out, the heavy cost often stole her breath away.

"And you?" Tabitha managed, quickly regaining her composure. "I couldn't help but notice the lovely mezuzah on the doorpost."

"Ah, yes," Tirzah nodded, tearing a piece of bread and thoughtfully popping it in her mouth. "My parents lived to please Adonai. After my father died, it was my mother's great faith that kept us afloat."

"She sounds like a remarkable woman," Tabitha observed, offering Laurel a small piece of fish.

"She was," Tirzah said, her tone boding no argument. "She taught me everything I know. I miss her every day."

"I'm so sorry for your loss." Tabitha's heart welled with sympathy, for she sensed Tirzah's great pain despite her cheery and stalwart persona.

With a brittle smile, Tirzah reached for another piece of fish.

Sensing her hostess didn't wish to expound upon the present subject, Tabitha changed course. "Have you a husband, Tirzah?"

"I did, once," Tirzah replied, clearly grateful to change the subject. "He was a sailor, like so many of the men around these parts. He died at sea many years ago."

"Oh, Tirzah," Tabitha sighed, instantly regretting her inquiry, "I'm so sorry."

Brushing aside her sympathy, Tirzah helped herself to another bite of fish. Tabitha couldn't help but notice the widow's reaction regarding her husband's demise lacked the raw grief of her mother's passing. "Trust me, I'm not the only widow of a sailor around here. There are hordes of us, I'm afraid."

Tabitha stared at the lovely widow in surprise.

"This is a seaport town, after all. And though beautiful enough to steal one's breath away, the sea can be a cruel master, caring little about who suffers at its hand," Tirzah murmured, her gaze distant and enigmatic as haunting memories danced through her mind. "Some *people* are like that, too," she added cryptically, "like the sea. Beautiful and alluring at first glance, though their deepest depths harbor dangers unlike anything one can possibly fathom."

Strangely unsettled, Tabitha drew Laurel just a bit closer. She couldn't help but wonder at Tirzah's hidden scars. Perhaps one day, the courageous widow would trust her enough to share her story, her heart.

"But enough of that," Tirzah quipped, dismissing the disturbing subject with an impatient wave of her hand. "You, too, have lost father, mother, husband. You know what it's like."

Nodding slowly in acknowledgment, Tabitha couldn't help but wonder if perhaps Tirzah had suffered a far more bitter cup than she.

"But if we widows squandered our days lamenting our fate, we'd all perish of starvation or simply drown in our own misery and self-pity," Tirzah added in her practical way. "And believe me when I say self-pity proves a far more dangerous force than the brutal waves claiming the lives of our men."

Rap, rap, rap!

Both women were taken by surprise at the unexpected eruption of sound as someone persistently—and impatiently—pounded on the front door. Exchanging looks of surprise and confusion, the two widows rose from the table.

Tabitha bent to retrieve her young daughter as Tirzah went for the door, her resolute stance indicating she would accept no nonsense from the dogged visitor, whoever it was. Amused, Tabitha smiled faintly as she cradled her sleepy daughter close to her heart.

Swinging open the door, Tirzah placed a hand on her hip, striking a somewhat patronizing pose as her knowing gaze swept over the disgruntled caller. "Well, Eli, what a pleasant surprise," she grinned with a playful tilt of her head. "To what do I owe the pleasure?"

"Ah, well, I am in search of—"

Fascinated, Tabitha drew behind Tirzah to gain a better glimpse of the unwanted intruder. There, upon the threshold, stood a red-faced Eli, the stiff overseer of Joram's impressive estate.

"Just look who it is, Tabitha," Tirzah teased, relishing the servant's discomfort. "Have you come all this way just to visit me, Eli?"

Clearing his throat uncomfortably, the servant's face reddened beneath his impressive turban. "The master has sent me to retrieve his niece, and he commanded me to say..." Eli's voice trailed off as his color deepened.

"Go on," Tirzah grinned, amused. "What deep, dark threat were you commanded to impart?"

"The master says you had no right to whisk away his niece, nor does he expect any argument from you, Tirzah, when I collect her and escort her to his estate," Eli finished, miffed by her condescension.

"Ah, your master should always expect argument from me," Tirzah replied, her bright eyes dancing with mischief. "As for you, Eli—do you always do as you're told, as Joram commands?"

"He is the master, and I but a servant," Eli supplied, annoyed.

"Ah, a pity, that. Now, why this sudden interest in Joram's niece?" Tirzah pressed, determined to ruffle him just a bit. "As you may recall, she was turned away at the door."

"That is none of your concern," Eli responded haughtily, attempting to mask his terror. Clearly, he feared returning to Joram's estate without his niece in tow.

"Oh, but it is," Tirzah replied, standing staunchly between her new friend and Joram's servant. "You see, Tabitha and her daughter are my guests, and as such, they remain under my protection."

"You needn't concern yourself about their safety," Eli argued, nearing his wit's end. "For heaven's sake, Tirzah, the master demands an audience with them!"

"*Demands?*" Tirzah repeated, a sharp brow arched in question. "Joram is in no position to demand anything from me—nor from Tabitha, for that matter. Contrary to his high opinion, Joram wields no power over us."

"It's all right, Tirzah," Tabitha interrupted, gently touching her arm, for she sensed the poor servant was about to strangle in agitation. "I will go with Eli."

"I told you he'd come groveling," Tirzah grinned, turning toward Tabitha and speaking just loudly enough for Eli to hear.

Wisely, Eli held his peace, though his tight expression betrayed his consternation.

"Thank you, Tirzah, for your gracious hospitality," Tabitha said, meaning every word. "It was an absolute pleasure meeting you, and I hope we can speak again soon."

"You can count on it," Tirzah promised, flashing Eli a triumphant smile.

"Come along now," the servant prodded, clearly anxious to be off. "The master awaits our arrival."

Stepping out the door, Tabitha held her daughter close, silently praying for wisdom, for guidance, and most importantly, for God's will to prevail.

CHAPTER 4

Kelila

Sychar

"I must admit," Kelila huffed, bending to secure a sturdy rope to a tent stake buried deep within the rocky ground, "this isn't quite how I envisioned our first few months of married life."

"No?" Grinning broadly, Kelila's husband, Philip, glanced up from securing a post on the opposite side of the small tent. "And how exactly had you envisioned it, love?"

"Oh, you know," Kelila said airily, straightening to brush the travel dust from her brightly colored tunic, "long, romantic evenings by candlelight, moonlit strolls along elegant avenues, tantalizing suppers shared in the privacy of our own home..."

"Cozying up beneath the stars of Sychar, wrapped snugly in my arms as I smother you in tender, romantic kisses?" Philip teased, coming around the tent to gather his lovely new bride in strong arms.

"Well, when you say it like that..." Kelila grinned as Philip bent to kiss her gently.

Blushing, Kelila pulled away, suddenly remembering the various passers-by traversing the narrow thoroughfare leading into the quaint Samaritan village of Sychar. "Philip! People are watching!"

"Sorry." Grinning, Philip tapped her nose before turning back to their canvas tent. "I couldn't help myself."

Rolling her eyes with dramatic good humor, Kelila knelt to inspect the fragile opening of their small, makeshift shelter. Tabitha had graciously offered to repair the aging canvas before departing for Joppa, expertly stitching multiple rips and mending an especially large tear in one of the front flaps. Thanks to the young widow's willingness and skillful handwork, Kelila and Philip should remain protected from the harsh, unpredictable elements, especially the blustery chill often ascending at nightfall.

"We've almost finished constructing the tent, Philip. What should I do now?" Kelila asked with a hint of boredom, rocking back on her heels and watching with lukewarm interest as her husband expertly adjusted the rough canvas over its wooden frame. She certainly hadn't expected their arrival in Samaria to unfold *this* way.

B*ut what* did *I expect?* Kelila thought testily. *A welcoming party of excited Samaritans desperate for the gospel? A palatial house all our own, with rows of stately marble pillars and a flowering garden, just awaiting our arrival?* Fleetingly, she thought of Tabitha, who was undoubtedly reveling in her rich uncle's posh Mediterranean manor. And she, Kelila, would spend yet another night in this confining traveling tent! Releasing an impatient sigh, she reminded herself that jealousy had no place in the life of a believer.

True, the events of Kelila's young life had unfolded far differently than she could have possibly imagined. It was likely she would spend many more nights in this rough canvas tent, sleeping on the hard ground and sharing her abode with all manner of unwanted, chirping, creeping insects—at least, until Philip obtained or built a house for them in Sychar. But deep in her heart, Kelila knew she wouldn't trade these circumstances for anything in the world, regardless of the momentary discomfort. For by God's grace, she had discovered her purpose in life, and she was determined to embrace it with her entire being. What a thrill to participate in this unrivaled moment in history by taking the gospel unto the ends of the earth, just as their beloved Jesus had instructed!

"How about gathering some sticks for the cook-fire?" Philip suggested in his calm, pleasant manner.

Blinking in confusion, Kelila turned large brown eyes upon her husband. Lost in thought, she had scarcely registered his practical suggestion.

Chuckling, Philip dragged their heavy traveling packs into the tent's narrow opening. "Didn't you ask what you should do next?" he asked, tickled by her blank expression.

"Oh, that's right," Kelila affirmed distractedly. "I did, didn't I?"

"Dusk will soon be upon us," Philip reminded her. "We'd best kindle a fire before dark."

Sighing, Kelila rose slowly, allowing her gaze to sweep across the fertile Samaritan plains, now washed in the magnificent golden glow lingering just before sunset. Where was the best place to search for dry sticks and brush around here, anyway?

Teeming with both pleasant villages and bustling cities, the land of Samaria had proven far unlike Kelila had anticipated. Whereas firewood had been plentiful in Jerusalem and the surrounding areas, in keeping with its unbearably dry desert climate, Samaria had already proven far more temperate, mild, and palatable. Even so, this presented a bit of a problem when dry sticks and brush were required on short notice.

Such commodities were found in abundance in Jerusalem, where everything is dry—including the age-old religion and traditions of its inhabitants, Kelila thought with a hint of a smile. But the culture and climate of this exciting new land drastically contrasted with the stern, ultra-orthodox atmosphere infiltrating the holy city. Nor was Samaria like Kelila's own native Cyrene, teeming with sophisticated philosophers, scholars, and intellectuals. No, this land seemed to present an aura all its own—nestled snugly within the heartland of the Jewish nation, and yet strangely held apart.

Kelila had learned quite a bit about the controversial region's birth and development during the arduous trek from Jerusalem. Philip's passion for world history had resulted in many interesting lessons along the way, as they passed by cultured Samaritan cities and smaller, agricultural villages. Though Kelila considered the subject of history one of the dullest topics known to man, even *she* found herself intrigued by the fanciful tales of ages past, captivated by the tumultuous and often bloody history of the land to which they were called.

Apparently, the mighty patriarch Jacob, by whom the nation of Israel had received its name, purchased land in nearby Shechem, now a thriving city in the Samaritan region. Locals still benefited from the well their ancestor had built, fondly referenced as Jacob's Well. Centuries later, after the nation of Israel had been divided, it was the famed King Omri of the Northern Kingdom who successfully established a desirable parcel of land located about six miles from Shechem as his capital city. Famous for its natural beauty and flourishing agriculture, the capital city, Samaria, boasted fine vineyards, thriving olive groves, and glorious, golden fields of grain. Verdant, terraced hills displaying rich layers of wild olives and lush figs bespoke the region's abundance. It was indeed a land of plenty, and Kelila could see why, in the days of old, ancient kings had coveted the proud city.

After a twelve-year reign, Omri's young son, Ahab, ascended the throne, and thus the grand history of Samaria became ominously darkened. Shortly before constructing a resplendent ivory palace for himself and successive rulers, King Ahab married a wicked Phoenician princess named Jezebel. An ardent worshiper of the fertility god, Baal, and a pantheon of pagan deities, Jezebel ushered in an era of blatant idolatry, besmirching the kingdom's reputation and influencing her subjects to indulge in all manner of unspeakable depravities. While bold, outspoken prophets like Elijah denounced the queen's debauchery, most fell prey to the deceptive, mystical lure of heathen idolatry. Beneath Jezebel's sensual and often hypnotic influence, the nation soon became entrenched in promiscuity and idol worship.

Naturally, Kelila had demanded to know the end of Jezebel's shocking tale. Had the Phoenician princess-turned-queen eventually repented, ruling God's chosen nation with justice and mercy? Or had she perished in her rebellion?

Unfortunately, according to Philip, the arrogant queen had persisted in gross idolatry. When the striking military commander, Jehu, rallied an army to seize the throne, ruthlessly slaughtering Ahab's descendants and destroying the abominable temple of Baal—along with all its heathen priests—Jehu's mission also included the brutal execution of the notorious pagan queen. Flung from a high window, the seductress of many souls was then trampled beneath the powerful hooves of warriors' horses and devoured by wild dogs.

Despite Jezebel's gruesome end, the nation's inhabitants refused to relinquish her pagan practices. Eventually, the Northern Kingdom of Israel, along with its resplendent capital city of Samaria, was conquered by savage Assyrians, just as the prophets tragically foretold.

"And this is why those who consider themselves 'true Judeans' have labeled the Samaritans a 'tainted' race," Philip had explained on their journey. "The Assyrian king colonized the newly conquered nation with Assyrian settlers, who soon intermarried with native Israelites, producing an entirely new race whom the Jews dubbed 'Samaritans.'"

Much to her surprise, Kelila had also learned that it was the Assyrian settlers who had requested priests be sent to Samaria to teach them about the

God of Israel. Thus, strict Judeans argued that the pure religion of their fathers had been polluted by the Samaritans, allegedly infused with pagan practices of foreign conquerors. Despite the Jews' harsh accusations, the Samaritans insisted they had remained true to the faith of their fathers.

And then there was the matter of where to conduct worship. While "true" Judeans considered the Samaritan temple crowning Mount Gerizim a sacrilege, observant Samaritans insisted theirs was the holy mount of God, thumbing their noses at the Jews' austere Temple complex upon Mount Moriah. Ultimately, the increasing hostility between the tenuous people groups erupted in violence when John Hyrcanus, a former Hasmonean high priest of Judea, destroyed the Samaritans' sacred temple. Over one hundred years later, the Samaritans retaliated by defiling the Temple in Jerusalem with dead men's bones.

Even to this day, the Jews and the Samaritans remain sworn enemies, entrenched in bitter rivalry, Kelila thought sadly. In her opinion, the situation was messy at best, impossible at worst. *Philip and I certainly have our work cut out for us,* she thought, her lips tilting in a rueful smile.

"Kelila?"

Snapping her attention back to the present moment, Kelila acknowledged her husband's address with raised eyebrows.

"The firewood?"

"Ah, yes. That." Wrinkling her nose, Kelila resigned herself to the performance of one of her least favorite tasks. "Once I have collected the wood, will you help me kindle the fire, Philip?" She was still a bit squeamish about performing the hazardous chore without assistance.

"You needn't worry about that, love. I will start the fire," Philip assured her, circling the tent for a final inspection.

Relieved, Kelila turned to perform the task at hand.

Wandering rather aimlessly about the grassy plain near camp, Kelila collected dry sticks and tufts of scratchy brush, contemplating the sober mission the Lord had set before them. Despite Philip's thorough history lesson, there was still so much she didn't know about the people to whom they were called. Though regal Samaria had claimed the coveted title of capital city for over one hundred and fifty years—until it was captured by the Assyrians over seven centuries prior—strict Judeans now loathed the very mention of its name. The Samaritans would undoubtedly prove wary and suspicious about the motives of a Judean evangelist and his Cyrenian wife.

The situation between the Jews and Samaritans had only worsened when Herod the Great rebuilt the magnificent city of Samaria, renaming it Sebaste to honor the powerful Roman emperor, Caesar Augustus. Herod's "improvements"—which included a smattering of pagan temples and a shrine dedicated to the emperor in distant Rome—had done little to endear Samaria to the Jewish people. Though Herod the Great was long dead, his thriving city lived on—a political powerhouse second only to Caesarea. Now, the city's title, Samaria or Sebaste, also encompassed the surrounding administrative district, greatly enlarging the city's reach.

Which explains why both the city itself and the surrounding region composed of various cities and villages all bear the name Samaria, Kelila thought, retrieving another spindly stick. Tucking it carefully into the heavy pile resting upon her forearm, Kelila returned to camp, her mind buzzing with questions and possibilities.

In her absence, Philip had hewn several thick logs to serve as benches, placing them near the smooth stones which would soon enclose a warm, crackling fire.

"Isn't this cozy," Kelila teased, dropping the pile of wood near the spot Philip had designated for the cookfire.

"You did well, Kelila," Philip smiled, squatting before the large pile of sticks and brush.

Beaming at his praise, Kelila lowered herself onto one of the log benches, her entire body aching from their travels.

"At first light, I will go into the city to inquire about more efficient lodging," Philip assured her, expertly arranging the sticks and brush within the crude border of stones.

"I like the sound of that," Kelila grinned, wincing as she stretched achy legs. "Although I'm not sure the tiny village of Sychar could rightly be called a *city.*"

Philip smiled, his attention upon his work.

"If only the Lord had called us to Sebaste or one of those elegant, sophisticated cities we passed along the way," Kelila sighed with a teasing air of long-suffering. "I've never been a country girl, you know."

"Ah, I'm aware of that." Stooping to blow upon the tiny flame he had expertly ignited with his flint, Philip glanced at her sideways. "But you'll learn. You may even find country living far more pleasing than the deafening cacophony of the big cities," he teased.

"I doubt it," Kelila put in with a wry smile, a slender brow arching in skepticism. "But the Lord called us here for a reason. Surely He knows best."

"He certainly does."

"Won't it be marvelous to build a home here, Philip?" she breathed, her dark eyes scanning the simple silhouette of the small town just ahead of them.

Tending the fire, Philip glanced up briefly, his smile strangely halfhearted.

Frowning, Kelila watched him work. Perhaps he didn't relish the idea of building an entire house from the ground up. She certainly wouldn't covet the laborious task. "Of course, we can always purchase a house rather than building one," she amended brightly. "Would you prefer that, Philip? We have ample funds after selling our house in Jerusalem."

"We do, indeed."

"I've always dreamed of a place all our own," Kelila sighed contentedly. "It will be such fun, won't it, Philip? Even if it *is* in a tiny Samaritan village," she added, her rumbling stomach reminding her she'd best see to supper preparations soon. "Won't it be exciting to finally put down roots?"

Rocking back on his heels, Philip's gaze betrayed a hint of…something.

Staring at him across the sputtering cookfire, Kelila's heart did a funny little flop inside her chest. "Philip? What is it?"

"It's nothing," Philip smiled, reaching for a spare stick to poke at the licking flames.

"It's obviously *something*," Kelila pointed out, wondering why her heart had suddenly picked up speed.

Coming around the crackling fire, Philip lowered himself onto Kelila's log bench, taking her hand in his. "Remember, beloved, the Lord has called us to *evangelism*. It is our purpose, our mission," he explained, his tone etched with weariness despite his best efforts to mask it.

"Well, of course, it is," Kelila acknowledged. "Our mission is *here*, in Sychar."

"For now," Philip agreed. "But as you've seen for yourself during our recent travels, Samaria is a big place, and we must reach as many as possible."

Kelila stared at him, confused. "But didn't God call us *here*?"

"He did," Philip responded without hesitation. "Jesus launched His ministry to the Samaritans here in Sychar, and I pray a few faithful followers remain to help us spread the Word. Even so, God may call us to new places, new lands, once we have accomplished His purposes here. We cannot know where He will send us tomorrow, or the next day, or even the next."

"Are you saying," Kelila began slowly, her heart pounding wildly in her chest, "that you intend for us to spend the rest of our lives living in that miserable tent?"

"All I'm saying," Philip chuckled, squeezing her hand, "is that the Lord has called us to take the gospel to *many* nations. We may not be settling down in any one place—at least, not anytime soon."

Stunned to her core, Kelila withdrew her hand from her husband's grasp. Surely Philip didn't intend to *live* on the road! Surely he had more sense than that! And *surely* he wouldn't deny the deepest longings of her heart! He wouldn't—*couldn't*—do that, could he? Willingly and happily, she had agreed to accompany him to Samaria, but it hadn't occurred to her then that Philip intended to reach the entire *nation* before settling down!

As rogue emotions began to spin out of control, Kelila closed her eyes, offering an emergency prayer for guidance and clarity. Philip's shocking announcement had shaken her more than she cared to admit. She wasn't quite sure how to respond, especially as indignation welled up inside her until she thought she would simply burst!

Lord, make him see reason! I refuse to spend the rest of my life in a tent, eating road dust for breakfast!

"I know it's difficult, my darling," Philip said quietly, sensing Kelila's silent withdrawal. "And I long to fulfill your wildest dreams—truly, I do. If your heart's desire is to settle down and build a house, I hope the Lord grants us that request. But perhaps—just perhaps—God has plans for us that far surpass our own."

"I just thought…" Blinking back tears, Kelila stiffened when Philip placed his arm around her. She couldn't help it. "I thought *this* was to become our home. I thought we would settle down, start a family, build a life together once we reached Samaria."

"And we will," Philip promised her, tenderly tipping her chin. "All in God's perfect timing."

Heart sinking, Kelila had a sneaking suspicion that the Lord's "perfect" timing would likely contradict her own. "So how long must we trek aimlessly about like wandering nomads?" she inquired, attempting to keep the edge from her tone. "When can we build a permanent home for *us*, for you and me?"

"You forget, beloved," he said, tenderly brushing her cheek, "at this very moment, Jesus is preparing a place for us—a permanent home, perfect in every way, far surpassing our deepest longings and desires."

Anxiously dropping her gaze, Keilia resisted the burning urge to argue with her husband. Of course, she knew the Lord was preparing their *eternal* home—but eternity felt rather distant at the moment, especially in light of her raging desires. She couldn't help but feel a bit put out with Philip. After all, she didn't need a *sermon* right now—she needed *reassurance*! Gazing into the steadily rising flames of the cookfire, she attempted to soothe her rising angst. As a child of God, she knew she mustn't be ruled by fragile emotions. What she needed was time to *think*, time to process all that Philip had revealed.

"Why didn't you mention this earlier?" Kelila lamented after a long, uncomfortable pause. Didn't Philip realize his plans impacted *her*, as well?

"I thought you were aware of the possibilities, especially when I received the call to missions," Philip replied slowly, his expression conveying his surprise and confusion. "I am an evangelist, Kelila."

"Stephanos was an evangelist, and yet *he* built a lovely home with Tabitha in Jerusalem," she pointed out.

"Yes, after years of travel and being on the road for months on end," Philip reminded her, ever patient. "Remember, the Lord sent Stephanos and me to preach in many towns and villages before he met

Tabitha."

"But after the wedding, Stephanos remained in Jerusalem with his wife." *Where he belonged,* she added silently, perturbed. "So why did Tabitha get to build a life with *her* husband? Why did *she* get special privileges?"

"I'm not entirely sure Tabitha would agree about receiving special privileges," Philip said gently, lightly brushing his knuckles against Kelila's cheek. "Stephanos is *gone,* beloved. Just imagine how she must miss him."

Though Philip's observation rang true, Kelila felt rebuked, condemned.

And annoyed.

Conscience burning like fire, Kelila reexamined her desires, wondering why she struggled so. After all, shouldn't her love for Philip be *enough?* Blinking back tears, she remembered the swelling joy she had experienced when Philip had asked her to become his wife. And even when he received the call to Samaria, requiring them to leave her home, her family, and her church to embrace his calling, she hadn't wavered in her devotion to him.

What had changed in the few short months since then? Where were those warm, tingly feelings *now* when she so desperately needed them? Had her faith weakened, somehow? Fighting tears, Kelila begged the Lord for patience and understanding she was far from feeling, recognizing how easily she could slip into old, sinful patterns of rebellion and self-pity—without the Lord's help, that is.

"Perhaps we should discuss this later," Philip decided gently, sensing his wife's deep unhappiness. "Besides, we may have placed the cart before the ox, as it were," he added with a rueful smile. "We cannot possibly know what God has in store for us, Kelila. He may have a home awaiting us here in Sychar, but He may not. The important thing, my bride, is to live one day at a time, obeying the Holy Spirit's leading, no matter where it does—or doesn't—take us."

Kelila held her tongue, though she preferred to argue further. Philip sounded so calm, so *in control*. Didn't he ever get worked up about *anything*, for heaven's sake? How could he—calm, cool, composed Philip—possibly understand what she was experiencing?

Somehow, Kelila held her peace. Mercifully, the sun had set amidst their lively debate, with the ensuing darkness veiling her mounting displeasure.

She was grateful for that.

"Now, how about some supper?" Philip inquired cheerfully, clearly hoping the touchy subject had been averted for the remainder of the evening.

Well, how nice of him to dash my hopes and dreams, and then candidly ask for his supper! Kelila thought, peeved. Though she could have gleefully smacked him, she somehow refrained.

With a curt nod of acknowledgment, Kelila bent to rummage through a leather satchel of provisions, mindful of her husband's questioning gaze upon her. She certainly hoped he fancied a handful of parched grain and dried raisins, because that's the best he was going to get tonight.

As for her, she would refrain from supper this evening. The thought of consuming anything sickened her.

It would seem her appetite had dissipated along with her shattered dreams.

CHAPTER 5

Tabitha

Joppa

Hoping to glean whatever information she could about her indomitable uncle on the way back to his impressive estate, Tabitha found herself keenly disappointed. Eli proved singularly unhelpful. When it came to his master, his lips were sealed more tightly than the clamshells washed up on the silver shores of the Mediterranean.

"Can you tell me what this meeting is about?" Tabitha dared as Eli paused before the same imposing double doors that had previously been slammed in her face. "Why did my uncle change his mind about seeing me?"

"I am not at liberty to speak of such things," Eli responded, ever guarded. Fumbling about his person, Eli eventually produced a large, clawed key. Inserting it into the lock, the heavy bolt was thrown back with a practiced twist of his wrist.

Mystified, Tabitha followed the servant through a stately vestibule and into a grand reception hall similar to the one in Mary's resplendent villa. Mentally comparing the two, Tabitha decided that Mary's house—exuding grace and simple elegance—proved far superior to Joram's somewhat garish estate, with its loudly frescoed walls, dizzyingly ornate patterns etched in the towering ceiling panels overhead, and bold, brightly colored mosaics swirling underfoot.

"Wait here, please," Eli said stiffly, offering a slight bow—almost an afterthought—before fleeing the scene.

As no one had offered to take her heavy traveling pack, Tabitha gingerly lowered it to the floor, propping it against the wall.

Taking Laurel by the hand, Tabitha settled onto a richly upholstered, straight-backed chair strategically placed among a smattering of luxe furniture arranged beneath a sprawling mural. Though the bold, gilded furniture was designed to be aesthetically pleasing, undoubtedly created to awe and impress, the hard chair proved exceedingly uncomfortable.

Hoisting her daughter onto her lap, Tabitha stroked the child's soft brown curls, praying silently as she waited. Within minutes, the little girl had fallen asleep, her head nestled trustingly against her mother's shoulder.

At first, Tabitha supposed it was her own impatience making time stand still. Soon, however, it became frustratingly apparent that Joram was in no hurry to see her. Irritated by the obvious slight, Tabitha forced herself to remember her mission: her uncle's soul was at stake. He was an old man, and

Tabitha highly suspected his health was declining. Should she abandon her cause now, it was likely Joram would eventually perish without knowledge of the Savior.

And yet, as the minutes dragged into hours, Tabitha's sympathy steadily dwindled. Though household servants hastened busily about the reception hall—darting in and out of grand entrances and disappearing down long corridors, seemingly doing their best to ignore her presence—Joram hadn't even bothered sending a maid to wash her tired feet, nor had he supplied the slightest hint of refreshment, not even a cup of water to ease her parched throat. Several hours after young Laurel should have been bedded down for the night, Tabitha was sorely tempted to rise from her chair and walk out the front door.

"The master will see you now."

With great effort, Tabitha suppressed her indignation as Eli emerged from a richly curtained entrance, his expression veiled. If he felt the least bit guilty about the poor treatment she had received, he showed no signs of it. But Tabitha held her peace, reminding herself that her witness before Joram and his household was at stake, and gently awakened her sleeping daughter. Rising from the uncomfortable chair required a bit of effort, for she was exceedingly stiff after many days of rigorous travel, followed by several hours of stationary sitting. Gently easing her daughter onto her own small, sandaled feet, Tabitha looked to Eli in question.

"You may leave your belongings here," Eli informed her, his gaze flitting distastefully toward her travel-stained pack leaning against the wall. "This way," he ordered curtly, gesturing for Tabitha to follow him through the lavishly curtained entrance.

Taking her daughter's hand, Tabitha heeded the overseer's request, amused by the way his ceremonious-looking robes swished in cadence with his hurried steps. Traveling the length of a frescoed corridor, Eli paused before an imposing entrance shrouded in luxuriant crimson tapestries. Parting the curtains in a practiced, dignified manner, Eli announced stiffly, "Your niece, Master Joram."

With a grand sweep of his arm, Eli ushered Tabitha and her daughter into Joram's regal office.

Leaning forward in an enormous, throne-like chair, Joram—like a watchful bird of prey—perched behind an astoundingly large cedar desk, one silken-sleeved arm draped indolently upon the golden-clawed armrest.

"Well, if isn't my long-lost niece." Scowl deepening, Joram's gaze bore into the lithe form of the lovely young woman approaching his desk, leading her young child by the hand.

At the mere sight of him, Laurel began to whimper, shrinking behind her mother and clinging to her garments for dear life.

"It's all right, my darling," Tabitha assured her daughter, perfectly calm. "Be at peace."

Joram's silver brows drew together in displeasure as Tabitha drew patiently before him, pausing in front of his desk. She didn't seem the least bit intimidated by his show of power and prestige.

Grant me Your words, Lord, not mine, Tabitha prayed, masking her nerves with great effort. *Lead this meeting as You see fit.*

Boldly lifting her gaze, Tabitha found herself

staring into a pair of hazel-green eyes startlingly like her own—and her departed mother's. Veiling her surprise, she maintained a confident posture, refusing to cower before the intimidation tactics of the indomitable old man.

"I judge your wait wasn't too uncomfortable?" Joram said coolly, clearly baiting her.

Though she would have preferred to lash out in retaliation, Tabitha held her peace. Rather than lashing out, she offered a calm, enigmatic smile.

"As you can imagine, I had urgent matters to address, matters far more pressing than this little *family reunion* you so kindly—and thoughtlessly—arranged," Joram said, his voice dripping with sarcasm. "I'm sure you understand."

Bristling inside, Tabitha held her ground with a calm, unruffled smile. Joram hadn't offered even a hint of apology for his deplorable treatment, but what had she expected? Working for the most prestigious woman of Jerusalem, Tabitha had encountered many powerful, arrogant aristocrats—her late husband's father, Amal, included. Enough to recognize her uncle's antagonistic antics for what they were: calculated and carefully staged—all intended to put her in "her place."

Lips lifting in amusement, Tabitha decided her uncle had finally met his match. He was a shrewd man, accustomed to fighting fire with fire and battling to the bitter death. But Joram hadn't the slightest idea about *love*—the pure, unconditional love Christ lavished upon His church, the kind of love He enabled His followers to bestow upon their friends and foes alike.

Joram wouldn't even know what hit him!

"What, may I ask, do you find so amusing, dear niece?" Joram growled, his silver brows knitting together in displeasure. "Should I find myself in your rather tenuous situation, I certainly wouldn't be smiling about it."

Dear niece, he had said, his rasping tone thick with sarcasm, but Tabitha refused to be cowed. "And why would you say my situation is tenuous?" Tabitha asked lightly, lifting a honey-colored brow in question.

"Well," Joram drawled, leaning back in his chair, "according to your letter, you've lost everything—father, mother, husband. In my estimation, your very existence is now entirely dependent upon my mercy and goodwill. With that in mind, you'd best tread lightly, dear niece."

"Ah," Tabitha responded, unperturbed. "I can see how you might reach that conclusion, Uncle. However, you are misguided in your assessment."

"Misguided?" Joram repeated cynically, arching a sarcastic brow. "And how is that?"

"You assume I came seeking your aid; however, I was employed by the wealthiest aristocrat in Jerusalem for nearly a decade. I have saved a tidy little sum, and I am in no need of financial assistance."

"No?" Joram drawled, his tone tinged with antagonism. "And what will you do when that so-called hefty sum of yours is depleted?"

"I shall fall back on the monthly income I receive from the property I shared with my late husband in Jerusalem," Tabitha replied without missing a beat. "Utilizing our chief asset as a rental property has provided additional income, may God be praised."

"You own *property*?" Joram questioned, his familiar hazel-green eyes bulging in surprise.

"In the heart of the holy city," Tabitha replied nonchalantly, secretly relishing his hidden amazement. "As you can imagine, such property is in high demand."

"And how do you plan to collect your tenant's rent, as you now reside on the opposite end of the province?" Joram barked gruffly, visibly miffed.

"Before leaving, I made arrangements with a friend of mine in Jerusalem. She collects the tenant's monthly rent in return for a small percentage of the renter's fee. If the need arises, I shall simply return to Jerusalem to collect the accumulation of monthly payments."

Joram stared at her, incredulous.

"Any more questions, Uncle?" Tabitha asked, a bit too sweetly.

"As a matter of fact, *yes*. How did you learn to operate in such a businesslike manner?" Joram demanded, attempting to mask his grudging admiration.

"As I previously mentioned, I worked for the wealthiest aristocrat in Jerusalem," Tabitha replied, enjoying his reaction. "As you can imagine, she taught me a thing or two about business."

"*She*?" Joram repeated, scandalized. "The wealthiest aristocrat in Jerusalem is a *woman*?"

"This surprises you?" Tabitha asked with a mischievous little smile.

"It would surprise anyone with a decent head on his shoulders," Joram grumped, absentmindedly shuffling through the paperwork on his desk.

As her uncle cleared his throat and attempted to regain his composure, Tabitha conducted a quick sweep of his impressive office, deciding the cold, stately chamber reflected the personality of its owner that even the cheery lamplight failed to soften. The luxurious suite was quite spacious, with frescoed walls boasting warm-toned paints of gold, silver, and crimson. Yellowing maps and ledgers charting sea trade routes were mounted upon the walls and spread across the massive desk. The entire western wall filled with neatly ordered cubby holes housed hundreds of scrolls, documents, and ledgers, while a set of gilded double doors on the opposite end remained slightly ajar, opening into a sprawling, torchlit inner court richly furnished with elegant furniture, ivy-laden trellises, and potted palms.

Allowing her gaze to return to the sour-faced man seated behind his ornate cedar desk, Tabitha wondered if Joram was even aware of his deep unhappiness. Would he ever recognize that all the money in the world could not buy joy or peace of mind?

"Well, regardless of your interesting little business venture," Joram interrupted condescendingly, folding his hands on the top of his desk with an air of finality, "you remain in my debt, Niece. Your husband is dead, and I am, after all, your last surviving relative. If you intend to lodge here on my estate, then you shall answer to me."

"Oh, that won't be necessary," Tabitha blithely assured him, surprising him even further.

"And where do you propose to stay, if not here?" Joram demanded, disgruntled. Clearly, he had no intentions of surrendering what he considered to be the upper hand.

"If you would be so kind as to direct me toward

suitable lodging, I can make arrangements for my-self and my daughter," Tabitha replied, bending to lift a quietly protesting Laurel and placing her on one of the regal chairs opposite her uncle's desk. She refrained from pointing out that he hadn't even invited them to be seated—another obvious slight. "I wouldn't dream of asking for your charity," she added a bit more tersely than she had intended.

"I find that rather difficult to believe, considering that your husband is dead and you have a child to care for," Joram observed coldly.

"*The Lord is my Shepherd*," Tabitha responded without missing a beat. "And by His grace, I shall not want."

"I suppose we shall see about that," Joram responded gruffly, leaning back in his throne-like chair. "Even so, the only available lodging in these parts caters to seafaring men and women of loose morals. As you might imagine, such establish-ments—infamous for gambling, drinking, and ca-rousing—are not fit for an honorable young woman nor for an impressionable child."

Well, at least he thinks I'm honorable, Tabitha thought snidely. But since she had no desire to lodge with her haughty, overbearing relative, the lack of appropriate housing posed a rather serious problem.

"I suppose I shall make some inquiries and see what I can find," Tabitha stated cheerfully, carefully concealing her concerns.

"And do you expect to stumble upon a decent establishment I have yet to discover after residing in Joppa all my life?" Joram groused with annoying logic. "You and the girl will stay here."

Joram's "suggestion" sounded far too much like a

demand for Tabitha's liking, and she couldn't help but wonder if it would be unwise to beholden herself to this imperious relative.

"Well?" Joram demanded gruffly. "Surely you don't expect to find accommodations nearly so luxurious elsewhere!"

Feeling deeply unsettled, Tabitha sent a silent prayer heavenward. *Lord, what should I do? If I accept Joram's offer to stay, he will surely lord it over me every single day!* The last thing she wanted was to grant her uncle the leverage he desired.

As cold and heartless as that man seems, I believe his heart craves acceptance and companionship—though he'd die before admitting it, even to himself... Unbidden, Tirzah's astute observation rang through Tabitha's mind, slicing through her tumultuous thoughts like a sharpened blade. Disturbed, she wondered if perhaps this was a sacrifice the Lord desired for her to make—to live in a place not of her choosing, to surrender her freedom—possibly even her *rights*—to minister to this cold, angry man.

But Lord, she silently protested, *how can I bear to accept charity from a man who will undoubtedly throw it back in my face every chance he gets?*

If anyone desires to come after Me, let him deny himself, and take up his cross daily, and follow Me.

But, Lord, is it wise? Tabitha protested in silence. *You call us to work willingly with our own two hands, to provide for those You have entrusted to our care. Show me a way to provide for my own daughter, Lord.*

Instantly, Tabitha knew what to do. After all, she'd done it before! Silently praising God for the Holy Spirit's guidance, Tabitha faced her uncle head-on.

"Hire me, Uncle, in exchange for room and board."

Joram stared at his niece in surprise. "I beg your pardon?"

"Hire me," Tabitha replied without missing a beat. "I am a capable maidservant, and I'm not afraid of hard work. In fact, I welcome it."

Studying his niece with a flinty expression, Joram's eyes narrowed in careful consideration.

"Well?" Tabitha prodded, anxious to see the matter settled. "What do you say?"

The two stood measuring each other with hazel-green eyes, each mentally evaluating the grit of the other. After a thunderous pause, Joram rose from his desk.

"We shall see if you're worth your salt, girl," he declared, his thin lips stretching into the semblance of a haughty smile. "You're hired."

"You won't regret it, sir," Tabitha assured him, grasping his outstretched hand in the same businesslike manner she had gleaned from her mistress.

"Eli!" Joram barked, loudly clapping his hands in summons.

"Yes, my lord?" Eli appeared so swiftly Tabitha knew he must have been lurking on the other side of the curtained entrance, undoubtedly eavesdropping.

"Show this young lady and her child to their new room," Joram directed with an impatient wave of his hand. "As of now, she is officially under my employ."

CHAPTER 6

Kelila

Sychar

It was a long, unpleasant evening. The conversation between husband and wife, though sparse, seemed stilted and unnatural as Kelila prepared Philip's supper and unloaded their traveling packs. Once she began readying the tent for bed, Philip wisely resorted to silence. There was, after all, safety in silence.

If Philip had enjoyed his sparse supper of dried fruit, parched grain, and nuts, he hadn't said so. Nor had he complained. He had simply seemed eager to bed down for the night after another long day of grueling travel. But Kelila absolutely refused to feel sorry for him. After all, *he* was the one determined to subject them to a nomadic lifestyle of constant upheaval and bodily strain! Surely the Lord wouldn't fault them for building a house, settling down, and starting a family—like every other "normal" couple in Judea!

Several hours later, Kelila lay on her back on the hard earthen floor, gazing up at the shadowy canvas tent ceiling and blinking back tears in the inky darkness. If Philip had desired her affections this evening, he'd wisely kept such thoughts to himself. Tucked in the farthest reaches of their confining shelter, Kelila didn't wish to be anywhere near him. Had it not been for the night's unwelcome chill and her somewhat irrational fear of wild beasts, Kelila would be sleeping outside!

Oh, Lord, Kelila prayed, her cheeks stained with humiliation, *You know what I am feeling right now. And though my thoughts are willful and selfish, You understand my weakness. You, too, were tempted as we are...as I am.* Closing her eyes, Kelila resisted the warm tears threatening to spill down her cheeks. *But, You, Lord, were without sin. You resisted temptation, Lord, setting Your face like a flint to do Your Father's will,* she continued, wondering at her keen disappointment. *Please help me follow Your example, standing firm in Your holy calling.*

Releasing a quiet sigh, Kelila studied the flickering shadows cast by firelight dancing across the canvas tent flaps, relieved Philip would keep vigilant watch over the fire burning a safe distance from their tent. Beyond the sturdy shelter, wind whistled through low-hanging branches, tickling verdant leaves overhead and vibrant patches of spring flowers gracing the sprawling plains. It was an idyllic night, with brightly burning stars splashed across a dark velvet sky, the silver moon towering into the heavens and washing the earth beneath in a soft, otherworldly glow.

Recalling previous starry nights spent in this very tent, tucked snugly in her husband's eager arms, Kelila stiffened in rebellion. Had she known Philip's intent all along, he would've been warming his own bed!

As an unexpected gust of wind tore at the tent flaps, Kelila was tempted to rise and tie them shut, though she rather enjoyed the small sliver of beauty visible just beyond the canvas flaps, despite the chill evening breeze. After a brief, silent debate, she decided to stay put. If she rose now, Philip would know she was awake. Since he hadn't yet elapsed into his familiar pattern of soft breathing, she knew that he, too, was awake.

Candace warned me this would happen, Kelila thought petulantly, suddenly aching for the wisdom of her older sister. *But when Candace said we would experience disagreements, I thought she meant over little things—like what to have for supper, or when to go to the market!* Why, she and Philip disagreeing about anything—least of all, anything *serious*? The thought had seemed utterly absurd!

Until now.

Oh, Candace, if only you were here! Kelila's heart cried, longing to grace the feet of her discerning older sister, absorbing her godly wisdom and guidance. After all, Candace had been happily married for over a decade! Surely *she* would know what to do!

And here I am—stranded in a tent in the middle of nowhere—with no one to help, no one to turn to, Kelila bemoaned, defeated.

Have you so soon forgotten the Spirit of truth who will guide you into all truth, beloved?

Kelila's eyes snapped open as the revelation hit

her full force! In her fierce agitation, she had entirely forgotten about the Helper, the Holy Spirit, whom Christ sent to lead and to guide His followers!

Precious Lord, I'm so upset! she confessed, dashing angrily at her tears. *I want to be angry at Philip, but deep down, I know he is simply honoring Your calling on his life. But how can I shake this disappointment, Lord? What can I do?*

You can trust.

Squeezing her eyes tightly shut, Kelila grit her teeth in frustration. *Trust,* the Spirit soothed. But how was she supposed to do that when God's "perfect" plan likely contradicted her own burning desires?

Sighing, Kelila turned over on her side. She didn't feel any better than before.

"My love, are you awake?"

Groaning inwardly, Kelila considered ignoring her husband's poignant inquiry and feigning sleep. But to do so reeked of deception, so instead she responded with a curt, "Yes. Do you need something?"

"Yes," Philip responded a bit hoarsely, lying flat on his back in the darkened tent. "I need *you.* I need my wife."

Peeved, Kelila somehow withheld a terse response.

When Philip spoke again, Kelila sensed rather than saw his wry smile in the growing darkness. "*Therefore, if you bring your gift to the altar, and there remember that your brother*—or wife, I suspect—*has something against you, leave your gift there before the altar, and go your way. First be reconciled to your brother*—or wife, yes?—*and then come and offer your gift.*"

"I don't see any gifts nor an altar in this tent," Kelila observed, presenting a rigid back to him.

"No," Philip conceded wanly, "but as I lay here, praying silently—offering up a gift or sacrifice of praise, if you will—the Holy Spirit brought this instruction to mind."

Kelila said nothing, for she didn't trust her own voice. Her tone would surely betray the stubborn rebellion coursing through her entire being.

"So," Philip said, clearing his throat a bit uncomfortably, "is it safe to assume that my wife has something against me?"

"It's not *you*, Philip," Kelila finally said, releasing a sigh of frustration. "Your plans caught me off guard tonight, that's all."

"I haven't made any plans, beloved," Philip assured her, his voice floating upon the darkness. "But I do believe *God's* plan may involve some traveling evangelism, at least for a time."

"I find it interesting you didn't breathe a word about this—until now."

"I thought we had the same idea."

"You said *Samaria*, Philip!" Kelila argued, beginning to wish she'd simply pretended to be asleep rather than engaging in this maddening discussion! "How was I supposed to know you intended to travel the entire globe?"

"I didn't say that," Philip reminded her, scooting just a bit closer. "Truly, my love, I haven't the slightest idea what God has in store for us. I just want to be willing, available, to heed His call. That's all I was trying to say."

Kelila stiffened when Philip's strong hands reached for her. She didn't wish to be held. Deeply unsettled, she rolled onto her back, turning her head to look at him. She could barely discern his familiar profile in the inky darkness of their tent. "When you asked me to marry you, Philip, I never imagined our lives would look like this."

"Like what?" Philip asked, seeking to understand.

"Traveling from place to place, living in a tent, never knowing when—or if—we will settle down, put down some roots, and start a family," Kelila said, tears rolling down her cheeks.

"Can anyone truly know how their life will unfold?" Philip gently reminded her, brushing away her tears. "We walk by faith, not by sight, Kelila. But if we take matters into our own hands, we only rob ourselves of the joy and fulfillment God longs to give us."

"You should have been more transparent," Kelila argued accusingly. "Instead, you made me fall in love with you, married me, and dragged me out here to the middle of nowhere, only later to divulge your true plans!"

"Is that really how you feel?" Philip asked quietly, hurt.

"Yes!" Kelila snapped, her temper getting the best of her. "That's exactly how I feel!"

A deafening silence hung in the air following Kelila's unfair outburst, a silence so dreadful she wondered how long she could bear it. But she refused to revoke her impassioned accusation. She refused to back down without a fight.

When Philip finally spoke, his voice conveyed the deepest kind of sorrow. "I never intended to deceive you, Kelila."

Turning her head, Kelila refused his extended

olive branch.

Sitting up in the darkness, Philip said quietly, "Do you regret it?"

Forcefully pushing herself up to a sitting position, Kelila squinted through the thick darkness obscuring her husband from view. "Do I regret *what*?" she huffed, ready to defend herself to the bitter death.

"Do you regret marrying me, Kelila?"

Philip's gentle whisper was like a punch in the gut, instantly bringing her attitude into focus. For the first time since the disagreement began, Kelila felt utterly ashamed.

"Oh, Philip." Going into his arms, Kelila wept softly upon his shoulder. "I'm so sorry. I don't know what came over me."

Breathing an immense sigh of relief, Philip cradled her in his arms.

"I will never regret marrying you," she insisted, her heart breaking in her chest. "I *want* to be your wife. I *want* to join you in this sacred calling, even if that means constant travel."

"I can't tell you how happy I am to hear you say that," Philip confessed, kissing her forehead.

"I don't understand what came over me," Kelila whispered. "Had I taken but a moment to calmly evaluate our discussion…"

Philip smiled in understanding as her voice trailed off in dismay. "You were simply caught off guard by an unexpected turn of events, Kelila, and exhausted after far too many days of hard travel."

"Even so, that doesn't excuse my behavior nor my hostile reaction," Kelila groaned, mortified. "How could I so soon forget our purpose, Philip?"

"Always remember, the enemy is ever watchful,

lurking about like a roaring lion, and he hates the mission we've been assigned," Philip reminded her, swiping away her tears with his thumbs. "He knows our triggers and our weaknesses far better than we. Like a savage predator, he seeks to destroy us when we are weak."

"And I kicked the door wide open for him, didn't I?" Kelila sighed, defeated.

"But you chose to heed that still, small voice instead," Philip reminded her, pulling her close. "And by God's grace, the enemy failed to cause permanent division between us. Had he succeeded, the people to whom we are called would have undoubtedly sensed our hypocrisy and shrank from our message."

"The devil didn't waste any time, did he?" Kelila observed wryly. "He tried to wreak havoc before we even began our new mission."

"And we must always be aware of that," Philip agreed. "Perhaps this is a good sign. The enemy doesn't waste his ammunition. Clearly, he doesn't want us here, Kelila."

"Which makes me all the more determined to stand our ground."

"That's my girl," Philip grinned, kissing her cheek.

"Forgive me, Philip. I was wrong."

"Shhh," Philip soothed, pulling her close. "It's forgiven and long forgotten."

Closing her eyes, Kelila felt the tension draining from her body as Philip bent to kiss her gently. Tightening her grip around him, she eagerly returned his affection, suddenly oblivious of the snug little tent and the distasteful conditions she'd *thought* she despised only moments earlier.

What was I thinking? she thought, delighting in the sensation of her husband's warm lips brushing against hers, his strong arms encircling her waist. *God has blessed me with a wonderful man, the perfect man for me. It doesn't matter if we are living in an empty barrel or in the emperor's ivory palace— the important thing is that we are together, united in thought and purpose, determined to love each other as Christ first loved us.*

In that sacred moment, the chill breeze, creeping insects, and the confines of the musty tent no longer mattered, for all of it paled in light of her sacred mission and the tender love God had ordained between a husband and wife.

CHAPTER 7

Tabitha

Joppa

Though Joram's mansion boasted a fine collection of luxuriant suites, Tabitha was granted what appeared to be a small, empty storage room, of sorts, near the servants' quarters on the first floor and at the back of the palatial home. Wryly, Tabitha imagined this was her uncle's way of demonstrating she shouldn't expect any special treatment from him.

Though Tabitha didn't mind the sparse accommodations, she feared that Joram had—perhaps intentionally—placed her in an undesirable position in the household. Had he assigned her to the servants' quarters, she would have been placed on equal footing with the household staff. And had she been granted a suite, she would have simply been regarded as Joram's niece.

But here, in her own separate chamber held apart from the servants' quarters, Tabitha was neither servant nor family, having been designated some sort of tenuous position in between.

Having already bedded Laurel down for the night, Tabitha kissed the sleeping child's soft cheek before rising stiffly, her weary gaze sweeping over her new quarters, which left much to be desired. With a cold stone floor, bare, windowless walls devoid of paint, and a damp, musty atmosphere, the darkened chamber possessed the warmth and cheer of a stone dungeon.

Well, I suppose this is home—at least, for now, she thought glumly, crossing the room and lowering herself onto the scratchy straw mattress resting on a narrow, wooden frame placed against the farthest wall. Apart from the makeshift bed, the small room also boasted a single wooden nightstand, several straw mats neatly rolled up and placed in one corner, and a row of empty stone jars lining one wall. She had utilized one of the straw mats to create a sleeping space for Laurel, using the only blanket she could find—the thin, worn one gracing her bed—to gently tuck her in.

I suppose I must simply endure the damp chill, as my uncle has failed to supply adequate bedding, Tabitha thought, too exhausted to care. Perhaps, in the morning, she would request a second blanket. She would make no requests tonight, as Eli had made it abundantly clear he hadn't appreciated having to lug her heavy traveling pack down the labyrinth of stone corridors leading to the back of the house.

Thank You, Lord, for guiding my steps today, Tabitha prayed, reverently folding her hands as her eyes drifted heavenward. *These accommodations are certainly not of my choosing, and yet I have peace because I know You have led me here.*

Already, Tabitha's creative mind buzzed with ideas to brighten up the dank little chamber. She certainly didn't intend to suffer the intense gloom of her new environment, especially for Laurel's sake. *A few colorful rugs and hanging tapestries will work wonders in this dreary space,* she decided. *And more oil lamps are certainly in order!* The few lamps mounted on the bare walls did little to dispel the heavy darkness. Perhaps, in time, she could afford to purchase some soft mats and plush pillows to scatter about for comfortable seating.

Smiling faintly, Tabitha realized she was probably getting ahead of herself. After all, she hadn't the slightest idea how long her uncle would permit her to stay, working in exchange for her room and board.

It was an odd sensation, believing she had been *sent*, and yet knowing so little about her mission.

Abraham must have felt something like this, Tabitha thought in wonderment, *for God simply told him, "Get out from your country, from your family and from your father's house, to a land that I will show you." Abraham knew next to nothing about his mission, and yet he obeyed—day by day, one step at a time.*

Gazing upon her sweet little daughter, her small back rising and falling gently in time with her steady breathing, Tabitha felt a dreadful wave of homesickness sweeping over her as the enormity—and possibly, the *finality*—of her calling hit her full force.

Abraham hadn't been permitted to return to his family in Ur of the Chaldeans. He and his lovely bride eventually died in the land God had promised to give them, far removed from family and friends, though confident in His perfect will. But what did God have in store for *her*? What if the Lord had no intention of leading her back to Jerusalem, back to her dear Mary, her beloved church family, and all that she adored?

What if she was called to live the remainder of her days in this dreadful little chamber under her uncle's suspicious and watchful eye?

Oh God, grant me strength, she prayed, battling against the bitter waves of anxiety sweeping over her. *Use me for Your glory, Lord. Show me what to do.*

Attempting to redirect her anxious thoughts, Tabitha thought of Tirzah, the cheerful widow who had shown them such kindness. She would need to find a way to properly thank her for her hospitality.

Lord God, I believe Tirzaḥ will be receptive to the truth about Your Son. Please, Lord, open her heart to You. As a staunch Jewess, it was likely Tirzah would desire to examine the claims about Jesus for herself, rather than blindly accepting His Messiahship. The Jews had waited thousands of years for Messiah to come, and most had lost heart, convinced He wouldn't make His appearance during their lifetime. Why should Tirzah be any different?

Tabitha assumed the woman would take a bit of convincing.

Perhaps I should have spoken about Christ's sacrifice when we broke bread together, she thought, second-guessing herself. When was the proper time to evangelize, anyway? Should she launch into a detailed gospel exposition right away, or simply give it some time, living by example first?

Oh, Lord, Stephanos was the evangelist—not me! she thought, bordering desperation. *I don't even know how to go about this!* Drawing a calming breath, Tabitha tried to remember her husband's manner of evangelism. He had always insisted that it was important to establish a trusting friendship with someone before introducing a faith that would likely turn their entire life upside down. Most potential converts were reluctant to embrace a faith that would instantly ostracize them from their family, friends, and religious community. *First, they must know you have their best interest at heart,* Stephanos used to say. *Until trust has been established, they have no reason to believe anything you say.*

Perhaps it was wise to give it some time—not only for Tirzah, but for Joram also. For now, Tabitha recognized it was exceedingly important to demonstrate the life and message of Jesus through her *actions*. She was undoubtedly under inspection, and arrogant men like Joram would be bent on disproving her credibility.

Swinging her legs up onto the bed, Tabitha decided she'd best get some sleep. It was late, and Joram would undoubtedly expect her to begin her shift early in the morning. She had no intentions of shirking her tasks. She would earn her keep.

Tabitha had expected sleep to claim her immediately after her evening prayers. But despite her overwhelming exhaustion, sleep remained maddeningly elusive. She tossed and turned, attempting to get comfortable on a bed that was much more like a bench. To make matters worse, she was cold and had nothing with which to keep warm. Eventually, she rose from the bed, rummaging through her bag until she found her spare tunic. Climbing back onto the rough mattress, she draped the thin garment over her shoulders, but it did little to dispel the growing chill.

Frustrated, Tabitha flung aside her tunic, swinging her legs over the side of the bed. "Merciful Father, I'm not sure I can do this," she whispered, vacillating between waves of homesickness and sheer frustration. "I have left so much behind—the dear woman whom I love like a mother, the sweet fellowship of my church family, a beautiful villa with my own bedchamber, beautifully and comfortably furnished...all of this have I forsaken—just to reach a mean, stubborn old miser who detests my very existence."

I, too, left all behind—My righteous Father, the adoration of angelic courts, and paradisal streets of gold. I understand, and I AM here.

Tabitha's heart constricted as the familiar voice whispered deep within her heart. Though soothed, she still possessed many questions. *But, Lord, Joram doesn't even care about the sacrifices I have made for him.*

Did you, when first I came, beloved? I surrendered all for you, to reach you while you were yet in sin. Before you knew you needed Me. Before you even loved Me. And this, because I loved you first.

Covering her face with her hands, Tabitha drew a steadying breath. The sacrifices she had been called to make paled in comparison with all her Savior had suffered for her sake, for the sake of the entire world. She couldn't imagine how Jesus must have suffered, having abandoned Heaven's glory and splendor to enter a filthy, broken world.

Oh Lord, I have no right to complain. Please grant me the strength to follow in Your steps.

Releasing a steadying breath, Tabitha received the consolation the Holy Spirit so graciously offered. She was about to attempt sleep once again when a surprising thought flittered across her mind, catching her off guard.

What had Tirzah said in her modest little house that day?

Trust me, I'm not the only widow of a sailor around here. There are hordes of us, I'm afraid.

There are hordes of us! Hit by a shocking recognition, Tabitha realized the Lord had—once again—expertly arranged every single circumstance in fulfillment of a masterful plan. Having been orphaned as a child and later widowed as a young woman, Tabitha possessed a burning desire to reach orphans and widows. But when God had called her to Joppa, she had sadly assumed that particular ministry had drawn to a close in her life, at least for a season.

I should have known You would have already worked everything out for good, Lord, according to Your perfect plan and purpose! Not only had God led her to the seaport town of Joppa to reach a floundering relative drowning in his own selfish greed, but He had strategically planted her right in the midst of countless widowed women and orphaned children, their husbands and fathers having become victims of the sea's capricious whims!

Shaking her head in amazement, Tabitha finally settled onto the bed, her heart overflowing with excitement and gratitude.

Perhaps the Lord had more than just her uncle in mind when He led her here!

CHAPTER 8

Tabitha

Joppa

Rising long before the sun, Tabitha spent the first half hour of her day in prayer and thanksgiving before briefly awakening her sleeping daughter.

"Good morning, my darling girl," Tabitha whispered, kneeling beside Laurel's straw pallet and stroking her soft brown curls. "Mama must begin the daily chores now. Would you like to rest here until I come for you?"

Bleary-eyed and exhausted from many days of hard travel, Laurel groggily nodded her consent before pulling the covers over her tousled head.

Chuckling warmly, Tabitha bent to kiss the fair forehead peeking out from under the worn blanket. "Mama will come awaken you when it's time for breakfast," she promised, rising to begin her workday.

With a cursory sweep about the dimly lit chamber, Tabitha suddenly realized her uncle hadn't provided fresh water nor a basin to wash her face and hands. Rolling her eyes in annoyance, Tabitha went to her traveling bag and retrieved her comb. After a quick brush, she replaced the comb, weaving her honey-gold tresses into a simple braid. Reaching for her head covering, she slipped it on before heading out the door.

Working her way down the confusing labyrinth of lamplit corridors, Tabitha wondered where she might locate Joram. Perhaps the opulent office where her interview of the previous day had occurred? She wouldn't dare approach him in his private suite, for the wealthy shipping tycoon would certainly consider such an act unseemly and presumptuous!

Perhaps she should find Eli first. As the overseer of Joram's estate, he would surely be qualified to guide her in the proper direction, possibly even assigning her daily responsibilities.

Rounding a sharp corner, Tabitha nearly collided with the man she sought.

"You really must watch where you're going, miss," Eli said impatiently, nearly dropping his writing tablet and fancy stylus. "What, pray tell, are you doing up at this hour?"

"The same as you, I would imagine," Tabitha replied with a hint of mischief. "Making myself useful."

"By lurking about dark corners and catching me unaware?"

"I was *looking*, not *lurking*," Tabitha amended, amused by Eli's obvious chagrin. "Looking for *you*, actually."

"Whatever for?"

"My uncle hired me, did he not? Any maidservant worth her salt wouldn't dream of sleeping in and leaving all the hard work to the others."

Eli studied her with a hint of suspicion. Clearly, he didn't trust her.

"I need to know what responsibilities I have been assigned," she plunged ahead, eager to begin the workday. "Where might I find my uncle?"

"In his bed, I would imagine," Eli responded, miffed. "Disturb him at your own peril."

"Joram doesn't rise early?" Tabitha asked in surprise, considering her former mistress who rose long before dawn.

"Long ago, yes," Eli replied with obvious impatience. "That has changed in recent years."

"I see," Tabitha mused, suspecting her uncle's age and poor health had something to do with that. "In the meantime, what shall I do to be useful?"

"You must consult your uncle about that when he awakens," Eli replied tersely, attempting to slip past her in the narrow corridor.

"Until then, have you any suggestions for me?" Tabitha asked, turning around to look after him.

"You should speak with your uncle about the matter."

"All right," Tabitha sighed, peeved. "In the meantime, does there happen to be a place I can freshen up? I wasn't provided any fresh water, nor a wash rag or basin."

"I do apologize if your accommodations weren't to your liking," Eli responded coolly, his tone implying he wasn't the least bit sorry. "There is a washroom, of sorts, near the servants' quarters. You may freshen up there."

With that, the overseer turned and hastened down the long corridor, clearly eager to escape her unwanted questions.

Watching him go, Tabitha released a small sigh of impatience. Eli had proven to be one of the most difficult and unobliging manservants she had ever encountered.

But never mind him, she thought, mentally calculating her course of action. First, she would wash her face and freshen up. Then she would see about assisting in the kitchen until her uncle awakened. In her experience, most kitchen staff began their chores long before dawn.

***

Kelila

Sychar

Located on the broad southern plain of Moreh near Mount Gerizim's majestically sprawling slopes, Jacob's well overlooked flourishing fields of grain and the sleepy little town of Sychar nestled snugly upon the lower ridge of Mount Ebal on the farthest edge of the grassy plain.

Huffing after a long, hot walk from camp, Kelila dropped her empty water jug rather heedlessly upon the grassy earth, straightening as she wiped the glistening sweat from her brow with the back of her hand. She didn't even want to think about the long walk back to camp, toting a full, heavy water jug uphill along the beaten path ascending toward the settlement!

I suppose it's my own fault, she thought, leaning forward and resting both delicate hands upon the well's cool stone ledge. *After all, Philip tried to convince me to come draw water at dawn.* But the mere prospect of encountering dozens of Samaritan women at the village well was a daunting thought—daunting enough to drive Kelila out during the heat of the day, when no one else was crazy enough to make the hike! She was certainly in no hurry to introduce herself to an intimidating group of potentially hostile women, especially not without Philip's aid and powerful, conciliatory presence.

But *I made it,* Kelila thought, a small, triumphant smile flickering about her lips. *I made the entire trip to the village well without encountering any hostile Samaritans along the way!* Spreading her fingers wide, Kelila savored the coolness of the stone ledge now saturating her warm palms as an unexpected breeze tickled her garments, tugging at her bright head covering and soothing her flushed face.

Delighting in the beauty of the day, Kelila lifted her face heavenward, basking in the warm sunshine deliciously contrasting with the cooler breeze, suddenly aware that her Savior had once stood in this very spot. Here, in this sacred space, He had met a Samaritan woman—an outcast by society's standards but precious in the sight of God. Reveling in the wonder of the moment, Kelila could almost *taste* the Spirit's presence here—it was so real, so acutely intense, she marveled.

God was at work—she could feel it in her bones! And He would complete the good work He had begun in Sychar. What an unspeakable privilege to participate in His magnificent plan!

"You're not from around here, are you?"

Stiffening in trepidation, Kelila's knuckles whitened as she gripped the stone ledge before her. Turning cautiously on her heels, she found herself face to face with a Samaritan woman.

Unsure how to respond, Kelila wondered if the woman's frank question constituted a threat. She supposed her heritage was rather obvious, with her exotic features, smooth, dusky skin tone, and a sea of cascading ebony curls.

Did Samaritans hate Cyrenians, too, or was their hatred centered strictly upon the Jews?

"Well?" the Samaritan prodded frankly, crossing her arms over her chest.

"My husband and I have only just arrived—" she fumbled, catching herself before disclosing the inconvenient fact that they hailed from Jerusalem.

"Ah," the woman replied, shaking her head with a wan smile. "The last time I encountered a foreigner at this well…" Her voice trailed off, though not soon enough to mask the heavy sorrow of her tone. Crossing over to one of the ancient stone benches scattered near the well, the woman lowered herself upon it, folding her hands in her lap.

Unsettled, Kelila wondered if she should simply proceed with the task at hand, hastily drawing her water then making a swift retreat back to camp. But the woman didn't appear dangerous or hostile. A deep compassion stirred within Kelila at the sadness mirrored in the Samaritan's serious brown eyes.

Attempting to be discreet, Kelila reached for her discarded water jug, cautiously watching the Samaritan from the corner of her eye. Though the woman was far from beautiful, she was striking in many ways. Her coloring was dark, with long, waist-length hair nearly the color of a crow's wing, intense brown eyes, and a deeply tanned complexion. Something about the woman's haunted eyes and tight lips hinted at a difficult past. The firm set to her jaw and the purposefulness of her posture implied both a fiery determination and a passionate disposition. Though it was hard to tell, Kelila guessed her to be nearing her thirtieth year of life—perhaps a bit more or less, but she couldn't be sure.

It suddenly occurred to Kelila that the woman had no means by which to draw water. Had she simply forgotten her jar at home? Was she in need?

"May I offer you a drink?" Kelila dared, trembling inside. She could only pray that the woman would not be offended by her charity.

The Samaritan turned to look at her then, her eyes conveying deep surprise...and something else. Something Kelila couldn't quite decipher.

Overcoming her initial shock, the Samaritan woman released a low chuckle. "I have not come to draw water today. No, often I come at this hour—the sixth hour—to think, to reflect, to pray."

Tingling with a strange sensation, Kelila tilted her head in wonderment, mesmerized by the sing-song cadence of the woman's low tone, sensing that *something* was about to happen.

"Once, I stood right there as you do now," the Samaritan continued, an enigmatic smile fluttering across her face. "And a Stranger sat upon this very bench, asking *me* for a drink. I regret to say my response was rather scathing. And yet no judgment sprang to His eyes, and there was no condemnation in His tone when He spoke to me."

"What did He say?" Kelila asked, entirely forgetting that the woman to whom she spoke was supposed to be a threat, an enemy.

The woman smiled, tilting her head to one side. "*He said, 'If you knew the gift of God, and who it is who says to you, "Give me a drink," you would have asked Him—'*"

"*—and He would have given you living water,*" Kelila finished with her, lost in a familiar story she'd often heard from the apostles' own lips.

The two women stared at each other, stunned, wide-eyed, and openmouthed, as Kelila wondered how a heathen woman knew of the apostles' sacred story, and as the Samaritan wondered how Kelila knew her own.

And then suddenly it dawned upon them both, a revelation so shocking, so grand and so glorious, they could only marvel.

"You're the Samaritan woman!" Kelila gasped, grasping the woman's arms in amazement. "The woman at the well!"

"And you," the Samaritan woman declared, her brown eyes sparkling with unshed tears, "are the answer to my prayers of many, many years."

CHAPTER 9

Tabitha

Joppa

The kitchen, a massive rectangular workspace bustling with activity, was located just off the sprawling dining hall as Tabitha had suspected it would be. The two chambers were connected by a practical swinging door, which the servants utilized during dinner parties, carrying tantalizing trays and steaming dishes to the polished table in the dining hall. Though Joram's estate was more traditional in style and less Hellenized than Mary's, Tabitha noted the setup in the vast dining hall still reflected triclinium-style seating arrangements, with plush, upholstered couches surrounding three sides of a U-shaped table.

The moment Tabitha entered the buzzing chamber, the servants exchanged nervous glances. Tabitha knew how swiftly gossip spread among household staff, and she imagined they were uncertain about how to relate to her. Was she to be treated like a fellow servant, or a lady of leisure?

However, after a cheery introduction, the kitchen staff—composed of six matronly women and two younger men—had reluctantly accepted her offer to assist.

After several hours of cheerful diligence, Tabitha sensed her fellow servants' relief and admiration had overtaken their initial wariness. Clearly, they had expected Joram's niece to be a haughty, spoiled young woman determined to be waited upon, not someone willing to roll up her sleeves and get happily to work!

Elbow deep in floury bread dough, Tabitha was laughing and sharing a lively conversation with Martha—the rotund, matronly head of the kitchen staff—when the swinging door burst open with such force it slammed against the opposing wall.

The entire staff froze in place as Joram loomed in the doorway, his countenance fearsome to behold. Eli stumbled just behind him, anxiously clutching his writing tablet.

"What do you think you're doing?" Joram growled, his flashing hazel-green eyes locking upon his niece.

Noting that the kitchen staff was visibly cowering in fear of him, Tabitha refused to be intimidated. "Have I done something wrong?" she asked lightly, casually wiping her hands on her floury apron.

The staff exchanged more nervous glances, pitying her.

"You had no right to assume responsibilities you had not been assigned!" Joram seethed as Eli came around him, desperately attempting to pacify.

"My lord, though I instructed her to await your

orders, I assume she was simply trying to help—"

"Haven't you work to do?" Joram snapped, his gaze flashing toward his errant overseer.

"Yes, my lord," Eli amended, his gaze flitting somewhat accusingly toward Tabitha.

"Then see to it!"

As Eli made his hasty retreat, Joram turned his attention back to his niece. "It was presumptuous of you to select a task of your own preference, rather than taking orders from me," he growled, his tone dripping with condescension.

"And it would have proven more favorable had I squandered the entire morning lying abed, simply awaiting your instructions?" Tabitha dared as the entire kitchen staff held their collective breath in fear.

"We shall discuss your present duties in my office," Joram said imperiously, stalking from the tension-thick kitchen with an air of finality.

Calmly removing her flour-dusted apron, Tabitha slung it over her shoulder as her fellow servants watched her with wide eyes and reluctant admiration. "Thank you for a marvelous time," Tabitha smiled, eliciting nervous chuckles from the staff. "I look forward to working with you again soon."

Slipping out the door, Tabitha held back a small smile. The poor, tyrannized staff likely doubted they would ever see her again after her appointment with the relentless Joram.

***

Making a brief side trip to check on her sleeping daughter, Tabitha was relieved to find Laurel catching up on some much-needed rest. Soon, the girl must eat, but she would see to that after debriefing with Joram, since Laurel was still nestled contentedly upon her mat of straw. After assuring the groggy toddler that she would return within the hour to see about some sustenance, Tabitha rose, squared her shoulders in resolve, and marched straight to her uncle's imposing office.

Pausing before the heavily curtained entrance, Tabitha wondered if she should make her presence known in some way or simply barge right in. Joram hadn't provided any instructions about that, and Eli was conspicuously missing—probably still in hiding.

"You may approach."

Wondering at her uncle's ability to sense her presence beyond the curtained entrance and marveling at the princely arrogance with which he spoke, Tabitha drew a steadying breath, somehow presenting a cheery smile as she parted the crimson curtains and entered the regal space.

As expected, Joram was seated behind his massive desk, loads of parchment paperwork and ledgers organized in tidy stacks upon the polished surface. Coldly meeting his niece's gaze, Joram impatiently tapped an elegant stylus upon the desk's smooth surface.

"Good afternoon, Uncle," Tabitha smiled sweetly, supposing it to be at least noon. Time had passed swiftly and pleasantly working alongside Joram's capable kitchen staff.

"Uncle, you say?" Joram drawled, his tone dripping with satire. "I still find it interesting you suddenly insist upon emphasizing our family connection now that you are in need."

"And I find it interesting you are so determined to classify me as a widow in need," Tabitha replied without missing a beat. "Should it set your mind at ease, Uncle, I would be happy to show you my financial documents. Though I am far from wealthy, by the grace of God I am certainly not in need."

Joram studied her coldly, his scowl deepening.

"Has it occurred to you that perhaps I call you 'uncle' because you are the only true family I have left?" she smiled gently.

"You have a daughter," Joram huffed, absent-mindedly shuffling through the documents on his desk. "So let's not be dramatic."

Tabitha could have told him that, though she undoubtedly loved Laurel as if she had borne the child herself, the adopted little girl was not related by blood. But since she didn't see that as any of Joram's business, she held her tongue.

"From this point forward, you may address me as 'my lord' or 'master,'" Joram said coolly, catching Tabitha by surprise. "That is entirely appropriate, as I am your employer. Why should we harbor special feelings toward one another simply because—by some senseless accident of nature or biology—we share the same blood?"

"God knits families together with a very special purpose in mind," Tabitha reminded him softly. "Our kinship is no accident—my lord."

Joram arched a sardonic brow.

"But if it so pleases you, I will no longer refer to you as my uncle," she agreed, deeply saddened.

"It so pleases me," Joram responded gruffly, shifting a bit uncomfortably behind his desk.

"Now if you have a tablet and stylus or parchment

to spare, I am prepared to chronicle my daily duties," Tabitha informed him in a businesslike manner, attempting to ease the crackling tension in the room by referencing the matter at hand.

"You can write?"

"Indeed," Tabitha replied, hiding her amusement. "In several languages."

"And how is that?" Joram demanded, appalled. "Your mother was an uneducated heiress who fell in love with a common laborer!"

"Is that why you disinherited her?" Tabitha asked, curious about her family history. "Because she married a commoner?"

"I disinherited her because she was a fool," Joram spat bitterly. "Our old father—God rest his soul— would have turned over in his grave had I handed over the family fortune on a silver platter—to a witless peasant, of all things."

Tabitha stared at her uncle in disbelief. Had he truly such low regard for her father, the humblest, kindest man she had ever known? Had he no respect whatsoever for the deceased?

"Your mother was a charming woman, whimsical and carefree," Joram admitted grudgingly, interrupting her train of thought. "But she thought she could have the best of both worlds when she fell in love with a man far below her means. I warned her that marriage to a common laborer would result in the loss of the family fortune—at least, for her."

"My mother never wanted your money," Tabitha declared stoutly.

"Well, that's a confounded good thing, because she never got it!" Joram declared, temper flaring.

"My mother fell in love with my father because he

was a godly man," Tabitha quietly explained, struggling to maintain her composure. She was sorely tempted to put the arrogant man in his place—and likely shatter her Christlike witness in the process!

"And she couldn't have bagged a *godly* man within the reputable upper class?" Joram demanded. "No, my sister was bent on having her own way, even if it meant shaming the family name and forfeiting a grand fortune."

Tabitha couldn't help but wonder if perhaps her mother had been wise to distance herself from her greedy brother, for Joram seemed to value money at the expense of all else. Fleetingly, she wondered if the grandparents she had never met had proven as pompous and overbearing as their son! She certainly hoped not, for such a thought utterly shattered her fond imaginings of the dear, old relatives who had passed long before her birth.

"Now tell me," Joram demanded, drawing Tabitha back into the conversation. "How did an orphaned maidservant such as yourself become literate?"

"My father taught me to read and write before he died," Tabitha said, her hackles rising as Joram's eyes narrowed in derision. "He was an intelligent man."

"He was a *poor* man," Joram nearly spat, his face reddening as old memories resurfaced in his mind. "Your mother was a fool to marry him. I warned her against such a mistake, but she was every bit as headstrong as you are."

Suppressing a small smile, Tabitha decided to take that as a compliment.

"As for your duties," Joram groused, roughly changing the subject, "be seated while I compose a list for you. I expect every item on that list to be completed at each day's end. Negligence is utterly inexcusable."

"Yes, my lord," Tabitha replied, carefully concealing her irritation. Her uncle spoke as if he fully expected her to fail him. Quietly taking a seat on one of the gilded chairs across from Joram's desk, Tabitha waited as her uncle scratched out a lengthy list of tasks and responsibilities. Completing the list with a flourish of his hand, Joram thrust it across the desk, his glowering gaze commanding her to rise and retrieve it. He would not stoop so low as to rise from his desk for a common maidservant.

Suppressing her annoyance, Tabitha accepted the long list, her intelligent eyes briefly scanning its contents. She supposed she shouldn't be surprised that Joram had assigned her the dirtiest, most unpleasant and grueling tasks.

Fully recognizing that Joram was likely anticipating—possibly even relishing—an argument from her, Tabitha folded the thick parchment, tucking it away into a hidden pocket sewn into her simple garment. "Thank you, my lord. I shall begin as soon as I see to my daughter's breakfast."

Stunned by her cheerful compliance, Joram's eyes flickered slightly, betraying his confusion...and disappointment. Yet again, he had failed to nettle her.

"As I agreed to work for you in exchange for room and board, is it safe to assume meals are included in this arrangement?" Tabitha asked, pausing before the heavily curtained entrance.

"You may partake of the staff's common portion," Joram said gracelessly, his gruff tone daring her to argue. "But you shall not pester my kitchen staff by making any demands or special requests. You shall eat only what is provided for the staff, nothing more."

Ah, gracious to the last, Tabitha thought, wondering if there was any hope at all for this disagreeable man.

"Thank you, my lord." Dismissing her keen dislike—which required quite a bit of effort—Tabitha forced a cheerful nod of compliance before parting the heavy curtains and slipping gracefully from his office.

Joram remained seated in his impressive chair for quite some time, his hard gaze fastened upon the gently fluttering curtains by which Tabitha had taken her leave. Brooding and utterly perplexed, he eventually managed to pull his attention back to the open ledger upon his desk.

CHAPTER 10

Kelila

Sychar

"Philip! *Philip!*" Kelila shouted, slamming back to camp with the Samaritan woman close on her heels. Straightening near a pile of freshly cut wood, Philip's brown eyes sought his wife's in question. Water sloshed from her large stone jar as she hastened toward him, radiant with joy. With her bright eyes, flushed cheeks, and beaming expression, he was certain he'd never seen her quite so excited before. Questioningly, he looked back and forth between the two women as they hurried to cross the distance between them.

"Philip!" Kelila cried out again, laughing as she bent over to catch her breath. "You'll never guess who I encountered at Jacob's well!"

Turning to look at the serious-looking woman standing at his wife's elbow, Philip's eyes softened in understanding, for he had seen this woman before—

in a vision, hungrily absorbing the Savior's teaching.

The vision in which God had called him to Samaria.

"I know exactly who this is." Philip smiled, marveling at the power of God.

"You do?" Kelila asked, looking a bit put out. "Then who is she?"

"The woman who met Jesus at the well," Philip supplied, shaking his head in amazement. "You're the one who shall help us win your people, aren't you?" Philip asked, directing his question toward the staid young woman.

"You will never know how long I have waited for this moment," Adorina breathed, her eyes sparkling with tears. "All this time...I was often tempted to doubt, so afraid that help would never come—"

"But it has," Philip assured her, fondly placing an arm around Kelila and drawing her close. "Perhaps our calling is in response to your prayers and faithfulness of many years."

Dropping her gaze, the Samaritan woman bit her lower lip, attempting to compose herself.

Heart going out to her, Kelila reached for the woman's wrist, pulling her just a bit closer. "Philip, this is Adorina. She and her husband live on Sychar's main thoroughfare."

"I would love to meet your husband, Adorina," Philip said sincerely. "Is he, too, a believer?"

"He is," Adorina answered, her low alto quavering just a bit. "He will be so happy you have come."

"And are there other believers among you?" Philip asked hopefully, eager to learn the lay of the land.

"There are a few halfhearted stragglers among us," Adorina answered honestly. "Quite frankly, many lost faith shortly after Jesus left. We had no one to instruct us in the Way. Without instruction or accountability, many have fallen away."

"Well, then," Philip replied, his tone and expression sure, "we'd best remedy that."

Adorina's eyes shone with hope. "You must begin teaching the people right away!"

Philip chuckled at her eagerness. "As my wife and I hail from Jerusalem, we may need someone to help ease doubts, suspicion, and misgivings. Can I count on you to introduce us to your neighbors and friends?"

"Absolutely," Adorina replied without hesitation, exchanging a knowing look with Kelila. "After all, I've done it once before. By the end of the day, every man, woman, and child in Sychar shall know your name."

***

Adorina wasted little time conducting Kelila and Philip to the modest home she shared with her husband in Sychar. The persistent woman had eventually persuaded Philip to pack up their belongings, helping husband and wife to deconstruct their small canvas tent and the entire encampment with surprising speed and efficiency.

"You will no longer need this tent, for you shall stay with us," Adorina had insisted, her tone boding absolutely no argument. "I insist."

Now, as Philip pushed the heavy cart bearing all their worldly possessions, Kelila strolled alongside the stoic Adorina, unsettled by the sea of curious eyes upon them as they traversed Sychar's bustling main thoroughfare. Merchants ceased hawking their wares as their gazes fell upon the unlikely group traveling down the street. Women with babies on their hips and baskets of produce on their arms paused, exchanging looks of avid interest. Even the small children playing a lively game in the street halted their mad antics, clearly fascinated by the newcomers.

Relieved, Kelila noted that most of the prying eyes appeared curious rather than hostile. Even so, she was relieved when they eventually reached Adorina's humble abode.

Funny, Kelila thought as Adorina showed Philip where he could leave the cart just outside the gate. *There was a time when I adored being the center of attention. Now, it unsettles me.*

"Come in, come in," Adorina invited with a flourish as she opened the gate. "My husband Ephraim won't return from the fields for several hours yet. In the meantime, I can help you both get settled in."

Kelila was impressed with the well-maintained outer court enclosed with formidable stone walls towering high above her head. "I just adore all your late spring flowers!" Kelila exclaimed, marveling at the intricate tendrils of green ivy climbing the walls and painted trellises. Pausing near an arched niche chiseled in the stone wall, Kelila bent to smell the aromatic flowers spilling over a pot-bellied jar carefully set within the wall.

"Thank you," Adorina replied, watching as Kelila fingered one of the delicate blooms. "Though it's the jar that holds far more value to me than the lovely flowers in it."

"This jar?" Kelila asked, confused. It was certainly nothing special, chipped and stained from use and age.

"Sometimes appearances can be deceiving," Adorina smiled fondly. "I was once like that stone jar—broken, marred, and stained. Every single person in my life insisted I was useless, broken beyond repair. And then I met *Him...*"

Taking Philip's hand as he drew alongside her, Kelila's eyes brightened with interest.

"That was the jar I carried to the well, day after day, in the searing heat," Adorina explained as Kelila's eyes widened in wonder, Philip's, in intrigue. "But then Jesus offered me living water, and I've never been the same. He changed me, Kelila."

Awed, Kelila reverently touched the old stone vessel. What a treasure it was!

"Now I proudly display that jar—though most would consider it nothing more than an ancient stone relic—to remind me of the day that everything changed. It's like a sign to me—a visible sign of the miracle that transpired in my heart so long ago. It is, indeed, quite valuable to me."

"I can see why," Kelila affirmed, marveling that this had been the very jar from which her dear Savior had requested a drink.

"I was dying of thirst the day I met Jesus," Adorina said, her eyes distant, her smile enigmatic. "I had hewn broken cisterns that could hold no water, exhausting all my own resources attempting to quelch that thirst. But only Christ with His living water could truly satisfy."

Kelila and Philip nodded in agreement, marveling at God's presence at work in the life of this strong woman. Undoubtedly, He had led them to the right person, to the right place.

"And this is the message I long to share with my people," Adorina said decisively, her dark eyes flashing with great conviction. "This is the message they need."

CHAPTER 11

Kelila

Sychar

Adorina's husband, Ephraim, was a capable-looking young man with olive-toned skin, hair the color of midnight, a closely cropped beard, and a disarming smile. A man of the fields, he possessed a lean, wiry build and sported simple, practical garments that somehow emphasized his strength and comeliness.

He and Philip hit it off right away.

By candlelight, the small group of believers remained safely sequestered in Ephraim and Adorina's unassuming home, gathered around a wooden table, clutching mugs of warm vegetable stew seasoned with garlic and onion, mint and thyme—compliments of Adorina, a skilled cook.

"How did you learn to cook like this?" Kelila asked her new friend in amazement, wrapping her fingers around her clay mug and savoring its delightful warmth.

"My mother died when I was scarcely weaned," Adorina explained, her eyes flickering ever so slightly with emotion. "I learned to cook as soon as I was old enough to hold a spoon—out of sheer necessity," she added with a faint chuckle.

"So what you're saying is you've had plenty of practice?" Philip implied, a twinkle in his brown eyes.

"At times, more than I'd care for," Adorina admitted as her husband draped an affectionate arm about her slender shoulders.

"When it comes to our marriage, I believe it's safe to say I received the better end of the bargain," Ephraim teased, exchanging a playful look with his wife.

"Absolutely not," Adorina interrupted emphatically. "Sometimes, I still marvel you were crazy enough to even consider pursuing me after my... past history."

"And that's exactly what it is," Ephraim reminded her tenderly. "*History.*"

Exchanging a knowing smile with Philip, Kelila couldn't help but be warmed by Ephraim's obvious devotion toward his wife. If she had to guess, she decided it was safe to assume that Ephraim was a good five years younger than Adorina. Though she was dying to ask about their love story, she supposed it wasn't polite to pry—at least, not yet. Perhaps, in time, the friendship between the four of them would flourish, inviting shared secrets and confidences.

"And how about you, Kelila?" Adorina asked, tearing her gaze from her husband and blushing deeply as if suddenly remembering her guests seated across the table. "You must be an excellent cook."

"Excellent may be a bit of an exaggeration," Kelila admitted, swatting Philip's shoulder when he chuckled in amusement. "I only learned to cook a few months before Philip asked me to marry him."

"Now how did you manage that?" Adorina declared, leaning forward with interest and resting her chin upon a closed fist. "You must have worked rather hard to avoid it."

"I was born into a wealthy family in Cyrene," Kelila explained, flushing slightly. "I'm afraid I was quite spoiled, with a fleet of servants to dote on me—the youngest of a large brood."

"My!" Adorina exclaimed, shaking her head in amazement. "The Romans would say you were kissed by the gods."

"Or cursed," Kelila laughed. "All that doting and spoiling certainly didn't do me any favors. I had to learn some very hard lessons later on—including how to cook!"

"But I must say," Philip added, drawing his wife a bit closer, "during our travels, you've become quite the expert at roasting lentils over an open fire!"

"Ah, lentils," Kelila mused, a wry smile teasing her lips. She could only hope that she'd eventually learn to appreciate the despicable little legumes, as they were affordable, shelf-stable, and travel-safe. Based on their calling, she had an unwelcome feeling she wouldn't be seeing her last lentil for quite some time.

"Truly, we cannot thank you both enough for your hospitality," Philip explained, leaning forward on the table. "This is the finest lodging we've enjoyed in several weeks."

"It's our pleasure to host you," Adorina said with great feeling. "We have waited for so long—for teaching, for instruction. Our people are dying of thirst, just as I was. They are seeking fulfillment in all the wrong things. My heart breaks for them."

"Soon, that will change," Ephraim assured her, gently patting her hand. "God has sent this wonderful couple to remedy that."

"If only you'd allowed me to shout their presence from the rooftops," Adorina said with a rueful smile. "The entire city should know of their arrival, Ephraim!"

"And they will," Ephraim reminded her. "Simply allow this travel-weary man and wife one evening to get settled in. Then you can shout out their presence to your heart's content."

"You can be sure I will," Adorina informed him wryly. "At first light, everyone shall know they have come to help us."

"We are honored by your kind reception," Philip told her sincerely. "However, I think we must prepare ourselves for the possibility that not everyone will be quite as eager as you to receive our message."

"But this is what they *need*!" Adorina insisted, rapping her empty mug on the table for emphasis.

"I agree," Philip said warmly. "However, there are centuries of bad blood between Samaritans and Jews. Understandably, some may be hesitant to receive us."

"Jesus demolished the barriers between Jew and Samaritan here in Sychar," Adorina insisted. "Perhaps in other Samaritan regions, you might encounter opposition. But I truly believe my village will happily receive you, Philip."

"May it be so," Philip said. "What can you tell us about the people of your village, Adorina? What exactly are we up against?"

Ephraim and Adorina exchanged a brief look of concern that wasn't lost on Philip.

"Our people are hungry for truth," Ephraim said carefully, folding his hands on the table's rough wooden surface. "However, this hunger has motivated some to seek fulfillment in forbidden places."

Kelila glanced at Philip in concern. What exactly did Ephraim mean by that?

"Some still believe Jesus is the Messiah," Ephraim assured him, "though there are precious few of us, I'm afraid. Even those who do believe have fallen from their first love."

"Jesus encountered great opposition in Jerusalem because the Jews' understanding of a Messiah is so different from ours," Adorina explained earnestly. "Just as the Jews believed the Messiah would be a mighty conqueror—a warrior-king, of sorts—the Samaritans have always believed the Messiah would be a spiritual teacher. For this reason, our people instantly recognized Jesus as the ultimate Teacher, the Teacher of teachers, and eagerly embraced His message. But many years have elapsed since He instructed us here, and memories are short. When word reached us that Jesus had been crucified in Jerusalem, then resurrected to ascend to His Father in Heaven, many lost heart. After all, how could they continue in the Way without a shepherd to guide them?"

"And, in Christ's absence, the people have turned to another for guidance," Ephraim sighed, disheartened.

"Another?" Philip repeated, surprised. "A fellow believer, perhaps?"

"If only that were so," Ephraim sighed, looking to his wife.

"Who, then?" Kelila asked, a strange, unwelcome tingling creeping up her spine.

"A man called Simon," Adorina supplied, her dark eyes flashing in indignation. "A sorcerer."

"A sorcerer?" Kelila blanched in horror. The dark jungles of her homeland boasted hordes of such deceivers—men who had given themselves entirely to demonic forces in exchange for wealth, power, or fame. Wielding the forces of evil like a sword, such men had plagued entire cities and villages with their black arts.

"Tell us more about this Simon," Philip said, leaning forward. "We need to know what we're up against."

"He's a wily one, that Simon," Ephraim admitted, shaking his head in dismay. "He's a very wealthy man, owning several estates scattered throughout many regions. We know very little about his past, although he claims to have perfected his craft in Alexandria."

"From whence does he hail?" Philip inquired intently.

"No one knows for sure," Ephraim responded uneasily. "Some have speculated that he's a native of the Samaritan village of Gitta, while still others insist he hails from Cyprus. Frankly, he could be Jew, Gentile, or Samaritan—he'll never tell, and perhaps that's how he's managed to dazzle all three groups in various regions. Even so, Simon's true heritage remains unknown, which has only further cultivated the mystery enshrouding his person."

"He possesses no known relatives," Adorina

explained, "and his lineage is strangely elusive, prompting many to ignorantly argue that perhaps he is the Messiah, heaven-sent."

"I see," Philip nodded, amused. "But surely the people understand the Messiah's lineage is distinctly emphasized in Scripture. It was long foretold the Messiah would come from the tribe of Judah. This should silence any further speculation regarding this elusive Simon."

"And this is exactly why we need your instruction!" Adorina exclaimed, grasping Ephraim's arm in excitement. "Our people are not familiar with most of the Hebrew Scriptures, Philip. They accept only the five books of Moses, and thus remain ignorant pertaining to so much regarding the Messiah! But you can help clear up these matters of confusion."

"I do hope so," Philip replied with a wry smile. "Though I doubt the sorcerer will host a welcoming party to propagate our teachings. In fact, he may stir up great opposition."

"Never mind Simon and his cursed arts," Adorina declared forcefully. "He cannot stop us, Philip. Who is he to silence the *true* power of God?"

"What doctrine does he teach?" Philip asked as Kelila watched him with anxious eyes.

"A strange concatenation of a religion all his own," Ephraim supplied wanly. "Mostly, he's combined popular religious thought with pagan philosophies, incorporating both Jewish principles and Greek mythology."

"So he's offering a little something for everyone," Philip observed with a hint of sarcasm.

"Exactly," Adorina agreed in disgust. "He possesses an opulent booth on the central square, selling charms and potions along with his pagan philosophies and ideologies, claiming the power to prescribe magic potions to reach desired ends—to promote health, healing, wisdom, and even claiming he can make one person fall in love with another."

"For an outrageous fee, of course," Ephraim added, his tone tinged with sarcasm. "Apparently, love is an expensive commodity. Simon's wealth increases by the day."

"And you say he travels from city to city promoting his heresies?" Philip clarified.

"He does," Ephraim surmised. "Though he seems quite content here in Sychar. Though he takes brief traveling stints with Helena and a small string of disciples, he seems to favor our little village for the time being. He's built a rather lavish living space behind his magic stall."

"Who is Helena?" Kelila asked, intrigued by the mythical and foreign-sounding name.

"A pagan enchantress, if you ask me," Adorina huffed, her striking features hardening in the flickering lamplight. "If the rumors can be trusted, Simon stumbled upon her in a brothel in Tyre and became utterly smitten."

"So he married her?" Kelila asked, stunned that a man of Simon's station would wed a former prostitute.

"Of course not," Adorina said, sickened. "But he did purchase her, and now the pair boldly and openly flaunt their promiscuous relationship."

"Adorina often jests that they're a perfect match," Ephraim added, a mischievous twinkle in his eyes. "Helena is in love with his money and mystic powers, while he is devoured with lust for her."

"This Simon sounds like very bad news," Philip observed, leaning back in his chair and taking Kelila's hand to reassure her.

"He is," Adorina finished, her dark eyes flashing in contempt. "And he's convinced half the people of Sychar that the power of God rests upon him, even leading some to believe he is the Messiah."

"Many have been deceived by his mystery, charisma, and charm, not to mention the mastery of his dark craft," Ephraim added grimly.

"We shall take this situation before the Lord in prayer," Philip assured them, squeezing Kelila's hand. "As difficult as it is to believe, God loves Simon and desires his salvation, as well."

The heavy silence lingering across the table was proof enough that Adorina strongly disagreed.

Smiling warmly, Philip tactfully changed the subject. "Ephraim, how might I go about obtaining lodging for me and my wife?"

"Are you looking to rent or to buy?" Ephraim asked practically.

"To rent, for the time being," Philip answered forthrightly.

"You don't plan on staying in Sychar?" Adorina asked, alarmed.

"Rest assured, we won't even consider moving on until our mission is complete," Philip promised. "Surely, our desire is to remain here in Sychar, but as an evangelist, I must remain open to the Spirit's leading."

"Of course," Ephraim replied as he and his wife nodded in understanding. "I do know of a place, but it leaves much to be desired, I'm afraid."

"We're far from choosy," Philip chuckled. "We'll

take whatever is available."

"Well, it's not a *house*, exactly," Ephraim explained slowly. "It's a vacant market stall in the central square, but the previous owner built an adjoining living space directly behind the booth. It's a bit rundown, but I'm sure with a few minor repairs—"

"We'll take it," Philip laughed.

"All right, then," Ephraim nodded. "I shall accompany you to make the proper arrangements at first light."

"Thank you, my good friend," Philip said wholeheartedly. "You are a godsend."

Dropping her gaze and twisting her hands nervously in her lap, Kelila attempted to swallow her keen disappointment. A rundown shanty adjoining a vacant market stall on a noisy street corner wasn't anything like the cozy little home she had dreamed of sharing with Philip! Heart sinking, she reminded herself that her situation was in the Lord's hands. She had far too many blessings to waste another moment feeling sorry for herself or mourning what could have been.

Squaring her shoulders, Kelila lifted her gaze, resolved to see this through. After all, she had the Lord. She had Philip. She had these wonderful people to reach! Perhaps in time the Lord would provide a place for them to call home.

But for now, she would remain content in His calling and their current mission.

CHAPTER 12

Tabitha

Joppa

Falling into bed, Tabitha was quite certain she hadn't felt more exhausted in her entire life. After a day of grueling labor in her uncle's mansion, she felt positively bone-weary. Nerves stretched thin, Tabitha's gaze drifted toward her sleeping daughter nestled contentedly on her straw pallet in the corner.

It had been quite a day! Her uncle had watched her every move with obvious disapproval, a deep scowl, and a critical eye. It was unnerving, laboring beneath the icy glare of one determined to detect the slightest flaw in her work ethic.

To make matters worse, Laurel had thoroughly disapproved of Tabitha's new assignment, shouting out her angst to the entire world at the top of her lungs. The girl's ear-piercing fits had nearly driven her—and the entire household—to distraction. Flustered beyond comprehension, Tabitha had done her best to soothe the toddler's outrage, to no avail. Utterly mortified by her daughter's behavior, Joram's disapproving scowl and degrading comments only heightened Tabitha's mounting tension. Every servant in this house must consider her a completely incompetent mother! After all, how could they know that Laurel had only come into her life a few short weeks ago?

Now, deep in peaceful slumber, Laurel's previously strained features had relaxed into a seraphic smile. Shaking her head in dismay, Tabitha wondered how on earth she was to train this poor child. She hadn't the wisdom or experience to raise a daughter alone! She hadn't the slightest idea what she was doing, for Heaven's sake!

Rolling onto her back, Tabitha stared up at the dark ceiling, blinking back tears of defeat. She hadn't known how impossible it would be, working all day without the proper care for her daughter. At Mary's villa, Rhoda had happily volunteered her services to care for the girl, allowing Tabitha to tackle her daily chores with ease. Looking back, Tabitha recognized she hadn't even begun to realize what a blessing that had been. She certainly hadn't expressed the proper appreciation to Rhoda! She regretted that now.

Oh, Lord, her heart cried in anguish, *what am I to do? How can I possibly perform the grueling chores I've been assigned with an angry, defiant two-year-old in tow?*

In that trying moment, Tabitha was sorely tempted to pack her meager belongings, awaken her sleeping daughter, and vanish into the night. She longed for Jerusalem, for the cozy little house she had shared with her precious husband, for the dwindling church family she dearly loved, and Mary's welcoming arms.

Oh, Mary, she thought dejectedly, *if only you were here! You would know exactly what to do!*

Shivering slightly, Tabitha realized—far too late—that she had forgotten to request a second blanket. Just the thought of shivering through another chilly night nearly brought her to bitter tears. Cold, miserable, and utterly defeated, Tabitha wondered if perhaps her ambitions had proven a bit too lofty, unattainable.

Why did I think I was capable of reaching a stubborn old goat like Joram? she thought, chagrined. *And how did I expect to work from dawn until dusk with a two-year-old in tow? And not just any two-year-old, but a child who has endured unimaginable trauma and heartache! Simply raising Laurel would have proven challenging enough! But to raise her alone while working full-time to support us—not to mention ministering to a cold, uncaring relative... What was I thinking, Lord?*

Turning her head, Tabitha gazed upon her peaceful daughter, her angelic features sweetly tranquil in the softly burning lamplight. The poor mite had endured so much, having lost her entire family and witnessed the slow, excruciating decline of a dying mother, only to be thrust upon total strangers while far too young to comprehend or understand her situation.

Do you remember the one who bore you, beloved? Tabitha thought, her eyes misting with tears as she studied her daughter's sweet features. *Do you miss her as desperately as I ache for my beloved husband?*

Turning over on her pathetic straw mattress, Tabitha squeezed her eyes tightly shut, fighting her despair. At this point, she was sorely tempted to doubt her calling, though she knew the Lord had led her here.

How can I do it, Lord? How can I possibly accomplish all I've set out to do? Covering her face with her hands, Tabitha lay very still, her heart pounding dully in her chest. *I can't do it, Lord. I can't do this on my own.*

And then a faint impression whispered its way into her mind, so practically, wonderfully true, she sat up in bed.

I know you can't do it, beloved. You needn't remind Me of that, as I already know it. But I'm glad you see it; for now, you can turn to Me in faith, quietness, and trust.

Releasing a tremorous sigh, Tabitha clung to the Spirit's gentle admonition with all her might. Perhaps these were the moments when faith flourished like spring flowers—the moments when one must lean entirely upon the Lord, relinquishing the illusion of one's own competence or control.

Turn to Me. I can accomplish mighty things through you.

Righteous Father, I place this impossible situation in Your hands. Lifting her own slender hands in a posture of prayer and submission, Tabitha relinquished her struggle to God. *I don't know what to do about these many problems, Lord, but I choose to believe that You already have a solution for each and every one of them.*

Releasing a ragged breath, Tabitha made a conscious decision to relinquish her fears and doubts, choosing instead to wait for guidance from the Lord.

Please show me what to do.

***

Dragging herself out of bed, Tabitha murmured her morning prayers aloud in a desperate attempt to shake herself awake. Accustomed to hard work, Tabitha suspected the bone-numbing weariness lingering over her like an ominous storm cloud had far more to do with her deep discouragement than the taxing labor of the previous day.

It certainly hadn't helped that she had tossed and turned half the night, shivering in the damp chill. A good night's rest would have certainly proven helpful. Today, she would not forget to request a blanket before retiring!

Gritting her teeth in angst, Tabitha dismissed a wave of steadily building resentment against her uncle. Recalling a familiar parable of Jesus, she supposed her bitterness would only serve to snuff out the light her Savior instructed her to shed upon this difficult household.

No one, when he has lit a lamp, puts it in a secret place or under a basket, but on a lampstand, that those who come in may see the light, Jesus once explained. Sighing, Tabitha reminded herself—once again—that her witness for Christ was at stake.

Despite the heavy sense of dread lingering in the air, Tabitha resolved to rise above it. Kneeling beside her sleeping daughter, she brushed aside the soft brown curls, bending to kiss the smooth forehead. *Help me, Lord,* she prayed. *I may not have an earthly husband to provide a home and sustenance for this little one, but You, Lord, are my ultimate Bridegroom, the Lover of my soul, the One who sees me and provides. I trust You.*

After briefly awakening Laurel to assure her that she would return to check on her soon, Tabitha rose woodenly to her feet, squaring her shoulders in firm resolve. Though she shuddered to even consider plunging headfirst into another day like the previous one, she would wait for the Lord to provide a solution.

Thankfully, Laurel would sleep for several more hours yet. That fact alone was a blessing!

For now, I must simply trust—and pay attention, she reminded herself as she quickly brushed her long hair, tying it at the nape of her neck, and slipping a covering over her head. *Perhaps the Lord has an answer right in front of me, one I haven't yet considered.*

Making a quick side trip to the washroom in the servants' quarters, Tabitha washed her face, hands, and feet. Ruefully, she noted that she would soon need to wash her garments as well—preferably at the day's end. She had but one change of clothes, and the arduous, sweaty work of the previous day had left its mark. *Several, actually,* she thought wanly, smoothing the soiled folds of her apron.

Making her way down the labyrinth of stone corridors emerging from the bowels of the dark house, Tabitha made up her mind to speak with Eli before tackling her daily assignments. First, she would request a blanket to ward off the night's oncoming chill. Second, she would ask about obtaining the proper materials to write a letter to Mary. Though she'd have to wait weeks and possibly even months to receive a response from the wise widow, Tabitha was certain her former mistress would undoubtedly have many wonderful suggestions about parenting an obstinate, traumatized child.

Confident in her mission, Tabitha took a sharp turn, nearly plunging headfirst into a very flustered Eli.

Taking several steps back, Eli smoothed his billowing robes, resembling a rather large, agitated bird. "Miss Tabitha! Please watch where you're going!"

"Forgive me, Eli," Tabitha responded, holding back a smile. "And, please, call me Tabitha. I'm not sure Joram would approve of you bestowing any special titles on a common maidservant."

"Do you plan on making a habit of this?" Eli hissed, glossing over her humble observation in his agitation. "Barreling into innocent pedestrians in darkened corridors?"

"Absolutely not," she replied, her bright eyes twinkling with mischief.

"Well, I'm glad to hear it," Eli replied, his tone clipped.

"Eli," Tabitha said warmly, earning a suspicious look from the stringent overseer, "may I please request an extra blanket? We have only one, and—"

"I shall have one sent to your quarters."

"Thank you," Tabitha said sincerely. "One last thing."

Eli's expression conveyed his impatience.

"I'd like to write a letter to my loved ones back home," Tabitha explained, amused by his air of endurant long-suffering. "How might I obtain ink and parchment to do so?"

"I shall present your request before the master," Eli responded, his tone indicating that her chances of obtaining what she desired was doubtful at best.

"Thank you, Eli," Tabitha replied, flustering him with another friendly smile. "I shall tend to my duties now."

"Very well," Eli responded tersely, slipping past her and resuming his passage down the corridor.

Wondering if her request would truly see the light of day, Tabitha hastened down the corridor, bracing herself for the strenuous chores awaiting her.

CHAPTER 13

Tabitha

Joppa

Trying not to think of the dozens still awaiting her attention in Joram's opulent seaside mansion, Tabitha was relieved she had eventually succeeded in hauling a monstrosity of an elaborate Persian rug into the large, enclosed stone courtyard reserved for the servants' dirtiest jobs. Somehow, she managed to drape the heavy finery upon the enormous wooden frame intended to secure the rug in place while a servant beat the dust and dirt from it.

Having found no particular instrument or paddle designated to aid her in the trying task, Tabitha supposed she was expected to beat the rug by hand. She didn't relish the idea at all. It would be a messy job, and she'd undoubtedly inhale several servings of grit and fine, powdery dust in the process.

"*Ahem.*"

Glancing over her shoulder in surprise, Tabitha saw Eli standing in the unadorned stone doorway behind her, his expression conveying his glaring irritation.

"Hello, Eli," Tabitha managed cheerfully, wondering what in the world she had done wrong this time.

"You have a guest awaiting you in the outer court," Eli informed her, his tone characteristically clipped and lacking good humor.

Tabitha stared at him in confusion. "A guest?"

"That *is* what I said, isn't it?"

"At this hour?" Tabitha asked in disbelief, glancing up at a pale gray sky. The sun had barely begun its slow ascent into the misty, morning skyline.

"The master isn't going to like it," Eli muttered, wringing his hands as if caught in an awkward dilemma. "I don't suggest you make a habit of this."

"Who is it?"

"I suggest you make your way to the outer court to see for yourself," Eli retorted. "And make haste about it. The master will have both our heads if he learns you were entertaining guests when you should have been working!"

Tabitha was warmed, sensing that Eli was risking Joram's wrath for her sake. Hurrying to the door, she paused long enough to lightly touch his arm. "Thank you, Eli. I will not tarry."

Slipping past him, Tabitha felt his eyes upon her even as she disappeared into the dark vestibule leading into the kitchen.

***

"Tirzah!" Tabitha exclaimed, both surprised and delighted to see her new friend waiting impatiently in the outer court.

"I was about to come track you down myself,"

Tirzah declared with a rueful grin, readily return-ing Tabitha's warm embrace. "Eli looked like he was going to self-implode when I demanded to see you. I wasn't entirely certain he would summon you."

"He risked my uncle's wrath to announce your arrival," Tabitha smiled, warmed yet again by the thought. Perhaps she was making some headway, after all!

Glancing over her shoulder, Tirzah's glance flickered toward the armed guards standing at stark attention at the gate. Turning back to her friend, she leaned in a bit closer, her light brown eyes tinged with a hint of reluctance. "Listen," she said, lowering her voice, "I hope you don't think I'm insane, but I didn't sleep a wink last night…"

Tabitha stared at Tirzah in confusion as the young widow's voice trailed off in obvious hesitation.

Appearing to steel herself for Tabitha's reaction, Tirzah met her friend's questioning gaze head-on.

"Tabitha, I think I'm supposed to ask you some-thing."

***

"Absolutely not!" Joram roared, slamming a closed fist upon his desk for emphasis. "No stranger comes into my home uninvited."

"Oh, please," Tirzah huffed, rolling her eyes in exasperation. "I'm hardly a stranger, Joram. You've known me since I was in my mother's womb, for heaven's sake!"

"And is that fact supposed to endear you to me in some nonsensical, illogical way?" Joram snapped, rising from his chair to face the young widow's challenging stare.

"I wouldn't expect you to harbor particularly fond feelings toward anyone but yourself," Tirzah responded coolly, completely unintimidated. "But you have known me my entire life, not to mention the fact that I worked for you after my father died. So you know that I am entirely trustworthy."

Standing opposite Joram's impressive cedar desk, Tabitha glanced at her friend in surprise. Tirzah had once worked for her uncle? She never would have guessed!

Dismissing her initial surprise, Tabitha forced herself to focus on the matter at hand. Watching the interaction between the unyielding Joram and a fiery Tirzah, Tabitha decided this meeting wasn't going well. Not at all. She had respectfully waited to arrange the meeting until Joram had awakened, dressed, and been served a luxurious breakfast. Clearly, her thoughtfulness had gone unnoticed.

"I knew hiring a relative would prove disastrous," Joram growled, glaring at his niece in accusation. "You've been with me less than two days, and already you have stirred up all manner of mischief."

"Actually, this was *my* idea," Tirzah responded sharply, putting Joram in his place. "Tabitha had nothing to do with this."

"And yet, here she stands—by your side, demanding you join my staff to pacify her shrieking brat."

"Far from it," Tirzah shot back, one hand planted firmly on the curve of her hip. "The last thing I want is to join *your* staff, Joram. I would be working solely for Tabitha, caring for her daughter a few hours each day so she can better perform the tasks you have assigned her."

"Yet you would be working for her here in *my* house!" Joram reminded her, peeved. "No doubt partaking of *my* resources!"

"I shall bring my own provisions if you're concerned I would dare touch the soggy lentils and grudging supply of water you deign to bestow upon your poor, malnourished staff."

Sensing that Joram was about to strangle in rage, Tabitha swiftly stepped in. "Ultimately, this is *your* decision, my lord," she said in a pacifying tone. "After all, it *is* your house, and I am under your employ. But when Tirzah offered to care for Laurel several hours each day, enabling me to grant my full attention to my work, I considered it a very wise suggestion. This way, I can more fully devote myself to the tasks you have assigned."

"And I imagine I shall be expected to compensate this potter woman for her services?" Joram hinted, his tone drenched in sarcasm.

"Absolutely not," Tabitha replied with confidence. "I shall compensate her from my own wages."

"You don't earn wages," Joram reminded her coldly. "You work in exchange for room and board."

"My, how generous," Tirzah huffed, receiving another glare from Joram, which she swiftly returned with gusto.

"She will be compensated; you needn't worry about that, my lord," Tabitha assured her uncle, tactfully tugging his attention from his icy stare-down with Tirzah.

Grudgingly, Joram glanced back and forth between the two widows, stroking his chin as if deep in thought. It was obvious he enjoyed wielding his power over them, which only further sharpened

Tirzah's tongue.

"Might I remind you," she pointed out, eliciting another hard stare from Joram. "It is highly unlikely Tabitha will remain on your staff without proper care for her daughter. And considering that your chances of finding someone else to do the job she's been assigned—in return for the mere pittance you have offered her—you may want to consider doing everything in your power to keep her on your staff. Not to mention the fact that her productivity will undoubtedly increase dramatically if her child is properly tended, freeing her to perform your bidding without distraction or hindrance—not that the girl is a hindrance," she swiftly amended, receiving an understanding smile from Tabitha.

"Well," Joram drawled, slowly lowering himself onto his throne-like chair. "It would seem you both have everything all figured out."

"Absolutely," Tirzah responded, "and the wisdom of our proposition is undeniable. Now the question is this: are you on board, Joram?"

Glancing back and forth between her glowering uncle and her tenacious friend, Tabitha hoped Tirzah wasn't pushing too hard, too fast. Praying silently, she awaited Joram's response.

"You may do as you wish," Joram finally growled after a long pause laden with tension. "But if this arrangement interferes with the productivity of my staff or the goings-on of this household, Tirzah, you're out."

"Gracious to the last, just as I expected," Tirzah grinned, filling Tabitha with trepidation. She feared this woman was far too bold!

Wrinkling his silver brows in disgust, Joram

dismissed the young women with a condescending wave of his hand.

Mighty God, Tabitha prayed, her heart bursting with gratitude as she turned to take her leave. *I asked, and You answered. You saw my need, and You swiftly provided. How great You are! How merciful, Father!*

Exchanging knowing smiles, the two young widows departed from Joram's office in triumph.

CHAPTER 14

Tabitha

Joppa

"Here you are, darlin'," Martha, Joram's matronly head cook, offered Laurel a warm piece of fresh flatbread as Tabitha gently set her on the sprawling stone countertop functioning as the kitchen's main workstation. "My, she's a sweet little mite, isn't she?" Martha beamed, watching the happy child as her little legs swung contentedly back and forth while she munched.

"She is *now*," Jonas, a servant Tabitha hadn't yet met, quipped, peeking his head through the swinging kitchen door. "Let's hope she stays that way. Yesterday, she was—"

"*Jonas!*" Martha harrumphed, planting flour-coated hands on her ample hips. "The girl's only just arrived in a brand-new environment, having been plucked from her childhood home and all she holds dear. Give her time."

Surprised, Tabitha glanced back and forth between the hefty lady cook and the sheepish manservant peering around the door. It was unusual for a woman to address a man in such a brusque manner. Glancing at Tirzah, Tabitha held back a wry smile. Well, in *most cases*, it was unusual. Tirzah certainly hadn't hesitated going toe-to-toe with Joram in his office!

"That's Jonas," Tirzah whispered, sensing Tabitha's confusion. "He's Joram's bookkeeper...and Martha's husband."

"Ah," Tabitha laughed, watching the heated exchange between husband and wife. "That makes sense now."

"What are you wanting, Jonas?" Martha grumped, reaching for a rather threatening-looking rolling pin.

"Just checking to see about the midday meal," Jonas muttered, his expression downcast.

"It will be ready when *I'm* good and ready," Martha shot back, turning her attention back to the little girl happily munching her flatbread on the edge of the counter. "In the meantime, I have work to do. I'll let you know when it's prepared."

Defeated, Jonas retreated with a halfhearted nod and a *good day* murmured in the general direction of the two widows and his wife's bustling helpers.

As Martha set aside her rolling pin, *oohing* and *aahing* over little Laurel and evoking shy giggles from the pretty toddler, Tabitha turned toward Tirzah, speaking loudly enough to be heard over the clattering clamor of the bustling kitchen. "I had no idea you worked for my uncle!" she exclaimed, fascinated. "I assumed you've always been a potter."

"I have," Tirzah supplied with a slight lift of her shoulder. "I've always loved the craft. But when my father died, my mother and I found ourselves in dire straits. While she sold her pottery and worked any odd jobs she could find to make ends meet, I went to work at age five or six—I've forgotten now."

"You worked for my uncle as a *child*?" Tabitha asked, even more surprised.

"Indeed. I was his wife's chambermaid."

"His wife?" Tabitha repeated, shocked. "Joram was *married*?"

Instantly, the clamor of the kitchen ceased. Tabitha's question hung in the air like an ill omen as several cooks glanced up from their work, uneasy.

"We are forbidden to discuss it," Martha said tersely, her expression commanding the eavesdropping servants nearby to get back to work. Reluctantly, they did so; however, Tabitha noticed their ears remained pricked with interest.

Surprisingly, Tirzah heeded Martha's stern rebuke, though her twinkling eyes promised to discuss the forbidden subject later. Inexplicably intrigued, Tabitha resisted the urge to ply Tirzah with questions right then and there, despite Martha's watchful eye.

"I suppose I must return to my chores," Tabitha sighed, her countenance lighting at the sight of her daughter giggling at the silly faces Martha made at her. "May we discuss your wages at the day's end, Tirzah? And establish a consistent schedule that works for you?"

"Absolutely," Tirzah readily responded. "But, Tabitha, we're not just neighbors—we are also *friends*. Truly, you needn't pay me to spend a few hours each day with your delightful daughter. It will be an absolute joy."

"That means more than you know," Tabitha told her, warmed by Tirzah's selfless service. "But I know what it's like to be undervalued...and underpaid," she added with a teasing smile. "You are losing time you could be at your potter's wheel—or selling your wares—to help me during this trying season. And as the Lord has provided the means for me to compensate you for your time, then I believe it's only right to do so."

"So, tell me," Tirzah grinned, her eyes lighting with anticipation. "How shall little Laurel and I spend our first day together?"

"Well, she'll need an afternoon nap," Tabitha mused. "But, until then—it's a beautiful day, so feel free to enjoy the sunshine and the fresh air! My uncle's gardens are lovely—I'm sure she would enjoy a stroll through them. Oh, and I'd like her to help me with some of the simpler chores after her nap," she added, mentally calculating which tasks a two-year-old could perform. Even if Tabitha had to heavily assist, it was important for Laurel to learn about diligence, responsibility, and work ethic.

"We are going to have a wonderful day!" Tirzah declared, scooping little Laurel from Martha's soft arms, much to the matronly woman's huffing protests.

"Mama must get back to work, little one." Stroking Laurel's fluffy brown curls as the child clung to Tirzah's neck, Tabitha's heart constricted at the prospect of missing a delightful day of fun with her daughter. She couldn't help but envy Tirzah, just a bit. But unless she intended to take another husband—which she absolutely had no desire to do—then she must continue to provide for her little girl.

Sighing somewhat dismally, Tabitha wondered if married women recognized what an unspeakable privilege it was to be at home with their precious little ones. What she wouldn't give to do so herself!

"Well, I have an engagement with a few dozen Persian rugs, so I'd best be going," Tabitha teased, kissing her daughter's forehead. "Thank you, Tirzah. And, Martha, thank you for so graciously providing Laurel's breakfast."

"It's a downright pleasure, it is," Martha insisted, returning her attention to a basket brimming with fresh produce from the market.

With another wistful smile, Tabitha left to resume her chores.

***

Kelila
Sychar

Sychar's spacious central square was hemmed in on all sides by long, rectangular-shaped stone buildings with rows and rows of sellers' booths and market stalls lining the entire perimeter. Most of the market stalls boasted adjoining chambers buried beneath the broad, pillared porticoes gracing the front of each sprawling building, which housed rows of unadorned doorways carved into the rough stone. Each doorway marked a shallow chamber corresponding with the individual booths. Despite the early hour, merchants had already begun conducting the day's business, re-stocking their shelves, counting jingling coins, and loudly hawking their wares. Passers-by responded with lukewarm interest, some lingering near the sellers' booths while others ignored the merchants completely, going about their affairs as usual.

Standing upon a raised curb within the central market square, Kelila was utterly speechless as she gazed across the dusty road at a dilapidated old structure soon to be called home. Attempting to calm her uncooperative emotions, Kelila drew a steadying breath, quietly assessing the damage.

The makeshift dwelling in question couldn't possibly be any further from her cherished hopes and expectations! Cringing inwardly, she noted the rundown storefront with its drooping, discolored canopy, broken-down wooden shelves, and jagged shards and remnants of pottery dusting the dirt floor and crooked shelf space. Empty, rotting crates were upturned every which way, scattered beneath the pathetic bit of shade provided by the sagging canopy.

She didn't even want to think about what the inside must look like!

Glancing sideways at Philip, she realized she should probably say something encouraging. He must be just as demoralized as she. Surely he felt inadequate, having nothing better to provide for his new bride than this miserable shanty! Taking his hand, Kelila was about to offer her gentlest consolation when Philip's bearded features stretched into a broad grin.

"It's *perfect*!" he exclaimed, shaking his head in

amazement.

"*What?*" Kelila gasped, utterly dumbfounded. Had she been studying the wrong structure, perhaps?

"Just look at it!" Philip declared, his brown eyes twinkling in joyous anticipation.

Following his excited gesture, Kelila's heart sank. She had, indeed, been looking at the right booth. So what on earth did he have to be so excited about? It looked like a dilapidated old hovel.

"Kelila, it's right on the main square! Right on the road!"

Exactly, Kelila wished to retort. *Planted amidst squawking chickens, braying donkeys, hawking merchants, and the creaking and rattling of a dozen carts!*

"With so much open space available to us, just imagine how many will gather to hear the Word!" Philip explained, his tone conveying his excitement. "We can easily instruct them from the booth—once we spruce it up a bit. Since ours is the last stall on the end, there will be plenty of room for spillover crowds, as well. And just think—right here on the broad public square! God is good!"

Though Kelila certainly wouldn't deny God's goodness, she couldn't help but assume Philip should have chosen a worthier argument than the provision of a rundown hovel to support that claim!

"This is far better than we could have hoped for, love," Philip confessed, drawing Kelila close to him.

Somehow, Kelila managed to keep her opinion to herself.

"Ephraim has gone to locate the owner so I can sign the documents and make it official," Philip informed her, beaming.

Good for him, Kelila thought, peeved. Maybe Ephraim would get lost along the way! She could certainly hope.

"What do you think of it?" Philip asked, clearly oblivious to her silent angst.

"It's..." Kelila stammered, attempting to conceal her keen disappointment. "It's really something," she finished lamely.

"Indeed!"

"Do other people live here, as well?" Kelila asked weakly, observing how the long buildings framing the central square housed dozens of doorways, none of which possessed an actual *door.* Most of the gaping entrances remained wide open or partially obscured with a hanging curtain or tapestry, of sorts.

"A few," Philip responded, "although the rooms behind the booths weren't designed for housing. Rather, they are intended to be used as storage spaces to stock merchandise, store equipment, protect perishables from bad weather—that sort of thing."

Just great, she thought, miffed. *Our first house is a storage room!* Well, at least it was a step up from the canvas tent...sort of.

Allowing her gaze to sweep across the entirety of the bustling square, Kelila noted a large corner booth on the opposite end of the sprawling stone structure housing the chamber Philip planned to rent. Unlike all the others, it boasted its very own door—and a very fine one, at that, with polished handles and an impressive golden knocker. In fact, the entire setup was impressive, with an exotic-looking canopy swirling with rich hues of scarlet, amethyst, sapphire, silver, and gold, elegant Grecian urns overflowing with fresh flowers, and plush, colorful rugs scattered around the booth. The area surrounding the booth had been neatly and professionally paved in stone, unlike the rest.

Why hadn't Philip looked into *that* one?

As if on cue, the sparkling gilded door bowed inward. Curious about the owner of such an opulent stall, Kelila watched as the tenant gracefully emerged, softly closing the door behind her. Rather than turning around, the woman remained poised in front of the door, delicately sliding a large bronze key into the lock.

Jaw dropping in shock, Kelila gaped at the most brazen-looking woman she had ever seen.

Glaringly Greco-Roman in style and appearance, the woman's wardrobe was shockingly provocative with a sheer, sleeveless white gown sporting a plunging neckline and thigh-high slits that teased shapely legs. A thick, jewel-studded golden belt strapped about her slender waist emphasized a lush, hourglass figure. Her slender wrists, arms, and throat were heavily adorned with glittering gold and sparkling gems. Rather than a modest head covering, she proudly donned a glittering crown woven of leaves overlaid in gold. With her striking presentation and almost unbelievable cascades of golden curls billowing over her back and shoulders, the woman appeared much like the glorified and often exaggerated descriptions of Greek and Roman goddesses.

Instantly unsettled, Kelila glanced over at Philip. She saw in dismay that he, too, had noticed her. His gaze remained riveted upon her—not in admiration, but in sheer disbelief. He, too, must be wondering if his eyes deceived him.

Doused in a heady fragrance that floated upon the morning breeze, the young woman pocketed her key, then, sensing eyes upon her, dared a coy glance over her bare shoulder. Somehow overlooking the throngs of animals, merchants, pedestrians, and shoppers, the woman's gaze fell instinctively upon the newcomers at the far end of the square. Kelila's insides twisted in alarm as her sultry gaze brushed over Philip with obvious interest. Turning icy blue eyes upon Kelila, her mouth contorted into a condescending smile.

Feeling rooted in place and strangely mesmerized by the woman's cold blue eyes, Kelila's stomach churned in mounting discomfort. For one long, distressing moment, the blonde woman held her gaze in challenge, and Kelila's heart pounded wildly in response.

Then, just as quickly as she had appeared, the woman turned and left, her hips swaying gracefully as she strode down the dusty, bustling street, swiftly vanishing amidst the crowd.

Instantly, a cold realization dawned, sending Kelila's heart pounding in trepidation; for It would seem she had just encountered a close neighbor.

Helena.

The sorcerer's muse.

CHAPTER 15

Mary

Jerusalem

Her brother's cheerful countenance was like a breath of fresh air.

Reclining upon a richly upholstered lectus in the lavish family triclinium, Mary smiled fondly across the table as Barnabas teased her sixteen-year-old son, John Mark. They were a lively pair—Barnabas, with his twinkling brown eyes and playful banter, and John Mark, with his swift comebacks and boyish charm. While John Mark reclined upon his lectus with practiced ease, Barnabas remained seated upright, his casual stance betraying the fact that, despite his elevated social status, he was far more accustomed to dining with commoners. Mary had always admired his unpretentious nature and gentle humility.

"It is a pleasure to dine with you, my brother," she said earnestly, silently thanking God for preserving

Barnabas throughout his lively and often dangerous travels. "You must tell us all about the churches you have visited throughout Judea and Galilee. Do our brothers and sisters fare well?"

"Better than well!" Directing his attention toward his younger sister, Barnabas' eyes sparkled with enthusiasm. "And our Savior's blessed message is no longer confined to the Judea province, nor even in Galilee. The message is spreading like wildfire, taking the empire by storm."

Mary leaned forward on her elbow, amazed. "Is the church growing so fast?"

"Faster," Barnabas chuckled, shaking his head in disbelief. "We are seeing churches springing up in regions as far as Antioch, Ephesus, Corinth—even Rome!"

"Believers in *Rome*?" John Mark quipped as a stream of servants entered the triclinium bearing steaming trays of food. "I'd like to see that!"

"John Mark, Rome is a wicked city, brimming with immorality, debauchery, and licentiousness," Mary said sternly, turning to smile her appreciation as the servants placed their trays upon the polished table.

Hiding a wry smile, Barnabas looked somewhat amused at his sister's rather abrupt description of the Imperial City.

"You must tell us more about these new churches, Barnabas," Mary invited eagerly, reaching for her goblet as the servants fluttered away. "But, first, will you honor us by blessing this meal?"

It was a delight and a privilege to hear Barnabas pray. Taking the bread from the table, he lifted it in the same manner their Savior so often had, reciting the traditional blessing over it. Then, in his calm, easy way, he thanked the Lord for His faithful provision, conversing as easily as if Jesus sat beside him. Mary couldn't help but feel as if the Lord Jesus shared their table once again when Barnabas communed with Him, for His presence lingered so heavily in the air she was almost tempted to reach out and touch it.

Once the blessing had been pronounced, Mary and Barnabas exchanged looks of amusement as John Mark partook of the feast with boyish zeal.

"I'd be the size of a sailing vessel if I packed away so much food," Barnabas chuckled fondly, ruffling John Mark's dark hair.

"That, I'd like to see," John Mark shot back as he helped himself to another rounded loaf of flatbread piled high with goat cheese, aromatic spices, and spring onions. "But if you became a huge sailing vessel, Uncle, then you wouldn't have to bother arranging passage on all those ships to accommodate your travels!"

"I said I would be the *size* of a sailing vessel, not that I'd *become* one," Barnabas returned drolly. "I would sink like a brick with all that extra weight!"

Mary shook her head in consternation as John Mark rewarded his uncle with a wide grin.

"Somehow, that boy eats and eats without gaining an ounce," she sighed. At least, not in the wrong places. To her great delight—and trepidation—her son was fast becoming the spitting image of his father with broad shoulders, a lean, muscular build, handsome, aristocratic features, and a winning smile. At times, Mary worried that her son didn't take life—or his relationship with Christ—quite seriously enough. Charming and dangerously attractive, John Mark could easily be led down the wrong path—a life without structure or discipline, one that promised ease and pleasure above all else. With Roman thought and influence permeating even the farthest reaches of the empire, many young people were falling prey to an Epicurean lifestyle.

Shaking herself from her troubling reverie, Mary forced a sociable smile, determined to enjoy her brother's company. After all, he had become so actively involved in his travels, she rarely saw him.

"Now about these churches cropping up all over the empire," Mary prodded, reaching for a vine-ripened cluster of red grapes. "Tell me everything, my brother."

"Well, they are still very small," Barnabas admitted, taking a thoughtful sip of scented water accented with flower petals. "No more than half a dozen believers in most of them. They meet in private homes, mostly in secret, at this point."

"Are they all former members of the Jerusalem church?"

"Most of them, but some simply heard Jesus' preaching during pilgrimages to Jerusalem for the feast days. Others were here when Peter addressed the great crowd at Pentecost. Those who accepted his teachings returned to their homelands, excited about their faith."

"They must greatly appreciate your instruction, Barnabas," Mary said, smiling warmly as young Rhoda emerged from the entryway bearing another tray.

"Oh, I don't offer any instruction," Barnabas amended, looking surprised. "I am not an apostle,

Mary."

"Neither was Stephanos, but that didn't stop *him*," Mary pointed out wryly, lifting her goblet to emphasize her point. "In fact, deacons regularly instruct the believers here, along with the apostles."

Barnabas' smile was rueful. "I'm far more inclined to simply encourage the brethren," he admitted. "Planting and building churches, well, it's a sacred calling, Mary."

"Don't be so certain God won't call you to do that very thing," Mary teased.

"He very well might," Barnabas mused with a faraway look that wasn't lost on his perceptive sister.

Despite her avid curiosity, Mary decided to drop the subject...for now.

"May I interest you in baked apples glazed with honey, cinnamon, and cloves?"

Mary's head came up as Rhoda's soft, dulcet voice wafted over the long table. The servant girl stood beside John Mark, blushing prettily, as she dipped her sweet-smelling tray within his reach.

"Don't you always?" John Mark grinned, watching her intently as she gracefully lowered the tray so he could make his selection. "Which one do you recommend?"

"Whichever most pleases you," Rhoda responded shyly, her large brown eyes filled with girlish admiration.

"I'd be hard-pressed to find one as sweet as *you*, wouldn't you agree, Uncle Barnabas?" John Mark teased, inviting his relative to participate in his playful banter. Clearly, he adored the servant girl just as an older brother might idolize a younger sister.

"I certainly couldn't argue that point," Barnabas

responded mildly, carefully observing his sister's reaction. "I will take one as well, Rhoda."

"Yes, my lord," Rhoda answered softly, hesitantly moving away from John Mark.

Once the apples had been served, Rhoda lingered near the table with her empty tray, clearly hesitating to return to the kitchen.

"Thank you so much, dear Rhoda," Mary said, smiling graciously. "That will be all for now."

"Yes, my lady," Rhoda replied, her soft tone tinged with disappointment.

Watching her go, Mary wondered if she should have corrected Rhoda for serving John Mark before attending their guest. The starry-eyed maidservant's infatuation with the dashing John Mark had grown rather than waned over time. Though Rhoda hadn't once behaved in an unseemly manner, Mary wondered if she should address the issue or simply leave it be.

Oh, but wouldn't the poor girl be devastated when it was time for John Mark to take a wife? Astounded, it suddenly occurred to Mary that her son was of marriageable age! Was she ready to consider arranging a marriage for him? The mere thought made her entire being grow cold.

"Is something on your mind, dear sister?" Barnabas quipped, his brown eyes sparking with mischief.

"Oh," Mary managed, unaccustomed to being caught off guard. "I am quite all right, Barnabas," she responded, watching dully as John Mark devoured the remainder of his dessert. It suddenly occurred to her that she desperately needed some time to speak with her brother—alone.

"Have you completed your studies for the day,

John Mark?" she asked, forcing a cheerful smile.

"Not yet. Tobias allowed me to join you and Uncle Barnabas for the midday meal," he replied, cringing inwardly.

"Then I suppose you'd best return to the bibliotheca and resume your work," Mary responded, her tone boding no argument.

Crossing the room, Mary paused before a tall window, gazing quietly into the lush gardens beyond as John Mark and Barnabas exchanged their goodbyes in the form of good-natured ribbing and a smothering bear hug.

"You've raised a good boy, Mary," Barnabas told his sister once John Mark had left the elaborate chamber, closing the distance between them and pausing just behind her.

"He's no longer a boy, Barnabas," Mary sighed, turning to gaze up at him with intense gray eyes. "Somehow, he became a man...when I wasn't even looking."

"It happens to all of us, I'm afraid." Barnabas chuckled softly, sensing his sister's inner turmoil. "You seem troubled, Mary."

"I suppose I am," she answered honestly, crossing her slender arms. "I must admit, I feel somewhat... lost."

"*You*?" Barnabas declared, incredulous. "Lost?"

"I know, it sounds ridiculous," Mary admitted, turning to look out the window once again. "But so much has changed in such a brief time. Many whom I love most have died or been forced to flee for their lives. And then I see my grown son, Barnabas, and I recognize that, all too soon, John Mark will take a wife and move on with his life, as well. Just like the others."

Fleetingly, Mary thought of Stephanos, their dear evangelist, who had sacrificed his life for the salvation of souls. And her beloved Tabitha, now ministering to her uncle miles away in Joppa. How she missed Kelila's vibrant smile and Philip's gentle warmth! *Praise God,* she thought, *at least Candace and Simon shall soon return from Cyrene!* How deeply she missed her brothers and sisters, now seemingly scattered over the face of the whole earth.

And then there was the painful absence of her beloved husband, Mark. The sting of loss was keen, even all these years later. Mark would have known how to find a worthy wife for their son. How she ached for him during trying moments like these!

Precious Lord, I praise You for the hope of Heaven, she thought, longing for that blessed day when those loved and lost would be sweetly reunited for all eternity.

"Ah," Barnabas said, recognizing his sister's quiet struggle. "I wouldn't be so sure about John Mark moving on now," he teased, lightly touching her arm. "It would seem he has quite the little admirer right here in your own house."

"Rhoda?" Mary gasped, her present troubles evaporating in her great surprise. "Barnabas, she has a girlish crush. It is nothing more than that."

"Are you sure about that, Mary?" Barnabas pressed, his brown eyes twinkling merrily. "She has adored your boy for years, and her love has only grown over time."

"Please, Barnabas," Mary protested, strangely unsettled by her brother's observation. "Rhoda is but a child! Far too young to know the first thing about marriage! Why, John Mark considers her a doting little sister."

"How old is our dear Rhoda, Mary?"

"She is twelve, soon to be thirteen," Mary mused, mentally calculating how many years the beloved maidservant had been with them. "She was but eight years old when we rescued her from that wicked slaver."

"Twelve or thirteen," Barnabas grinned. "Many young women are betrothed to be married by that age."

"Well, just because they *are* doesn't mean they *should* be!" Mary said firmly, clearly dismissing the matter. "The poor girl is still a child, Barnabas. She certainly needn't be thrust into a betrothal long before she is ready."

"Of course," Barnabas chuckled, amused by his sister's uncharacteristic reaction. Mary was typically so composed! He decided it was best to change the subject. "Isn't John Mark training to take over the family business someday? That, too, will encourage him to remain in Jerusalem, no?"

"I worry for him," Mary confessed, thankful the Lord had orchestrated this special time with her understanding older brother. She hadn't realized how desperately she needed a listening ear, and Barnabas was the best listener she had ever met.

"He is incredibly bright and has everything going for him," Barnabas reminded her.

"Perhaps *too* much going for him," Mary murmured, placing a delicate hand upon the window ledge. "Have I spoiled him, Barnabas? Have I given him too much?"

"John Mark has undoubtedly enjoyed some of

the finer aspects of living," Barnabas said frankly, "but you have never been easy on him, Mary. The moment he began to speak, you started training him in the Scriptures. His education was thorough and rigorous. He was educated by the most respected scholars until he was thirteen years old. And for the past three years, he has received adept training in matters of business. You have given him considerable responsibilities, grooming him to step into his father's former position once his training is complete."

"A role in which he seems utterly disinterested," Mary sighed, almost wishing she could shake her son into submission. "However, he *is* ready to assume the role Stephanos previously occupied as my personal secretary, but it's obvious he would rather be doing anything else."

"In time, he will learn to appreciate his work."

"I do hope so," Mary murmured, attempting to dismiss her mounting concern. "At times, I fear he isn't interested in anything except having a good time."

"He's still young, Mary," Barnabas soothed, squeezing her shoulder in encouragement. "But God has a way of getting our attention, instilling important lessons that no human instructor can rightly impart."

"I suppose I can only hope those lessons won't prove too painful for him," Mary observed with a rueful smile. "The school of hard knocks is seldom pleasant."

"But quite effective," Barnabas grinned.

Turning laughing eyes upon her brother, Mary smiled, somewhat encouraged. "I sense there is something you wish to ask me, Brother."

"Ah," Barnabas chuckled, running his hand through his wavy curls. "I should know better than to attempt subtlety with you. You are far too perceptive."

"Is something on your mind, Barnabas?"

"In recent travels, I have encountered numerous communities in which believers dwell in peace and safety," he explained, treading somewhat carefully around a sore subject. "And my offer still stands if—at any time, for any reason—you desire to join a community of believers elsewhere, outside of Jerusalem."

Barnabas held up a pacifying hand as his sister's eyes narrowed in dismay. "I would be happy to escort you and John Mark to any city of your choosing, should you decide to relocate. I am especially impressed with the church in Damascus. It is flourishing like—"

"The Lord has placed me *here* in Jerusalem, Barnabas," Mary interrupted without hesitation. "I cannot leave."

"If I may be so bold," Barnabas dared, taking her hands in his. "You have just mentioned feeling lost, Mary. Perhaps this is the Spirit's prompting to—"

"It isn't," Mary responded, unmoved. "I've felt this way before, Barnabas, when I lost Mark. But I mustn't be swayed by my *feelings*, for they come and go, waxing and waning over time. It is only natural to feel lonely and unsettled amidst such great upheaval and loss. But God will see me through it. I must simply trust that He is orchestrating far greater things than I can imagine, despite appearances."

"You are a steadfast, courageous woman." Barnabas smiled, squeezing her hands affectionately.

"And you are a very sweet—though biased—older brother," she teased, pinching his bearded cheek.

"All right, then," he sighed, his eyes conveying his disappointment. "If you are certain you're supposed to be here, then I shall not press the matter any further."

"Thank you, Barnabas. As long as I maintain my husband's business holdings, believers meeting in this house are still guaranteed a slight measure of safety, since the religious leaders are reluctant to disrupt the Temple commerce dependent upon Mark's enterprises. I must remember what's truly important, though I must confess, it is tempting to be led by my feelings, at times."

"For all of us," Barnabas affirmed. "But what you are doing here, Mary, is truly remarkable. Keep up the good work."

Sensing that Barnabas was preparing to take his leave, Mary grasped his hand, gazing up at him with earnest eyes. "Please keep the matter of John Mark's training, as well as his future, in your prayers. As for arranging a betrothal with a worthy bride, I don't even know where to begin. If I am entirely honest, I'm somewhat daunted by the thought."

"You oversee half a dozen profitable businesses scattered throughout multiple regions, Mary," Barnabas grinned, tweaking her shoulder. "You are more than capable of arranging your son's betrothal!"

"Quite frankly, the thought terrifies me," Mary confessed, shaking her head in dismay. "And you know I don't scare easily, Barnabas."

"I think all of Judea knows that," Barnabas chuckled, amused. "Just remember," he reminded her gently, his light brown eyes alight with peace, "our gracious Father already knows what is best for John Mark. Let *God* arrange his marriage and his future, Mary."

"Are you implying that I simply sit back and do nothing?" Mary asked, surprised.

"I'm not sure you are capable of that, Mary," Barnabas laughed, taking her arm as they crossed the room.

"Then what are you saying?"

"I'm saying, seek Him first and keep your eyes open. At the proper time, you will know what to do."

CHAPTER 16

Kelila

Sychar

Contrary to Kelila's high hopes, Ephraim located the owner of the marketspace without delay. Once Philip signed the paperwork and produced money for the payment, Kelila knew there would be no escaping the inevitable: the neglected market stall and adjoining storage room located on the bustling central square had indeed become her new home.

Standing inside the dimly lit storage room located behind their new booth, Kelila surveyed the damage, battling her own despondency. How on earth would she turn this tiny little space into a worthy *home*? With a perfectly square floor plan, the shallow chamber boasted only two small windows with sagging shutters—one looking out onto the street, the other placed on the end wall. She supposed she should be grateful they had rented the booth on the corner; otherwise, the storage room would have only one window facing the central square, like the others. Fleetingly, Kelila wondered how many lamps would be required to brighten the gloomy living space, especially at night. The entire left wall was lined with ancient wooden shelves, although most of them were sagging or broken. Though the shelves were intended to store merchandise, Kelila decided she would utilize several of them to house at least a dozen oil lamps, perhaps more. As her gaze swept over her newly acquired surroundings, Kelila noted there wasn't any kitchen space, nor was there a speck of furniture to be found. Allowing herself a final sweep of the undesirable space, she wondered what to do about the hard-packed earthen floor and the absence of a front door.

"Well, what do you think?" Philip asked, drawing alongside her with a broad smile. "Are you already making plans?"

Yes, Kelila thought snidely. *Plans to pack up our few measly belongings and hurry right back to Jerusalem!* Just thinking about the adorable little house a few doors down from her beloved sister—the beautiful home they had sold to pursue their calling—made her heart ache just a bit. Especially in light of their most recent acquisition.

"Well?" Philip prodded, bending to plant a kiss on her cheek.

"It's going to need a bit of work," she managed bleakly.

"I think we're up for the challenge," Philip grinned, turning her around to face him. Reaching for his wife, he smiled down at her, his eyes filled with love. "I cannot wait to share this calling with you, beloved."

Since she didn't trust her voice to mask her deep concerns, Kelila tried for a convincing smile instead.

"Kelila! Philip!"

The couple turned their heads toward the entrance as Adorina burst into the small room, her dark eyes nearly wild with excitement. "Come, come! You *must* see this!"

Exchanging a look of confusion with Philip, Kelila trailed rather aimlessly behind him as he followed the excited Samaritan woman out the doorway.

Stepping out into the blinding sunshine, Kelila squinted as her eyes adjusted to the drastic change from darkness to light. Coming around their market stall, she nearly bumped into Philip, who stood stock still before the sprawling street.

"Can you believe this?" Adorina declared, taking Kelila's arm.

Following Adorina's awe-filled gaze, Kelila stifled a gasp of utter shock. For there before them, filling the entire street and spilling over on all sides, was one of the largest crowds she had ever seen.

"Where did they come from?" she gasped, her eyes grazing the sea of curious, eager Samaritans.

"I may have mentioned your arrival." Adorina grinned, crossing her arms before her chest. Cocking her head toward Philip, she added, "These people are hungry for the Word, Brother. Are you ready to feed them?"

Stunned to his core, Philip managed a slow nod before moving under the partial shade provided by their drooping, discolored canopy. Mortified, Kelila wished Adorina had allowed them time to repair their new abode before inviting the entire city to their doorstep! What must the Samaritans think of them now?

"Stop worrying," Adorina encouraged, as if sensing the direction of Kelila's thoughts. "They wouldn't be here if they didn't want to hear what you have to say."

Drawing a calming breath, Kelila nodded her agreement. Bowing her head, she committed her husband's speech into God's hands. *Lord, grant him the words to reach these people and usher them into Your kingdom!*

With one last nervous glance toward his wife, Philip faced the crowd and smiled. "My dear friends," he said, his soothing voice saturated with warmth, "thank you for this kind welcome."

The crowd erupted with cheers, catching Kelila entirely off guard. She hadn't dared to hope for this kind of reception!

"Now," Philip began, his nervousness melting away as the Spirit moved within him, "I'd like to tell you about a Man you met many years ago. His name is Jesus. Perhaps you remember Him."

At these words, the Samaritans released a shout of sheer joy, waving their fists in excitement and loudly crying out their encouragement.

Grasping Adorina's arm, Kelila blinked back tears, overwhelmed by the Samaritans' shocking reception. Their joy was like a mighty rumble so great it shook the very ground beneath her sandals.

***

Tabitha

Joppa

Dusk was settling upon the azure waters of the Mediterranean when Tabitha finally stumbled into the washroom to freshen up and tidy her messy hair.

She desperately needed to wash her soiled garments, but Tirzah was undoubtedly waiting for her, and the mere prospect of tackling another strenuous chore was daunting at the moment. *I shall wear my spare tunic tomorrow and rise early to wash this one*, she decided. Feeling dead on her feet, she traveled a now-familiar stone corridor and slipped into the small room she shared with Laurel, bathed in the rosy glow of evening lamplight.

Seated on the floor beside Laurel's straw mat with her back pressed against the wall, Tirzah greeted the weary maidservant with a knowing little smile, lifting a finger to her lips.

Tabitha's eyes softened at the sight of her sleeping daughter, nestled contentedly under the blanket. Tirzah was stroking the child's back in a motherly fashion, clearly fond of the little one.

"How long has she been asleep?" Tabitha asked softly, lowering herself beside her new friend. The stone wall felt deliciously cool against her stiff back after a day of grueling physical labor.

"Not long," Tirzah replied, crossing her legs at the ankles as if settling in for a nice, long chat. "How was your day?"

"Busy," Tabitha chuckled, relieved it was nearly over. "I couldn't do this without you, Tirzah. Truly, your presence is an answer to prayer."

"Nonsense," Tirzah said, brushing aside Tabitha's praise in her usual manner. "Besides, I can't take credit for something I knew I had to do."

Tabitha looked at Tirzah in surprise.

"Tabitha," Tirzah mused, her brows drawing together as if she was deep in thought, "is it strange to say I felt like God told me to do this? To help with

Laurel?"

"Absolutely not," Tabitha responded, warmed by Tirzah's honesty and vulnerability. "Especially since I was praying for help the very moment you felt God's conviction."

"It's the strangest thing," Tirzah remarked, shaking her head in wonder. "I have served the God of Abraham all my life. And yet, this is only the second time He has ever spoken to me."

Tabitha smiled, deeply touched.

"It felt…unreal," Tirzah confessed. "I heard no voice, no resounding trumpet blast. But somehow, I just *knew*. I sensed you needed help. How, you may ask? I will never know."

"The Holy Spirit moves in mysterious ways," Tabitha mused, caught off guard by the strange look Tirzah gave her.

"The *what?*" Tirzah asked blankly.

"The Holy Spirit," Tabitha repeated slowly, suddenly aware of the fact that Tirzah probably hadn't the slightest idea what she was talking about. *Oh dear,* she thought, her heart springing into her throat in the most unpleasant manner. In Jerusalem, she had been surrounded by Jews who had embraced Jesus as their long-awaited Messiah. But here in Joppa, her people knew nothing of Jesus, much less the Holy Spirit!

For the very first time, Tabitha found herself reluctant to share the truth. If Tirzah, a staunch Jewess, considered Tabitha's doctrine blasphemous, she would likely walk away and never look back. The thought of losing the only friend she had in this strange new city was daunting; yet, even worse was the prospect of relinquishing the help she so desperately needed with Laurel.

Cheeks burning in shame, Tabitha loathed her own weakness.

Oh, Lord, forgive me! she prayed, her stomach churning in apprehension. *Forgive me for even considering silence, Lord. I will not be afraid to proclaim Your name, Your truth. Help me, Lord. Help me.*

"Tabitha?" Tirzah pried, studying her friend with a hint of suspicion. "Are you all right?"

"I am now," Tabitha replied, relieved the Lord had spared her the shame of denial. "I nearly allowed fear to silence my tongue."

"Fear?" Tirzah repeated blankly, looking as if she was beginning to question Tabitha's sanity. "Fear of what?"

"Tirzah, this is going to sound strangely out of place in this conversation," Tabitha warned her, meeting her gaze with intensity. "But you asked about the Holy Spirit, and I cannot keep silent. I must tell you the truth."

"All right." Shifting a bit uncomfortably, Tirzah offered a slow nod, clearly measuring her distance to the door.

"You may have heard rumors about a famous Rabbi called Jesus of Nazareth—"

"Ah, Jesus of Nazareth. You are one of His followers, aren't you?"

Tabitha stared at the perceptive young widow in shock. "How did you know?"

"We've heard all manner of stories about your Rabbi. He instructed His students to love their enemies, no? To do good to those who persecute them and to pray for those who spitefully use them."

"He did," Tabitha responded, utterly amazed.

"Well," Tirzah decided, turning earnest eyes upon her friend, "only the follower of a Man like that would forsake all they have ever known to reach a miserable old tyrant like Joram."

CHAPTER 17

Tabitha

Joppa

Tears springing to her eyes, Tabitha couldn't help but laugh aloud at Tirzah's astute conjecture. She should have known the perceptive young widow would eventually guess at her dearly held faith and allegiance. She just hadn't expected her to guess so soon!

"Are you people as crazy as everyone says?" Tirzah asked in her forthright manner, her eyes twinkling with a hint of mischief.

"I suppose you will have to decide that for yourself," Tabitha told her with a knowing smile. "That is, if you decide to stick around after what I have told you."

"I'm not going anywhere *now*," Tirzah replied stoutly. "After all, I'm curious about what you will do next."

"Frankly, so am I." Tabitha laughed merrily, enjoying the sweet fellowship of her new companion. "I've been here but two days, and already my uncle has nearly driven me to distraction!"

"You've lasted far longer than most," Tirzah pointed out ruefully. "I couldn't bear five minutes under his employ."

"Clearly, you lasted far longer than that. In his office, you mentioned working several years for him," Tabitha prompted, turning to look at her friend. "If you don't mind me asking, how did such an unlikely arrangement come about?"

"Ah," Tirzah acknowledged, her large hazel eyes taking on a faraway look. "That feels like ages ago. But then again, I suppose it was."

"Are you willing to discuss it?" Tabitha asked gently. "I imagine you could offer a great deal of advice."

"Possibly," Tirzah acknowledged wryly, "although I imagine my own counsel is worth next to nothing."

"I highly doubt that."

Releasing a somewhat tremorous sigh, Tirzah rested her hands upon her knees. Clearly, it was difficult for her to divulge her past trials.

"We needn't speak of it if it unsettles you," Tabitha assured her, touching her hand.

"No," Tirzah responded, shaking her head with great purpose. "If my blunders or misdeeds or even the pain of my past can aid others in their present circumstances, it would be wrong to still my tongue."

Tabitha stared at the widow with new respect. Tirzah was a strong, courageous woman. She could hardly fathom how the Holy Spirit would work through her, should Tirzah choose to accept Christ as her Lord and Savior.

Please, Father, Tabitha prayed earnestly, *through*

the power of Your Holy Spirit, grant me the wisdom and ability to reach this woman for Your kingdom!

"As I mentioned earlier, I didn't really work for Joram," Tirzah spoke quietly, interrupting Tabitha's silent intercession. "I worked for his wife, Peninah, serving as her chambermaid."

"Peninah." Softly, Tabitha repeated the name of the aunt she had never met. "What was she like?"

"Oh, Lady Peninah was an angel," Tirzah assured her, smiling faintly at the memory of the gracious woman, her childhood idol. "She was a kind, gentle soul. Her hair was a like a vast sea of curly red tendrils, and her complexion was soft and fair like the pearly white sand upon the shore. Your uncle worshiped her," she added, shaking her head in amazement. "He called her Pennie."

"Pennie," Tabitha repeated, smiling softly. Try as she might, she couldn't imagine her growling, brooding uncle in love with *anyone*. To even consider him using a pet name was almost absurd! "When did this take place, Tirzah?"

"Oh, it must have been at least thirty years ago," Tirzah replied, her brows drawing together in consideration. "Possibly even longer."

"So my uncle was a young man then?"

"In his thirties, I would imagine."

"And you?" Tabitha asked, intrigued. "How old were you?"

"I was very young, six or seven at the most," Tirzah replied. "When my father died, Lady Peninah took pity on us. She hired me on the spot, insisting she was in desperate need of a chambermaid. Looking back now," Tirzah smiled, her eyes shimmering with a faint sheen of tears, "I see she only sought to help support us in our time of need. Lady Peninah had an entire fleet of servants to wait upon her; even so, she hired *me*—a grieving, inexperienced child."

Shaking her head in awe, Tabitha wondered how her uncle could have possibly married a woman so diametrically opposed to his own character.

"But Lady Peninah would have rescued every needy soul in Joppa, had her husband allowed it," Tirzah chuckled, warmed by fond memories of her former mistress. "The earnest prayer of her heart was that, someday, this mansion would become a refuge for the needy and destitute."

"And how did Joram feel about *that*?" Tabitha grinned, amused.

"Surprisingly, he wasn't against it at the time," Tirzah responded, utterly surprising her. "Lady Peninah was an impeccable, gracious hostess. She hosted large dinner parties often, intentionally inviting those most in need. Joram would serve as host on those occasions, basking in his wife's glowing presence. She was happiest when she served others."

"My aunt sounds like a truly remarkable woman," Tabitha mused, her heart aching just a bit. "How I wish I had met her."

"It was an honor to serve your aunt, Tabitha," Tirzah said with great feeling. "I loved her like a second mother. She was such a comfort to me after the loss of my father."

But then she, too, was taken, Tabitha thought sadly, her heart breaking for Tirzah. Truly, the poor widow had experienced unspeakable loss throughout the course of her life.

"When Lady Peninah discovered she was finally with child, she and Joram were over the moon," Tirzah said, resuming her story with growing sadness and shaking Tabitha from her thoughtful reverie. "Truly, I have never seen two people more excited about welcoming a child into this world. They were just beside themselves."

"Joram? Excited about *anything*?" Tabitha declared, incredulous. She simply couldn't imagine her harsh, overbearing uncle as an excited father-to-be.

"Joram insisted that if the child was a girl, she would be as beautiful as her mother. And if it was a boy, then he would become a man of business, like his father," Tirzah explained. "But Peninah didn't have a healthy pregnancy, Tabitha. She suffered nearly every day, succumbing to fierce tremors, fainting spells, debilitating nausea, and all manner of dreadful symptoms. Even as a very young child, I couldn't help but fear her difficult pregnancy might be an omen of what was to come."

"And what happened?" Tabitha asked, fearful she wasn't going to enjoy the rest of the story.

"Joram invested a fortune in dozens of expensive physicians, all of them promising a cure," Tirzah sighed, her expression downcast. "He even sent for highly trained, well-known doctors from as far away as Ephesus, Athens, and Alexandria. But despite his dwindling coffers, none of them produced a cure."

"Poor Joram," Tabitha murmured, feeling the first stirrings of sympathy toward the impatient older man. "He must have felt so frightened and desperate."

"He became more and more distrusting as the months slipped by," Tirzah confessed, haunted by dark memories of desperate times. "Soon, word of your uncle's situation reached others. All manner of supposed physicians and self-proclaimed 'healers' sought him out, promising a worthy cure—for a price, that is. And Joram, desperate to save his wife and unborn child, spared no expense to find a cure. Even so, the physicians grew richer as Lady Peninah grew worse."

Blinking back tears, Tabitha wondered how such a crisis must have impacted her uncle, then just a hopeful young man desperately in love with his wife and soon-to-be child.

"When Lady Peninah went into labor, the entire household held its collective breath," Tirzah recounted sadly, her haunted expression conveying the unforgettable trauma of the incident. "As her chambermaid, I assisted the physician throughout the entire process. We all hoped and prayed she would birth a healthy child, putting an end to the terrible suffering she had endured during her pregnancy."

"But she didn't, did she?" Tabitha asked sadly.

"No," Tirzah sighed regretfully. "During three days of hard labor, Joram never left her side. He knelt by her bedside, clinging to her hand like a lifeline. But despite our fervent prayers and best efforts, she died just before sunset on the third day. Joram lost his beloved wife and child, and I must confess, I will never forget the expression on his face when it happened. It haunted me for years."

"Oh, Tirzah," Tabitha whispered, her eyes filling with tears. "I am so sorry you had to experience that. It must have broken your heart."

"It did, for a time," Tirzah admitted a bit woodenly. "After all, I hadn't yet recovered from the somewhat recent loss of my father, though I was blessed by the faith and strength of my mother and Lady Peninah, both of whom helped me grieve his loss and move on with life. Ironically, many of the lessons Peninah taught me during the three or four years I worked for her enabled me to face her death with strength and courage. Otherwise, I'm quite certain I would have fallen apart."

"God's ways are truly higher than ours," Tabitha breathed, having experienced the same unexplainable miracle when she lost her husband, Stephanos.

"But when Lady Peninah died, Joram didn't *grieve*, Tabitha, he *raged*—against this household, against the world, against life itself," Tirzah remembered, her eyes flickering with fierce emotion. "Before Peninah's death, Joram seemed to be a decent, reasonable man—certainly no prize, in my opinion, but *acceptable*. Yet, when she died, he became *unbearable*. It was as if part of him—the good part—died along with her. He became angry, bitter, and obsessed about getting his affairs in order, including his will."

"And that's when he decided to disinherit my mother," Tabitha realized, putting together the broken pieces of a story she had never fully known. "That would have been a few years before I was born, I suppose."

"Most likely," Tirzah agreed. "Your mother was living in Jerusalem at the time."

"Yes," Tabitha nodded. "She met my father when she visited Jerusalem for the Feast of Tabernacles. They fell in love, but my uncle disapproved of the marriage because my father was a commoner."

"Why doesn't that surprise me?" Tirzah quipped rather drolly.

"So did Joram terminate your employment after his wife died?" Tabitha asked, still processing her uncle's tragic past.

"Not at first," Tirzah replied. "But he became desperate to cleanse this place of all memories of her. He sold every trace of her belongings, leaving nothing behind. He even sealed off the bedchamber they had shared, the room in which she perished in childbirth, threatening us servants within an inch of our lives should we choose to venture into it."

"It must have been a very difficult time for everyone."

"It was," Tirzah agreed. "Most of Joram's staff departed, seeking employment elsewhere. Martha and Jonas chose to stay, and Eli, as well. But the rest went their separate ways, forcing Joram to hire new help. Since then, he's had trouble keeping his staff—for obvious reasons. He's not exactly a stellar employer."

"Were you forced to leave, as well?"

"I eventually left because Joram's behavior became intolerable," Tirzah replied, her expression indicating such memories remained distasteful to her. "He cut my pay in half, insisting that most of my services were no longer needed after his wife's passing. And yet the tasks *he* assigned were ten times harder than anything *she* had expected of me. Frankly, I think he just wanted to get rid of me. Looking at *me* only reminded him of his precious Pennie. I think it hurt him to see his wife's chambermaid moving about the house without her."

"I understand," Tabitha nodded, deeply saddened by the dreadful tragedy. "Based on what you have shared with me, my aunt seemed to be a woman of great faith."

"She was," Tirzah assured her. "Her faith was very much like my mother's—steadfast and unwavering, even at the end."

"But Joram didn't share his wife's belief?"

"In name only, perhaps. He attended synagogue services with her and kept the Law. Back then, he even kept the pilgrimage feasts. After her death, he became somewhat slack in his observances. Though he believes God exists, I think he resents Him for taking his wife."

"Oh, Joram," Tabitha sighed, saddened. "If only he had shared Peninah's faith. Perhaps, then, he could have recovered from his great loss." Having suffered the paralyzing sting of bereavement herself, Tabitha resolved to show her uncle nothing but kindness, even when he was most incorrigible.

It won't be easy, she thought, considering his glowering hostility and glaring condescension. *But Joram doesn't even know his Messiah has come. The rigid observance of laws and customs apart from an intimate relationship with God failed to mend his gaping wounds, and perhaps that is why he has forsaken them.*

Only Jesus could ease his pain and bring forth healing. And now Tabitha knew with absolute certainty that God—in His wisdom, love, and care—had sent her to arrange a divine introduction.

CHAPTER 18

Kelila

Sychar

Bone-weary, Kelila unrolled a simple sleeping mat, spreading it upon the dirt floor of her new abode. Despite her keen exhaustion and rankling dismay about her current housing situation, her lips pursed into a knowing little smile as she reached for a worn blanket, dropping it lightly on the pallet.

You really are at work here in Sychar, aren't You, Lord? she thought, still in awe several hours after Philip's powerful address. *The Samaritans drank in Your Word like thirsty wanderers in a barren desert land.*

Kelila hadn't dared to hope for such a welcoming reception from a people at odds with hers and Philip's Jewish heritage. But the Spirit of God had readied the way, sending Adorina ahead of them to prepare the hearts and minds of her people to receive the Good News. Kelila was convinced the

Samaritans would have remained stationed at their booth the entire night, hungrily absorbing Philip's every word, had Ephraim not joined him under the canopy near dusk, graciously announcing the meeting's end.

"I am sure our dear evangelist will be more than happy to speak again tomorrow," Ephraim had promised the sweeping crowd, casting a playful wink toward Adorina and Kelila waiting patiently in the doorway. "Until then, we must allow him some rest and the opportunity to settle into his new home."

With great reluctance and unveiled disappointment, the crowd had hesitantly dispersed—but only after Philip promised to speak again the following afternoon.

"That sleeping mat looks incredibly inviting right about now," Philip teased, drawing up behind Kelila and playfully nuzzling her shoulder. "I feel dead on my feet."

"I can see why," Kelila smiled, enjoying her husband's affections as he wrapped his arms around her waist from behind. "You had a busy day."

"And you, as well," Philip reminded her, gently kissing her temple. "Did you imagine we would see such crowds so soon?"

"Never," Kelila responded wanly as Philip released her, lowering his strong body onto their sleeping mat. Accepting his outstretched hand, she followed suit, smiling to herself as Philip held her close, fitting his lean body around hers.

For one delicious moment, Kelila closed her eyes, savoring the silence of their small abode. Adorina had graciously lent them several oil lamps, now faithfully flickering from their perches upon the rickety wooden shelves, and Ephraim had happily assisted Philip in delivering their few belongings to their new home. Even so, the small chamber felt vacant and threadbare, begging for Kelila's attention.

Opening her eyes, Kelila allowed herself a thorough sweep of their quiet surroundings. The heavy curtain Philip and Ephraim had nailed above the doorframe served as a temporary barrier between their small abode and the outside elements, though Kelila was quite certain it would do very little to keep out unwanted insects, wandering animals, or dangerous intruders. Every possible surface—the shelves, the windowsills, and even the floor, seemed to be coated in a fine layer of powdery dust. She would need to give the place a thorough cleaning and scrubbing. Would she have time to begin cleaning, unpacking, and settling in before the eager crowds reconvened outside the following day?

Smiling to herself, Kelila remembered a time when she wouldn't have dared to stoop so low as to perform menial tasks such as cooking or housework! She was thankful the Lord had shaken her from her sense of self-importance and selfish pride.

Well, mostly, she thought with a small sigh, considering her grudging attitude toward this dwelling the Lord had graciously provided for them.

Perhaps she was still a serious work in progress, after all.

"It was so kind of Ephraim and Adorina to insist upon helping us get settled in tomorrow morning," Philip spoke into the gathering darkness, pulling his wife just a bit closer. "Ephraim has volunteered to help with the repairs, as well."

Well, we certainly need all the help we can get, Kelila thought drolly, wisely refraining from voicing her skepticism.

"What shall we tackle first, love?"

"We need a door, a *real* door," Kelila informed him without hesitation. "I must admit, I've been on pins and needles—first, sleeping in that canvas tent with no means of protection, and now here, with no ability to shut and bolt a secure, sturdy door."

"So I am assuming now is not the time to remind you that our security lies in the Lord's protection?" Philip grinned.

"No, now is not the time," Kelila shot back, bemused. "Besides, it is also written, *You shall not tempt the Lord your God*!"

"Ah, pitting Scriptural truths against each other, are we?" Philip teased, playfully nuzzling her neck. "You needn't worry, love. Ephraim and I will see to it first thing in the morning."

"You are wonderful," Kelila breathed, feeling a bit better already. "Thank you, Philip."

"Speaking of wonderful," Philip grinned, turning her over to face him in the cozy lamplight, "I am so proud of you, Kelila."

"Proud?" Kelila repeated blankly, draping an arm behind her head as she gazed up into her husband's sincere face. "Of *me*?"

"Don't sound so surprised," Philip chuckled, bending to kiss her nose. "I know this place certainly wouldn't be your first choice for a home, Kelila."

Or my second choice, or third, or fourth, or tenth... she thought, resisting the urge to voice her dismay.

"And yet, you have made the best of our situation,

love," Philip continued, tenderly brushing the lush raven-black tendrils from her smooth forehead. "Not once have you complained."

Almost instantly, Kelila was bombarded with guilt. Though she hadn't vocalized her deep displeasure to Philip, she had most certainly brooded and stewed about the matter privately. Her thoughts had proven less than lovely.

"You really shouldn't be proud of me, Philip," Kelila sighed, her color deepening in shame. "I may have held my tongue, but my thoughts have been far from honorable."

"Oh?" Philip asked a bit playfully, scooping her into a closer embrace. "How so?"

"Well, I haven't been very happy about living here," she admitted, unable to meet his gaze. "Frankly, I have barely come to terms with the fact that we may be called to traveling evangelism rather than putting down roots. I'll confess, this old market stall certainly hasn't done much to lift my spirits or ease my disappointment."

"I'll bet you're glad we won't be putting down roots *here*," Philip teased, receiving a withering look from his wife.

"Honestly, Philip, *everything* about our life has proven drastically unlike I've imagined it, thus far," Kelila conceded, amused by his good humor.

"It has, indeed," Philip responded in quiet agreement. "But I suppose we shouldn't have expected it to be otherwise."

"Why not?"

"Well, the life of a believer constitutes the daily decision to *follow*—to follow in the footsteps of Christ, wherever He may lead," Philip mused, rolling onto his back and gazing up at the flickering shadows writhing upon the low ceiling. "Oftentimes, He selects the paths we least expect. In fact, when Jesus first came here to Sychar, his disciples were against it. They thought He should take the longer route which circumvented Samaria. And yet, despite their vehement protests, Jesus chose to journey through Sychar."

"And I suppose, now, we can see why," Kelila admitted, considering the vast sea of eager listeners of that afternoon. Jesus had planted the seeds for their salvation long ago—much to the disciples' shock and displeasure, at the time—by taking an unlikely, beaten path and arranging a meeting with a dejected outcast by the well.

"If one truly desires to follow Jesus," Philip continued, shaking Kelila from her reverie, "then he or she must be ready to relinquish their own plans in order to embrace the will of God. Jesus warned us of this time and time again, saying, '*If anyone desires to come after Me, let him deny himself, and take up his cross daily, and follow Me.*' And yet, every single time, we are baffled and mystified when we are actually called to *do* that very thing—to deny ourselves in order to choose His will above our own."

"Why is it so difficult to remember what's truly important, Philip?" Kelila sighed. "Jesus hadn't even a place to lay His head. Having no home of His own, He was completely dependent upon the hospitality of others. And yet, I was tempted to abandon our mission simply because I didn't *like* the house God provided for us."

"We all face these challenges and temptations, Kelila," Philip reminded her gently. "The important thing is you *obeyed* despite your negative feelings."

"Not without a struggle," Kelila confessed, disheartened.

"Nonetheless, you *did*," Philip smiled, tucking stray ringlets behind her delicate ear. "And when you are tempted to feel dissatisfaction or despair, turn to Jesus, beloved. Immerse yourself in the power of His presence, and He will strengthen your heart and bolster your resolve."

CHAPTER 19

Tabitha

Joppa

Tabitha awakened with a cheerful heart and a spring to her step, eager to begin her workday. Having carefully crafted a practical and sustainable schedule with Tirzah the previous evening, Tabitha was confident her workday would progress smoothly this time. It had taken over an hour to produce a satisfactory schedule, one that enabled Tabitha to accomplish her chores even while parenting a young child. As a new mother, she knew her first priority must be the care and training of her daughter. After all, God had brought the orphaned little girl into her life for a reason. And though Tabitha deeply desired to reach her uncle with the gospel, she knew she must be vigilant against neglecting her highest calling—raising a child according to God's principles. By His grace, she must learn to parent young Laurel, minister to her patronizing uncle and his household, and work to support herself—all at the proper time, in the proper order.

Though it was a daunting assignment, Tabitha felt quite certain the Lord would see her through. Hadn't He already sent Tirzah to assist her during her busiest hours? In time, Tabitha knew—with the Lord's help, of course—she could learn to properly balance her priorities and responsibilities.

Oh, but the sacrifices I must make won't be easy, Tabitha thought as she smoothed the wrinkles from her fading tunic, brushed her long hair, and twisted her golden locks into a simple, functional braid. One such sacrifice involved awakening at this early hour, long before the rest of the household even began to stir, to get a head start on her chores. If she began laboring several hours before the sun came up, then she should complete her chores much earlier in the day, resulting in more time to spend with Laurel. Tabitha was quite certain she could complete at least half her workday before Laurel awakened for breakfast. Then, she would cease working long enough to begin Laurel's day with prayer, to wash and dress the little one, and to serve her a simple breakfast.

Tirzah had agreed to arrive at Joram's mansion just as Laurel was finishing her morning meal so Tabitha could get back to work. Tirzah had suggested she and Laurel stay nearby, encouraging the little one to play in whichever room Tabitha happened to be working. This way, mother and daughter could interact throughout the day, exchanging smiles and conversation. If everything went according to plan, Tabitha would have finished the most grueling tasks by the time Laurel awakened from her afternoon nap. Then, the little girl could easily "assist" her mother with the remaining chores, freeing Tirzah to return to her potter's wheel somewhat early in the afternoon. Thankfully, her services would only be required a few hours each day.

After kissing her sleeping daughter's soft forehead, Tabitha straightened and slipped from the dimly lit chamber. She had quite a bit of work to accomplish before dawn if her schedule was to unfold according to plan.

***

John Mark

Jerusalem

Stationed upon the prominent northwestern corner of the Temple Mount and overlooking the magnificent, gleaming Temple compound, Antonia Fortress—the Roman garrison responsible for the peace and preservation of Jerusalem—boasted an impressive cohort of highly trained Roman soldiers whose sole assignment was to maintain order in the Temple courts below. The garrison's founder and builder, Herod the Great, had insisted the purpose of the highly fortified garrison was to protect the beloved Temple, but his claim was a screaming farce. The long-deceased monarch's thirst for power and control—every bit as notorious as his deadly reputation—had proven legendary. Any Jew worth his salt knew the fortress had been established by the late, great Herod to *command* rather than protect the Temple complex.

Wandering somewhat aimlessly about Jerusalem's crowded streets, John Mark paused amidst a bustling cobblestoned way, gazing up at the distant watchtowers crowning Antonia's seamless perimeter. Four stately towers ascended heavenward, with the fourth surpassing the others in height by at least twenty cubits and commanding an impressive view of its sacred charge below, now humming with priests and Levites, worshipers and thrill-seekers, pious Jews roaming the inner courts and curious Gentiles craning their necks to see past the forbidden walls.

Ah, those forbidden walls had aroused both resentment and raging curiosity for untold years. The barrier of separation between Jew and Gentile angered some, humbled others, and piqued the burning interest of most.

Tearing his attention away from the Temple compound looming upon the eastern horizon, John Mark's gaze fell upon yet another set of forbidden walls—the steep, stone enclosure of Antonia Fortress. The citadel was like a miniature, thriving Roman city, with in-house lodging for respected officials and separate barracks for lower ranking soldiers, ambling pillared cloisters, glittering baths, and broad, paved courtyards where soldiers gambled and told crude jokes during their leisure hours.

John Mark knew that staunch Jews detested this unholy Roman quarter, intrusively abutting the northwestern corner of their sacred Temple compound. Even the businesses and market stalls lining the shady streets near the garrison catered to the Romans' taste, boasting an impressive array of drinking establishments and brothels.

Naturally, John Mark had always been warned

against venturing too close to the Roman quarter. Not only was it unsafe; it was also unwise, his mother had often warned him.

Even so, John Mark couldn't shake his fascination with the Roman way of life. True, the younger Roman generation had seemingly given themselves to wanton passions and wasting idleness. But there were also many great leaders of the Roman breed—commanders who led their troops in victorious triumph through battle, bringing entire nations to their knees. Such men of action captured his young imagination as he sat cloistered behind his mother's massive desk, calculating tedious rows of numbers while Tobias peered vigilantly over his shoulder.

True, his mother possessed a mind for mathematics, numbers, and figures. Though undoubtedly a woman of action, Mary seemed unbothered by the mind-numbing hours of clerical work required of her in the painfully silent bibliotheca. And though John Mark hadn't dared to voice his feelings aloud, he could hardly stomach the thought of wiling away the remainder of his days crunching numbers behind a desk.

No, he sensed adventure beckoning just around the corner, daring him to set aside his dull ledgers, casting caution to the wind and partaking of all the excitement life had to offer. He wanted to see the world, like his Uncle Barnabas. He wanted to fall in love with a beautiful woman. He wanted to make the most of every treasured breath God gave him.

Hesitating slightly, John Mark paused before a slight fork in the road—one so subtle he might have missed it. Taking that subtle turn would place him dangerously close to the Roman quarter, and he was a young Jewish man…traveling alone.

It's *highly unsafe,* he thought, wincing slightly as he considered what his mother would have to say about his willful disobedience. After a slight inward battle, John Mark turned off the market thorough-fare, stealing down a shadowed lane rimmed with questionable establishments.

He couldn't help but notice the stark absence of his Jewish neighbors as the Roman presence thick-ened in the streets. Armed soldiers passed to and fro, their metal-clad uniforms clanking in time with leather, hobnailed sandals. Bold, unveiled Roman women posed on tall balconies and teased darkened doorways, their painted eyes flashing clear invita-tions toward the uniformed soldiers passing by.

Feeling a strange coiling sensation tightening in the pit of his stomach, John Mark decided it might be best to turn back. He was beginning to stick out like a sore thumb—a lone, modestly attired Jew sur-rounded by throngs of ostentatious Romans. Fleet-ingly, he wondered at the obvious depravity of the area, for it conspicuously lacked the pomp and gran-deur he had expected to encounter after glimpsing the proud, richly adorned Romans traversing the broad marble lanes of the Upper City. John Mark had always been intrigued by the distinct aura they conveyed—the way they took pride in their heri-tage, their glistening armor, their powerful steeds, their relentless army, their Imperial City, and their emperor upon his throne. But here in this seedy Roman quarter brimming with grinning rogues and brazen, ill-clad young women, John Mark was singularly unimpressed. Repulsed, even.

Nervously drawing his embroidered cloak over

his dark hair, he turned to leave.

"Hello there, stranger."

John Mark froze, his sandaled feet planted firmly upon the cobblestones, as a young woman's enticing voice pinned him in place.

Turning slowly on his heels, John Mark found himself face to face with the most startlingly beautiful young woman he had ever laid eyes on.

"I haven't seen you around here before," the young woman teased, her azure blue eyes searching his face with avid and seemingly innocent curiosity.

Clearing his throat, John Mark wondered if he should dare speak to this stunning beauty. Already, his palms were sweating.

Blinking nervously, he glanced over his shoulder, half expecting his mother to materialize out of thin air to scold him and warn him against "the flattering tongue of the seductress" which the wise old Solomon had so vehemently cautioned against.

"You are no Roman," the girl observed, tilting her proud head and placing a delicate hand upon her hip. "What is a nice Jewish boy like you doing on this side of town?"

A *nice Jewish boy?* Grimacing, John Mark wondered how he must appear to this exotic Roman girl. *Probably like the prudish, bumbling student of a stuffy Jewish rabbi,* he thought, peeved.

"Well?" the young woman probed as her lush black lashes fluttered in question. "Can't you speak?"

In deepening frustration, John Mark wondered what had happened to his voice, desperately attempting to keep his eyes in his head. He was certain he had never seen a young woman of such radiant and unrivaled beauty. With piles of lush golden blonde curls pinned atop her proud head in an elaborate Roman style, intricately woven with glittering jewels and pearls, her soft features appeared dove-like with loose, curly blonde tendrils framing an exquisite face. Her curvy frame was draped in sheer, gauzy fabric—perhaps imported silk—and belted at the waist, emphasizing her alluring shape.

"Of course, I can speak," John Mark finally managed, wondering how his confidence had evaporated in an instant. Half the Jewish maidens of the city were in love with him, and yet one beautiful Roman girl had rendered him utterly speechless!

Attempting to reclaim his usual charm, John Mark feigned an ease he was far from feeling. "I was simply out for a stroll after visiting a good friend of mine."

"In the Roman quarter?" the girl challenged, her slender brows drawing together in amusement. "Jews don't make friends with Romans."

John Mark could have argued that point. After all, his mother insisted upon bestowing the love of Christ upon *all* men—even Romans. Although he couldn't help but consider the fact that she certainly wouldn't approve of this exchange with a daring, unveiled Roman girl...

"My friend resides near the Temple complex," John Mark responded somewhat defensively. He didn't dare divulge the fact that his best friend was the grandson of Gamaliel, the most respected teacher of all Judea.

"You've strayed rather far from the religious district, have you not?" the girl pointed out, her eyes and expression playful.

"A bit farther than I intended," John Mark admitted, drawn to her flirtatious manner. She was obviously interested in him, to his great astonishment!

"Best watch where you are going next time," the girl teased, boldly drawing aside his cloak to gain a better view of his handsome features. "A lone, defenseless Jewish boy in the Roman quarter—"

"I don't need a bodyguard," John Mark assured her, straightening just a bit. "I can take care of myself."

"I'm sure you can," she cooed, her gaze flitting boldly over his lithe form. "Even so, one can never be too careful."

"And you?" John Mark cut in, unwilling to be made a defenseless victim. "What is a lovely young woman like yourself doing on this shady avenue, alone?"

"You think I am lovely?"

John Mark flushed at the look she gave him.

Laughing musically, she lifted coy blue eyes to his. "Everyone knows my father is a powerful Roman official and wouldn't dare lay a hand upon his daughter."

"I see," John Mark responded, his curiosity further aroused.

"My father is a good friend of the tetrarch, Herod Antipas," she continued casually. "Currently, we are residing in his guest rooms at the Jerusalem palace."

"And if you are staying at the palace at the far end of the Upper City, what are you doing *here* at the opposite end of town near the Temple district?" John Mark asked, attempting to beat her at her own game.

"Perhaps, I, too, was visiting a friend," she replied, her eyes dancing with mirth. At the look John Mark gave her, she added sweetly, "All right, I was check-ing on my father at the Antonia Fortress. He buries himself in work, and since the tetrarch has planned a feast in his honor this evening, I thought it best to remind him of his social obligations."

John Mark stared at her, taken aback. *This* girl was to participate in one of Antipas' legendary ban-quets! She was proving more and more fascinating!

"What is your name?" the girl asked frankly, pulling John Mark from his distracting thoughts.

"I am John Mark," he responded, flattered she even cared. "And you?"

"Aurelia," the girl replied with a flawless smile.

Aurelia. The name was as graceful and lovely as the girl who bore it.

"And is this the part when you ask if you shall ever see me again?" Aurelia prompted, drawing close enough for him to smell the scented ointment upon her fair skin.

Despite the caution bells going off in his mind, John Mark found himself consumed with the desire to spend more time with this girl, to win her heart and possibly even her hand. The thought was truly shocking, and for a brief moment, he was taken aback by his own desire. Though dozens of eligible Jewish girls frequented the church meetings hosted in his mother's house each week, he hadn't been drawn to any of them in the way his entire being longed for this exotic Roman girl.

"Well?" she pressed, her expression betraying her desire.

"All right," John Mark quipped against his better judgment, his confidence bolstered by her obvious attraction to him. "When shall I see you again, Aurelia?" How he loved the sound of that name!

"By the looks of you, is it safe to assume you reside in the Upper City?"

"It is," he grinned broadly.

"Well, then," she replied, gazing up at him through thick, tilted lashes. "Meet me after Herod's banquet tonight. I can sneak you into his palace gardens. They are quite delectable—"

"I couldn't leave my mother's estate after dark," John Mark protested, alarmed by her suggestion.

"Ah, we wouldn't want to upset your mother, would we?" Aurelia teased, a hidden edge sharpening her tone. "Tomorrow, then? You can meet me at the Upper Market before the palace of Herod Antipas. That is, if your mother approves," she added with a knowing smile, and John Mark couldn't quite decide if she was teasing or condescending.

"I'll be there." John Mark had frequented the prestigious market catering to wealthy Upper City clientele hundreds of times, most often running last-minute errands for his mother. "What time?"

"Meet me in the cool of the morning beneath the southern colonnade," Aurelia told him, her eyes glowing with anticipation and something else... something that both stirred and unsettled him. "I'll be waiting for you." Standing on tiptoe, she planted a firm kiss on his cheek. "Until then."

Mesmerized, John Mark watched as Aurelia slipped past him and gracefully resumed her stroll, scarcely able to comprehend what had just happened.

Tonight, he knew he would dream of a golden-haired angel with graceful curves, deep blue eyes, and a flawless smile.

CHAPTER 20

Tabitha

Joppa

Tabitha and Laurel were finishing a simple breakfast of warm lentils and flatbread when Tirzah burst into the kitchen clutching a cumbersome wooden crate laden with curious-looking objects.

"Good morning, everyone," Tirzah nearly sang as the door swung shut behind her.

The kitchen staff, busily at work, glanced up in greeting—some even offering shy smiles in return—before resuming their tasks. It was obvious they appreciated the sunny presence of the two young widows, having grown accustomed to Joram's glowering countenance and their formerly cheerless environment.

"Good morning, Tirzah," Tabitha smiled, warmed at the sight of her spirited friend. "What's that you have there?"

"Looks like a box of junk to me," Martha grunted,

eyeing Tirzah with displeasure as she dropped the crate rather heedlessly upon the kitchen counter.

"Far from it," Tirzah responded, plunging eager hands into the wooden crate. "On the contrary, I've brought a bundle of treasures just waiting to be discovered," she grinned, producing a very worn-looking doll and holding it up for Laurel to see.

Squealing her delight, the child held out her arms to receive the thrilling treasure.

Happily, Tirzah handed the little doll to Laurel, who inspected the old toy with shining eyes.

Reaching further into the crowded crate, Tirzah drew forth several wooden blocks, some of them still bearing traces of brightly colored paint. "I thought we could have some fun with these," she explained, smiling just a bit shyly. "These toys belonged to me when I was a little girl. Most of them were handcrafted by my father."

"Oh, Tirzah," Tabitha breathed, coming around the counter and taking one of the intricate little building blocks in her hand. "These are beautiful."

"Well, they're not in the best of shape," Tirzah admitted, her eyes betraying deep, hidden sentiment. "But they are sturdy, nonetheless. They've held up these many years."

"How kind of you to share these precious treasures with Laurel," Tabitha exclaimed, touched. "She hasn't any toys of her own. Truly, thank you, Tirzah."

"These baubles and trinkets are simply *begging* to be played with," Tirzah responded, brushing aside the praise in her typical manner. "They certainly weren't getting any use rotting in this old box on a shelf. Now, where will you be working today,

Tabitha?"

"I must begin by scouring the walls and tiles of the outer court," Tabitha informed her a bit ruefully.

"Ah, your uncle isn't going easy on you, is he?"

"If you ask me, that man don't have a gracious bone in his body," Martha harrumphed, turning back to the dough rising near the glowing stone oven.

Exchanging knowing grins, Tabitha lifted Laurel off the countertop as Tirzah retrieved the box of toys.

"Well, then," Tirzah decided, her eyes glittering with fun, "Laurel and I shall join you in the outer court. The fresh air will be nice."

"That sounds wonderful," Tabitha replied, balancing a beaming Laurel on her hip.

"Now," Tirzah grinned, tweaking Laurel's rosy cheek, "shall we take this box with us and dive into this delightful treasure trove of toys?"

Squealing her delight, Laurel clutched the little doll close to her heart.

"All right, then," Tabitha smiled. "We have a plan."

***

Kelila

Sychar

Pausing to delicately dab at the sweat on her brow, Kelila surveyed the progress within the tiny chamber she now called home. She couldn't deny the obvious transformation, despite the sparsity of the furnishings.

Ephraim and Adorina had arrived on Philip and Kelila's doorstep mere moments after dawn, eager and well-equipped to tackle the daunting task of repairing the dilapidated old market stall and adjoining tenement-style chamber behind it. Ephraim came armed with a sturdy cart piled high with his best tools and spare building materials, while Adorina had boasted a steaming kettle of hearty gruel. After sharing a simple but joy-filled meal, the young couples tackled the impossible project with efficiency and determination. While the men first busied themselves installing a sturdy wooden door and mending the broken shutters, the women thoroughly scoured the walls, shelves, and even the hard-packed earthen floor until the entire space fairly shone.

"We are making good time," Adorina decided, wringing out a filthy cloth over the jar designated to collect the dirty water. "I suppose we should step outside and see about mending that pathetic little canopy shading your market stall."

Straightening with a bit of effort, Kelila forced a weary smile. She was having a rather difficult time keeping up with the inexhaustible Samaritan woman, who was clearly accustomed to grueling physical labor. "Perhaps we should take a moment to rest," she suggested, crossing the room to wring out her own dirty wash rag. "You have been so kind to help us, Adorina. I wouldn't want you to overexert yourself—"

"Nonsense," Adorina chided, drying her hands on the worn apron expertly tied around her slender waist. "I am accustomed to such work."

Obviously, Kelila thought, the muscles in her

arms burning like fire.

"Besides," Adorina pointed out, "we needn't waste any time. Once Philip's ministry takes off, it is doubtful we will have even a spare moment to tend to such matters."

Oh my, I certainly hope not! Kelila thought, alarmed. After all, Philip had become a respected spiritual leader in Jerusalem without his ministry consuming every spare second of his time! Why should it be any different here in Sychar?

"Come along," Adorina instructed, swinging open the somewhat creaky door Philip and Ephraim had installed. "We must—" Adorina froze upon the threshold mid-sentence, unprepared for the sight that met her intense dark eyes.

"Adorina?" Kelila questioned, glancing toward the men who had now halted their work on the sagging shelves, their curiosity piqued by the young woman's reaction. "What is it?"

"Come see for yourself," she responded, pulling the door open wider.

Drawing alongside her friend, Kelila covered her mouth in surprise as their husbands appeared behind them, exchanging questioning glances.

Already, a sea of eager Samaritans lined the street before their market stall, clearly unwilling to miss even a moment of Philip's preaching. Many had brought family members, friends, and young children. Some had even set up makeshift canopies and spread blankets upon which to recline, while others happily munched on dried fruit or flatbread they had brought along with them.

The moment the Samaritans glimpsed Philip's sturdy frame in the doorway, a shout of greeting rang out, echoing and resounding through the dusty streets.

"Is it time?" several Samaritans asked, the excitement evident in their voices. "Will you address us now?" others asked while many sprang to their feet and waved their hands in exuberance.

Stepping past the women in surprise, Philip smiled warmly at his audience, raising a hand in greeting.

The response was nearly deafening as throngs of eager Samaritans joined those already gathered in the street, exchanging looks of joyous anticipation.

"Tell us more about this Jesus," several shouted, straining to be seen above the crowd. "Is He truly the Messiah, as He promised? Is He coming back? Will we see Him again?"

Exchanging knowing looks with his wife and two friends crowded in the doorway, Philip turned toward the crowd, his entire being resonating with confidence. "You know," he replied with an enigmatic smile, "I'm glad you asked. Let's talk about the imminent return of Jesus Christ, the Son of God, our Savior."

CHAPTER 21

Kelila

Sychar

Philip addressed a spellbound crowd late into the afternoon. All activity within the bustling market square came to a screeching halt as merchants closed up shop to join the rapidly growing crowd, curious about Philip's simple, practical teachings. The Samaritans absorbed his instruction with avid intensity, deeply convicted as memories of another unusual Jewish Man who turned a willing smile and outstretched hand upon them penetrated their hearts and minds. Undoubtedly, they remembered how their hearts had burned within them as Jesus had addressed them, the peace of God shining upon His face.

Amazed, Kelila leaned against the doorpost, watching her husband from behind as he addressed the eager crowd with confidence and skill. The Lord had truly gifted Philip for evangelism, and she was proud of him. He was carrying on the Lord's work with fervency and zeal, and the looks upon the faces of his listeners was ample proof that his obedience was producing abundant fruit.

Patiently, Philip explained who Jesus was according to the Scriptures, and how His death and resurrection had fulfilled the age-old testimonies of the ancient prophets.

"Jesus returned to Heaven to prepare a place for us," Philip explained. "And He will prepare a place for each and every one of you, if you will believe upon Him, accepting His shed blood upon the cross as the final atonement for your sins."

As quiet murmurs of acceptance rippled through the crowd, Kelila's heart swelled within her chest. It was truly humbling to witness so many hungering for truth, eager to embrace the Savior of mankind, the only hope of the world.

"Before He returned to Heaven," Philip continued, standing beneath the partial shade provided by the broken-down canopy, "Jesus imparted this life-giving word, saying, 'I am the way, the truth, and the life. No one comes to the Father except through Me.' Friends, Jesus is the *only way* to the Father. We cannot be reconciled by our own strength, nor by our own good works. Nor is there any other name under Heaven by which we can be saved. When our sinless Savior took our transgressions upon Himself, suffering an agonizing death upon the cross, He took the penalty we deserved. Just as in ages past the Temple priests symbolically transferred the sins of man upon an innocent, spotless lamb, slitting its throat and shedding its blood upon the altar, so, too, our sinless Savior took our filthy sins upon Himself, shedding His precious blood in place of our own. Only by accepting this unfathomable exchange can we be saved from the penalty of sin, which is eternal death, for sin cannot exist in the presence of a holy God."

Heart nearly bursting within her, Kelila glanced toward Adorina, who was seated upon an upturned wooden crate a few paces away, thirstily absorbing Philip's every word. Her striking features were utterly transformed, her countenance alight with understanding as Philip answered the deepest questions of her heart, her prayers of many years.

Humbled by her friend's passion and sincerity, Kelila was suddenly reminded of the joy and conviction she had experienced at her own conversion. She remembered being overcome with the burden of her sins and overwhelmed by her need for Christ's pure cleansing as the Apostle John had preached about the prodigal son in the Upper Room. After Mary had assisted her in her prayer of repentance and acceptance of Jesus Christ, an unimaginable weight had lifted from her shoulders. In an instant, she had been freed from her self-inflicted prison of discontent and self-absorption. In that one unthinkable moment, her life suddenly made sense. She had known without a doubt that God had a plan for her life, and no sacrifice was too great to serve the One who laid down His life for her, tenderly loving her long before she even knew Him.

Blinking back tears, Kelila suddenly realized that somewhere along the beaten path between shining Jerusalem and the small town of Sychar, she had unwittingly relinquished that burning passion, that quavering excitement she once experienced in the presence of her God. Amidst the twists and turns and unexpected cares of this life, she had somehow lost her first love.

Bowing her head in unspeakable grief, Kelila silently repented and earnestly sought the Lord.

Please forgive me, Lord, she prayed, clenching her fists at her sides in anguish. *The rigors of travel, the homesickness for my church and family in Jerusalem, my disappointment with present circumstances, and fear of the unknown have undoubtedly taken their toll. I have allowed such things to steal my joy and peace, fixating upon earthly things rather than heavenly ones.*

Lifting her eyes, Kelila's gaze swept over the sea of shining faces, every single one of them fixed upon the evangelist addressing them from the market stall.

Precious Lord, this *is why we came—to share Your love with these dear people!* her heart cried in both repentance and sweet jubilation. *Forgive me, Lord, for losing sight of what is truly important. Rekindle my first love for You and the mission You have entrusted to us! Set my heart afire for these precious sheep to whom we have been called!*

As Philip continued preaching, confidently assuring the Samaritans that Jesus would, indeed, return for His people at the appointed time, many men and women stood, lifting their hands in triumph and shouting out their enthusiasm. Kelila watched, utterly spellbound. Burrowed in frustration and self-pity, she had nearly missed this breathtaking moment in church history, underestimating the magnitude of her calling.

Thank You, God, for waking me up! Thank You

for revealing Your truth to my heart.

"Since we do not know the day or the hour of Christ's imminent return," Philip continued earnestly, "we must always be ready. We must forsake the sins that so easily ensnare us, and we must fix our eyes upon the Lord Jesus. Are you ready to forsake your sins and turn to God?"

"We are ready!" the Samaritans cried out, lifting their hands in worship and surrender. "We renounce our sins! We want to receive the Lord Jesus Christ! Let us be baptized!"

The clamor rose until it fairly shook the streets, resounding through the market square like a fervent battle cry.

Righteous Lord, Kelila prayed in triumph, *Your name is glorified even here! In a land regarded as unholy and unclean by those of importance and prestige, You have filled us with Your presence, reigning in the hearts of men!*

Turning to exchange smiles with Adorina, Kelila saw that she was crying. Her husband, Ephraim, drew behind her, dropping a comforting hand upon her shoulder as cleansing tears slipped down her cheeks.

Dabbing at her wet face with the corner of her shawl, Adorina met Kelila's gaze in awe, shaking her head in joyful wonder.

After years of fervent intercession for her people, revival had finally come.

CHAPTER 22

Tabitha

Joppa

Tabitha sailed through her chores with efficiency and skill, overwhelmingly grateful for Tirzah's cheerful presence and her kind assistance with Laurel. The little girl seemed to be thoroughly enjoying Tirzah's company, Tabitha noted with a huge sigh of relief. Typically, Laurel was shy and rather guarded around strangers. The lively pair shadowed Tabitha throughout the day as she went about the great mansion, efficiently accomplishing each allotted task.

"I believe we have stumbled upon a routine that works well for everyone," Tirzah decided, reaching for her leather bag of provisions and preparing to take her leave.

"I cannot possibly thank you enough for all your help today, Tirzah," Tabitha declared, watching as her daughter played happily on her straw mat with the little worn doll.

"It was my pleasure," Tirzah responded, her tone boding no argument. "I think I shall leave the little box of toys here in your room, if you don't mind. It might prove a bit cumbersome toting them back and forth each day."

"I hadn't thought of that," Tabitha agreed. "You can certainly leave them here with us, although I don't think I will allow Laurel to play with them during your absence. This way, the toys will be something specially set apart for her time with you each day."

"Ah, excellent thinking," Tirzah responded, reaching for her threadbare shawl and draping it over her capable shoulders. "This way, Laurel will look forward to our time together rather than dreading the hours her mother is unable to bestow her full attention upon her."

"Exactly."

"My mother used to do that very thing on Sabbath, but with stories rather than toys," Tirzah reminisced, smiling in fond recollection.

"Oh?" Tabitha asked, walking Tirzah to the stone doorway of her small, unadorned chamber. "How so?"

"Well, my mother had a collection of scrolls that my grandfather compiled as a young man—stories about our faith, our people, our heritage. She liked to take them out—but only during Sabbath hours—and read them aloud to me."

"What a marvelous idea!" Tabitha exclaimed, making a mental note to institute the same special custom with her daughter. Even if she hadn't direct access to the Scriptures, she knew many of the stories by heart and could share them with Laurel in a fun and engaging manner.

"Looking back now, I see her great wisdom in doing so," Tirzah said with a faint smile, her eyes poignantly distant. "While the neighbor children mourned and bewailed Sabbath's swift approach, I stood outside in the outer court waiting for the first star to appear at sunset, ushering in the day of rest. The moment I spotted that star, I would burst into the house, reminding my mother that it was time to light the Sabbath candles."

"It sounds wonderful," Tabitha encouraged gently, sensing that it was difficult for her friend to discuss such things.

"It was," Tirzah nodded, pulling her thoughts back to the present moment with obvious effort. "But enough of that. Those days are long in the past."

"But forever in your heart," Tabitha reminded her, gently touching her friend's shoulder. Sensing that Tirzah was little comforted, Tabitha decided to change the subject. "Speaking of the Sabbath, Eli said something about a synagogue when I first arrived. With the seventh day fast approaching, I'd best inquire about where to locate your house of worship."

"House of worship?" Tirzah released a graceless snort. "We do have a local synagogue, but, unfortunately, the body of worshipers remains as stone cold and utterly lifeless as the lofty building in which they gather. I can already tell you, Tabitha, they won't take too kindly to the new Messianic doctrine of your sect."

Fleetingly, Tabitha recalled the cold reception her husband had received at the Synagogue of the Freedmen located in the ancient City of David. The religious leaders had opposed him every step of the way, eventually instigating his horrific and untimely death. Shuddering, she pushed aside such troubling memories.

"Tabitha? Are you all right?" Tirzah asked quickly, sensing Tabitha's hidden anxiety.

"I'm fine," Tabitha responded with a smile she hoped looked sincere. "Regardless of the reception I may receive at the synagogue, I would like to join you in worship on Sabbath—if that's all right with you, of course."

"You are welcome to accompany me anywhere you wish," Tirzah assured her. "But, please, don't take offense if the religious leaders are cold and severe in their appraisal. They look down their long noses at everyone. Trust me, you wouldn't be the first."

"Nor the last, I imagine," Tabitha supplied wanly. "I have one last question, Tirzah, before you go."

"Ask away."

"How might I send a letter of correspondence to Jerusalem?" she asked frankly. "Eli supplied me with materials just this morning, so I scratched out a hasty letter before breakfast."

"You wish to send word to Jerusalem?"

"Yes, to my former mistress. She abides in the Upper City."

"Ah, yes." Tirzah nodded after a moment of consideration. "Fortunately, Jerusalem—especially the Upper City district—is important enough to receive correspondence, even if the system is unreliable," she acknowledged with a wry smile. "I will take the letter and see that it is received by the proper hands."

"Oh, thank you, Tirzah!" Tabitha nearly squealed,

utterly delighted. "You are an absolute gem!"

"Flattery won't get your letter there any faster," Tirzah teased as Tabitha hurriedly retrieved the sealed scroll from her bedside stand.

"Truly, thank you," Tabitha said with great feeling as Tirzah accepted the scroll. "This means more than you know."

"It's nothing," Tirzah assured her, slipping the scroll into her leather bag. "Now, I must be off to tend my potter's wheel. The poor, neglected thing must be thinking I've forgotten all about it by now!"

***

After Tirzah left for the day, Laurel seemed quite content to "assist" her mother with the simpler chores that remained. The little girl was clearly tired and subdued after many hours of animated, lively play with her new companion.

Delighted with her progress, Tabitha completed her final task an hour earlier than she had anticipated. Now she could see to a leisurely supper with Laurel before bathing her and dressing her for bed!

Mother and daughter were enjoying a quiet supper of vegetable stew and warm flatbread when Joram barged into the kitchen, the veins bulging in his neck.

"I should have known I would find you in here—shirking your responsibilities!" he sneered, coming around the counter to face his niece.

Stunned and frightened, Laurel dropped her flatbread and sent up a howl capable of waking the dead. Reaching for her, Tabitha stood and cradled her close, raising level eyes toward her glaring relative. "Please lower your voice," she requested, unruffled. Stroking her daughter's small back, the toddler buried her face in her mother's soft tunic, sobbing in fear. "You are frightening the child."

"Make her stop screaming!" Joram shouted, covering his ears in outrage.

"You are screaming louder than she is," Tabitha pointed out calmly, drawing a cackle of amusement from Martha and looks of sheer terror from her bustling kitchen helpers. "Please, calm yourself, my lord," Tabitha politely implored him, "then I assure you she will stop crying."

Fists clenching at his sides, Joram glared down at his plucky niece as she comforted the frightened little girl, gently patting her quaking back. Soon, the toddler was hiccupping softly, calmed by her mother's quiet strength.

"Now," Tabitha responded, meeting her uncle's fiery gaze head-on. "What did you wish to discuss, my lord?"

"Your work ethic is deplorable," Joram snarled, drawing confused looks from nearby servants. "You have no right to enjoy a leisurely supper at this early hour when there are chores to be done!"

"I have completed them, my lord," Tabitha assured him, offering Laurel a piece of flatbread to serve as a distraction from the brooding man before them.

"Completed them?" Joram repeated, his eyes flickering in suspicion. "That is impossible, unless you rushed through them in a slipshod, careless manner!"

"You may inspect my work if you wish," Tabitha responded, striving for calm. "I believe you shall find my work satisfactory."

"And how did you manage to complete your tasks in this unbelievably timely manner?" Joram demanded, his eyes betraying his misgivings.

"She got up and set right to work several hours before the rest of us, my lord," Martha cut in, clearly peeved by her employer's behavior and emboldened by Tabitha's courage.

Joram raised a brow in question. "Did she, now?"

"If you don't mind me saying so, she's quite a busy little bee, my lord," Martha responded in defense. "I've never seen one more diligent than she."

"Is that so?" Joram growled, turning cold eyes toward his niece. "Pray tell, why would begin working at such an ungodly hour? So you can lounge about like a queen and order the rest of us about in your spare time?"

"No, my lord," Tabitha responded evenly. "Rather, so I can spend adequate time with my daughter during her waking hours. She is, after all, my first responsibility."

Brows drawing together in distrust, Joram shook his head in obvious exasperation. Turning to leave, he cast a final glare toward the kitchen staff before slipping out the swinging door. "Get back to work."

Anxiously, the servants resumed their tasks, exchanging nervous glances after the door swung shut behind their glowering employer.

"My, my!" Martha clicked her tongue chidingly, plunging floury hands into a large batch of dough. "Have you ever known a man more determined to be unhappy?"

Glancing up in surprise, Tabitha realized that Martha was right. Joram was downright determined to be incorrigible. His deep unhappiness was a clear *choice*, a conscious, deliberate decision.

But why? Why was he so resistant against faith, hope, love, and trust? True, his past was genuinely tragic, and Tabitha understood the agonizing sting of loss better than most. Seldom did a day pass when her heart did not ache at the keen absence of her beloved Stephanos, her tender yet fiery evangelist. But the Lord had enabled her to push past the gnawing pain, embracing the future He had in store for her with faith and confidence.

Precious Lord, she prayed, settling Laurel back on the counter and attempting to reclaim her fleeing appetite, *I don't know how to help that man, but You do. Please grant me the wisdom and patience required to reach him.*

CHAPTER 23

Kelila

Sychar

"The reception we have received here in Sychar is far better than we could have possibly hoped for!" Philip declared, still overwhelmed by the throngs of Samaritans begging to receive Christ that afternoon. "Truly, God is at work here."

"Jesus was right when He told His disciples that the fields were ripe for harvest here," Kelila smiled, carefully spreading their bedroll near the rows of shelves adorned with flickering oil lamps. "Hundreds received Christ today, Philip—all of them asking to be baptized as soon as possible!"

"Adorina knows of a small stream within reasonable walking distance," Philip mused, drawing a stack of thin blankets from one of the shelves he had repaired with Ephraim earlier that day. "Ephraim agreed to take me to see if it is a suitable place to host the baptisms."

"Wouldn't that be exciting?" Kelila dared, her dark eyes sparkling as she accepted the folded blankets her husband offered her. Kneeling before the sleeping mat, she spread out the first one to provide a bit more cushion for their aching backs.

"The excitement about Christ's message is spreading like a wildfire," Philip observed. "I spoke with several men after today's meeting. They met Jesus here in Sychar when He arrived with His disciples several years ago. They remember Him and regret relinquishing their faith so quickly."

"And now they believe He is the Messiah?" Kelila asked, draping another blanket on top of the first one.

"They do. They were among the many who received Christ this afternoon."

"Praise God," she smiled, pleased for them. In a way, she envied them, for she had lived in distant Cyrene when Jesus walked among His people in Judea and Galilee. Unlike Philip, Ephraim, and Adorina, Kelila hadn't been privileged to meet the Lord Jesus before He ascended to Heaven. Oh, but how she wished she had!

Even so, I am an exceptionally blessed woman, Kelila reminded herself, inspecting the sleeping arrangements she had laid out. *Jesus Himself said, "Blessed are those who have not seen and yet have believed."*

"Shall we call it a night, beloved?" Philip asked with a playful wink, settling onto the sleeping pallet and drawing the top layer of blankets over his muscular form. Invitingly, he patted the empty space beside him.

Allowing herself one final sweep of her new living space, Kelila decided she was ready to retire for the evening. Though her entire being longed to continue readying their small home, even the steadily burning oil lamps didn't provide enough light to justify working late into the night. She would simply rise early the next day and get a head start before Philip's preaching commenced again.

Lowering herself onto the sleeping pallet, Kelila slipped beneath the blanket, smiling as Philip wrapped strong arms around her, drawing her close.

"What are you thinking about?" Philip grinned, tucking a long, unruly tendril behind her ear. "I can literally see the wheels turning in your head."

"Is it so obvious?" Kelila laughed, appreciating the way Philip understood her.

"Only because I know you so well," Philip chuckled, planting a kiss on her cheek as she nestled close to him. "What is it?"

"With your permission, Philip, I would like to browse the market stalls and make a few purchases tomorrow," she said forthrightly.

"That's not a bad idea," Philip mused, nodding his approval. "The Samaritans will appreciate the fact that we do business with them."

"Oh, I hadn't thought of that."

"What do you wish to purchase?"

"A washbasin with a stand, an accompanying stool, and fresh towels for hand and foot washing," she readily replied. "I'd like to set up a wash station near the door so guests have easy access to it. Oh, and a small table with a few mats for seating. And a nightstand. And several oil lamps so we can return these, as Adorina may need them soon."

"That's quite a lengthy list," Philip teased. "But

purchase whatever you need, love. I trust you to make wise selections, and you know far better than I what is required to make a house a home."

"Oh, thank you, Philip!" Smiling to herself, Kelila couldn't help but feel excited about furnishing their new home. Though she hadn't initially approved of this unusual living arrangement, her acceptance of God's will had enabled her to focus on the more positive aspects of the humble abode. First, it would be ridiculously simple to keep the place neat, clean, and tidy! In addition to that, little expense would be required to furnish such a small space. And even though she wasn't thrilled about living in the crowded town square, she was only a short walk from Adorina's house, which was located on the main thoroughfare near the bustling market.

"The men I mentioned earlier," Philip spoke into the darkness, pulling Kelila from her silent musings. "They remembered the apostles, as well. Of course, the apostles were called *disciples* back then."

"Wouldn't they be thrilled to see the legacy Christ left behind?" Kelila smiled, shaking her head in wonder.

"They'd never believe it," Philip laughed. "Which is why our new brothers have offered to visit them, bringing a report of all that has happened here."

Turning over on her side, Kelila propped herself up on her elbow, staring at her husband in shock. "Samaritans are going to see the *apostles?* In *Jerusalem?*"

"A few brave souls have volunteered to do so," Philip replied, his voice betraying his excitement. "Not only that, but they plan to ask if any of the apostles will return with them to bring more instruction."

"Wouldn't that be wonderful!" Kelila gasped, amazed. The mere thought of seeing the brethren from beloved Jerusalem brought tears to her eyes. "But, Philip, will they come?"

"That is up to the Lord, I suppose," Philip chuckled. "But I have no doubt the apostles will seek Him in this matter."

"Well, of course, they will," Kelila agreed, attempting to suppress her mounting excitement. After all, she shouldn't get her hopes up until they knew for certain.

Another thought suddenly occurred to her, one that intruded upon her enthusiasm. "Philip," she asked slowly, somewhat reluctant to voice the question, "if the apostles come to Sychar, will they... well..."

"Yes?" Philip prodded, a playful smile teasing his lips.

"Well," Kelila stammered, slightly ashamed to voice her concern. "What if they steal the attention of your flock? You have only just begun to garner the Samaritans' interest."

"Oh, beloved," Philip chuckled merrily, pulling her onto his firm chest. Tucking her hair behind her ears, he smiled in understanding. "The apostles walked beside the Lord Jesus for three and a half years. They are far more experienced than I, and far more knowledgeable."

"Well, I wouldn't say that," Kelila interrupted protectively. "You are a powerful, gifted evangelist, Philip."

"I am *nothing* without the Lord, dear one," he reminded her tenderly. "Like all believers, I am but an empty vessel to be filled with the power of the Holy Spirit. Only when He directs my hands, my feet, my words, my thoughts, can I be useful in His kingdom."

Studying his features in the dim light of the gently flicking oil lamps, Kelila saw that his brown eyes kindled with sincerity.

"Frankly," Philip continued honestly, "I am thrilled the apostles may come. Just imagine how greatly the Samaritans will benefit from their preaching!"

"So you're not upset?"

"Not in the least," Philip assured her. "On the contrary, I rejoice; and I hope it comes to fruition."

Kelila smiled, warmed by her husband's obvious humility.

"The kingdom of God is not a house of competition, beloved," Philip added with a knowing little smile. "A true minister of the gospel welcomes the aid of other believers without resentment or a competitive spirit. May God forbid that kind of attitude from creeping in among those He has chosen to shepherd His flock."

Nodding slowly, Kelila contemplated her husband's wisdom. If only *everyone* shared his humble perspective!

"Philip," Kelila suddenly exclaimed, grasping his hand in excitement as another thought hit her. "May I send word to Jerusalem with the men who depart?"

"I don't see why not," Philip assured her. "Do you wish to write a letter to your sister's family?"

"Oh, yes!" Kelila exclaimed, tears springing to her eyes. "And I want to write Mary, too. I promised her I would keep her informed about the mission work here."

"Of course," Philip agreed. "That's an excellent idea. But I wouldn't tarry, beloved. The men plan to leave within a matter of days."

Heart pounding in her rising excitement, Kelila contemplated what she would say to her sister, Candace, and her beloved mentor, Mary. "Do you suppose Simon, Candace, and the boys have returned from Cyrene yet, Philip?"

"Perhaps," Philip answered. "They set sail even before we departed for Samaria."

"That's true," Kelila agreed, mentally calculating how long the voyage to and from Cyrene by cargo ship would take. How long had it taken when she made the trip from Cyrene to Judea? Ten days? Two weeks? She couldn't remember. All she remembered was how desperately she had longed to get off that deplorable, smelly ship!

"Even if your sister's family hasn't yet returned," Philip continued, interrupting her silent calculations, "the Samaritans can leave Candace's letter with Mary for safekeeping until they arrive in Jerusalem."

"That's a good idea," Kelila decided, aflutter with anticipation. How would she ever sleep tonight with all this exciting news?

"What will you write about?" Philip smiled, sensing her restless energy and elation.

"I will tell them all about our journey here," Kelila decided, her eyes sparkling with enthusiasm. "And I will tell them about our new friends, Ephraim and Adorina, and the joyous reception we have received. I may even tell them about that bizarre enchantress we encountered when we first arrived at this market stall."

"The enchantress?"

"That bold-looking blonde woman," Kelila clarified, pleased that the sensual beauty clearly hadn't left a lasting impression on Philip.

"Ah, yes," Philip chuckled lightly. "I remember now. But I'm not entirely sure she is an enchantress."

"She lives with a sorcerer," Kelila responded airily, as if that explained everything.

"Ah." Clearly, Philip considered it best not to argue.

"Perhaps Adorina's fears were irrational," Kelila mused, enjoying her husband's arms around her as they conversed.

"What do you mean, irrational?"

"She seemed to think the sorcerer would create quite a stir when we arrived," Kelila reminded him. "But he hasn't even bothered to leave his fancy little house."

"That's because he isn't here," Philip told her.

"What?" Kelila blinked, surprised and disturbed.

"Ephraim said he set off on one of his mysterious ventures a few days before our arrival, but he is expected to return any day now."

"I see," Kelila murmured, displeased. "Well, his hold upon the people must have been tenuous, at best. Why else would so many renounce their sins and embrace the Way?"

"We can certainly hope and pray that is so," Philip nodded, though his expression conveyed his doubts.

"What?" Kelila dared, her anxiety mounting. "Do you think he will stir up trouble?"

"I certainly hope not."

"But?" Kelila prompted, sensing there was something Philip hadn't said.

"When the enemy has established a stronghold, he doesn't often just step aside and surrender his prey without a fight," Philip warned her, thoughtfully stroking her lush, curly hair. "Even so, we may ask the Lord to protect us, guarding the hearts of these tender new converts. He will prepare us for whatever opposition may—or may not—lie ahead."

Dark brows drawing together in dismay, Kelila contemplated her husband's sober words.

Sleep didn't come for a long, long time after that.

CHAPTER 24

John Mark

Jerusalem

Aurelia emerged from the deep shadows of the southern colonnade, the sunlight catching the streams of golden hair flowing over her shoulders and down her slender back. Her garments, composed of the finest Egyptian linen and accented with soft touches of coral with golden trim, fluttered gracefully in the early morning breeze as her slender arms sparkled with jewel-studded golden bracelets matching the elegant girdle belted at her waist. With a coy smile and a slight wave of her hand, she acknowledged the handsome young man approaching from the sprawling, marble-paved market square, his brown eyes filled with swelling admiration.

"I wondered if you would show up," Aurelia purred, her blue eyes glowing with desire as John Mark drew before her, his wide eyes betraying his captivation.

"I keep my word," John Mark informed her, attempting to appear at ease, in control. The truth of the matter was, the mere sight of this girl sent his heart racing, his palms sweating, and his mind reeling with breathless possibilities.

"A man of his word?" Aurelia teased, pausing to trace his chiseled jawline with a smooth, manicured finger. "I like that."

John Mark's heart sprang into his throat, nearly overcome by her touch. Her cool fingertips upon his flushed skin felt utterly delicious, arousing all manner of forbidden thoughts.

What would it be like to win an exciting young woman like Aurelia? he wondered. Perhaps, if she embraced the Way, his mother would approve of his intentions. But did he have the courage to share his faith with this beautiful creature? And even if he did, how would she respond? What would a sophisticated Roman think of a provincial Jew's religion, especially one dubbed heretical by his own religious leaders?

"Shall we stroll?" Aurelia asked boldly, surprising him. He wasn't accustomed to forward women taking the lead. Even so, the idea of strolling arm in arm with this lovely woman suited him.

"Anything your heart desires," he grinned, offering his arm in a chivalrous manner.

"Anything?" Aurelia purred, her thick lashes fluttering enticingly. "I may hold you to that. After all, you are rather desirable."

John Mark nearly came out of his skin when she took his arm, leaning heavily upon him as if she was already his own. Fleetingly, he wondered what would happen if they encountered a fellow believer or one of his mother's associates. Should that occur, word of his clandestine meeting with a pretty Gentile girl would surely reach his mother! The thought was bad enough to turn his stomach.

Frantically, he offered a silent petition heavenward. *Please don't let my mother learn about this yet!* Surely the Lord understood his raging desire. Hadn't He himself said it wasn't good for man to be alone? Well, for the first time in his young life, John Mark had discovered a woman that suited him. She was beautiful, enticing, mysterious, and utterly fascinating. Besides, perhaps he, John Mark, was her only hope for salvation! It was entirely possible, after all.

Hadn't his mother taught him to share the gospel with his peers? Well, Aurelia now presented the perfect opportunity to do so.

"Now, tell me about yourself, John Mark."

Drawn from his inner turmoil by her melodious voice, John Mark forced a confident smile he was far from feeling. "Well," he drawled easily, catching himself before he could say, *There isn't much to tell.* How would *that* sound to a sophisticated and exciting young woman like Aurelia? She ran in powerful circles with incredibly important people! Her days were surely spent mingling among wealthy Roman aristocrats, her nights marked by royal banquets in the halls of kings!

"Well?" Aurelia prodded, strolling alongside him at a leisurely pace, a delicate hand upon his arm. "I want to know everything about you."

"And I want to know about you, Aurelia," John Mark shot back, saving himself the humiliation of recounting his own boring existence to this interesting and exotic creature. "Yesterday, you mentioned that you are a guest of Herod Antipas. Do you plan to stay in Jerusalem?"

"That depends," Aurelia said flirtatiously, tossing her hair over her shoulder in a rather flippant manner. "My father and I hail from Rome, but his career takes him all over the empire. I love traveling abroad, so I often accompany him."

R*ome!* John Mark thought, his fascination battling keen disappointment. It was highly likely Aurelia would soon return to the Imperial City with her father. The thought sickened him. *But perhaps,* he thought, grasping at straws in his desperation, *if she has a reason to stay—*

"You must be wondering why the daughter of a successful Roman official has taken an interest in a Jewish boy," Aurelia grinned, and John Mark was flabbergasted by her bold admission of interest.

"Tell me," John Mark responded with an easy smile, desperately attempting to keep his cool.

"You intrigue me, John Mark," Aurelia replied, leaning in so close his senses were clouded by the heady scent of her strong perfume. "When I stumbled upon you in the Roman quarter, I knew there was something different about you. Somehow, I knew fate had brought us together. And now," she said, turning to take his hands and gaze directly into his eyes, "I am positively desperate to discover *why.*"

Fate, she had said. Secretly, John Mark wondered if a force far greater than fate had arranged their meeting. Aurelia, a Gentile from Rome, wouldn't know anything about the Holy Spirit's leading. But, clearly, she felt it, too—it was like a magnetic, driving force, drawing them together. Perhaps the

Lord had indeed orchestrated this unlikely meeting between them! After all, it wouldn't be the first time God had blessed a union between a Jew and a Gentile. Ruth married Boaz, didn't she? And Salmon took Rahab to wife!

Forcing a calming breath, John Mark attempted to compose himself despite the unfamiliar desires raging within him, shaking him to his core. He was certain Aurelia could hear his heart pounding in his chest like a war drum as she gazed up at him with unveiled desire. For one fleeting moment, he considered cupping her face and kissing her, for her clear blue eyes dared him to do so.

But the perfect moment was obliterated when an unexpected clatter followed by an explosion of angry shouts erupted across the Upper Market. Snapping his head in the direction of the ruckus, John Mark saw several Roman soldiers descending upon a thief near a jeweler's booth. In the process, several tables had been overturned, the expensive merchandise clattering to the tile floor as the jeweler shouted in outrage.

Saddened, John Mark watched as the young thief was shoved against a table by several uniformed soldiers, his hands roughly bound behind his back.

"Never a dull moment in this dusty little province," Aurelia quipped sarcastically, peeved by the unwanted interruption.

John Mark glanced at her in surprise, for her dulcet tone lacked even the slightest hint of sympathy. It was likely the captured thief would pay for his transgression with his life, and yet she watched the ensuing violence with an air of annoyance.

As the jeweler scrambled to upright his scattered

tables and gather up his merchandise, the thief was pushed roughly past throngs of gaping shoppers, his head bowed in shame. John Mark watched the disturbing scene, strangely unsettled.

"You look pale as death. Surely you have seen a man arrested before!"

Mortified by Aurelia's observation, John Mark cleared his throat, turning his attention to the striking beauty at his arm. "My apologies, Aurelia. I was lost in thought."

"Clearly."

"I suppose I should be returning home," he managed, deeply unsettled by the thief's plight. What could have possibly motivated a Jew to rob a fellow countryman? Was it sheer desperation? Or a temptation too great to resist?

"You must leave? Already?" Sensing that perhaps she had misspoken, Aurelia turned on the charm. "But you've only just arrived," she exclaimed, wearing a pretty pout. "Must you leave me so soon?"

"We can meet again, another time," John Mark promised her, distracted. Right now, he needed some time to think and sort through his tumultuous emotions.

"Tomorrow, then," Aurelia responded, sensing his slight withdrawal. "I want to see you again, John Mark. And soon."

Drawn by her intensity, John Mark turned to meet her gaze. Once again, he found himself utterly captivated by her beautiful blue eyes and poignant expression. His chest constricted at the thought of losing her.

"I will see you again, Aurelia," he said firmly, hoping he sounded more confident than he felt. "But not tomorrow."

"Why not tomorrow?" she demanded, petulant.

"It is the Sabbath," John Mark replied, uneasy. He had a feeling she wouldn't like what he had to say.

"You're not allowed to have fun on the Sabbath?" she asked pointedly.

"Of course, we have fun," John Mark declared, embarrassed and defensive. "But it is to be a day of rest and restoration. On the Sabbath, we celebrate the glory of God's creation, worshiping and feasting with family and friends."

"But it doesn't have to be Saturday. You can rest any other day of the week," Aurelia suggested impatiently.

"I couldn't do that," John Mark managed, squirming inwardly. She wasn't making this easy!

"Why not?"

"Because God blessed the *seventh day* and hallowed it. In His Word, He commands us to keep the seventh day as a Sabbath day of rest and worship. The Scriptures even tell us we will keep the Sabbath in the age to come, after Jesus returns for His followers and makes everything right," he explained, wondering if he was making any sense.

"But what makes one day more special than another?" Aurelia argued in answer to his silent question. "It's just *time*."

"Romans observe festivals and holy days, too," John Mark pointed out, drawing upon what little knowledge he had of pagan customs. "How is our Sabbath observance any different than the venerable day of the Sun celebrated on the first day of the week by heath—*ahem*, I mean—by Greeks, Romans, and such?" he asked, somehow catching himself before he referenced her people as *heathen*.

"Greeks and Romans do worship on Sunday if they so choose," Aurelia admitted, losing patience. "But our religion is far less stuffy and rigid than yours. We worship at our own convenience, regardless of the day. And we only give offerings or make vows in exchange for requests granted by the gods."

"Like...like a bribe?" John Mark asked, surprised.

"Something like that." Aurelia laughed, not the least bit bothered by the concept. "Regardless, Romans worship as they please, without condemnation or a long list of rules about how to do it. We live for pleasure, not misery. You Jews could learn a lot from us."

Feeling defeated, John Mark wondered if Aurelia considered him as "stuffy" and "rigid" as his religion.

"There's so much more to this world than what you have been taught, John Mark, locked behind those cold stone walls of your little synagogue," Aurelia informed him, her blue eyes sparkling with fun. "I look forward to teaching you a thing or two. With me, you will experience excitement and pleasure and wild sensations beyond your greatest imaginings. Trust me." Grasping his neck, she drew his head down, planting a firm kiss on his mouth.

Dazed, John Mark stared at her, speechless, as she pulled away, a knowing smile gracing her lips.

"You were made for me," she smiled, emboldened by his captivation. "And I, for you. But, first, you'll have to find yourself, John Mark. All your life, you have been blindly following in the footsteps of ancestors long dead. But that is about to change."

Intrigued, John Mark watched as Aurelia reached behind her neck, unclasping the delicate golden pendant gracing her slender throat. Taking his hand, she tucked it into his palm, carefully closing his fingers over it. The metal felt cool and pleasant in his sweaty palm.

"Keep it," she purred, caressing his closed hand with manicured fingers. "This way, you shall always have me with you. Even when we are apart."

Rendered utterly speechless, John Mark managed a slow nod as she gently released his hand.

"We shall meet here in the Upper Market on the first day of the week, since the seventh is off limits—for now," she informed him with a teasing little smile. "Good day, John Mark."

Swallowing hard, John Mark attempted to steady his beating heart as he watched Aurelia gracefully crossing the sprawling Upper Market, her sights set upon the magnificent palace towering regally above the paved square.

Dropping his gaze, he stared at his own closed fist, his fingers wrapped around the golden keepsake Aurelia had placed in his hand. Gingerly, he opened limber fingers, squinting at the heavy pendant resting in his palm, fascinated by the strange etchings upon its gleaming surface.

This way, you shall always have me with you, Aurelia had said.

Taking a closer look, his heart skipped a beat in recognition. Engraved upon the pendant was a twisted serpent, its ruby-studded eyes glittering in the golden sunlight.

CHAPTER 25

Kelila

Sychar

Seated upon an upturned crate at the edge of their sagging market stall, Kelila listened as her husband addressed a sea of shining faces before him. The crowd had doubled and possibly even tripled since the previous day, and Kelila was excited to see so many seeking the truth about the gospel.

Dabbing at her brow with her pale green shawl, Kelila glanced up at the sun rising steadily in the sky. Though it was still early, the day was quite warm. At least she *felt* warm...and fatigued. Perhaps she simply hadn't slept well. She had lain awake long into the night, dreading the sorcerer's return. What if his arrival dampened the joy and eagerness of these precious new converts? What if he came against them in fury?

"Is something wrong?" Adorina whispered over her shoulder, seated on a straw mat near Kelila's makeshift chair. "You look troubled."

"Oh, it's nothing," Kelila quickly assured her, trying for a convincing smile. She certainly didn't wish to appear unsettled or disturbed before her husband's audience!

"Are you well?" Adorina persisted.

"I'm fine," Kelila promised. "A little tired, perhaps, which is unlike me."

"You've only just arrived from an arduous trek," Adorina reminded her. "I'm sure that is to be expected."

Their whispered interlude was suddenly cut short by a blood-curdling scream that tore across the central square, throwing the entire gathering into a state of fearful apprehension and frenzy. Instinctively, Philip halted his preaching as men and women rose hesitantly, scanning the perimeter of the town square in question and exchanging nervous glances.

Heart springing into her throat, Kelila grasped Adorina's arm as chills of premonition tingled up and down her rigid spine. "What was that?"

Another ear-splitting scream pierced the air, so fierce and dreadful Kelila was tempted to run and hide.

Adorina's eyes narrowed in recognition. "The demoniac."

"The *what?*" Kelila gasped as several people in the crowd fled in sheer panic, some of them screaming or crying out in terror. Mothers shielded their small children, looking toward their husbands in earnest fear. Frantically, Kelila's gaze fell upon Philip, who remained standing confidently beneath the canopy's partial shade, his brown eyes serious as he swiftly assessed the situation.

Following his gaze, Kelila detected a ragged and bloodied entourage of Samaritans dragging a raging, shrieking demoniac toward the crowd…and toward her husband. Gasping in fear, Kelila sprang to her feet in protest. "What are they doing?"

"Stay calm." Adorina rose along with her, maddeningly composed. "That young man is possessed by a slew of demons."

"So I gathered!"

"His family must have heard about Philip's ministry," Adorina surmised, watching grimly as the chained demoniac battled against his captors and his iron chains, bellowing his outrage.

"Why…why would they bring him here?" Kelila stammered, her panic rising as the struggling demoniac was dragged closer toward their market stall and the anxious gathering.

"Why else?" Adorina smiled knowingly, her eyes luminous with anticipation. "To be healed."

"*Healed?*" Kelila gasped, taking several steps back as the demoniac's perseverant relatives dragged him within a few feet of the undaunted evangelist.

Throwing his head back, the demoniac released another frightful roar that chilled Kelila to the bone. Grasping Adorina's hand like a lifeline, she watched with bated breath as the demoniac's weeping mother fell at Philip's feet, begging him to restore her son as the young man raged against the grasp of four strong male relatives. Clawing and biting at his captors, he attempted several powerful kicks with bound limbs that rattled his chains in the most frightening and foreboding manner.

Wide-eyed with fright, Kelila held her breath,

praying silently, fiercely, as the demoniac was dragged directly before a tall and confident Philip. Ephraim drew protectively alongside the evangelist, his powerful form posed for action. Clearly, he was ready and willing to intervene, if needed.

Now a mere stone's throw away from the demon-possessed man, Kelila allowed herself a cautious inspection, both shocked and repulsed by what she saw. Looking away in revulsion, she was quite sure she had never seen anything so diabolical or gruesome. Bulbous, bloodshot eyes darted about like that of a savage beast. The demoniac's bearded face was covered in foam as blue veins bulged from his taut neck and forehead and shaggy dark hair fell across his rage-filled eyes, partially obscuring his view. His jagged fingernails still bore the blood drawn from his suffering relatives. Forcing another look, Kelila saw that the madman's family bore many scars along with fresh wounds as they gritted their teeth and bore the brunt of the young man's fierce struggling. With another rabid cry, he arched his back, bowing up against his restraints.

What if he should break free from their grasp? she thought, terrified. *What chance does Philip stand against a raging beast possessed by devils?*

"God will protect Philip," Adorina whispered, as if reading Kelila's frightened thoughts. "Have faith."

Embarrassed, Kelila nodded firmly, glancing nervously toward the crowd. Had the presence of the demoniac frightened them away? Surprisingly, she saw anger and indignation reflected upon many faces, though fear was certainly present, as well.

"How dare you interrupt the teacher's instruction?" a hard-looking man standing near the front shouted at the distraught woman still huddled at Philip's feet. The crowd was quick to join in, snarling insults and demanding that the demoniac be forcefully removed.

But Kelila saw the expression upon the face of the young man's heartbroken mother, her features riddled with desperation and pain. Her family was clearly in a bad way, for the clothes upon her back were little more than soiled rags. She, too, bore many angry scars, but Kelila realized the most painful ones were likely hidden, buried deep inside. Suddenly and quite unexpectedly, Kelila's heart went out to the poor woman so desperate to find healing for her son.

Oh, God, help! Kelila could think of nothing else to pray. The moment was far too tense, the fear and anguish much too real. But God knew her heart. And He knew what was needed most.

As the crowd continued to shout their indignation and rage against the writhing demoniac and his relatives, Philip's brown eyes swept over his audience, a look of deep sorrow on his somber face. Holding up a powerful hand, he silenced them without a word.

Turning toward the weeping mother crumpled at his feet, Philip bent and gently reached for her, drawing her up by the elbow. "Peace," he said, his powerful voice rising above the heart-stopping shrieks of the demoniac. "Do not be afraid."

"The woman is a widow. She lives with her brother, three grown sons, and her fourth son, the demoniac, on the outskirts of the village," Adorina revealed to Kelila in a low whisper, leaning in to be heard above the din. "It is rumored the poor woman has tried every possible cure for her son. She even sought the sorcerer's services, paying him an outrageous fee to concoct some ridiculous potion to promote healing."

"We have tried everything," the woman explained to Philip, confirming Adorina's statement and struggling against her tears. "Even Simon with all his power could do nothing. After many failed attempts, he concocted a final potion, but I could not bring myself to administer it."

"What kind of potion?" Philip asked quietly, his expression indicating he already knew.

"It was…" the woman stammered tremulously, "… it was meant to put my son out of his misery and end his sufferings."

Gasping in horror, Kelila was sickened and appalled by what the wicked sorcerer had suggested. Looking to her friend, she saw Adorina's dark eyes harden in indignation.

"Simon said there was no other way," the woman tried to explain, tears pouring down her leathery face. "He said it would be an act of mercy to end his sufferings."

"But you didn't go through with it," Philip gently observed. "Why?"

"I…I just couldn't," the woman rasped, her thin shoulders hunching over as great, rending sobs shook her small frame. "He is my son. He wasn't always this…this *monster*. He was my *son*."

"Amen," Philip breathed, taking her by the shoulders and forcing her to meet his burning gaze. "Praise God, you heeded the still small voice within, sparing his life."

"I never met your Teacher," the woman breathlessly confessed as her son continued struggling violently behind her. "But it is said He worked miracles and cast out demons. It is also said He has granted such power to His apostles, enabling them to do the same."

"Dear woman, your faith gladdens His heart and mine," Philip smiled warmly, drawing whispers of fascination and speculation from the crowd. "Indeed, there is hope for your son."

Clinging to the stoic Adorina's arm like a lifeline, Kelila's heart pounded wildly in her chest as Philip stepped past the weeping woman, pausing before the raging demoniac.

Oh, God, she prayed, nearly frantic with fear. *Preserve my husband. Protect him, Lord!*

The instant Philip drew before the demoniac, he released a mighty roar so terrible Kelila thought she would faint. It was as if the evil spirits plaguing the poor man sensed the Holy Spirit of God within the courageous evangelist and sought to wage war against him.

"I am not afraid of you," Philip breathed, bending to meet the seething demoniac's gaze head-on. "The Spirit of the living God dwells inside of me. You have no power here."

Baring his teeth, the demoniac lunged at Philip, barely constrained by his now trembling captors.

Standing his ground, Philip grasped the demoniac's powerful shoulder, shouting with great authority, "In the name of Jesus Christ, the Son of God, I command you—*all* of you—to come out of him and enter him no more!"

The crowd was on its feet as the young man violently convulsed, dropping to his knees and crying out in anguish.

Heart pounding furiously in her chest, Kelila wondered if she had only imagined the sound of flapping winged creatures retreating in terror and defeat, chased away by a gust of mighty wind.

Going instantly limp, the young man fell upon his face before Philip, utterly still.

"Is he..." Kelila breathed, too frightened to say the rest aloud. *Oh, God, is he dead?*

His mother must have thought so. Releasing a cry of anguish, she rushed the lifeless form of her grown son, scooping his limp body in her arms. Kneeling beside her, Philip gently turned the young man over on his back. Kelila and Adorina breathed immense sighs of relief when the former demoniac gazed up at Philip with wide, frightened eyes—completely subdued.

"Don't be afraid," Philip encouraged, slowly helping the young man ease himself into a sitting position. "Your torment has ended."

Face crumpling in tears, the woman threw her arms around Philip and her restored son, sobbing her relief and gasping out her gratitude. "Oh, thank you, thank you!"

"All glory goes to God," Philip told her, accepting her fierce embrace. Glancing up at her stunned brother and sons now gathered around in awe and gaping confusion, Philip smiled. "As you have all seen, He alone is our Healer."

Breathless with amazement and sheer relief, Kelila realized she still clutched Adorina's arm like a lifeline. Laughing sheepishly, she loosened her grasp, excited to witness what would surely follow. She had no doubt Philip would lead the young man to Christ after such a shocking miracle!

However, her thoughts were interrupted when the crowd erupted with enthusiasm and zeal, shouting out their excitement, waving their hands, and dancing in the street.

"The man is healed!"

"It's a miracle! A *miracle*!"

"Can you heal my mother? She has been ill for weeks—"

"My father is blind. Please, restore his sight!"

And suddenly, the enormous crowd rushed Philip and the former demoniac's family, begging and pleading for miracles of their own, for healing for themselves and their loved ones. Kelila had never heard anything like the joyous cacophony which followed as men and women rejoiced in the obvious miracle, savoring the thought of even more to come.

Jostled by the rambunctious throng as it pressed around Philip from all sides, Kelila allowed Adorina to draw her away from the market stall and further from the ensuing madness. Folding her arms over her chest, Adorina watched as her husband, Ephraim, helped Philip organize the clamoring Samaritans into neat, orderly rows.

Did Philip truly intend to heal them *all*? Checking her line of thought, Kelila reminded herself that *Philip* hadn't the power to heal them—only God could do that. And *He* would decide whom to offer healing, and who should glorify Him through suffering, instead.

Clasping her hands over her heart, Kelila marveled, for the Spirit of God was truly at work among these people. Nothing—absolutely nothing—could douse the soaring happiness swelling within her chest.

At that moment, Adorina grasped her arm, her expression instantly alert. Following her friend's burning gaze, Kelila's heart nearly stopped at the sight of a commanding form—a tall, powerfully built man watching solemnly from a distance, his magnificent, crimson-colored robes fluttering in the breeze and emphasizing his eerily still form. His swarthy complexion suited his neatly oiled, styled salt-and-pepper beard and dark, fathomless eyes—blazing eyes which seemed to look within the very souls of men.

Releasing a shaky breath, Kelila fought against the shudder passing through her body, every fiber of her being tingling in premonition. Instinctively, she knew who this strikingly impressive figure must be.

The sorcerer had returned.

CHAPTER 26

Kelila

Sychar

Stunned by the sudden appearance of a likely enemy, Kelila swallowed hard, not even feeling Adorina's fingers digging into her arm. Glancing anxiously toward her friend, the two exchanged looks of concern, but also resolve.

How long had the sorcerer been standing across the market square? How much had he observed? Had he witnessed the healing of the demoniac whom he had been powerless to aid?

Turning back toward the indomitable figure, Kelila's heart sprang into her throat. He was gone! Though she supposed he must have simply crossed the street and slipped into his own elaborate market stall on the opposite end of the square, she couldn't help but wonder if perhaps he had evaporated into thin air.

"Now what do you suppose that was about?"

Adorina mused, her sharp eyes scanning the dusty street where the sorcerer had watched them with grim severity. "Why would he simply stand there, staring?"

"He probably wanted to know what all the fuss was about," Kelila guessed, hoping it was nothing more than that. "How long was he standing there?"

"I haven't the slightest idea," Adorina admitted. "I assumed he was still off seeing to matters of business, and I let my guard down. But it won't happen again."

"Do you think we should be concerned?"

"Absolutely," Adorina responded, surprising her. "Simon is an agent of darkness, employing forbidden arts to obtain his own desired ends. He is not going to like another man interfering on what he considers his own turf."

Kelila's pulse quickened as she contemplated this unwanted fact.

"Even so," Adorina reminded her staunchly, "God has far more power than one foul magician. We needn't fear him."

Easier said than done, Kelila thought, her stomach churning with apprehension. If only she possessed Adorina's grit! Very little seemed to disturb or frighten her.

"Let's forget about him," Adorina decided, turning serious eyes back toward Philip and Ephraim as they assisted the large throngs of people vying for their attention. "Just look what God is doing here! We mustn't allow Simon to steal our joy or dampen our happiness."

Following Adorina's gaze, Kelila watched as streams of eager Samaritans joined the crowd pressing around Philip and Ephraim, bringing sick relatives and friends to receive healing. Philip was laying hands on a frail, bearded man leaning heavily upon a gnarled walking stick. Raising his eyes heavenward, Philip sought healing in the name of Jesus. Immediately, the elderly man flung his walking stick aside, lifting his hands and dancing like a delighted child. The crowd resounded with shouts of jubilation and amazement as Philip bowed his head, publicly thanking God for His abundant mercy.

"Come." Adorina smiled, nodding toward their husbands at the front of the market stall. "Let's get a bit closer, shall we?"

Nodding her agreement, Kelila followed Adorina around the outer fringe of the large gathering, emerging near the long, limestone structure housing the merchants' respective storage rooms. When Adorina lowered herself onto the edge of Philip's empty cart, Kelila followed suit. *This is a rather nice perch from which to observe the meeting,* she decided. Why hadn't she thought of it before? Here, near the entrance of her new home, they were close enough to witness the healings, though also somewhat removed from the thick of the crowd.

Smiling, Kelila noted that the former demoniac hadn't left Philip's side since his miraculous healing. His mother stood proudly beside him, her once downcast features truly radiant and alight with joy.

When a former paralytic stood upon his own two feet for the first time in his life, the crowd went wild with joy, nearly overcome. It was truly staggering to see family, friends, and neighbors of the small, tightly knit community restored to health and wholeness. Kelila was touched by their sincere happiness for each other.

"I see we have a great healer in our midst." Suddenly, a sultry voice rang out over the crowd, both musical and strangely mesmerizing. "By what power do you invoke such mighty wonders?"

Craning their necks, the crowd turned to see the sorcerer's muse standing calmly upon a raised curb, her clear azure eyes fixed upon the evangelist.

Heart springing into her throat, Kelila sensed rather than saw Adorina's entire body tense as her spine went rigid. Had the sorcerer sent Helena to interrogate Philip? Was she simply curious, or had she come to challenge his authority?

Exchanging a quick look with Ephraim, Philip gazed over the heads of those assembled before him, boldly making eye contact with the brazenly dressed woman. "I am not a healer," he said firmly, ready to defend his position.

"No?" Helena mused, a cascade of lush golden curls falling over one shoulder as she tipped her head in seemingly innocent question. "Your actions speak otherwise, Jew."

"These men and women have been healed in the name of Jesus Christ, the Son of God, through the power of the Holy Spirit," Philip testified, unruffled by her obvious challenge. "By my own strength, I can do nothing."

"Oh, I have no doubt about that," Helena replied coolly, stepping off the curb and walking gracefully toward the gathering.

Heart pounding in her chest, Kelila watched in horror as the crowd parted like the Red Sea, reverently creating a wide path for the strange enchantress. What power she must wield over them to elicit such a response!

Pausing directly before Philip and Ephraim, Helena's painted lips tipped rather smugly. "Our people have suffered enough," she said coldly, her blue eyes flashing a clear warning. "We needn't one more *false* prophet touting *false* hope and a *false* religion, stirring up trouble here in our little hamlet."

"*Our* little hamlet?" Adorina scoffed loudly enough to be heard by all, instantly on her feet, her challenging glare closing the distance between herself and the fierce enchantress.

Kelila's pounding heart nearly stopped, unprepared for her friend's fiery challenge, as many in the crowd drew back in apprehension as the enchantress stiffened, turning scornful eyes toward Adorina. Clearly, the Samaritans both feared and revered the queenly looking young woman, her charming smile masking the eyes of a viper. Had the people witnessed her power at work, or was their fear simply driven by rumors and hearsay?

"This isn't *your* little hamlet, Helena, nor have you any right to dictate what happens here," Adorina reminded her, her dark eyes blazing. "Everyone knows you are from a Phoenician city, the land of Jezebel! Is it any wonder you now follow in her footsteps? You are no Samaritan, nor have you the right to govern us."

"Foolish woman," Helena clicked her tongue as if chiding an errant child. "Have you forgotten who you are dealing with?"

"Absolutely not," Adorina shot back. "You are a witch and the kept woman of a deceitful magician. Your power is from the evil one, and we refuse to be deceived any longer."

Gasps of fear and shock rippled through the crowd, but Adorina wasn't swayed by the mounting apprehension nor the tension crackling heavily in the air. "If you wish to place your faith in magic spells and potions, so be it," she said bravely. "But I refuse to let you lead my people astray any longer, Helena."

"You will regret this."

Shuddering, Kelila knew those cold blue eyes would haunt her dreams.

"No, Helena," Adorina responded stoutly, boldly crossing the distance between them and coming face to face with the seething young woman. "But *you* will, unless you repent and turn from your wickedness." When Ephraim touched her shoulder in silent entreaty, Adorina refused to deviate from her course. "If you would like to sit quietly and listen to Philip's instruction like all the rest of us, Helena, we would be honored to have you remain. Otherwise, I must ask you to leave."

With a smug little smile that sent tiny shivers up and down Kelila's spine, the enchantress turned on her elegantly clad heel, stealing quietly through the crowd. Pausing at the elaborate double doors of her opulent quarters, she cast an unsettling smile toward Philip, her coy expression indicating that he hadn't seen the last of her yet.

After Helena's scornful and dramatic exit, the gathering waited in tense, uneasy silence. What seemed to be a very long, very awkward pause followed, until Ephraim forced a sheepish smile. "Well, that was exciting!"

With several nervous chuckles, the Samaritans relaxed ever so slightly as Philip offered a reassur-

ing smile. "I apologize about that untimely interruption," he said humbly, his gaze traveling toward
Adorina, her cheeks still ruddy with passion. "Are
you all right, my friend?"

"I'm sorry, Philip," Adorina confessed, her tone
indicating otherwise. "But that woman has caused
enough trouble. And I refuse to stand idly by, allowing her to lead our people astray. We have waited
long enough for the truth to reach this land. I will
not let that foul witch destroy it."

"She cannot destroy the truth, beloved," Ephraim
gently reminded his wife, guiding her toward an upturned crate and helping her settle upon it despite
her obvious protests. "Our God is greater."

Hopping off the wagon, Kelila closed the distance
between herself and her friend, touching her shoulder in encouragement. While she admired Adorina's
grit, she hoped the passionate woman hadn't unwittingly made things worse for the new believers.
What if her bold stance against Helena's influence
only increased the sorcerer's hostility against them?
Glancing nervously between Philip and Ephraim,
she wondered if their thoughts mirrored her own.

"Based on Helena's reaction," the former demoniac's uncle scoffed loudly, addressing Philip, "I'm
guessing you are not in league with the sorcerer
despite the mighty healings you perform."

"Absolutely not," Philip responded firmly, though
Kelila noticed his tone was laced with understanding rather than judgment. "You must understand,
friends, that neither I nor the sorcerer possess any
real power of our own. Our bodies are empty vessels
meant to be *filled*. Some choose to be filled with the
power of God, while others cling to the deceptive

powers of Satan."

"Are you saying that Simon receives his power from the *devil*?" the mother of the restored young man asked timidly, clearly stunned by the revelation.

Kelila looked to Philip, wondering how he would address this honest question without causing offense. They were treading upon dangerous waters, and it made her exceedingly uncomfortable. What if the sorcerer lurked nearby, eavesdropping upon Philip's unpopular, straightforward teachings?

"Repeatedly, the Scriptures forbid witchcraft or sorcery of any kind," Philip patiently explained, his kind eyes traveling over the troubled faces of his audience. "It is written, *There shall not be found among you anyone who makes his son or daughter pass through the fire, or one who practices witchcraft, or a soothsayer, or one who interprets omens, or a sorcerer, or one who conjures spells, or a medium, or a spiritist, or one who calls up the dead. For all who do these things are an abomination to the Lord.* When God gives us a clear command like this, it is because He knows the grave danger of indulging in these sins. He knows when a man or a woman dabbles in witchcraft or sorcery of any kind, they become susceptible to great deception, possibly even demon-possession."

"Are you saying that Simon's power is *real*?" another curious Samaritan asked. "I have always believed sorcerers to be nothing more than deceitful frauds."

"Some *are* tricksters and frauds," Philip soberly affirmed, "extorting others by employing clever trickery and cunning illusions. Even so, others have truly given themselves over to evil and demonic spirits, receiving power from these dark entities. We must constantly be on guard, standing firm against this wickedness."

"But if Simon has great power granted by evil forces, why was he unable to cast out the demons in my son?" This, from the restored young man's mother.

Kelila leaned forward just a bit, fascinated by the sincere questions swirling around her husband. Silently, she prayed the Lord would grant him wisdom to answer these honest inquiries.

"After they witnessed Jesus casting out a mute spirit, the Pharisees began spreading rumors that He cast out demons through the power of Satan," Philip replied, his brown eyes serious. "But Jesus knew their thoughts and addressed their mistake by saying, '*If Satan casts out Satan, he is divided against himself. How then will his kingdom stand?*' It would be utterly contrary to the devil's mission to free an imprisoned soul from bondage. And though the enemy undoubtedly wields great power through Simon, the sorcerer, I don't find it plausible that the devil would work against himself and his own dark agents, do you?"

Quietly, the crowd contemplated this unexpected piece of wisdom, undoubtedly processing all they had witnessed at the hand of their local sorcerer.

Sensing the direction of the Samaritans' thoughts, Ephraim voiced the question he knew they must all be thinking. "I have heard many—Simon himself included—claim that he practices only 'good magic'. He insists that his magic promotes good rather than evil, harming no one. How would you refute this argument, Philip?"

"There is no such thing as 'good magic.' Period. End of story."

Kelila was surprised by the finality of her husband's statement. Was there no room for argument? Not even a little?

"The use of magic of *any kind* involves the employment of supernatural forces to obtain a desired end," Philip went on to explain. "Sadly, we have become desensitized to the dangers of sorcery and witchcraft, mostly because our theaters and stadiums abound with compelling entertainments arousing our interest in this deadly subject by glamorizing and romanticizing the craft."

Cut to the heart, Kelila considered the shows and performances she had once obsessed about, sneaking out of her father's house to watch hours of foul entertainment in Roman theaters. *Why, I practically worshiped the celebrated actors and actresses performing in the shows I adored!* she thought, thanking God for freeing her from that bondage. Her addiction to ungodly forms of entertainment had undoubtedly shaped her mind and worldview contrary to His Word. At the time, she hadn't known the danger of such influences. Unwittingly, she had flung a door wide open to an evil presence determined to fill her mind with propaganda from the pit of hell. Even many seemingly "innocent" performances had harbored subtle subliminal messages that contradicted and even mocked the Word of God.

Oh, Lord, forgive me for falling prey to that deception, Kelila repented anew, overwhelmingly grateful the Lord had rescued her from an ungodly obsession. Considering the pounding music, the breathless wonder, and the riveting nature of such compelling entertainments, Kelila realized it was all a lure intended to capture one's attention, ultimately ensnaring the soul.

"Despite the seemingly irresistible allure of these popular entertainments," Philip continued, drawing Kelila's attention once more, "we must consciously *choose* to obey God's clear command to reject forbidden practices. As devout Samaritans, you are all familiar with the first five books of Scripture penned by God's faithful servant, Moses. In it, God said, '*the person who turns to mediums and familiar spirits, to prostitute himself with them, I will set My face against that person.*' My friends, we must seriously take this to heart. When we indulge in such things—whether practicing the craft ourselves or delighting in those who do—we have prostituted ourselves to our own hurt and disadvantage."

"It's true."

The crowd was aghast when the formerly possessed young man spoke for the very first time. Kelila, too, felt her own ears prick as Adorina leaned forward in her makeshift chair.

"I beg you, heed the words of this evangelist," the young man continued. "Once the darkness has overtaken you, it is often too late to turn back. Trust me, I know. Philip speaks the truth."

Placing an encouraging hand on the young man's shoulder, Philip smiled his understanding. "Thank you for your testimony. May I ask your name?"

"My name is Jothan."

"Brothers and sisters," Philip said, his eyes drifting over those gathered before him, "please heed the testimony of our new friend, Jothan. I repeat, there is no such thing as 'good magic,' for the devil is the source of all these deceptions. If he can woo us with seemingly innocent, 'harmless' magic, then we have allowed him a dangerous foothold."

Sensing that Philip's message was changing hearts and renewing minds, Kelila closed her eyes, thanking God for His wisdom and guidance.

"In closing," Philip smiled, his shining brown eyes conveying the great love he had for his listeners, "I'd like to remind you of the warning God gave us before ushering our fathers into the Promised Land. This is what He instructed Moses to tell the people: *'The nations which you will dispossess listened to soothsayers and diviners; but as for you, the Lord your God has not appointed such for you. The Lord your God will raise up for you a Prophet like me from your midst, from your brethren. Him you shall hear.'* Brothers and sisters, it is my deepest joy to announce the arrival of that promised Prophet—the Man Jesus Christ!"

Shouts of victory and applause rang out in the town square, lifting Kelila's spirits and filling her heart with thanksgiving. Turning to Adorina, she tweaked her shoulder, receiving a wan smile in return. Her people had not been swayed by Helena's untimely challenge. Their hunger for truth remained.

"As children of God," Philip closed, "we must choose to heed the voice of God in all things. Jesus Christ has shown us the Way, and now we must purposefully walk in it."

Resounding amens rippled through the square as new believers resolved to practice the evangelist's exhortations.

"Brothers and sisters, the prophet Isaiah warned us against following the dictates of our own hearts. Whereas the gospel of Satan grows increasingly deceptive, urging us to follow our hearts rather than the commandments of God by encouraging us to dabble in forbidden arts to achieve happiness and success, there *is* another Way, the only Way to life."

"Jesus is the Way!" several shouted triumphantly, drawing a warm smile from Philip.

"Amen," he agreed. "And as your relationship with Jesus flourishes and deepens, the dangerous practice of magic will become far less appealing. The alluring deceptions of this life will utterly pale in comparison with the truth and knowledge of God as revealed in His Son, Jesus Christ."

CHAPTER 27

Tabitha

Joppa

"Do you and Jonas attend the Sabbath services at the synagogue, Martha?"

Martha glanced up sharply as she drew a tray of steaming flatbread from the massive stone oven in the kitchen. "Sabbath services?" she repeated, her veiled eyes betraying questions. "Why do you ask?"

Easing Laurel onto the immaculate stone countertop, Tabitha sensed she had made Martha uneasy for some reason. "I plan to join Tirzah for the morning service," she replied, extremely excited to worship with her people in the local synagogue despite Tirzah's somewhat cynical warning.

"We attend," she responded simply. Setting aside the tray of flatbread, Martha's eyes flickered with hidden doubts.

"Oh, that's wonderful," Tabitha exclaimed, delightedly clasping her hands. "May Tirzah and I sit with you and Jonas tomorrow morning?"

Dropping her gaze, Martha appeared to inspect the steaming loaves of flatbread, though Tabitha knew she was mulling over something else. "You can sit with me," she responded, gingerly selecting a loaf for Laurel's breakfast. "But Jonas will be seated with the men."

The fact that the men and women—even husbands and wives—were expected to sit on opposite sides of the synagogue indicated that services were obviously structured in a very traditional, conservative manner.

"Laurel will be so happy to sit with you," Tabitha affirmed, hoping to ease Martha's obvious discomfort. "It will be good for her to be surrounded by familiar faces in a new environment. Thank you, Martha."

"Mm-hmm." Offering Laurel some flatbread with a motherly smile, Martha turned and reached for a crate of fresh produce. Selecting a large cucumber, she reached for a paring knife and began to carefully peel away the vibrant green skin, carefully avoiding Tabitha's gaze.

"Have I upset you, Martha?" Tabitha dared, sensing something was wrong. "You seem distracted."

Finally turning to face the younger maidservant, Martha planted a hand on her hip, her other hand still wielding the paring knife. "Has Tirzah told you anything about the synagogue?" she asked.

"A little," Tabitha admitted, recalling Tirzah's caution with a rueful smile. "Why?"

"It's just that…well, they don't take too kindly to newcomers at the synagogue," she muttered, shaking her head in concern. "You might consider bracing yourself for that."

"Aren't they pleased to meet new people seeking the Lord?"

"Well, they *should* be," Martha harrumphed, turning her attention back to the cucumber. "But they're a zealous bunch, quick to run out anyone contrary to their interpretation of the Law."

"I see," Tabitha nodded, a small smile playing about the corners of her lips. "I have encountered such people before."

Martha lifted a brow, clearly doubtful.

"Don't worry, Martha," Tabitha chuckled, lifting Laurel from the counter once she had finished her bread. "I'll be careful not to step on any toes."

"We'll see about that," Martha muttered under her breath, her knife fairly flying as she expertly chopped the peeled cucumber and reached for another. What would the religious leaders think of this beautiful, spirited young widow and her shy little daughter?

Smiling to herself, Tabitha balanced a contented Laurel on her hip, mentally calculating which task to tackle before Tirzah's soon-expected arrival. Their new arrangement seemed to be working beautifully, with Tirzah keeping an eye on Laurel as Tabitha performed her hardest tasks of the day. Even Laurel's raging tantrums had subsided, and Tabitha desperately prayed they were gone for good.

"I always enjoy this brief time with you in the kitchen when the rest of your staff is busy at the market or tending other chores," Tabitha said sincerely, pausing near the swinging exit door. "Thanks for your advice about tomorrow's service, Martha. I shall do my best to keep the peace."

Speaking of keeping the peace, she thought snidely as Joram barged through the door, red-faced and impatient.

"I thought I would find you in here," he sneered, his hazel-green eyes wandering accusingly toward his head cook. "A word," he addressed Tabitha curtly. "In my office."

"As you wish," Tabitha replied, unruffled. "Martha, may I leave Laurel with you? Tirzah should arrive any minute to relieve you —"

"Absolutely not," Joram spewed angrily, disgruntled. "Martha has *work* to do. You will not burden my staff by dumping your child—"

"Nonsense," Martha interrupted tersely, to the great surprise of both Tabitha and Joram. "This little one is an absolute *dear*, not a burden. She can help me wash the vegetables." Taking Laurel in eager arms, Martha cuddled the toddler against her ample bosom before placing her on the counter near the crate of fresh vegetables.

Clearly taken aback by Martha's newfound boldness, Joram appeared to be contemplating the severity of her fate when Tabitha cut in sweetly, "Shall we be going?" With a final glare in Martha's direction, Joram turned reluctantly on his heel, following his niece out the door.

***

"So," Tabitha asked lightly as Joram irritably settled into the large chair behind his broad desk, "what have I done now?"

Arching a silver brow, Joram's scowl deepened.

"Are you dissatisfied with my performance?" she

teased.

"You seem rather flippant for one whose employer might be dissatisfied with her work ethic," Joram growled, watching her with cold, hardened eyes.

Tabitha merely smiled, casually folding her hands behind her back as she awaited the lecture that was surely to come.

Further nettled by his niece's calm composure, Joram became even more combative. "You have been completing your chores quite early in the day."

"Yes," Tabitha agreed, a bit confused. "Tirzah and I designed a schedule to free my afternoons and evenings, allowing me time with my daughter. Haven't we already discussed this?"

"And now we shall discuss it again," Joram shot back, annoyed. "You forget, I am the employer—and you, the servant dependent upon my goodwill. As such, we shall discuss whatever I wish, as often as I wish."

"Then by all means, go on," Tabitha quipped, her pacific smile still in place. "I am listening."

Further chagrined, Joram plunged roughly ahead. "I have decided to increase your workload. I don't appreciate indolent servants dilly-dallying about with nothing to do. A few additional chores should decrease your overabundance of spare time."

Though Tabitha's entire being balked at Joram's suggestion, she refused to betray her raging feelings. To do so would only fuel his determination. "That won't be necessary," she replied in a businesslike manner. "My daughter requires the bulk of my 'spare time' in the afternoons and evenings, so you needn't rack your brain to come up with more chores to keep me busy. My time is, indeed, occupied and I certainly won't be dilly-dallying around if that's your concern."

"I am not asking your *opinion* on this matter!" Joram barked. "I did not hire you so you could lounge about my estate in ease and idleness! I hired you to *work*!"

"And work, I have," Tabitha responded, unfazed. "Not only have I completed every daily task we agreed upon, but I have also worked the hours consistent with a full shift. The only reason it may appear otherwise is because I begin my workday so much earlier than the others, and therefore complete my tasks sooner. Please feel free to consult Eli about this if you doubt my word."

"I shall feel free to consult whomever I wish," Joram snapped, distractedly shuffling through some parchment paperwork on his desk. Clearly, he had not expected a calm, composed rebuttal.

Tabitha simply smiled.

"Despite your tidy little argument, I will not have servants lazing about my estate. I value efficiency, and your empty afternoon hours are currently unproductive. If you wish to remain in my employ, then you shall either alter your schedule to correspond with the rest of my staff, or you shall assume more tasks to occupy your spare time," Joram said dogmatically, determined to nettle her. "The choice is yours."

"Thank you for explaining your concerns, my lord," Tabitha responded after a silent prayer for guidance. She was becoming increasingly grateful for the years she had served her brilliant mistress in Jerusalem, observing Mary's humble yet masterful dealings with shrewd, incorrigible businessmen like

Joram. "However, I must disagree with your assessment of my time," she continued, her tone conveying both humility and confidence. "The hours I spend with my daughter after work are not 'unproductive,' as you have suggested. On the contrary, this is the most productive and valuable part of my day, for God Himself ordained my sacred position as Laurel's mother."

Despite the fact that Joram resembled a seething volcano on the brink of eruption, Tabitha plunged ahead, careful to remain calm and unperturbed. "I will gladly serve the hours of a reasonable workday, accomplishing the chores we have agreed upon, as this allows me to properly raise my daughter and make a living, as well. But I cannot alter my schedule nor fill my evenings with additional responsibilities, as that would hinder my ability to parent my daughter as I believe I should. If this arrangement is displeasing to you, I can seek employment elsewhere, my lord. I do not wish to trouble you."

"This isn't a negotiation!" Joram nearly shouted, leaning forward on his desk. "What on earth gives you the idea—not to mention, the *arrogance*—to assume you have a say in this matter?"

"Would you prefer I seek employment elsewhere, then?" Tabitha asked gently, her demeanor maddeningly composed despite her hidden exasperation. Should Joram fire her, she realized her chances of reaching him with the gospel were next to nothing. Very likely, she would have to pack up her few belongings and return to Jerusalem in defeat.

"You seem to consider yourself a valuable asset of this estate," Joram said through clenched teeth. "Pray, tell, why you haven't yet realized you are but one insignificant maidservant, entirely expendable?"

"My value is not found in or of myself," Tabitha replied, surprised by the overwhelming calm she was experiencing despite Joram's raging hostility. Only the Holy Spirit of God could have administered such great peace. "I am a cherished child of God, my lord, a child of the King. Therein lies my true value, which is why the opinion of man fails to move me."

Unprepared for such a response, Joram leaned back in his chair, flustered and increasingly frustrated.

"If I may be so bold—"

"Are you asking my permission to proceed with boldness?" Joram interrupted her, peeved. "If so, this would be the first time!"

"My lord," Tabitha said imploringly, her kind eyes beseeching him to understand, "yours is the most luxurious estate in all of Joppa. Your existence is couched in success and luxury. You possess a fleet of servants to wait upon you hand and foot. And yet, you remain so very unhappy—"

"What's your point?" Joram growled, his eyes burning like angry coals.

"Despite your great success in life, perhaps you lack the most important thing of all."

"Oh?" Joram patronized, a heavy brow arching in sarcasm. "And what is that?"

"Love," Tabitha responded simply, cringing inwardly at the look he gave her. Even so, she refused to be dissuaded from her course. "You say I am expendable, but surely you know your staff submits to your demands out of fear or grudging obedience. But, my lord, I am here because I *care*. I care about *you.* We are family, and my heart's desire is to bridge the gap between us. Do you understand?"

"I am not a child," Joram fumed, rising from his desk in agitation. "Thus, you needn't speak to me as such. And might I remind you *again* that we are not family! I have no family, nor have I any need of one! I am perfectly fine on my own—"

Tabitha's brows drew together in concern when Joram, red-faced and breathless, swayed dangerously. "My lord?"

Dropping heavily into his chair, Joram covered his face, rubbing his forehead with wooden fingers.

"My lord?" Tabitha repeated, deeply concerned. "Are you all right?" she asked, coming around the desk to meet him.

"Leave me be!" Joram barked, jerking away when she touched his shoulder. "I don't need any help from you."

"Are you unwell?" Tabitha dared, refusing to be intimidated.

"I'm fine!"

Sensing that his health was fragile at best, Tabitha somehow refrained from prying any further. She knew it would only further pique Joram's ire. Besides, he wouldn't tell her anything, anyway. He was the most distrusting, suspicious, stubborn old man she had ever met!

"Go," Joram snarled, his forehead beaded with sweat. When Tabitha hesitated, he lifted his head, his eyes flashing fury. "I said, *go!*" he shouted, outraged.

"Shall I summon a physician?" Tabitha dared, pausing at the heavily curtained entryway.

"A worthless, good-for-nothing physician is the last thing I need!" Joram railed, his hard jaw clenching in rage. "And if you suggest such a stupid thing again, you can pack up your squalling little brat and hurry on back to wherever it is you came from."

Though her pride stung at Joram's scathing declaration, Tabitha saw nothing but pain and hopelessness reflected in his eyes. And, somehow, the Holy Spirit filled her heart with compassion rather than indignation. Recalling her uncle's tragic past and the senseless death of his wife and unborn child, Tabitha resolved to demonstrate the boundless, undeserved mercy of Christ, though it would have been far easier to lash out in anger.

What had Tirzah said about her uncle's despair over Lady Peninah? *Joram, desperate to save his wife and unborn child, spared no expense to find a cure. Even so, the physicians grew richer as Lady Peninah grew worse...*

"Forgive me, my lord," Tabitha said quietly, realizing far too late that she had unwittingly rubbed salt upon an open, festering wound. "Should you need any assistance, you know where to find me." With that, she slipped out the door, leaving Joram to contemplate the unsettling similarities between this kind-hearted, compassionate young woman, her deceased mother, and his beloved, departed wife.

CHAPTER 28

Rhoda

Jerusalem

Humming quietly as she went about her chores, Rhoda decided there was nothing quite like Preparation Day—the sixth day of the week—which was designated to make oneself and one's household ready for the sacred Sabbath. How she savored the satisfaction of completing a productive day's work each Friday, readying Mary's villa for Sabbath worship at sunset! How she cherished the sweet Sabbath fellowship with her God and her beloved brothers and sisters! How satisfying it was to know that her toil must come to a screeching halt upon the seventh day, freeing her to rest, worship, and commune with God and fellow believers. What sheer joy the Sabbath had become to her young heart!

Dusting the sprawling reception hall in which her lady received her guests, business associates, and fellow believers, Rhoda paused after polishing the smooth surface of a large, oval-shaped mirror positioned on a neatly paneled and frescoed wall. Glancing shyly at her own reflection, she wondered at her appearance. She was fast becoming a young lady, which both frightened and delighted her. Dark, gentle curls graced her shoulders, framing a peaceful face with a creamy complexion and soft brown eyes tinted with flecks of hazel and gray. Her lips matched the color of dusty rose petals staining her gracefully curved cheeks, and her smile reflected her compassionate, gentle nature. Delicately adjusting the sheer white head covering which matched her simple linen tunic, Rhoda blushed at the realization that, soon, she would reach marriageable age.

The thought was both exhilarating and petrifying. Though her girlish heart longed for love, she would likely be betrothed to a man she did not know or love.

Oh, John Mark, she thought sadly, thinking of the young man who had held her heart since childhood, *if only our circumstances were different!* She had adored Mary's laughing, teasing, good-natured son ever since her arrival at the Jerusalem villa, and though her heart yearned for him, she knew he would be foolish indeed to take an orphaned maid to be his wife. She desired far better for him, though it would be painful to watch him fall in love with someone else. Lowering her eyes in deep sorrow, Rhoda reminded herself—yet again—that she must undoubtedly brace herself for the inevitable.

Bam! Bam! The sound of massive double doors slamming open resounded through the marble hall, giving Rhoda a terrible fright. Nearly dropping her dust rag, she tore her gaze from the mirror, anxiously smoothing the folds of her pale tunic. Only one person in this house barreled through the heavy gilded doors in such an impetuous manner!

Heart picking up speed, she waited anxiously, nervously twisting the dust rag in trembling fingers.

A moment later, John Mark emerged from the frescoed vestibule across the room, an eager spring to his step, as always.

Heart pounding at the sight of him, Rhoda admired how well he carried himself with broad shoulders thrown back and handsome head held high. Though his mother insisted he dress in a modest, unadorned manner, he still bore himself with the confidence of a prince.

As John Mark made a hasty beeline for the marble stairway, Rhoda cocked her head in quiet observation, her spirit strangely unsettled. Something wasn't quite right, though she couldn't place what it was. Mounting the broad marble stairs, he remained completely oblivious to the quiet maidservant watching him from the other side of the room, his features betraying his elation…and a hint of misgivings, as well. A glittering gold chain dangled from his tightly closed fist, tickling Rhoda's interest and curiosity.

Taking the stairs two at a time, the handsome young man soon vanished from sight, the sweet smell of scented oil lingering in the air behind him.

Scented oil? Crinkling her nose in repugnance, Rhoda found it highly suspicious that John Mark had anointed himself with a sweet-smelling fragrance before leaving the house. He had never troubled himself with such things before…

Apprehension mounting steadily, Rhoda returned

to her dusting with a heavy heart. She couldn't help but suspect something was amiss. Grappling against swelling disappointment, she realized John Mark hadn't even noticed her presence.

***

Tabitha

Joppa

"Tirzah? Is my uncle...well, is he sick?"

"Sick in body or sick in the head?" Tirzah grinned, swinging a heavy cloth bag over one shoulder as she prepared to take her leave.

"I was referring to his health." Smiling wanly, Tabitha rose from her place beside Laurel's sleeping pallet, where her daughter played contentedly with Tirzah's old doll. "He experienced something rather like a fainting episode while berating me in his office this morning. He grew very weak and fell back into his chair. It was very sudden, entirely unexpected."

"Serves him right," Tirzah huffed, pausing in the doorway, "since he treats his own family like dirt."

"What do you mean?"

"*This*, for example," Tirzah declared with an emphatic sweep of her arm, encompassing the small, sparsely furnished, windowless chamber Joram had assigned to Tabitha and Laurel. "In exchange for your backbreaking labor, *this* is the room he provides you! You work for room and board, Tabitha. For the quality of work you perform, you should be residing in one of his upper floor suites with a panoramic view of the Great Sea!"

"I must admit, that sounds nice," Tabitha confessed with a teasing smile. "But this room has sufficed. We have food, clothing, shelter, and a wonderful new friend," she added, affectionately squeezing Tirzah's arm. "The Lord has faithfully met each of our needs."

"No thanks to your Uncle Joram," Tirzah grumped, unappeased.

"Remember, we are not supposed to call him that," Tabitha chastised playfully, her eyes twinkling with fun. "Not for any reason. To us, it is strictly, 'my lord' or 'master.'"

"He isn't *my* lord or master," Tirzah huffed. "In fact, he isn't my *anything*—except an intolerable pain in my side."

"He *is* your neighbor," Tabitha pointed out.

"Not by choice," Tirzah shot back, her sparkling brown eyes betraying mirth despite the sobriety of her tone. "As for his health, he does appear rather gaunt. Also, a bit pale. I haven't thought much about it. He is aging, after all."

"That's true," Tabitha agreed. "But the fainting spell did trouble me."

"Why?" Tirzah asked bluntly. "If the man drops like a rock and goes in the way of our fathers, your problems would be solved!"

"How so?" Tabitha asked, horrified.

"Well, he wouldn't be here to boss you around and watch your every move with his infamous condescension. And if he died, you would inherit this beautiful estate, would you not?"

"Oh, no," Tabitha assured her, shocked at Tirzah's suggestion. "Joram would never even consider leaving his wealth to me. First, he scarcely knows me.

Second, he doesn't trust me. And last, he detests the very air I breathe!"

"Ah," Tirzah agreed with a shake of her head. "I suppose you're right. It's a pity, though."

"Perhaps not," Tabitha responded thoughtfully. "If Joram thought the only reason I came to Joppa was to wait around for him to die so I could inherit his wealth, well, my testimony would mean nothing to him. Since I have nothing to gain, he knows I truly care."

"But *why?*" Tirzah asked honestly, propped against the sturdy doorframe. "Why *do* you care? Joram is an incorrigible old man. He had the nerve to disinherit your mother, and now he treats you— her daughter, his niece—like rubbish. It seems to me you would be far better off without him."

"Perhaps," Tabitha admitted, "but what of *him*, Tirzah? He has no faith, no family, no friends. Should he depart from this life, would he be ready to meet his Maker?"

"That, I'd like to see!"

"I believe that Jesus is the only way to Heaven, Tirzah," Tabitha honestly explained. "And I believe that God has led me here to reach my uncle with that very truth."

"The religious leaders around here would consider that statement about your Rabbi blatant blasphemy," Tirzah observed without condemnation. "A mere man cannot claim to be the bridge to Heaven."

"No," Tabitha agreed, "a mere man cannot. But Jesus Christ, the Son of God, can."

"I admire your staunch convictions," Tirzah told her. "I really do, although I'm not quite sure what to think of them. Even so, I am concerned for you,

Tabitha. You have placed yourself and your daughter at the mercy of a cruel, selfish old man. Though your intentions to 'save' him are noble, I'm not sure this is a practical aspiration."

"Perhaps not," Tabitha confessed. "But God can do extraordinary things. Besides, Joram has shown some signs of softening."

"Oh?" Tirzah asked a bit snidely. "Such as?"

"Such as allowing you to help me with Laurel for several hours each day. We never thought he would agree to that," Tabitha reminded her.

"Nonsense," Tirzah shot back, chuckling. "Joram is shrewd - he knows your productivity will be tripled without having to chase after a toddler all day. That is the only reason he consented!"

Tabitha only smiled.

"As unlikely as it may seem," Tirzah ventured, her brown eyes serious, "I think you should consider the possibility that Joram may live another twenty or thirty years, then die without faith. If that happens, is it worth all the bitter sacrifices you are having to make right now?"

"Absolutely," Tabitha responded without hesitation. "God has called me here. I have no doubt about that. And obedience to God is always worth the sacrifice."

"Forgive me for speaking so freely," Tirzah said frankly. "If I wasn't your friend, I would hold my tongue. But I worry for you. I don't wish for you to look back later, deeply regretting the fact that you wasted the best years of your life on a worthless, self-centered oaf like *I* d—" Halting abruptly, Tirzah looked away.

"Like you did?" Tabitha finished for her, very

gently.

"Yes," Tirzah sighed loudly, annoyed she had spoken so carelessly. "I don't wish to discuss it. You understand."

"Of course, I do," Tabitha assured her. "And we shan't discuss it if that's what you wish."

Visibly relieved, Tirzah nodded.

"Thank you for caring so much, Tirzah," Tabitha said wholeheartedly. "I appreciate your willingness to speak frankly with me and I know you are just trying to protect me. But the Lord can do that far better than you or I, can He not?"

"You know I can't argue with that," Tirzah said ruefully.

"So please don't worry about me," Tabitha smiled encouragingly. "Just see how God has blessed me! Why should I be dismayed? I have a beautiful earthly home to return to in Jerusalem should the need arise, and a home in Heaven incomparable to even the most stunning or luxurious estate on earth! What more could I possibly ask for?"

"You say the strangest things," Tirzah grinned, shaking her head in amazement. "On that fanciful note, I suppose I must be going to prepare for Sabbath."

"Thank you for your help today, Tirzah," Tabitha told her with great feeling. "You truly are a Godsend. Shall I see you in the morning for Sabbath service?"

"You shall, indeed," Tirzah responded wryly, slipping out the door. "Prepare yourself for a lively morning, my friend. I pledge to stand by you, whatever happens."

Tossing a wink over her shoulder, Tirzah cheerfully took her leave.

CHAPTER 29

Tabitha

Joppa

After Tirzah's departure, Tabitha knelt beside her daughter, smiling warmly. "All right, my darling. It's time to put your little doll back in her box. Our friend, Tirzah, has gone home."

Laurel glanced up at her mother with innocent brown eyes. After a cursory inspection of Tabitha's face, she went back to playing with her doll.

Perhaps she did not understand me, Tabitha thought, dismayed. She was still uncertain about Laurel's level of comprehension. Recently, Laurel had begun using short, single-syllable words sparingly, responding to simple sentences, and answering questions with a brief *yes, no,* or nod of her tiny head. But how much did the toddler truly comprehend?

Oh, Lord, Tabitha prayed for the umpteenth time. *I know so little about children, and yet You have called me to motherhood! Please help me.* If only Mary was nearby! What a wealth of godly instruction she could provide! Tabitha ached for the kind, intelligent widow's Scriptural wisdom and practical advice, especially concerning the care and training of young Laurel. More than anything, Tabitha desired to instill in Laurel a deep, unshakable love for God. Out of such love sprang obedience, sacrifice, and surrender. Had Stephanos lived, he would have partnered with her in the daunting endeavor of training their child in the way she should go.

Oh, Stephanos, how I miss you! How my heart aches to share these moments with you. Closing her eyes, Tabitha drew a steadying breath. She hadn't time to contemplate the tragic past, nor ponder heart-wrenching what-ifs. There were still chores to be done, not to mention the preparation of her mind and heart to usher in the Sabbath rest at sunset.

"Laurel," Tabitha said gently, "please give the doll to Mama. It's time to finish our chores."

Glancing suspiciously at Tabitha's outstretched hand, Laurel shifted her little body in defiance, clutching the doll close to her heart.

"Laurel," Tabitha repeated, sensing her daughter's rebellion, "give the doll to Mama."

Laurel responded with a withering look of sheer defiance.

"Oh, how very sad, Laurel," Tabitha said quietly, wondering how she should respond to her daughter's blatant rebellion. "You must obey Mama." Reaching for the doll, Tabitha's heart leaped as Laurel sent up a piercing shriek that could have shattered glass.

"Laurel!" Tabitha exclaimed, shocked and dismayed. "Hush, child."

Snatching the doll from Tabitha, Laurel's little legs pounded the floor as she rushed for the corner, planting her bottom on the cool flagstones and presenting a rigid back to her mother as she clutched the doll to her heart.

Stunned to her core, Tabitha went after her. "Laurel, your behavior is unacceptable." Taking the doll, she cringed as Laurel released another ear-splitting scream. "Laurel, *no*. You mustn't scream like that."

Singularly unimpressed by her mother's instruction, Laurel only raised her voice, stamping the ground with angry little feet as she threw a rather impressive tantrum.

O*h, Lord, what do I do?* Briefly, Tabitha was tempted to give the doll back just to silence the unbearable screaming. But she knew to do so would only encourage and condone such behavior. Laurel must learn obedience, even at this early age.

S*tay calm,* Tabitha reminded herself, crossing the room and placing the doll in the wooden crate of handmade toys. Hoisting the box up on her hip, Tabitha turned to face the screaming child. The outraged toddler continued to shriek like a wounded banshee, kicking and pounding at the floor. *Oh dear,* Tabitha thought, completely flustered. *I need answers, Lord, and preferably sooner rather than later!*

A*t* this rate, Laurel would soon alert the entire household to her willful tantrum! What would Joram have to say about this unpleasant episode?

Suddenly, Tabitha recalled something she'd once heard her dear friend, Candace, say while training her headstrong little Rufus. *I have discovered that screaming temper tantrums have a tendency to cease once an angry child has lost his audience and realizes his antics have failed to impress them...*

Oh, Lord, thank you! Tabitha thought in relief. *Please, let this work!*

Looking evenly at her red-faced, raging child, Tabitha said calmly, "Mama has work to do, Laurel. When I come back, I hope you have a happy face." Leaving the room, Tabitha paused a few feet down the corridor, listening intently. Devoid of her captive audience, Laurel's screaming instantly ceased. Tabitha could almost sense her daughter looking around the room in confusion, wondering what had just happened. With a knowing little smile, Tabitha decided to wait several minutes before returning to her. Hopefully, in a much calmer state, Laurel would prove more receptive to her mother's instruction.

***

As Tabitha completed the remainder of her chores, she prayed that Laurel had comprehended the quiet talk they had shared shortly after the girl's willful tantrum. In simple, basic terms, Tabitha had explained the importance of obeying God's commandments. And the fifth commandment required children to obey their parents. Tabitha had tried to explain the glory of this command, for it was the first commandment with a promise: *Honor your father and your mother, that your days may be long upon the land which the Lord your God is giving you.* Obedience was not required to impede upon one's freedom or make life miserable; instead, obedience established one's safety, security, and well-being, ultimately leading to happiness and fulfillment.

Though it was doubtful Laurel absorbed everything she had said, Tabitha could only pray the Scriptures would sink deep within the girl's heart and mind, eventually taking root and bearing fruit as the child grew in age and maturity.

The remainder of the afternoon passed smoothly, and Tabitha was grateful to complete her chores with plenty of time to usher in the Sabbath rest. As the sun, a fiery ball of burnished bronze, appeared to slip below the golden-tinged waters of the majestic Great Sea, Tabitha settled onto her straw mattress and drew her daughter onto her lap. Though she yearned to take Laurel upon one of the mansion's graceful balconies overlooking the breathtaking sunset reflected upon the undulating waters of the Mediterranean, she didn't wish to stir up trouble with Joram, who already watched her every move with burning suspicion. Instead, she thanked the Lord for providing a chamber suitable to their needs, despite the absence of comfortable furniture, an inspiring view, or a cozy ambiance. There, in the flickering lamplight, Tabitha quietly prayed the customary Sabbath blessings as her daughter nestled close. Though she had no Sabbath candles to light, she sensed the light of the Holy Spirit enshrouding her small chamber, filling her heart with the peace of God's comforting presence.

Eager to begin a new Sabbath custom with young Laurel, Tabitha had already decided which ancient story to share with her. After all, there was no better place to start than the beginning! Tonight, she would tell the glorious story of Creation, when the blessed Sabbath Day was instituted by God Himself, His gracious gift to mankind.

"*In the beginning God created the heavens and the earth.*" Animatedly, Tabitha launched into the beautiful Creation story, knowing the words by heart. "*The earth was without form, and void; and darkness was on the face of the deep. And the Spirit of God was hovering over the face of the waters. Then God said, 'Let there be light'; and there was light.*" Pausing briefly, Tabitha was completely unprepared for the tidal wave of loneliness sweeping over her soul. Suddenly, in the dim, lonely light of flickering oil lamps, she was reminded of many sweet Sabbaths past, nestled in the safety of her husband's strong arms. How often had they met with Mary, Candace, Simon, Philip, Kelila, and a slew of dedicated believers to celebrate the sacred occasion? How she ached for their sweet friendship and cheerful camaraderie now! Alone in this dank stone chamber, far removed from fellow believers and the light they bore for Christ, Tabitha keenly felt their absence.

Taking a deep, steadying breath, Tabitha refused the swelling, aching loneliness filling her soul. *You are not alone,* she staunchly reminded herself. *The Lord is always with you, and He has blessed you with a precious child and new friends, as well.*

Dismissing fragile feelings, Tabitha made a conscious decision to stand upon the truth of God's Word. She would not allow the enemy to steal her peace of heart and mind. To do so would only allow him to rob her of this precious opportunity to teach Laurel about the joys of Sabbath, the blessed day of rest and communion with the Lover of her soul.

CHAPTER 30

Tabitha

Joppa

Pausing before an imposing set of elaborate, gilded doors on the upper floor of Joram's seaside mansion, Tabitha bore a heavy tray boasting an impressive breakfast spread.

O*h, Lord,* she prayed, her heart thudding heavily against her ribcage, *I hope I won't regret this!*

Taking a deep breath, Tabitha turned, skillfully using her back to push open the large double doors. After a brief protest, the heavy doors bowed inward, granting her entrance. Allowing herself a brief, cursory sweep of the enormous bedchamber, Tabitha observed a mammoth four-poster bed on the farthest wall, appearing like a slumbering beast in repose and boasting the finest of Egyptian linens. Plush, richly upholstered furniture was meticulously arranged upon thick Persian rugs sporting mesmerizing middle eastern patterns. Tall bronze lamps burned brightly despite the wide-open double doors of an elegant balcony at the far end of the chamber, now flooding the entire room with bright morning light. With its expensive hanging tapestries, suspended candelabras, gilded furnishings, and luxe, imported finery, the imperious chamber was truly fit for a king.

Allowing herself a moment to compose herself, Tabitha crossed the vast chamber with confidence, emerging at the wide double doors leading onto the balcony. The view that met her gaze was truly exquisite, stealing her breath away. Beyond the towering city walls loomed the dazzling waters of the Mediterranean, washed in golden sunlight and an otherworldly light. Snowy white gulls released mournful dirges as they swooped above the gently lapping waters, showcased against a deep blue sky and fluffy, billowing clouds. The day was truly glorious, as if nature itself praised its Creator by demonstrating the greatest of pomp and splendor.

"*Shabbat Shalom*, my lord," Tabitha smiled, expertly placing the breakfast tray upon the intricate table where her uncle sat on the balcony in angry, brooding silence. "Happy Sabbath!" At the sound of her cheerful voice, Joram jerked a withering glare over his shoulder, his silver brows knitting together in dismay.

"What are you doing here?" he demanded, outraged. "You don't belong up here!"

"It's a pleasure to see you, too," she grinned, snatching a pitcher from the breakfast tray and easily filling the goblet he clenched in white-knuckled fingers. "I am delighted to serve you this morning, my lord."

"Where is Gad?"

"Do not punish him, my lord," Tabitha said in a motherly tone, already protective of the gangly teenager assigned the dreaded task of presenting Joram's meals each day. "After quite a bit of wheedling, I convinced him and Martha to allow me the privilege of serving your meal. Gad assured me you were always decent and fully clothed for breakfast, so I wasn't concerned about that."

"You have no right to rearrange the tasks I assign my staff!" Joram growled, the veins in his neck bulging in both anger and embarrassment. "Who do you think you are?"

"Your maidservant, of course," she responded lightly. "Is this not what maidservants do? Serve their masters with cheerful diligence?"

Grudgingly, Joram watched as she arranged the breakfast items on the table before him, though he would never admit that her skill and efficiency put poor Gad to shame. "You don't wish to *serve* me," he sneered, feeling lightheaded with frustration. "You only wish to snoop about my mansion, poking around and sticking your nose where it doesn't belong."

"Frankly," Tabitha responded, folding her hands humbly before her, "I desired to wish you a happy Sabbath, and to invite you to join me in worship at the synagogue this morning."

"Ha!" Joram snorted contemptuously, his volume competing with that of the protesting gulls nearby.

"You might enjoy it," Tabitha grinned, subtly gauging his reaction. "Will you at least consider it?"

"Not in a million years."

"But why not?"

"I haven't set foot in that dreaded place since—" Joram's voice cut off sharply, and Tabitha realized she had unwittingly broached a sore subject—yet again.

"My lord," she said kindly, daring to touch his bony shoulder, "I would be incredibly honored should you choose to join me in worship."

"Well, you won't be receiving any such honors from me," Joram said with a brittle smile, jerking his shoulder away. "You can beg on your knees till kingdom come, and I assure you, it won't make a bit of difference nor change my mind."

"And that's exactly what concerns me," Tabitha readily responded, surprising him. "Eventually, God's Kingdom *will* come, my lord, descending from Heaven as a bride beautifully adorned for her husband. But when that day comes, will you be ready for it?"

"What right have *you* to question *me?*" Joram demanded haughtily, slamming a closed fist upon the table so hard it rattled the contents of his tray. "Do *you*—a pathetic, widowed serving girl with hardly a penny to her name and entirely at the mercy of a cold, cruel world—consider yourself above *me?* God has lavished His favor upon me in the form of wealth and success. Who are you to argue with such proofs?"

"God makes His sun rise on the evil and on the good, and sends rain on the just and the unjust," Tabitha reminded him gently.

"And I suppose you consider me to be an evil, unjust man?"

"Wealth isn't always a sign of God's favor, my lord," Tabitha responded carefully, praying silently as she spoke. "For some, it can prove to be a terrible stumbling block."

"You speak boldly for one in your precarious position," Joram hissed, deeply offended.

"I speak as one who cares for you, my lord," Tabitha said earnestly, her hazel-green eyes boring into her uncle's matching ones. "Which is why I must ask—do you still serve the God of your fathers?"

There was a long, tension-thick pause, punctuated only by the shrill cry of the swooping gulls. As the moments dragged by, Tabitha wondered if her uncle had simply refused to dignify her question with an answer. "My lord?"

Joram's eyes hardened as he met Tabitha's relentless gaze. "I pay Him homage in my own way," he said coldly, his fingers tightening around the stem of his goblet. "Not that it is any of your business."

"I see," Tabitha replied, her quiet tone laced with the sadness reflected in her soft eyes.

"Now go, and leave me be," Joram growled, avoiding her gaze in an uncharacteristic display of unease. "I wish to enjoy my meal in peace."

"As you wish, my lord," Tabitha replied obediently, surprisingly encouraged by the barely discernible traces of remorse Joram had so carefully concealed. Perhaps, later, he would consider their discussion. Perhaps—just perhaps—there was still hope for him! With a soft, hidden smile, Tabitha turned to leave.

"Enjoy the morning service at the synagogue, worshiping with like-minded hypocrites such as yourself," Joram tossed patronizingly over his shoulder, his tone dripping with amused sarcasm.

Pausing on the balcony's elegant threshold, Tabitha squared narrow shoulders and drew a calming breath. Refusing to be provoked by Joram's caustic barbs, she offered an unperturbed, seraphic smile before fully turning on her heel and leaving him in peace.

CHAPTER 31

Kelila

Sychar

It was a joyous procession that traveled the meandering, olive tree-shaded path leading to a distant, sparkling spring beyond the tiny village of Sychar. Gathering along the water's edge with Adorina at her elbow, Kelila watched proudly as her husband waded into the waist-deep spring, excited to baptize new converts.

Unlike the stringent Jews Kelila had encountered in Jerusalem, the Samaritans hadn't seemed the least bit bothered by the lengthy walk required to reach the scenic spring in which the baptisms would be conducted. In Jerusalem, the Pharisees zealously monitored their footsteps, unwilling to exceed the designated number of steps one was permitted to take on the Sabbath Day. But here, the Samaritans seemed less aware of the rigid traditions and lengthy additions Jewish sages had slowly but surely attached to the inspired laws of God.

Smiling, Kelila absorbed her verdant surroundings, delighting in the birdsong, the cool morning breeze, and the dazzling beauty of God's creation. As another gentle breeze whispered against her flushed cheek and tugged at her modest head covering, she couldn't help but feel as if she was observing the day of rest in Heaven's flower-strewn fields! What a joy to be surrounded by these sincere brothers and sisters, both new and old to the faith!

Glancing both ways, Kelila watched as throngs of believers drew along the riverbank, their faces shining with joy and anticipation. Cautiously, she dipped one sandaled toe in the cool, crystal waters lapping against the grassy bank. It felt utterly delightful! What a joy to gather here with these Samaritan worshipers, and how better to honor the sanctity of the Sabbath Day than to witness the commitment of dozens of new converts as they were baptized, symbolizing the death and burial of the old man, and the resurrection life one experienced through the redemptive power of Christ and the gift of the Holy Spirit!

After Philip led the large group in prayer, the gathering sang a hymn of worship, their joyous voices ringing out across the flowery meadow and carrying to the distant hills. Kelila was especially enthralled by Adorina's smoky alto voice, her husky tone both beautiful and unique. She realized her own clear, high soprano complimented Adorina's low alto in the most delightful way.

As the baptisms commenced, Kelila watched as Ephraim waded into the shallow water, drawing alongside Philip. She was impressed with Ephraim's servant heart and eagerness to assist Philip however possible without seeking prestige or recognition for himself.

"Your husband is a born leader," Kelila told Adorina in a low voice. "His help has proven invaluable to Philip."

"It's what made me fall in love with him," Adorina admitted quietly, her dark eyes serious. "Despite my hesitation about a sixth marriage when he proposed, I couldn't help but notice his quiet strength and able leadership. It's what I admire most about him."

Turning their attention toward the peaceful spring, the women watched as dozens of Samaritans were baptized, their faces shining with joy and sparkling with tears as they were lifted from the glittering waters. Kelila blinked back tears when the former demoniac waded into the spring, his mother and uncle close behind him. With a knowing smile, Philip placed one hand on Jothan's shoulder, raising his other hand heavenward as they prayed together. Turning to the young man, Philip declared, "Jothan, I baptize you in the name of the Father and of the Son and of the Holy Spirit." There was a loud splash as Jothan was dipped below the water's shimmering surface. When he came back up, he pumped his fists heavenward with a triumphant shout of victory and celebration.

Kelila and Adorina joined the enthusiastic applause as the crowd rejoiced over Jothan's repentance and restoration, many among them laughing heartily, touched by the young man's jubilation.

Amid the shouts, laughter, and applause of the joy-filled celebration, Kelila felt a strange, unwelcome shiver slither up and down her spine. Drawing her cloak closer about her slender frame, she turned her head, her dark eyes warily scanning her surroundings.

There, just beneath the tree line on a distant ridge, a darkened silhouette appeared—the powerful, confident form of a man, his mysterious and elaborate robes fluttering in the quiet morning breeze.

Kelila's heart skipped a beat, swelling with mounting apprehension. For despite the gaping distance between them, she instinctively knew who was lurking in the shadows of swaying branches, his stony gaze fixed upon the evangelist in the peaceful water.

Even in this quiet meadow, they had failed to escape the sorcerer's watchful, smoldering gaze.

***

Tabitha

Joppa

The local synagogue was a cold, drab affair constructed of crude gray stone and sturdy, unadorned pillars. Tabitha was fascinated by the ancient simplicity of the large structure, which had likely remained unchanged through many centuries of use. Joppa was an age-old city, and she imagined dozens of generations had met in this synagogue within the city borders throughout the fading centuries.

"Welcome to our humble house of worship," Tirzah quipped as they passed beneath one of the three rectangular stone entrances gracing the front of the square-shaped building, following closely on the heels of Martha and Jonas, both wearing their finest apparel. "It's not fancy, but it has weathered the test of time."

"I can see that," Tabitha replied with interest, balancing a very subdued Laurel on her hip. Shyly, the child buried her face on her mother's shoulder, anxious about their austere new surroundings. "Is this the only synagogue in the city?"

"This is Joppa's original gathering place," Tirzah informed her, following the flow of somber-looking women as they selected seats in their designated area. Mechanically, the men streamed in the opposite direction, seating themselves on the layers of cold stone benches lining bare walls. "In recent centuries, the city has spilled far beyond its boundary walls; thus, the need for more houses of worship resulted in the construction of many more synagogues. Unlike this one, some of them are rather elaborate."

Inconspicuously lowering herself onto a stone bench between Tirzah and Martha, Tabitha nodded her understanding. Sensing the unspoken demand for silence and the tension crackling heavily in the dank atmosphere, she refrained from voicing any further questions.

"May I hold the child?" Martha whispered, her eyes betraying a hint of apprehension.

"Of course," Tabitha smiled, hoping to set the middle-aged woman at ease. "Laurel," she whispered gently, "would you like to sit with Auntie Martha?"

Laurel responded by holding chubby arms out to the woman, who promptly gathered the toddler to her bosom. Comforted by the doting woman's embrace, Laurel nestled quietly in her lap, content.

Grateful her daughter seemed to be adjusting to

the unfamiliar environment, Tabitha allowed herself a curious review of the staid chamber. It was constructed in the same fashion as most Jewish synagogues, with a wide, rectangular floor plan flanked by layers of stone benches on all four sides. Unembellished oil lamps flickered faintly from their mounts on vertical gray walls. Thick stone pillars upheld heavy wooden beams, which in turn supported a towering sunroof cut into the high ceiling, providing both silver sunlight and additional ventilation for the otherwise stuffy chamber. A lone wooden stand placed upon a square block of hewn stone occupied the wide-open space in the center, where the scrolls of Torah could be placed for appointed elders to address the gathering.

Fascinated, Tabitha's gaze traveled across the room, where rows of solemn-looking Jewish men sat across from the women's quarter, awaiting the service's commencement. She quickly spotted Jonas among them, twiddling his thumbs like an anxious schoolboy. Fleetingly, she wished she was free to invite him to sit with them! He looked rather out of place and alone amidst the somber crowd until a very dignified-looking Eli appeared, taking the seat beside him. Holding back a smile, Tabitha supposed she shouldn't be surprised to see Joram's stuffy overseer in such a place.

Flanking both the entrance and the favored rows of seating nearest the speaker's stand were the religious leaders of the synagogue, all of them donning severe garments and even more severe expressions. Their dark eyes flickered over the sea of men and women gathered in the synagogue as they critically inspected new arrivals. Tabitha noted with amusement that her presence was acknowledged by several of them with unveiled suspicion. Not one of them attempted to greet her or even offer a welcoming smile.

After what felt like an eternity of silent intensity, a dark-robed Pharisee adjusted his prayer shawl and, with the practiced, swaying gait of a religious man, took his place behind the wooden stand. Tabitha watched in fascination as a simply dressed, white-capped scribe presented the designated scroll to the surprisingly young Pharisee. Both men were exceedingly careful not to touch to parchment scroll itself, making skillful use of the large bronze handlebars. Receiving the scroll with a practiced air of reverence, the Pharisee carefully fitted its bronze handles into carved notches on the stand. Reaching for a tapered ornamental rod of silver, he placed its pointed edge upon the upper right-hand corner of the scroll, preparing himself for the reading.

Crinkling her nose in revulsion, Tabitha's senses were instantly assaulted by a pervasive stench so foul she was sickened. The repugnant smell wafted throughout the entire synagogue, washing over horrified congregants like a foul tidal wave. As the gatherers exchanged questioning glances, the Pharisee behind the stand stiffened in outrage, his taut features contracting in fury as his fiery gaze swept over the congregation.

"Not again," Tabitha heard Tirzah groan beside her, shaking her head in both frustration and empathy. Swiftly, Tabitha spotted the unexpected offender near one of the bleak stone entrances. Intrigued, her gaze followed the large, broad-shouldered form of a deeply tanned, weathered older man attempting to slip amidst the congregants, unnoticed. Unfortunately, the repugnant odor clinging about his person and his large, muscular frame impeded his ability to remain secretively discreet.

As the powerful stranger's presence became increasingly obvious, the congregants drew back in panic and revulsion. A frightened hush fell over the entire gathering as each held their collective breath, awaiting the dreaded pronouncement from the religious leaders.

"You!" the Pharisee shouted, pointing his silver rod in accusation at the large, powerfully built older man. "You, there!"

The unwelcome stranger lifted cold, clear eyes to the Pharisee, his leathery, bearded features truly fearsome to behold. Fleetingly, Tabitha wondered if the Pharisee was half-mad to address the big, smelly man with blazing eyes and a fierce persona.

"You are *unclean*, a constant burr in our sides and a stench in God's nostrils!" the Pharisee shouted, his unintentional irony drawing chuckles of mirth from several nearby congregants. "Get out! You are not welcome here!"

"I only wish to sit quietly and observe—"

"Get out!" the Pharisee demanded, his stark white teeth bared beneath a dark, neatly styled mustache and matching beard. "You have desecrated this house of worship!"

"In accordance with the Law of Moses, you are deemed unfit to join us in this sacred space," and older religious leader dressed in far more opulent, colorful clothing drew alongside the agitated Pharisee behind the stand, his pretentious bearing indicating he was accustomed to wielding great authority.

"That's the ruler of the synagogue," Tirzah whispered, leaning toward Tabitha as she nodded her understanding.

Lifting large hands in surprising acquiescence, the older man turned and vanished through the nearest exit without argument, though his eyes burned in anger and protest.

Glancing back and forth between the livid young Pharisee, the flustered religious leaders, and the gaping congregation, Tabitha's heart went out to the poor man denied the right to worship with his people. Why was he ostracized in such a shameful manner? And why the rancid odor lingering about his person, and such outrage on the part of the religious leaders?

"Did anyone touch that man?" the Pharisee demanded tersely, jolting Tabitha from her silent questions. His dark eyes roved about the tense congregation in challenge. "I repeat, did he brush against any of you, or did his shadow fall upon anyone as he entered?"

Reluctantly, several congregants nearest the entrance raised their hands, their shoulders slumping in defeat.

"Then you are ceremonially unclean," the Pharisee pronounced coldly, his eyes narrowing in contempt. "Go. You must cleanse yourselves to become ritually pure again." When several hesitated, his cold eyes narrowed in dangerous challenge. "Go!"

Deeply saddened, Tabitha watched as several men rose to leave, glumly departing from the morning service. She could scarcely comprehend the hardness of these leaders' hearts, their utter lack of empathy or compassion. How did they expect to invoke necessary changes if they denied sinners access to the transforming Word of God?

Something is going to have to change around here, she decided, crossing her arms in indignation. *And soon!*

CHAPTER 32

Mary

Jerusalem

Spearheaded by the indomitable Saul of Tarsus, violence against the Jerusalem church continued to increase, rendering weekly attendance at local synagogues virtually impossible for followers of the Way. Though believers longed to reach their Jewish neighbors with the blessed gospel truth, they wisely recognized the synagogues in Jerusalem were no longer a safe outlet by which to share their faith. At least, not for the time being.

Seated with perfect posture beside her teenage son on a simple wooden bench in the Upper Room, Mary listened reverently as James, the Lord's brother, delivered an impassioned Sabbath sermon about the importance of rejoicing through trials, recognizing that the testing of one's faith produces patience. Folding elegant hands in her lap, Mary nodded her regal head in wholehearted agreement as James expounded upon the truths he had learned from Jesus, having been raised in the same household as his beloved Savior. Mary could scarcely fathom the fact that James had once lived in rebellion against Christ, refusing to accept His Messiahship—until Jesus rose from the dead! Now, James—a humble, practical craftsman—was swiftly rising to a prominent leadership position in the Jerusalem church. His staunch yet quiet faith emboldened those who felt called to remain in the holy city despite the ever-present threat of danger and persecution.

Stealing a glance toward John Mark, Mary noticed he seemed rather unsettled—strangely detached from James' wise sermon. Though he sat quietly beside her on the bench, his lean body remained tense, his posture restless. He was clearly distracted, but why?

Slender brows drawing together in concern, Mary wondered at his strange behavior. *I had best keep a close eye on him,* she resolved, strangely disquieted. *At his tender age, all manner of trappings and temptations harbor the potential to snatch up the seeds of truth sown by the Holy Spirit.*

She certainly had no intention of allowing that to happen.

***

Tabitha

Joppa

After recited blessings and a brief Scripture reading, the solemn congregation endured a laborious and stringent—not to mention, highly opinionated—exposition upon the Levitical Law. Once the Pharisee presiding over the meeting pronounced a rather lifeless benediction, relieved service-goers streamed out the three separate stone openings of the synagogue, filing back to their homes—some with an air of boredom, others, apathetic, and still others, with shoulders slumped in defeat.

Lifting her cool face to the morning sunshine, Tabitha was tempted to tear off her head covering to bask in the warm, delightful sunlight. Wouldn't it be fun to watch the religious leaders' frantic hysteria should she do such a thing? Hiding a smile, Tabitha reminded herself she was a follower of Jesus, called to *peace*. She would not willfully or intentionally cause offense by sowing seeds of strife. No, she was called to set an example for others—relentless obedience to Christ, fueled by the love of God and the power of the Holy Spirit. In a way, she pitied these cheerless religious leaders so determined to gain victory by futile works of the flesh. They were trapped in a vicious cycle of fruitless works, observing the mandates of fallible men, even at the expense of God's Word. No wonder they were so unhappy!

Smiling, Tabitha watched as Martha balanced little Laurel on her hip, with Jonas leaning in to tap the toddler's nose. Lingering a short distance from the entrance of the synagogue, Martha appeared to be proudly introducing the pretty child to another middle-aged couple, who were clearly delighted by the little one.

"It's a downright shame, isn't it?" Tirzah mused, drawing alongside Tabitha with sadness in her eyes.

"What is?" Tabitha asked, confused.

"That Martha and Jonas weren't blessed with children of their own."

"Oh," Tabitha sighed, saddened for the dear couple she already loved. "Indeed."

"Your little one has undoubtedly brightened their days."

"Tirzah," Tabitha said slowly, turning to meet her gaze as congregants slipped eagerly past them on the stone way, "who was that man? The one the religious leaders pronounced unclean."

"Ah," Tirzah responded knowingly. "That's Simon. He is a tanner by trade—thus, the awful stench that gives him away every single time."

"He's tried to attend services before?"

"He's persistent, I'll give him that," Tirzah quipped. "He tries to sneak in about twice a year. As you saw—or should I say, *smelled*—the foul odor lingering about his person gives him away every single time."

"I see," Tabitha acknowledged, deeply saddened. "Is there no way to purge the dreadful smell?"

"If there is, it's yet to be discovered," Tirzah replied wanly. "Leather-making is a messy, hands-on affair. The stench often permeates a tanner's clothes and skin, even after meticulous bathing and scrubbing. According to the religious leaders, a tanner's work renders him in a nearly permanent state of ritual uncleanness."

"But why?" Tabitha asked, unfamiliar with the trade.

"A tanner's craft involves the carcasses of dead, rotting animals," Tirzah responded. "It's a bloody ordeal. Not to mention the fact that most tanners handle the corpses of creatures deemed unclean by

288 | RACHAEL C. DUNCAN

Jewish Law."

"Does Simon?"

"We wouldn't know," Tirzah responded wryly. "The religious leaders haven't asked, nor have they provided him a chance to defend himself."

"How sad," Tabitha sighed, her heart going out to the gruff, older man. "He must be very lonely, shunned from worship and even society."

"Simon is as salty as the sea by which he resides," Tirzah responded, waving aside her concerns. "He can take care of himself."

"He lives by the sea?"

"That's right," Tirzah nodded. "Downwind, on the eastern side of town just beyond the city limits, as our zoning laws require. Why do you ask?"

"I imagine it has been quite a while since anyone has paid Simon a friendly visit," Tabitha grinned, her eyes dancing with mischief.

"I know that look," Tirzah said, her brown eyes narrowing in suspicion. "What's on your mind?"

"What if we paid him a visit, Tirzah?"

"He's a crusty old man, but I think he has a good heart," Tirzah replied slowly, clearly mulling over Tabitha's suggestion. "I would have invited him to dine with us after the service if it wouldn't render all of us ceremonially unclean."

"Jesus is a friend of outcasts and sinners," Tabitha told her, sensing the Spirit's gentle leading. "I believe we should reach out to him, Tirzah."

"The religious leaders will have a fit!"

"What they don't know won't hurt them," Tabitha grinned.

"Fine." Releasing a sigh of mock exasperation, Tirzah nodded her reluctant consent. "I will go with you, but only on one condition."

"And what is that?"

"That you and Laurel join me at my house for a Sabbath meal," Tirzah implored, always hospitable. "Martha and Jonas have already agreed to come. I would have invited Eli as well, but he's far too scared of your uncle to even consider such a thing."

Laughing, Tabitha nodded her agreement. "I can think of nothing I'd like better than to break bread with my dear friends."

"Perfect," Tirzah declared. "After our meal, perhaps we can decide how to go about meeting Simon. I sure hope you know what you're doing."

"Oh, I don't," Tabitha chuckled. "But the Lord does. And He has never led me in the wrong direction."

CHAPTER 33

Tabitha

Joppa

The Sabbath meal was a joyous occasion, and Tabitha silently thanked God for His boundless mercy and provision. Cradling her sleepy daughter in her lap, Tabitha allowed her gaze to sweep over the beloved faces flanking the low table. She was truly blessed to enjoy the sweet fellowship of these dear friends!

And to think they have yet to embrace the truth about Jesus, Tabitha thought, suddenly reminded of the urgency of her mission. Though Tirzah, Martha, and Jonas remained stalwart in their Jewish faith and heritage, they were unaware of the fact that the long-awaited Messiah had finally come to redeem His people. And that blessed fact made all the difference in the world!

"So, Tabitha," Tirzah grinned, leaning back contentedly on one arm after they had finished the simple but pleasant meal, "what did you think of our dear little synagogue?"

Tabitha noticed Martha and Jonas exchanging anxious looks at Tirzah's blunt question. Desiring to put them at ease, Tabitha responded lightly, "I'm so glad I went. Thank you for escorting me, Tirzah."

"*Really?*" Tirzah pried in disbelief. "So you're saying you wish to go back again?"

"Absolutely," Tabitha responded without hesitation.

"*Why?*"

"Why do *you* keep going back?" Tabitha inquired patiently, turning the tables on her mischievous friend.

"Because the Law requires corporate worship on the Sabbath," Tirzah shrugged. "I certainly don't wish to fall prey to God's judgment."

"I see," Tabitha responded, without criticism. "Like you, I choose to attend Sabbath services because the practice was ordained by God. In the Scriptures, it is written: *Six days shall work be done, but the seventh day is a Sabbath of solemn rest, a holy convocation.*"

"A *woman* reciting Torah?" Martha asked, impressed and somewhat scandalized. "How did you learn it?"

"My father insisted," Tabitha laughed. "He knew the Word of God like the back of his hand, and he taught me everything he knew. After his death, the kind woman who took me in shared his passion for the holy texts."

"Mercy," Martha huffed, amazed.

"I'd like to learn more about the Scriptures myself," Tirzah mused, causing Tabitha's heart to leap with hope. "You quoted that passage so easily,

Tabitha. And you brought the words to life, unlike the dull droning of the religious leaders. I've actually nodded off once or twice during their lengthy recitations!"

"That verse has always encouraged me to keep the Sabbath faithfully, in rest and corporate worship as God ordained," Tabitha acknowledged, humbled and encouraged. "The Lord knows how important it is for believers to worship together, strengthening each other, holding each other accountable, and being bound by a common purpose."

"As wonderful as that sounds, our synagogue is nothing like that—as I'm sure you noticed," Tirzah quipped wanly. "Frankly, sometimes I wonder why I bother attending so faithfully when I gain absolutely nothing from it."

"The religious leaders make a decent point every now and then," Jonas put in a bit timidly, receiving a sarcastic look from his wife. Even so, Martha held her tongue, clearly nervous about criticizing the "holy men." Tabitha offered her an encouraging smile, for she, too, understood the danger of judging others. For now, she would leave the haughty religious leaders in God's hands, focusing instead on setting a godly example and following the Spirit's leading.

"I've yet to gain anything of real value by attending synagogue services," Tirzah spoke up in her forthright manner, undaunted about voicing her thoughts.

"That's not entirely true," Tabitha disagreed with a hint of a smile, shifting Laurel in her lap, for the little one had drifted off to sleep.

"Oh?" Tirzah challenged, though her tone remained in good humor. "Name one thing."

"You have gained discipline, faithfulness, and obedience," Tabitha responded without missing a beat. "The Lord has helped you better understand and institute these principles through faithful attendance, even when you would prefer not to go."

Tirzah's expressive hazel-flecked brown eyes conveyed her surprise and enlightenment.

"Besides that, attending services is not always about what we can *gain*, but what we can *give*," Tabitha added, wondering if she was speaking too freely.

"What do you mean, *give*?" Martha asked, interested despite her initial hesitation. "We are humble, uneducated folk. What knowledge can *we* impart to others?"

"Perhaps it's best to leave the instruction to the holy men," Jonas suggested timidly.

"True, the religious leaders are appointed to conduct services, sharing Scripture and instruction with the congregants. And I am certainly not suggesting that we usurp their authority," Tabitha agreed. "But service-goers have much to contribute, as well. While there, we can encourage, uplift, and pray for each other, scouting out needs and finding creative ways to meet them."

"Sounds like quite a bit of work," Martha harrumphed.

"How did your Rabbi view such things, Tabitha?" Tirzah interjected, enjoying the lively discussion.

"Jesus always made a point of attending Sabbath services," Tabitha replied. "It was His custom. His disciples follow His example in this."

"Who's Jesus?" Jonas asked blankly, receiving

another look of exasperation from his wife.

Caught off guard by Jonas' frank inquiry, Tabitha's stomach fluttered with an unexpected flurry of nerves. Since her arrival in Joppa, she had prayed earnestly about the opportunity to share the truth about Jesus, although she hadn't been entirely sure how to go about it. Stephanos had been the great evangelist, not her! Repeatedly, she had wondered if she should simply dive right in with a detailed exposition on the gospel message, or rather live by example and hope those around her would eventually ask about her faith. But now, Jonas had unwittingly opened the door for her, and it remained wide open as three pairs of eyes fixed upon her, waiting expectantly for her response. *Lord, help me! I don't even know where to begin, how to explain how wondrous You are...*

"Jesus is the Prophet from Nazareth who raised such a ruckus in Jerusalem a few years ago," Tirzah responded in answer to Jonas' question, interrupting Tabitha's silent plea and drawing looks of concern from the older couple. "He was crucified on Passover."

"Yes," Martha nodded. "His tragic death set the world afire with rumors. Some even claim He rose from the dead."

"He did," Tabitha stated simply, her heart thudding against her ribcage as three speechless companions gawked at her as if she'd taken leave of her senses. "Truly, He did," she repeated with a bit more confidence. "I saw Him. In fact, over five hundred witnesses can testify to this."

"Five hundred?" Jonas repeated in shock, receiving yet another look of correction from an increasingly nervous Martha.

"Indeed," Tabitha nodded. "First, He appeared to various women at the garden tomb. Later, He revealed Himself to His apostles in my mistress's home. This is where I witnessed His victory over death."

"Wait a minute," Tirzah cut in, her eyes narrowing in disbelief. "I knew you followed Him when He was alive, but I had no idea you actually believed those outrageous rumors."

"But are they so outrageous?" Tabitha proposed, silently beseeching the Lord even as she spoke. "Did not the Scriptures foretell His coming? Including His death and resurrection?"

"Did they?"

"It was Isaiah, our nation's greatest prophet, who foretold the life, death, and resurrection of Jesus in shockingly accurate detail," Tabitha explained, trembling inside. "Remember, Isaiah said the Messiah would be wounded for our transgressions and bruised for our iniquities. *The chastisement for our peace was upon Him, and by His stripes we are healed.*"

"And what if Isaiah spoke of someone else?" Tirzah asked frankly.

"Isaiah went on to say, '*He was taken from prison and from judgment… He was cut off from the land of the living; for the transgressions of My people He was stricken.*' He even goes so far as to say, '*They made His grave with the wicked—but with the rich at His death.*' How could Isaiah have possibly known that the Messiah would be crucified with wicked men, then buried in a rich man's tomb? This evidence clearly points to Jesus as the Christ, the

Anointed One."

"And if it's a coincidence?" Tirzah persisted.

"Then consider the prophetic psalm of David," Tabitha suggested, praying for Tirzah, Martha, and Jonas even as she spoke. "By the power of the Spirit of God, David foretold the Messiah's crucifixion with supernatural clarity. Consider this passage, for example: *They shoot out the lip, they shake the head, saying, 'He trusted in the Lord, let Him rescue Him; Let Him deliver Him, since He delights in Him!'* And this is exactly what happened when Jesus was nailed to the cross. Scoffers gathered around him, shouting these insults word for word, unaware of the fact that in their derision, they were unknowingly fulfilling an ancient prophecy!"

Tirzah nodded in cautious consideration, though she didn't look convinced, while Jonas and Martha seemed increasingly unsettled by Tabitha's shocking claims.

"In addition to that, David describes Jesus' crucifixion experience centuries before the Romans perfected that cruel, detestable method of torture," Tabitha continued, deciding she had best make her case before she was dismissed as a raving madwoman. "*I am poured out like water, and all My bones are out of joint; My heart is like wax; it has melted within Me. My strength is dried up like a potsherd, and My tongue clings to My jaws... For dogs have surrounded Me; the congregation of the wicked has enclosed Me. They pierced My hands and My feet... They divide My garments among them, and for My clothing they cast lots.* King David penned these words centuries before Jesus arrived! How could he have known that brutal soldiers and wicked men would encircle Jesus, mocking and berating Him? How could he have known the excruciating signs of crucifixion? And how could he have possibly predicted that the Messiah's hands and feet would be pierced, and that wicked men would gamble for His clothing? The fact that these remarkable prophecies were fulfilled when Jesus died attests to His Messiahship. But even more than that, His divinity was proven for all time when He rose from the dead, conquering the grave."

"And this is why you believe that Jesus is the only way to Heaven?" Tirzah asked, her logical mind mulling over the facts her friend had just presented.

"It is," Tabitha responded without hesitation. "Jesus is the long-awaited Messiah, and He came to set us free. Many refuse to accept His Messiahship because they thought He would free us from the Romans. But that's not why He came. He came to free us from *sin*. By accepting His shed blood upon the cross as the ultimate sacrifice to cover our sins, we have peace with God and we are promised eternal life in paradise."

"Martha, Jonas," Tirzah laughed, "you both look white as a sheet!"

Glancing at the older couple, Tabitha saw that Tirzah was right. Undoubtedly, they considered her doctrine blasphemous but were far too polite to say anything. Wishing she possessed her late husband's gift for evangelism, Tabitha hoped she hadn't spooked them beyond repair.

"You'd best not say anything about this at the synagogue," Jonas dared, shifting in obvious discomfort.

Tabitha smiled at him, appreciating his earnest

concern. Sensing their growing uneasiness, she decided to refrain from further discussion—for now. Despite her glaring lack of confidence, she reminded herself that God had provided this opportunity to speak boldly for His name. In obedience, she had planted the seed. Perhaps, in time, the Lord would help it grow.

CHAPTER 34

Tabitha

Joppa

"Thank you for providing a delightful meal and sweet Sabbath fellowship," Tabitha said with great feeling, pausing on Tirzah's threshold to adjust her bleary-eyed daughter's position in her arms. "I had a wonderful time."

"And I, as well," Tirzah assured her, one hand resting casually on the open door. "Although I'm not entirely sure we can say the same about Martha and Jonas. They left rather promptly after the exciting little discussion about your dead Rabbi."

"He isn't dead, Tirzah," Tabitha said with a smile. "Remember, I saw Him. I know He lives."

"You *think* you saw Him."

"I know I did."

"It could have been wishful thinking," Tirzah suggested.

"Not unless the five hundred others who also saw Him were deceived by wishful thinking, as well," Tabitha pointed out, her hazel-green eyes twinkling.

"Well, don't worry too much about Martha and Jonas," Tirzah assured her, dismissing the controversial subject. "They may think you're crazy, but they also respect you. Allow them some time to mull over what you said."

"And you?" Tabitha smiled, stroking back her daughter's wispy brown curls. "Will you mull over what I have said, as well?"

"I've heard it said that true followers of Jesus refuse to rest until they have converted every person within a Roman mile of them," Tirzah chuckled, shaking her head. "Now, I see such rumors are true."

"Speaking of people within a Roman mile," Tabitha interjected, sensing it might be wise to change the subject, "didn't you mention the presence of many widows in this region?"

"Too many," Tirzah affirmed.

"How might I contact them?" Tabitha asked frankly. "Surely many of them suffer deep need. Perhaps I can help."

"Don't you have enough on your plate as it is?"

"Not yet," Tabitha smiled in response.

"The best place to start might be the tenement-style living quarters by the sea," Tirzah decided. "Near the docks, there are several large buildings constructed in the style of Roman insulae—you know, with shops and vendors located on the ground level, but hundreds of tightly packed apartments occupying the upper floors. The living conditions are filthy and overcrowded, but they're cheap; thus, the only living space most of the widows can afford."

"I see," Tabitha responded sadly. She'd heard many horror stories about the dangerous, poorly constructed Roman tenements. Disease spread rapidly in such close, squalid quarters, and fires were a common occurrence. To make matters worse, it wasn't unusual for the shoddy structures to collapse unexpectedly, crushing their helpless inhabitants. "I shall make plans to visit there as soon as possible."

"If you seek a decent starting point, you may wish to inquire about an old widow woman named Ruth," Tirzah said, her tone strangely veiled. "She's an ornery one, but she knows every widow in the city. She lost not only a husband, but also a son, to the sea's cruelty."

"Bless her heart," Tabitha murmured, a pang gripping her heart. "And she resides in the tenements near the docks?"

"Last I heard, she did."

"How do you know her, Tirzah?"

"*Know* her?" Tirzah repeated with an uncharacteristically bitter smirk. "She was my mother-in-law."

Tabitha was taken aback.

"It's likely in your best interest not to mention to her that I sent you," Tirzah added, her eyes flickering with something hidden. "We didn't get along."

"You didn't keep in touch after your husband died?"

"We didn't keep in touch when he was *alive*,"

Tirzah responded with a brittle smile.

Sensing that Tirzah had sacrificed a carefully guarded secret to assist her in her mission, Tabitha touched her arm. "I won't say a word."

"You know, I hadn't thought of that woman for years...until recently," Tirzah admitted. "Shortly before your arrival, she came to mind. And now, it's like the old crone plagues my constant thoughts."

Tabitha simply waited, sensing the Spirit at work.

"Well, perhaps the Lord is trying to get my attention," Tirzah finally sighed, exasperated. "Or perhaps He knows how stubborn I am, and He is sending you to assist Ruth in my stead."

Balancing Laurel on one hip and smiling her understanding, Tabitha gave Tirzah's shoulder a comforting squeeze.

"Well, enough about that," Tirzah said, abruptly dismissing the unpleasant subject. "Do you still wish to visit Simon the tanner?"

"Absolutely, yes!"

"I admire your enthusiasm, though you may regret it."

"I have yet to regret anything the Lord has led me to do."

"Well, there's a first time for everything," Tirzah teased. "Truly, it would be in our best interest to allow Simon a week or two to cool off before planning a visit. He is a proud man. If he even suspects we have come out of pity or offering charity, he will surely turn us away."

"I trust your judgment," Tabitha assured her.

"All right, then," Tirzah nodded solemnly. "It

sounds like we have a plan. And we had best be praying the religious leaders don't find out what we're up to."

**

John Mark

Jerusalem

"At last!" Gracefully lifting her flowing robes, Aurelia hastened toward the handsome young man crossing the bustling market square. Draping her arms over his neck, she stood on tiptoes to kiss him. "I thought I'd simply die waiting to see you again!"

Tingling with pleasure from head to toe, John Mark could hardly comprehend that this breathtakingly beautiful young woman longed for him! Emboldened by her desire, he took her hands in his, raising them to his lips.

"I hope you had a dreadful day without me," Aurelia teased, batting long lashes at him.

With a slight tinge of guilt, John Mark considered how the hours had dragged by the previous day. He had spent most of it impatiently monitoring the sun's position in the sky, longing for the day of rest to end. His mind had been clouded with thoughts of Aurelia, most of them far from virtuous.

"Did you wear my necklace?" Aurelia demanded, sending his heart into overdrive as her slender fingers reached to unclasp the first few buttons of his tunic, producing the gleaming piece of jewelry

304 | RACHAEL C. DUNCAN

beneath his garment. Cradling the heavy pendant in her palm, her glowing eyes traveled upward, meeting his gaze. "You did!"

"You were with me, even in our absence," John Mark assured her, pleased with the poetic-sounding nature of his sentiment.

"I want to be alone with you," Aurelia dared, her eyes conveying forbidden intent. "It's far too chaotic here in the market square."

Instinctively, John Mark knew it was a terrible idea. His mother would likely skin him alive for even considering it!

"Come," Aurelia purred, offering an extended hand. "I know just the place."

"Wh-where?" John Mark stammered, both desperate and reluctant to perform her bidding.

"I know of some lovely private gardens near the palace grounds," she soothed, offering a sultry smile. "It was built for Roman citizenry, but you won't be turned away if you're with me. This time of day, we shall have the place all to ourselves." Taking his hand, Aurelia led him past harried shoppers and rows of crowded market stalls, her gait both graceful and intentional.

Woodenly following her lead, John Mark's heart pounded in time with the ancient proverb tearing through his mind: *With her enticing speech she caused him to yield, with her flattering lips, she seduced him. Immediately he went after her, as an ox goes to the slaughter, or as a fool to the correction of the stocks...*

Despite the disquiet within his soul, John Mark

dismissed his rising doubts, overcome with desire for the most ravishing young woman he had ever laid eyes upon. What did it matter if she was a Roman? Should he marry her, she would be required to accept *his* religion, wouldn't she? And if she truly loved him, she would gladly dismiss her idols and pagan philosophies to become his wife.

Wouldn't she?

Do not let your heart turn aside to her ways, the Spirit warned. *Do not stray into her paths; for she cast down many wounded, and all who were slain by her were strong men...*

Somehow, in his desperation, John Mark convinced himself all would be well.

CHAPTER 35

John Mark

Jerusalem

John Mark wasn't in a hurry to get home.
After one glance at his guilt-ridden features, his exasperatingly perceptive mother would know something was amiss. Fumbling with the heavy golden chain beneath his tunic, his heart hammered against his ribcage as he aimlessly meandered Upper City streets, allowing himself time to gain his composure. Recalling the ardent kisses shared in the privacy of a quiet garden, his conscience burned in shame despite the rippling waves of pleasure he had experienced in the heat of the moment.

He had always believed his first kiss would be reserved for his bride on the eve of their wedding.

Shaking his head in confusion, John Mark couldn't help but question the nature of his relationship with Aurelia. She had stormed into his life like a whirlwind, drop-dead gorgeous, passionate, and full of life. Now, mere days after that fateful encounter, he couldn't bear the thought of living without her.

Spotting a familiar resting place with graceful stone colonnades, magnificent potted palms, and curved marble benches scattered about a gently splashing fountain, John Mark made a beeline for the familiar respite. Lowering himself onto the bench nearest the soothing marble fountain, he closed his eyes, resting trembling hands on his knees.

How was he to know—*really know*—if he had met the love of his life, the woman he was meant to marry? Though he'd heard plenty of romantic tales about love at first sight, his practical mother scorned the popular idea. "Love is a *choice*, not a sentiment," she often declared with annoying logic. "A person's *appearance* may attract one's attention, but his or her *character* must determine the course of the relationship." How often had Mary quoted Solomon's famous proverb about the fleeting nature of outward beauty and the dangerous deception of charm?

Well, his mother was a beautiful woman, wasn't she? His entire life, he'd heard men and women alike praising his mother's stunning beauty. Her regal bearing and bronzed complexion paired with luminous gray eyes and dark, waist-length curls was truly a striking combination. And yet, Mary was inarguably a noble, godly woman. Her beauty certainly did not render her evil or immoral!

Perhaps this was also the case with the lovely Aurelia. Just because she was stunning didn't mean she was innately evil! Instinctively, John Mark knew what his mother would have to say about the matter: "Beauty isn't the issue. The problem arises when one possesses beauty *without* godliness."

Dismissing the wise counsel he had long received at his mother's knee, John Mark cradled his head in his hands, deeply unsettled. Perhaps he should take the direct, practical route by frankly asking Aurelia to define the nature of their relationship. The thought was daunting…and troubling. Eager to justify his actions, John Mark attempted to convince himself that she, too, desired to wed. Why else would she be so eager to take liberties strictly reserved for marriage?

This line of thought sent him into yet another downward spiral of raw emotion. Aurelia's father was a wealthy, powerful Roman. Would such a man even consider arranging a betrothal for his daughter with an insignificant Jewish boy? With a flicker of anger, John Mark realized he felt entirely inadequate—a shocking sensation for one usually brimming with confidence. But what was the wealth of one Jew in comparison with a Roman's splendor? Aurelia's father had the riches of an empire at his disposal, not to mention the confidence of the tetrarch and the ear of the emperor!

Well, perhaps Mary's wealth and status would prove helpful in arranging a betrothal…that is, if she agreed to do so. But what if Mary disapproved of Aurelia?

Frustrated beyond comprehension, John Mark recognized the bleakness of his situation. It was highly unlikely his mother—or Aurelia's father—would cooperate with his desires.

Sitting up straight on the bench, John Mark lifted his gaze, his dark eyes flashing in uncharacteristic defiance. It would seem his love for Aurelia was utterly impossible.

Unless he decided to take matters into his own hands.

***

John Mark eventually returned home, feeling testy and depressed. His mother would surely expect him to get right to work with Tobias in the bibliotheca, and the thought rankled. The last thing he wanted to do right now was labor over endless rows of dull numbers and exasperating charts and graphs!

"Hello, John Mark."

Halting mid-stride, John Mark's gaze traveled across the vast reception hall, resting upon his mother standing motionlessly at the foot of the great winding staircase. The intensity of her gaze was unsettling.

"I'm glad you're home," she continued in her calm, regal manner. "What kept you away so long?"

"I was with Simon." He hadn't intended to lie, but the falsehood had escaped his lips before he'd even realized it. Now, it was too late to retract his dishonest statement without facing serious repercussions.

"How is Simon?" Mary staidly inquired.

"He is well," John Mark responded uneasily, wondering if his mother sensed his dishonesty. It would be unusual for his friend Simon, the son of a Pharisee and grandson of the mighty Gamaliel—president of the Great Sanhedrin—to be away from his religious studies for such a lengthy stretch of time.

"And Simon's grandfather? How is he?"

"He, too, is well." John Mark didn't quite understand the relationship between Mary and Gamaliel.

Though the revered teacher clearly respected Mary, her doctrine deeply concerned him. Given the circumstances, it was rather shocking he had allowed the friendship between his grandson and John Mark to continue.

"I'm glad to hear that," Mary said sincerely, carefully gauging her son's reaction. "Has Simon been enjoying his studies?"

"Simon is happiest when buried beneath a pile of scrolls," John Mark responded testily. Remembering Aurelia's snide comments, he added tersely, "But he'll never 'find himself' that way, blindly following in the footsteps of ancestors long dead."

"Did he say that?" Mary asked, tilting her head in concern.

"I'm just saying he has no idea what he wants in life," John Mark muttered, avoiding her gaze. "He's spent his entire life doing what everyone else tells him to do."

"And is that how *you* feel?" Mary prompted wisely. "As if you have no say in your future?"

John Mark couldn't bring himself to meet his mother's intuitive gaze.

"If you are dissatisfied with your life and your work, John Mark, then perhaps we should discuss it," Mary said soberly. "In the meantime, I would encourage you to consider the innumerable blessings God has gifted you."

"I just want to know who I am, Mother," John Mark dared, irritated by Mary's calm practicality. "I need to find myself."

"God help us should we truly 'find ourselves,'" Mary responded with a wry smile. "In and of ourselves, we are but filthy rags, John Mark—selfish, stubborn, willful sinners in desperate need of re-pentance."

John Mark looked away, angrily working the muscles in his jaw.

"But in Christ, we are complete," Mary remind-ed him gently. "In Christ, we are new creations, filled with the Holy Spirit of God and brimming with unimaginable possibilities. Perhaps, instead of seeking your own will for your life, you should seek God's plan for you. His ways are far better, far more wonderful, than anything we could possibly devise for ourselves."

"I should get to work," John Mark murmured, clearly dismissing his mother's wisdom.

"See to it, then," Mary said quietly, grieved by her son's terse response. Seemingly overnight, her cheerful, laughing, teasing son had become angry and disillusioned. Undoubtedly, the Lord's wisdom and guidance was needed in this matter. She couldn't imagine what could have possibly transformed her son's attitude in such a brief amount of time. Perhaps his friend, Simon, was becoming a poor influence. She would need to investigate that for herself.

As John Mark stalked from the marble hall, Mary was not alone in her distress. Young Rhoda stood silently beneath an elegant entryway, her soulful brown eyes fixed upon John Mark's retreating back. Clutching her hands near her heart, she lifted her gaze heavenward, making fervent intercession for the one she had always loved.

CHAPTER 36

Kelila

Sychar

"Oh, Philip!" Kelila cried, clutching a pair of slim parchment scrolls close to her heart and squealing with delight. "I can scarcely comprehend that we've received word from Mary and Candace!"

"Well, are you going to open the scrolls and read them, or shall you leave us in dreadful suspense all night?" Philip teased, his bearded features softening in the warm lamplight of their modest abode.

"Oh, I can hardly wait!" Kelila exclaimed, aflutter with excitement. "Which one should I choose first?"

"Can you tell the difference between the two?"

"Mary still uses her late husband's seal," Kelila explained, lifting the first scroll for Philip's inspection. Mary's elegant wax seal appeared deep scarlet in the dim glow of the oil lamps. "This one is hers."

"Ah," Philip nodded in recognition.

"I think I shall open Candace's first," Kelila decided, her slender fingers trembling with excitement as she broke the simple seal and unrolled the parchment. Instantly recognizing her sister's familiar, flowing script, her dark eyes filled with tears. Oh, how she missed her beloved family! She was overwhelmingly grateful to the kind Samaritans who had located the house of Mary in Jerusalem, having journeyed there to visit the apostles to update the persecuted church about the explosion of new converts in Sychar. She could hardly believe the brave Samaritan delegation had already returned with word from Jerusalem! The round trip—including their stay in Jerusalem—had occupied less than two weeks' time, to everyone's great relief. The villagers had nearly burst with hopeful anticipation while awaiting the delegation's return. And now the entire village was abuzz with excitement, for Simon Peter and John had agreed to visit Sychar as soon as possible!

Oh, won't it be like a piece of Heaven on earth, she thought dreamily, *welcoming brethren from Jerusalem and sharing their sweet fellowship once again!*

"Well?" Philip prodded, drawing her back to the present moment. "What has Candace written?"

"Quite a lot, actually," Kelila laughed, pleased her sister had taken the time to pen a lengthy letter.

"Come," Philip invited, lowering himself onto a mat near the low table and beckoning for her to join him. "Sit with me."

"Oh, I couldn't *sit*!" Kelila exclaimed, nearly bursting with happiness. "Not now!"

"All right, then," Philip laughed. "But can you see without the assistance of a lamp?"

"I can see well enough," she replied, her hands trembling in anticipation. "All right, are you ready?"

"Am I ready?" Philip laughed. "I'm about to explode with curiosity."

"All right," Kelila breathed, her heart racing with eager expectation. "Here's what Candace has written: *'My dearest Kelila and Philip,*" she read, her voice slightly tremorous. "*'How dearly you are missed! Please know you remain in our constant thoughts and prayers. Despite the geographical distance between us, we are bound by the unchanging, never-failing love of Christ! Nothing can separate us from His love, nor from each other. We have an eternity of perfection awaiting us, where we shall never be torn apart!*" With great animation, Kelila read pleasing updates about her sister, her brother-in-law, and her dear, sweet nephews—the loveable, rambunctious Rufus and his far more serious older brother, Alexander. Tears sprang to her eyes as she read aloud about the increasing persecution in Jerusalem, the bravery of imprisoned church members, and courageous Mary's ongoing ministry toward those in prison. Apparently, Saul of Tarsus continued nursing his hatred against followers of the Way, pursuing them with zeal and vengeance.

In her letter, Candace also recounted her family's trip to Cyrene and their prayerful determination to reach their relatives with the love of Christ. "Hmm," Kelila commented, glancing up at Philip. "Here, Candace speaks to me directly: *'Kelila, my dear sister, you will be so pleased to learn that Mother has returned to Jerusalem with us. She seems far more receptive to the gospel now'*—" squealing her delight, Kelila spun around the room in excitement, her colorful robes spinning about her ankles. "Philip! Mother has returned with Candace and Simon! She's in Jerusalem!"

"Yes," Philip chuckled, enjoying her enthusiasm. "Praise God!"

"Oh, how wonderful!" Kelila cried, nearly overcome with joy. "Perhaps, surrounded by so many faithful followers of Jesus, Mother will accept the truth for herself!"

"We will pray for this without ceasing."

"Hmm," she mused, returning her attention to the letter. "I wonder why Father did not accompany—" Kelila froze mid-sentence as her gaze returned to the parchment page.

"Kelila?" Gazing questioningly at his wife, Philip saw her entire countenance turn ashen as the blood drained from her face. "My love?"

Unable to respond through her swiftly closing throat, Kelila raised tear-filled eyes to her husband.

Quickly going to her, Philip steadied her, grasping her forearms and looking intently into her eyes. "Kelila, what is it, my love?"

"M-my father..." she breathed, overcome.

"Here, love," Philip whispered gently, guiding her toward a narrow wooden stool. "Please, sit for a moment." She looked as if she would drop dead on her feet!

Woodenly, Kelila did as her husband suggested, clearly in a state of shock as Philip eased her onto the rickety stool.

"What is it, Kelila?" Philip asked gently, kneeling before his distraught wife. Gently taking the letter from her, he set it aside and took her hands in his. "Something has upset you."

"It's my father," Kelila whispered, too stunned to even weep.

"Is he sick?" Philip asked gently, deeply concerned. "Has he been injured?"

"He's..." Kelila stammered, raising dull, lifeless eyes to Philip. "He's dead."

***

"I just can't believe he's gone," Kelila whispered, cradled in her husband's strong arms like a hurting child. "I can't even wrap my mind around it."

Philip shook his head sadly, feeling terribly inadequate to console his aching wife. He was just as stunned as she was! According to Kelila, her father had always been indomitable—strong and healthy, and a force to be reckoned with. Who could have possibly known he would pass away swiftly and unexpectedly in the late midnight hours?

Wrapped in the soothing comfort of her husband's embrace, Kelila desperately tried to grasp a seemingly incomprehensible fact: Her father was gone. She would never see him again—at least, not in this life. And possibly, not in the next. How could she possibly know if he had accepted the truth before his passing?

At Kelila's shaky request, Philip had bravely finished reading the letter aloud, but Candace had remained rather elusive regarding the matter of their father's salvation. More than likely, the stubborn man had perished in his sins.

Apparently, his death had been sudden. He had gone to bed far earlier than usual one evening, complaining about discomfort in his chest. Hours later, his wife had awakened beside him, only to find him utterly cold and still.

O*h, Mother,* Kelila thought, inexplicably grieved. *How terrible that must have been for you! I should have been there to comfort you!* Closing her eyes, Kelila listened to the sound of her husband's quiet breathing beside her, overcome with sorrow.

H*ow can death claim a soul so suddenly?* she thought, shivering despite a thick layer of blankets and the warmth of her husband's arms. They had lain upon their sleeping pallet this way, wrapped in each other's arms, for hours, and yet sleep refused to come for either of them. Rather, the night stretched on and on, the darkness seemingly closing in on all sides. Kelila nearly felt smothered by it.

H*ow can I sleep now?* Kelila thought, sickened. *My father is dead, and now I shall never be restored to him. He hated me, and for good reason.*

"I should have gone to him," Kelila finally mourned, turning from her husband's embrace and settling on her back. The ground felt hard and uncompromising beneath her shoulder blades. Blinking several times, her eyes adjusted to the darkness of their small chamber as she gazed up at the low ceiling. "I should have completely disregarded Father's orders and went to him, begging his forgiveness."

"He disinherited and disowned you, Kelila," Philip reminded her gently. "If such a person returns to their family without permission, the consequences can be dire."

"I should have gone anyway," she insisted stoutly, loathing herself. Why had she assumed her father would live forever? Why had she simply supposed that, in time, the situation would work itself out?

Had life ever proven so kind? "How could I be so foolish?"

"Sweetheart, you didn't know."

"But I should have!" she cried, her voice trembling. "And now...now I'll never have the chance to make things right. I hurt him, Philip. I hurt him deeply. And now...now..." Looking away, Kelila clenched her jaw, unable to voice the rising swell of bitterness filling her soul. There were simply no words to adequately describe her anguish. None at all.

"Philip," she said into the darkness, her tone firmly resolved. "Don't tell anyone about this. Not even Ephraim or Adorina."

The long pause hanging in the air was enough to assure Kelila that Philip disagreed with her request.

"I mean it," she emphasized, irritated by his silence. "We have a mission here, and I have no intention of burdening these people with my personal troubles."

"Love, that's what the body of Christ is all about," Philip gently reminded her. "We are to bear one another's burdens, comforting and strengthening each other."

"But *we're* supposed to do the comforting and the strengthening," she argued. "Not the brand-new converts."

"Ephraim and Adorina would wish to support you—"

"Don't tell them."

Sensing his wife's raw pain, Philip decided to honor her request. There would be plenty of time to discuss her reluctance later, after she'd had some time to grieve and process the tragic circumstances.

"Promise me that, Philip," Kelila persisted, her tone uncharacteristically harsh.

"I won't say a word without your permission," Philip assured her, squeezing her hand beneath the blankets.

Turning over on her side, Kelila battled against swelling shock, pain, and regret, bracing herself against merciless waves of emotion as they battered her wounded soul. How could so many emotions war against each other all at once? She felt as if her heart had been utterly ripped to shreds.

Though she desperately longed to cry—*needed* to cry, even—her tears refused to come.

CHAPTER 37

Tabitha

Joppa

Pausing on the cobbled street across from the towering Roman-style tenements near the bustling docks, Tabitha hoisted Laurel a bit higher upon her hip and adjusted the small basket she bore on her opposite arm. She had arrived completely unprepared for the nonstop activity of the docks, now flooding her senses like a raging tide. Offering her daughter a nervous smile, she briefly questioned her decision to bring Laurel along on this errand. Her uncle's seaside mansion, safely situated behind secure, mammoth stone walls, showcased the sea's beauty, brilliance, and tranquility even while safely removed from the chaos of the booming shipping and fishing industries. But here, so close to the water's lapping edges and the rickety, slap-shod docks boasting aging piers, beams, and fraying ropes, the quaint seaport town roared to life.

Breathing deeply of the fresh, salty air, Tabitha allowed herself a moment to get acquainted with her unfamiliar and shocking surroundings, unable to even partially track the frantic movements and frenetic activities of so many diverse people rattling off dozens of languages. The swelling chorus of foreign tongues sounded strange and unnatural to her ears. It seemed every possible station of life was represented among the people bustling about the docks as slaves, servants, and free working men scrambled up and down the long, wooden gangplanks of gargantuan sailing vessels, loading and unloading the ships' heavy cargoes with practiced ease despite the sweat glistening upon the brows and bare backs of poorly clad slaves. Turbaned overseers anxiously referenced their tablets as loads of cargo were carted swiftly back and forth, while well-dressed, stern-faced aristocrats grimly surveyed their chests of goods as they were brought forth from the bowels of the great ships. Smiling to herself, Tabitha saw that Laurel seemed utterly entranced by the majestic white sails billowing in the gusty sea breezes like enormous, symmetrical clouds. The toddler chuckled her delight as nimble sailors clambered up and down the swinging rope ladders running parallel to sturdy, towering masts, adjusting the sails.

In stark contrast with the mighty cargo ships of the great harbor were dozens of smaller fishing vessels gently bobbing in the azure waters. With a slight pang of homesickness, Tabitha was reminded of Simon Peter, Andrew, James, and John—dearly beloved apostles who'd once been humble fishermen before Jesus taught them to fish for men instead!

Fascinated, she watched as massive hauls of fish were dragged from crude sailing vessels by muscular, rough-looking fishermen, their nets straining against the weight of their catch.

If that wasn't enough to overstimulate one's senses, rows upon rows of ramshackle market stalls lined the docks, with merchants proudly hawking their wares. Cringing inwardly, Tabitha wondered if each shopkeeper was attempting to outshout his fellow sellers! The resulting cacophony was nearly deafening.

Lifting her gaze heavenward, Tabitha watched in breathless wonder as snowy white gulls dipped and swayed, swooping so low the feathers of their majestically spread wings nearly touched the water's crystal surface. Then, entirely unexpectedly, the gulls would change course, soaring headlong into the clear blue sky.

Mighty God, Tabitha's heart cried as she surveyed the wondrous seascape beyond, *surely Job was correct in his assessment so many centuries ago, when he said, 'But now ask the beasts, and they will teach you; and the birds of the air, and they will tell you; or speak to the earth, and it will teach you; and the fish of the sea will explain to you. Who among all these does not know that the hand of the Lord has done this, in whose hand is the life of every living thing, and the breath of all mankind?' Just look at the vastness of this shimmering sea, the depth of this clear blue sky, the majesty of the gulls above and the teeming fish below! What a brilliant Creator You are!*

With great effort, Tabitha tore her gaze from the panorama of blue sky, ocean waves, and the billowing sails of the mighty ships, focusing her attention instead upon the poorly constructed tenements a short distance from the docks. Shops lined the entire ground level, from which greedy merchants competed with the sellers nearer the docks, shouting out at distracted passers-by and holding up their wares for inspection. Tabitha wasn't looking forward to bypassing the exploitative shopkeepers and hoped they wouldn't delay her at their market stalls.

Taking a deep breath, she waited for several jouncing wagons to pass on the cobbled street before gingerly crossing over it, tightening her grip around her daughter's small waist. Pausing before the rows of shops on the first level, Tabitha craned her neck, gazing upward and counting at least four stories within the massive structure.

"May I assist you, miss?"

Glancing up in surprise, Tabitha found herself standing near a fruit vendor's booth. Barrels of ripe fruits and vegetables graced wooden tables and filled neatly stacked crates beneath the seller's brightly covered awning.

"You look a bit…lost," the vendor continued, his tone gracious rather than condemning. He wasn't a bad-looking sort at all, though his chestnut brown hair was a bit longer than Tabitha was accustomed to, as it nearly reached his shoulders. She had discovered that—apart from the synagogue, of course—many rugged men of this seaport town appeared a bit more casual in looks and attire than the brothers of her native Jerusalem.

With a self-conscious smile, Tabitha tucked a wayward strand of honey-gold hair behind her ear. Thank goodness she had secured the rest of her long locks in a tight knot at the nape of her neck, hidden safely beneath her head covering. Otherwise, this ceaseless wind would have surely made a mess of it!

"Perhaps you can point me in the right direction," Tabitha ventured cautiously, wondering if the handsome young merchant intended to trap her in conversation, hoping to convince her to make a purchase. "I am seeking a widow named Ruth. I was told she lives here."

"Ah, dear old Ruth," the merchant grinned fondly. "Are you a relation of hers?"

"A friend of a friend," Tabitha responded, sensing the young man's caution. Clearly, he didn't intend to arrange a meeting for Ruth without learning of Tabitha's intentions.

"Is she expecting you?"

"I'm afraid not," Tabitha responded honestly. "I have brought her some freshly baked bread from my friend's kiln," she added hopefully, lifting the delicate basket balanced on her forearm.

"You have quite an armload there," the young merchant observed, his warm brown eyes traveling from the basket of carefully wrapped loaves to the sweet child in Tabitha's arms.

"Indeed," she responded, chuckling lightly.

"Are you a skilled baker?" the merchant continued, and Tabitha sensed he was feeling her out in a casual manner meant to set her at ease. "That's quite a few loaves in your basket, there."

"I can bake, though I doubt my loaves are exceptional," Tabitha laughed, appreciating his concern for the older woman she intended to visit. "I work at Joram's estate, but Martha oversees his kitchen and does most of his baking."

"Ah, Martha," the young man responded easily, nodding his head in recognition. "She has been known to frequent this market quite often—even this very booth. You work for old Joram, you say?"

"I do," Tabitha responded, a mischievous twinkle in her eye. "In addition to that, I am his niece."

"His niece!" the young man declared in surprise. "Well, then, I suppose you can be trusted," he teased. "Joram is the wisest in his trade, though we see very little of him. How is the old man faring?"

Tabitha caught herself before automatically responding, *He is well.* Unfortunately, that wouldn't be entirely truthful. Joram was a frustrated, angry old man.

Recognizing her hesitation to elaborate, the young man laughed it off. "Never mind," he grinned. "That was an unfair question."

Smiling her relief, Tabitha thanked God for leading her to this pleasant, amicable young merchant. She had been rather nervous to inquire about a complete stranger, but this good-natured young man had set her at ease. With a sharp pang to her heart, she realized his kind, easy manner reminded her very much of her beloved Stephanos.

"I didn't ask your name," the merchant smiled, interrupting her thoughts.

"Oh, it's Tabitha, and this is my daughter, Laurel."

"Hi there, Laurel," the merchant grinned, clearly enchanted by the lovely child. Instantly shy, Laurel flashed a little grin before hiding her face in her mother's neck. "I am Adam," he informed her. Despite his warm brown eyes and ready smile, he was strongly built with a very masculine persona about him. Tabitha couldn't help but think he appeared somewhat out of place in the small seller's booth.

"Pleased to meet you." Nodding politely, Tabitha hoped Adam would now direct her toward Ruth's small tenement apartment. She hadn't much time to waste. Surely Joram would demand to know her whereabouts should she tarry too long!

"You will find Ruth on the highest level," Adam informed her, sensing her eagerness to depart. "The first door on the left."

T*he highest level.* Only the poorest and most destitute tenants lodged on the top floors of such structures, where the cheapest and smallest chambers were housed. Tabitha's heart went out to the poor widow woman she hadn't even met yet.

"Thank you very kindly," Tabitha responded with great feeling, relieved to have obtained the information she sought. "I appreciate your help more than you know."

"Anytime, miss," Adam responded with an easy smile, a mischievous flicker reflecting in his brown eyes. "Best of luck with Ruth."

Wondering about Adam's hidden amusement, Tabitha nodded once more before slipping past his stall and entering a narrow vestibule sheltering the first flight of dark stone steps.

CHAPTER 38

Tabitha

Joppa

Having climbed three flights of steep stone staircases, Tabitha was relieved to finally emerge at the top.

P*raise God, Ruth's apartment is the* first *door on the left,* Tabitha thought, unsettled by the darkened corridor that seemingly stretched on forever, as if into a whirling abyss. She had no desire whatsoever to travel any further down that disturbing, narrow hallway than necessary. Rickety wooden doors appeared to line the entire length of the shadowed hall, unsettlingly close together.

How small must these apartments be? Tabitha thought, pausing before the door she sought. *The tenants must not enjoy even a speck of privacy!* Shuddering slightly, she drew Laurel even closer and dared a quick tap on the door's grainy surface. She couldn't imagine living alone in a place like this, with shady staircases and lonely corridors. Every now and then, a cheap oil lamp was mounted upon the mud brick wall—almost like an afterthought on the part of the builder—providing the slightest glimmer of light. But Tabitha doubted the faint flickers served their intended purpose in the heavy darkness of night.

Hoping Ruth was home and would promptly answer her knock, Tabitha tapped at the door once again, a bit more assertively this time. After all, it was entirely possible the older woman was hard of hearing. Perhaps she hadn't heard the light rap the first time.

"Whatever you're selling, I don't want any! Go away!"

Startled by the gravelly shout resounding from the other side of the door, Tabitha wondered what to do. She hadn't come to sell anything, but how was she to convince Ruth of that? Timidly, she knocked once more.

"I said I don't want any!" came the terse response.

"Good day, Ruth," Tabitha called cheerily, hoping she could be heard well enough through the closed door. "I haven't come to sell any merchandise."

"Go away!"

"I am new in the area, and I'd like to introduce myself," Tabitha dared, wishing she possessed the charisma and boldness of her late husband. Undoubtedly, he would have already charmed the suspicious old woman!

The door swung open swiftly and unexpectedly. Filling the doorframe was the form of an obstinate old woman, her leathery features taut with keen displeasure. The old widow was surprisingly sturdy for her ripe age, with broad shoulders and a wide frame.

Her close-cropped gray curls still bore traces of fiery red, in accordance with her feisty and dogged temperament. Surprised, Tabitha noticed the woman hadn't even bothered to don a head covering nor remove her dilapidated, work-stained apron to greet her guest.

"What are you—deaf? Dumb?" the old woman demanded, her fists planted uncompromisingly on her hips. "Didn't I tell you to go away?"

This was Tirzah's former mother-in-law? Shocked, Tabitha attempted to mask her great surprise. Subconsciously, she had envisioned Ruth as a sweet, delicate older lady. Clearly, her fanciful imaginings couldn't have proven further from the truth!

Recovering with a bit of effort, Tabitha managed a gracious smile. "I apologize for the intrusion, my lady," she said humbly, addressing Ruth with the utmost respect. "My name is Tabitha, and this is my daughter, Laurel." Frightened by Ruth's fierce demeanor, the toddler hid her face in her mother's neck, clinging to her garments for dear life. "Having recently arrived in Joppa, I wished to get in touch with the widows of the region. As a widow myself—"

"What do you want?" Ruth snarled, her eyes narrowing in suspicion. "A handout?"

Struck by the familiarity of Ruth's accusation, Tabitha realized that haughty greed was not restricted to members of the upper class, such as Joram.

"Actually," Tabitha countered kindly, "I've brought you some fresh baked bread. I hope you will enjoy it." Tentatively, she offered the basket on her forearm.

Ruth eyed her with suspicion, one brow raised.

"What's the catch?"

"The catch?" Tabitha repeated, confused.

"You don't know me from Adam," the old woman sneered, "so why do something nice for me?"

"Actually, it was *Adam* who helped me locate you," Tabitha quipped, somewhat tickled by the coincidence and suddenly understanding the young man's secret amusement. *He could have warned me about Ruth's temperament,* she thought, peeved. *He sent me up here knowing full well what I was about to encounter!*

"Huh?" Ruth muttered, confused. "What are you babbling about?"

"The man at the vendor's booth," Tabitha supplied, wondering if Ruth's memory was failing. "Adam. He directed me to your apartment."

"He's going to regret that," Ruth grumbled, crossing her arms in disgust.

"May I come in?" Tabitha dared, certain she was about to be turned away. "I would love to break bread with you."

"I have no refreshments to offer."

"Remember, I've brought some bread," Tabitha pointed out with a persuasive smile.

Leaning heavily against the doorframe, Ruth surveyed the young woman with suspicion and displeasure. "Well," she finally muttered, gesturing for Tabitha to enter, "I guess it wouldn't hurt none."

With a resigned sweep of her arm, Ruth permitted Tabitha to cross her threshold with an anxious Laurel in tow.

"Thank you, Ruth." Stricken by the widow's abject poverty, Tabitha attempted to conceal her shock with a brave smile as she was motioned impatiently inside. Amazed, she realized the old woman's entire home was even smaller than the tiny storage room Joram had granted her at his estate. There were no facilities conducive for cooking or even relieving oneself. As for furnishings, the one-room living quarters boasted a few cracked stone jars, one low table, and a bed of straw in the corner, which Tabitha assumed must serve as the widow's bed. How the woman's old bones must ache with such a poor arrangement! Not to mention the three imposing flights of steps required to reach her paltry abode!

Perhaps that's why she remains mobile and strong, Tabitha thought, intrigued. *Ruth is a hard worker, in constant motion.*

"Sit down there, will you?" Ruth ordered tersely, indicating the bare table. "Want some watered wine? It's all I got on hand."

"Thank you kindly, Ruth, but I'm fine," Tabitha replied warmly, unwilling to partake of the widow's scanty supply. Seating herself before the low table, she helped Laurel get situated beside her. Sympathetic, she realized Ruth hadn't even simple mats to cushion the hard floor. An expert seamstress, she decided to do something about that—in time, of course, *if* she was able to gain Ruth's trust.

"Suit yourself," the widow grumbled, filling a clay mug for herself before joining Tabitha and Laurel at the table.

"My, what a lovely view," Tabitha exclaimed, glad to have found something to compliment the widow about. The door remained open to an extremely narrow, dilapidated wooden balcony overlooking the sparkling Mediterranean. Tabitha supposed the tenement's adjoining balconies were the only available place for tenants to dry laundry or perform chores requiring fresh air.

"Well, are we going to sample that bread you've been boasting about, or just sit here staring at it?"

Hiding a knowing smile, Tabitha reached into the basket she'd placed on the table, carefully unwrapping one of the golden loaves. "Will you do the honors?" Offering it to the crotchety old woman across the table, she smiled her encouragement.

Eagerly accepting the soft bread, Ruth broke it into three equal pieces, offering a piece to Laurel and Tabitha. Laurel's eyes widened in surprise when the old woman immediately tore into her bread, neglecting the customary blessing or prayer of thanksgiving.

Silently blessing her and her daughter's meal, Tabitha nodded to Laurel, encouraging her daughter to partake. Later, she would explain why Ruth hadn't blessed the meal.

"Not bad," Ruth acknowledged, enjoying the nourishment Tabitha had provided. "Are you a baker?"

"A maidservant," Tabitha replied. "I work on the estate of Joram—"

"My deepest apologies," the woman huffed in sarcastic interruption, rolling her eyes. "That man is a stubborn old goat."

Tabitha held back a smile.

"You said you're new around here?"

"Very," Tabitha replied. "I hail from Jerusalem. My daughter and I left after my husband passed away."

"Sorry for your loss," Ruth muttered, her tone far removed from feeling.

"As a widow myself, I find it quite healing to visit other widows," Tabitha explained. "Together, we can encourage, strengthen, and support each other—"

"Don't fool yourself," Ruth cut in, annoyed. "We widows support *ourselves*. Ain't nobody going to offer us even a sliver of charity, nor a handout."

Tabitha resisted the urge to point out that the bread in Ruth's hands was, in fact, an act of charity. Even so, she knew her behavior would have a far greater impact on Ruth than her words. And angry words would hinder rather than aid her mission.

"I didn't see you at the synagogue on Sabbath," Tabitha said lightly, changing the subject. "Were you unwell?"

"That's none of your business."

"I apologize," Tabitha said quickly. "I didn't mean to pry—"

"You didn't come up here to get me some religion, did you?" Ruth demanded, her thick brows raised in suspicion. "I've done just fine without it, mind you."

"I came because I wished to meet you and to offer any assistance, if needed," Tabitha answered honestly. "The same offer stands for the other widows of this region. I understand there are quite a few of them."

"More 'n there should be, that's the truth," Ruth mumbled, rising as quickly as her old bones would permit.

"I've been told the widows trust and respect you, Ruth," Tabitha told her, noting the flicker of interest in Ruth's blazing eyes. "I would greatly appreciate it if you would kindly pass along my offer to them. I am here if any of the widows need assistance, sustenance, or prayer."

"That's a mighty strange offer," Ruth observed, stalking over to the door and swinging it open wide. "You'd best be off now. Wouldn't want to overstay your welcome, would you?"

Smiling her understanding, Tabitha stood, bending to lift Laurel off the ground. Balancing her carefully on one hip, she crossed the cramped, little room, pausing at the threshold. "My offer stands. If the widows need any help at all, I can be found at Joram's estate." Without further ado, Tabitha slipped out the door.

"Wait," Ruth called after her, attempting to conceal her puzzlement. "You forgot your basket of goods."

"I didn't forget," Tabitha assured her, pausing in the dim corridor. "I brought it for you. May God bless you and keep you, Ruth." Turning on her heel, Tabitha steeled herself for a long trip down the dreaded flights of steps.

She could only hope and pray that Ruth would ponder all she had said. The poor woman was a lost, lonely soul. Only the love of Christ could break down the barriers she had painstakingly constructed around her stony old heart.

CHAPTER 39

Tabitha

Joppa

"How did it go?"

Glancing over her shoulder, Tabitha saw Adam standing behind the seller's booth, his hands folded behind his broad back and his brown eyes twinkling with mischief.

"You could have warned me," she commented wryly, gently lowering her daughter so the squirming child could stand on her own two feet. Taking Laurel's hand, she tipped her head to one side. "How long have you known Ruth?"

"As long as I can remember," Adam replied. "She's a tough old bird, isn't she?"

Smiling, Tabitha noted the fondness in Adam's tone.

"Did Ruth appreciate your visit?"

"Perhaps, in time, she will."

"We'll see about that," Adam said with an enigmatic smile. "She's not so bad, once you get to know her."

"I didn't think she was bad at all."

"Ah, she must have gone easy on you, then," Adam grinned. "That's a good sign."

Amused, Tabith resisted the urge to ply him with questions. "I suppose I must be going. Thank you for your help today, Adam."

"Don't mention it," he responded easily. "Always glad to help a fellow neighbor."

Acknowledging the kind young man with a sincere smile, Tabitha helped her little daughter cross the cobbled street.

***

Kelila

Sychar

A few doors down from her own market stall, Kelila stood before the baker's booth, savoring the aroma of freshly baked loaves and flatbread. Though she was becoming far more skilled in the art of cooking and breadmaking, Philip often encouraged her to make purchases in the local market, building both trust and bridges with the citizens of Sychar.

"Might I interest you in a few loaves today, my lady?" the baker, a rotund older man sporting a flour-dusted apron, asked brightly.

"Don't you always?" Kelila smiled, determined to present her best face despite the pain and regret clawing at her heart. "I shall take two loaves, please." Pressing several coins into the baker's ample palm, she offered another overbright smile.

"Two loaves, it is," the baker responded, turning to fetch two beautiful, golden loaves from a barrel beneath the shade of his canopy. "Anything else?"

"That will be all for today," Kelila responded lightly. "Thank you, sir."

"It is my pleasure to serve you and your husband, my lady."

Touched, Kelila thanked God for the salvation of this man and his entire family. They had been among some of the first to receive Christ when she and Philip first arrived in Sychar over a month prior.

"I see the sorcerer is still practicing his cursed arts," the baker mused, watching as the wily Simon placed a small, velvet satchel in the hands of a pale young woman. Taking both her hands in his, he kissed them before releasing her.

Appearing slightly unsettled but hopeful, the young woman turned away, carefully tucking the satchel within the leather pouch secured about her waist.

Suppressing a shudder, Kelila was glad Simon's booth was located at the opposite end of the long market strip. She didn't wish to be anywhere near his house of magic spells.

Suddenly realizing that the baker awaited her response, Kelila forced a calm smile she was far from feeling. "Perhaps, Simon, too, will believe someday."

"Ha," the baker snorted, skeptical. "It'll be a cold day in Hades before that happens."

Politely bidding the baker a good day, Kelila placed her newly acquired loaves in her basket and stepped onto the street. She was eager to return home where she could nurse her wounds alone, far from prying eyes and questioning stares.

Lord, try as I might, I just don't understand why You let my father die, she wrestled in silent prayer, battling against the warm tears burning her eyes. *How could You let him die without providing an opportunity for reconciliation? How, Lord?*

Nearing her own simple market stall, she released a wistful sigh. Philip and Ephraim had done a fine job repairing the sagging canopy and the dilapidated wooden frame. Now, Philip could easily address his listeners beneath the welcome shade provided by their recent repair. Situated on stacked crates near the entrance was an assortment of small stone jars in which Kelila had planted various herbs from Adorina's garden. Already, little green sprouts had begun to emerge from the moist earth caked within the little pots. At Adorina's instruction, she had also placed several large stone jars in strategic locations to capture rainwater, both for the plants and for personal use, as well. The place was beginning to feel more like home, though Kelila had certainly harbored reservations at the beginning.

Perhaps I was right in my hesitation, she thought, slipping under the canopy's shade and pausing to inspect the little green sprouts in the nearest jar. *Perhaps I should have gone to Cyrene with Candace before coming here. Philip would have fared just fine without me. If only I could go back in time and make it all right...if only...*

"You look deeply troubled, my lady."

Halting abruptly, Kelila's grip upon her basket tightened as her heart sprang into her throat. Instinctively, she knew to whom the mesmerizing voice belonged without even turning around.

"One might think you were losing faith."

Turning around slowly, Kelila found herself face-to-face with Simon, the sorcerer. Irritated by his cool insinuation, she straightened, proudly lifting her chin. "What a ridiculous thing to say," she responded evenly, hoping she appeared composed when, in fact, her insides quaked. She had never been within such close proximity to a sorcerer, and she was overwhelmingly thankful for the sturdy, wooden merchant's counter serving as a barrier between them. "I don't believe we have been formally introduced. You have yet to attend one of my husband's meetings."

"Ah," Simon acknowledged with dripping condescension. "I am Simon, known around these parts as the great power of God."

"And you are not disturbed by such a lofty title?" Kelila dared, angered by his suggestion.

"Unlike most, the truth does not offend me."

"Nor lies, apparently," Kelila shot back, her eyes flashing. "*Jesus* is the truth, Simon. He is the power of God—not you. He is the Messiah long promised."

"I suppose you are entitled to your opinion."

Drawing a calming breath, Kelila reminded herself that *no one* was beyond God's reach—not even Simon. She must be careful, for in her frustration, she might very well turn this man away from Christ.

"As you previously mentioned, we haven't been formally introduced," Simon continued, interrupting her train of thought. "Your husband is called Philip, yes?"

"He is."

"And you?"

"I am Kelila."

"Kelila," the sorcerer mused, and Kelila shuddered at the sound of her name upon his lips. "A lovely name for a lovely woman."

The sorcerer's dark eyes caressed Kelila's face and form in a way that made her skin crawl. Bolstering her courage, she returned his gaze without shrinking, refusing to gratify his lust to be feared. She could easily see why others revered him, for he carried himself with the air of a merchant prince of the mysterious underworld, brimming with confidence and dark charisma. Broad-shouldered and impressive in stature, he dressed to emphasize his physique with expensive, fitted garments and a glittering, gem-studded belt strapped at his waist. His clothes were truly magnificent, boasting rich, swirling colors and patterns. Though his dark hair and beard was beginning to turn gray, the salt and pepper appearance suited him well, lending him an even more sophisticated image. Snidely, Kelila wondered how much oil he must apply to his hair and neatly trimmed beard each day to achieve such a lustrous shine.

"Tell me," Simon drawled, folding well-shaped, swarthy hands in front of him, "why have you come to Sychar, Kelila? What is your mission, your purpose?"

"The Messiah has come," Kelila answered readily, silently begging God for assistance in this uncomfortable situation. "Even so, many remain unaware of His arrival. It is our mission to share this Good News with the world, that all who believe in Jesus might be saved."

"As I'm sure you've noticed," Simon replied, his lips parting in amusement, "there is no need for another spiritual leader in Sychar. It's a small place, and I have served the citizenry well for years."

"You have *deceived* the citizenry, not *served* them," Kelila coolly disagreed, fighting to maintain her composure.

"You cannot deny my power. I have worked signs and miracles."

"As did the Pharaoh's magicians when God sent Moses to free His people," Kelila reminded him, unwilling to be swayed. "Perhaps your intentions are good, Simon. I cannot read your heart—only God can do that. But the power you possess comes from the evil one, not from God. You cannot dabble in forbidden arts—sins God has clearly and repeatedly forbidden in His Word—and then claim to be His minister."

"The great success I have achieved vouches for me," Simon hissed, his dark eyes hardening in anger. "I am an agent of light, harnessing the powers of the earth to perform my will. The works I do enhance the lives of others."

"The devil himself masquerades as an angel of light," Kelila observed, sadly shaking her head. "Is it any wonder his ministers do the same? You may claim to work for God, Simon, but your deeds speak otherwise. Jesus taught us that a tree is known by its fruit. Any 'minister' claiming to do the work of God must be carefully evaluated, his fruit inspected. If his words or deeds contradict the unchanging Word of God, he is either deceived *or* deceiving others." Raising level eyes to his, she added with solid conviction, "Just as you are."

Dark eyes kindling in rage, Simon steadily returned her gaze. "And why, pray tell, are you *really* here?"

"If you truly have so much power, then why are you asking me?" Kelila shot back, her righteous anger overwhelming any previous concerns. "Concoct some magic potion of divination or consult the spirit world yourself!"

Turning on her heel, she prepared to take her leave. As far as she was concerned, this conversation was over.

"You don't believe I have power over you, do you?"

Pausing at her threshold, Kelila's back stiffened in anger. "None at all," she tossed over her shoulder, refusing to reward him with so much as a backward glance.

"You are wrong."

Ignoring him, Kelila reached for the latch on the door, eager to be rid of Simon's pompous company.

"Don't you wish to know if your father forgave you before his death?"

Instantly, Kelila froze with her hand on the door, her heart pounding in her throat with the fury of a dozen war drums.

"It's a pity—your lack of faith," Simon sighed, and she could imagine the sardonic smile stretching his swarthy features. "I have spoken with your father. He wants to see you."

Turning slowly on her heel, Kelila met his gaze, her dark eyes burning with anger. "My father is dead."

"But not to me."

Instantly understanding what he was implying, Kelila was utterly sickened—and strangely torn. Did Simon truly have the power to consult the departed spirits in the underworld? If so, had he *truly* been in contact with her father?

Trembling from head to toe, Kelila reminded herself of the holy Scriptures—all of which forbade the wicked craft of necromancing.

"I can make this happen for you," Simon soothed, his features washed with a carefully practiced air of compassion. "I can take away your pain."

Turning promptly on her heel, Kelila jerked open the front door. Barreling inside, she slammed it behind her with a resounding *thud*, leaving the smug sorcerer standing alone on the dusty street.

Leaning heavily against the door, Kelila burst into a flood of tears, breathing great, gulping sobs of pain and regret. Nearly reeling with nausea, she slid unsteadily to the ground, gripping her midsection with trembling hands and dissolving in bitter tears of lament.

CHAPTER 40

Tabitha

Joppa

"This is stunning," Tirzah pronounced, holding up a lovely, hand-sewn apron and inspecting it with delight. "Tabitha, you made this yourself?"

"I enjoy sewing," Tabitha replied lightly, brushing aside her friend's praise. "It's not much, but I wanted to thank you for all the help you have provided with Laurel since my arrival in Joppa."

"That isn't necessary."

"Oh, but it is," Tabitha readily replied. "You willingly sacrifice several hours each day just to help me. I appreciate you more than you know."

"I'm not exactly a saint for that," Tirzah responded wryly. "I do get paid, after all."

"You get paid very little," Tabitha reminded her, honored by Tirzah's humility. "I wish I could afford to pay even more."

"Your friendship is payment enough," Tirzah

replied, her tone boding no argument. Carefully folding the apron, she gingerly placed it on an empty peg near her potter's wheel. "But I'm not sure I can wear this at the wheel."

"Oh?" Tabitha asked, disappointed. "Did I do something wrong? I've never made an apron for a potter before."

"Wrong?" Tirzah repeated, laughing. "Of course not! It's just so lovely, I couldn't bear to smear dirty clay all over it!"

Sharing a knowing chuckle, the two friends prepared to set out. Reaching for the basket of baked goods on the low table, Tabitha watched as Tirzah closed the wooden shutters and reached for her shawl.

"Are you sure you want to go through with this?" Tirzah quipped, her eyes sparkling with mischief. "If the religious leaders find out, we'll be excommunicated for life!"

"How will they know?" Tabitha pointed out. "We will be far removed from the synagogue beyond the city walls!"

"They have eyes everywhere," Tirzah muttered, shaking her head in annoyance. "But I promised I would join you, and so I shall—if you still insist on going."

"I insist," Tabitha grinned, following Tirzah out the door and watching as she expertly secured the lock.

Pocketing the key, Tirzah shook her head and released a long-suffering sigh. "It was wise to leave Laurel in Martha's care," she decided, swinging open the gate of the outer court and allowing Tabitha to pass through. "I'm afraid old Simon might scare her senseless."

"I'm afraid he might scare *us* senseless, too," Tabitha noted, receiving a rueful glance from her friend.

"I'm not afraid of anything."

"I'm beginning to think that's true," Tabitha chuckled as Tirzah re-latched the gate behind them.

The journey to Simon's house and adjoining tannery was a pleasant one. Tabitha relished breathing deeply of the salty sea air and the cool gusts of wind tearing at her head covering and honey-gold braid. Though accustomed to the shining city of Jerusalem with its fashionably paved avenues, wondrous marble structures, and of course, its crowning gem—the breathtaking Temple compound—Tabitha decided that Joppa possessed a natural beauty all its own. The quaint seaport town boasted cobbled ways, magnificent views of the rolling ocean waves, colorful bursts of seasonal flowers and verdant tendrils of ivy climbing ancient walls and trellises, and towering green palms that seemed to touch the sky itself. Strolling along the jagged shoreline with Tirzah, Tabitha followed her friend's lead by removing her worn sandals and delighting in the warm, damp sand tickling her toes. It felt like something out of a dream—basking in the warm sunshine while traveling the foamy shoreline of the stunning Great Sea.

Their sojourn had proven so pleasant that Tabitha almost regretted their arrival at the house of Simon. It was a rather impressive affair for an outcast, with towering walls sheltering a large estate behind a mammoth iron gate. Despite its immense size, both the house and adjoining tannery were starkly bare and unembellished, rather like the simple man who operated the business, Tabitha decided. Sheltered from the sea by a semi-circular cove of jagged rocks, the property was still startlingly close to the water's edge. On a perfect day like this, Tabitha supposed that must be an enormous advantage, but she shuddered to think of how those waves must roar and crash against the jagged rocks on a wintry, stormy night.

"This is my first trip to Simon's abode," Tirzah admitted, pinching her nose and grimacing in distaste. "I must say, the smell is overpowering. Far worse than the odor that lingers about his person."

Battling waves of nausea, Tabitha nodded her agreement, wondering how on earth she would manage to carry a conversation with Simon when her stomach threatened to revolt at any given moment. The stench had floated upon the air long before their arrival despite the hearty sea breezes that dutifully carried it away on the wings of the wind. But the closer they drew toward the main gate, the more overwhelming the stench became.

"Good morning, sir," Tirzah called out cheerfully, startling Tabitha as they approached a stoic-looking guard at the gate. "We have come to see Simon, the tanner."

Amused, the guard's lips curved into a sardonic smile.

"Is he available?" Tirzah asked politely, ignoring his leering grin.

"If he isn't, *I* am," the guard responded wolfishly, looking both women up and down.

"Pardon me, sir," Tirzah responded, clearly peeved, "but this is a pressing matter, and I don't think your master would appreciate your delaying us."

"A pressing matter, indeed," the guard sneered, shifting his attention toward Tabitha and giving her a look that made her skin crawl.

"She's right," Tabitha spoke up, assuming a mask of confidence reflective of her spunky friend's. "Simon will wish to see us right away."

"And who is it, might I ask, that seeks the pleasure of his company?" the guard drawled, patronizing them.

"We are representatives of the esteemed Joram of Joppa," Tirzah shot back, relishing the guard's astonishment and ignoring Tabitha's look of surprise. "Shall we inform the mightiest shipping master of this region that Simon's guard turned us away at the gate? I'm sure your demise would prove amusing to him."

Swallowing nervously, the guard swung open the massive gate without further delay, gesturing for another nearby guard to escort them in.

Crossing the sprawling outer court on the heels of the second burly guard, Tabitha murmured under her breath, "*Joram* didn't send us here, Tirzah! We came of our own accord."

"Of course, we did," Tirzah shot back, her chin lifting in triumph. "But the guard doesn't know that."

"And if Joram discovers you tossed about his name to gain entrance here?"

"He won't."

"I wouldn't be so sure," Tabitha responded nervously, hoping Tirzah hadn't inadvertently damaged her witness for Christ with the mistruth. Regardless, they had been granted access to the elusive tanner and, praying silently, she resolved to make the most of this rare opportunity.

"Wait here," the guard barked, ushering them into an empty, stone reception hall. "I will alert the master to your arrival."

***

After what seemed like an eternity of anxious waiting, Tabitha and Tirzah were alerted to Simon's impending approach by the sound of heavy footfalls traveling rapidly down a nearby stone corridor. A moment later, a surprisingly tall and strongly built older man emerged from the mouth of a torchlit corridor, his features and bearing fiercely defensive.

"Simon," Tabitha greeted cordially, hoping she sounded natural and cheerful. "Good morning, sir. It is an honor to meet with you."

Doing a fierce double take, the tanner clearly questioned Tabitha's sincerity. Folding massive arms over his barrel chest, he glowered at the two widows with unveiled suspicion, his eyes flashing in disbelief. "Old Joram didn't send either of you here, did he?" he demanded, surprisingly astute.

Exchanging a look of concern with Tabitha, Tirzah spoke up boldly. "Forgive me, my lord. We do, in fact, hail from Joram's estate. This young woman is Tabitha, his niece, and I work with them in his home. But I had to stretch the truth just a bit to appease that overzealous guard of yours at the gate."

Simon arched thick gray brows in skepticism.

"We wished to speak with you, sir," Tabitha plunged ahead, deciding that the old man was even more intimidating up close. His flashing eyes and taut features framed by an impressive gray beard, his towering frame, and bloody apron was enough to arouse concern in the stoutest of hearts. In her silent trepidation, she nearly forgot about the foul stench permeating the house and surrounding grounds.

"Now why would two upstanding women such as yourselves wish to speak with me?" Simon demanded, his gray brows arched in challenge. "What do you want? Surely you know your presence here has already rendered you both unclean."

"We are not concerned about that, sir," Tabitha spoke bravely, ignoring his glaring skepticism.

"No?"

"No, sir," Tabitha replied, wondering if Tirzah was regretting their bold venture yet. They hadn't experienced a particularly warm reception!

"You—Tirzah, is it?" Simon spoke unexpectedly, clearly catching Tirzah off guard. "I've seen you in the synagogue often. You are faithful in your attendance."

"Indeed," Tirzah responded with a nod, unperturbed.

"But you," Simon added, his kindling gaze falling upon Tabitha. "You're new around here."

"That's right," Tabitha confirmed, quivering inside. "I relocated to Joppa with my daughter after my husband's death. Joram, my uncle, has agreed to let me work for him in exchange for room and board."

Simon nodded his understanding, and Tabitha realized he was the first person she'd encountered without something negative to say about her uncle. Perhaps, having been deemed an outcast by acceptable society, he didn't consider himself worthy to judge. Her respect for him increased.

"Why are you here?" Simon asked frankly, clearly eager to return to his work.

"Simon," Tabitha began, plunging ahead before her own apprehension could silence her tongue, "have you heard of Jesus of Nazareth?"

"Who hasn't?" Simon responded simply, obviously wondering what any of this had to do with him.

"Then you must know He is the Messiah we have all been waiting for," Tabitha dared, carefully watching Simon's reaction. "I came today because I thought you should know how deeply He cares about you. Jesus ministered to those considered the scum of society—widows such as Tirzah and myself—and outcasts, as well."

"You came all this way to tell me about a dead Carpenter?"

"He isn't dead, Simon. The rumors about Him are true—He rose from the dead."

"Hogwash."

"I saw His resurrected body myself," Tabitha assured him, her countenance alight with sincerity.

Studying her face intently, Simon evaluated the young widow's sanity, his eyes narrowing as she persisted.

"Jesus is the Son of God, Simon—the only way to Heaven," Tabitha insisted, wondering if Simon was about to order his guards to escort her off the premises. "Even if the religious leaders ban you from God's presence, they cannot keep you from His love."

Appearing to wrestle with his own thoughts, Simon finally shook his head in frustration. "I am unclean."

"And you say this because the religious leaders deemed you so?" Tabitha dared, sensing Tirzah's eyes upon her.

Simon stroked his abundant gray beard, remaining silent.

"The religious leaders often took issue with my Lord, as well," Tabitha patiently explained, her eyes begging Simon to understand. "The Laws of God, Jesus obeyed; for there was no sin in Him. But the manmade traditions of the scribes and Pharisees, He openly evaluated with honesty and practicality. As you can imagine, this angered the religious leaders." Sensing Simon's impatience, Tabitha plunged ahead. "On one such occasion, when the Pharisees accused Him, Jesus said, '*Woe to you, scribes and Pharisees, hypocrites! For you cleanse the outside of the cup and dish, but inside they are full of extortion and self-indulgence.*' He was pointing out that many of the religious leaders went to great lengths to appear righteous, meticulously following the manmade ordinances their ancestors had presumptuously attached to the Law of God. But in their hearts, they were full of pride, condescension, and greed. Jesus went on to say, '*First cleanse the inside of the cup and dish, that the outside of them may be clean also.*'"

"Are you implying that the laws of God don't matter?"

"The laws of God always matter, and we should obey them without question," Tabitha assured him. "But, Simon, it is the condition of the heart that matters to God. Submit to Him, and He will show you how to walk beside Him. He will make you clean."

Simon simply studied her, stroking his long beard.

Based on his fierce persona and restless, impatient demeanor, Tabitha was shocked he had permitted her to speak so freely.

After what felt like a very long, uncomfortable pause, Tirzah spoke up, surprising Tabitha. "Have you any questions, Simon?"

Tabitha held back a smile, pleased that Tirzah had joined forces with her. Oh, if only Tirzah, too, would come to a full understanding of Jesus as the Son of God!

"You both believe this...this theology?" Simon finally demanded, his eyes narrowing.

"I believe it with all my heart," Tabitha affirmed.

"I am still a student of hers," Tirzah replied, eliciting a look of surprise from her friend. A student? Was she truly considering accepting the gospel truth?

"Young woman," Simon said sternly, his intense gaze directed at Tirzah. "This young widow, Joram's niece, has nothing to lose by embracing this strange new doctrine."

"Neither do you," Tirzah shot back, unruffled. "Perhaps you should consider it."

Tabitha held back another smile, admiring her friend's grit.

"But you, Tirzah, have much to lose," Simon reminded her. "Your friends and neighbors, your livelihood, even your place in the synagogue is upheld by your reputation here. You might consider thinking twice before conforming."

Biting her tongue, Tabitha resisted the urge to point out that she had, in fact, lost a great deal already, despite Simon's opinion. She had surrendered her home, her church, and loved ones to embrace

God's calling, taking the gospel to new lands. She was not immune to suffering loss, either.

"I know what is at risk, sir," Tirzah responded without batting an eye, filling Tabitha's entire being with hope.

"And must I relinquish my profession to gain the favor of this so-called Messiah?" Simon asked pointedly.

"I know very little about your profession, Simon," Tabitha honestly confessed. "Unfortunately, I don't know what it entails. But if your profession—or *any* profession, for that matter—requires you to sin against God, then yes, you must deny yourself, take up your cross, and follow Him. But if your profession is guiltless in the sight of God, then, no. To receive Christ as Savior, you must repent of your sins and turn to God. Then, by the power of the Holy Spirit of God, He will enable you to walk in obedience."

Wrinkling his brow, Simon appeared to be processing all she had shared.

"I suppose we have taken enough of your valuable time today," Tabitha smiled, offering the basket she had been balancing on one arm. "We shan't overstay our welcome, Simon. But if you have any questions at all, you may send word for me at Joram's estate."

Reluctantly accepting the basket of baked goods, the burly Simon appeared somewhat comical, hesitantly cradling a delicate basket of sweet pastries.

"I don't imagine the religious leaders will take kindly to this strange doctrine of yours," Simon observed, watching as a guard entered the bare stone hall to escort the women past the gate.

"Please remember that salvation is in the hands of God, not men," Tabitha exhorted him, pausing at the arched stone entry. "Even if you are not permitted to worship at the synagogue, you can worship in your heart—in spirit and truth—no matter where you are."

"And why would you waste your time coming all the way out here to speak with an outcast, a complete stranger to you?" Simon demanded, perplexed.

"Because Jesus led me here to see you," Tabitha responded without missing a beat. "He longs to gather you unto Himself, just as a father welcomes his beloved child home." With an encouraging smile, Tabitha turned to follow Tirzah and the guard into the outer court, leaving Simon to puzzle over her unexpected arrival and bizarre presentation.

Watching them go, he was strangely touched by one young widow's surprising concern for him.

CHAPTER 41

Kelila

Sychar

Kelila spent the remainder of the afternoon pacing the floor, utterly sickened by Simon's offer...and her own lack of resolve. Though her faith and logic assured her that the sorcerer was a wicked liar and a shrewd deceiver, her heart reluctantly pondered his mysterious insinuation.

Simon said he had spoken with her dead father.

In that exchange, her father had revealed his true feelings toward his youngest daughter.

Simon said that she, too, could commune with her departed loved one.

Releasing a groan of frustration, Kelila grasped her pounding head in trembling hands. She was utterly sick of pondering everything Simon had said!

Worse than that, she was disappointed in herself. Kelila knew the Scriptures well, and the Word of God clearly forbade the black art of necromancing—

communing with the spirits of the dead. She also knew that, according to God's Word, the dead could not communicate with the living. Any illusion of communion with the soul of a departed loved one was merely a clever deception from the enemy.

Despite all this, one nagging question continued to gnaw at her heart and mind: If Simon hadn't truly encountered the soul of her dead father, then how did he know of her father's death? And even more than that, how did he know there had been a rift between them?

Recognizing the sound of Philip's gentle footfalls outside the front door, Kelila drew a deep breath, attempting to compose herself. All afternoon, she had been tempted to go snatch her husband from his work in the fields alongside Ephraim, so eager was she to voice her nagging question. But knowing that Philip was earning income to help support them in their ministry, she had somehow resisted the urge to do so.

"Did you tell anyone about my father?" Kelila demanded the moment the heavy door creaked open and her husband stepped inside the lamplit room.

Looking at her in surprise, Philip closed the door behind him, dropping the latch in place. "Of course not," he responded, his eyes betraying questions. "Why?"

"Not even Ephraim or Adorina?" Kelila persisted, almost hoping her husband had betrayed her trust. At least then she wouldn't be given further reason to believe the sorcerer's outrageous claims! "You've told no one?"

"No one," Philip replied, bending to wash his dusty, work-stained hands with the clay pitcher and basin near the door. "I gave you my word I wouldn't speak of it."

Huffing in frustration, Kelila turned from him, resuming her frantic pacing.

"Why?" Philip repeated, perplexed. "Has something happened?"

"Simon knows about my father," Kelila tersely informed him, shaking her head in frustration and confusion.

"Simon the *sorcerer*?"

"Yes, the sorcerer," Kelila supplied bitterly. Pausing in the middle of the room, she was annoyed by Philip's look of surprised concern.

"When did you speak with the sorcerer?"

"He sought me out this afternoon on my way home from the baker's booth," Kelila replied, miffed by her husband's inquiry. "I certainly didn't go looking for him!"

"And he knew your father died?"

"Yes," Kelila sighed, feeling exhausted and on edge. "Worse, he claimed my father 'visited' him and desires to speak with me."

"Merciful God," Philip murmured, coming to his wife. Taking her hands in his, his brown eyes sought hers earnestly. "Kelila, Simon is a wicked man. We mustn't fall prey to his schemes."

"Are you saying it's all just a cruel, clever trick?"

"It could be."

"But if he didn't actually commune with my father, then how did Simon know he was dead, Philip?" Kelila demanded, dissatisfied with her husband's assessment of the situation. "And how could he possibly have known there was a rift between us, that I am tortured by the thought that Father may have died without forgiving me?"

"Sorcerers and magicians are highly trained and skilled in the art of reading people, Kelila," Philip assured her, squeezing her hands in his. "Naturally, Simon assumed your father was dead based on his observations of us."

"Why would he assume that?"

"Because you are a cultured, beautiful woman, Kelila," Philip responded without hesitation. "You carry yourself with the air of a lovely princess. What wealthy Cyrenian in his right mind would allow his daughter to marry a poor, unimportant Jew like myself? Of course, Simon would assume you were at odds with your father."

"Even if that were so, how did Simon know Father may have died harboring a grudge against me?"

"Your mere presence here would indicate such," Philip pointed out. "You are living in an unpopular, far-flung province, married to a poor traveling evangelist. It doesn't take a genius to realize your father wouldn't be thrilled about this arrangement, Kelila."

"I think you are grasping at straws," Kelila told him, withdrawing her hands and turning away. "You can't possibly understand how I feel! This uncertainty is tearing me apart, Philip! I've prayed and prayed for answers, so what if this is God answering my prayer? What if this is the Lord's way of assuring me of my father's forgiveness? Or providing a way for me to make amends one last time?"

"In light of your pain and uncertainty, I can see how tempting it is to believe that," Philip said gently, going to his distraught wife. Tipping her chin, he looked steadily into her eyes. "But God doesn't contradict His Word, Kelila. The Scriptures clearly forbid communion with spirits of the dead."

"But how can we know that for sure?" Kelila persisted, wanting to weep. "What if we have simply misinterpreted the Scriptures about it? What if we're wrong and I am missing an opportunity to make amends with Father?"

"Kelila, that opportunity perished with your father," Philip said gently, hurting for her. "Remember, the Scriptures tell us, '*the dead know nothing…their love, their hatred, and their envy have now perished; nevermore will they have a share in anything done under the sun.*' Could the Scriptures be any clearer than that? Once a person dies, they have nothing more to do with this temporal world. That's why it's so urgent that we embrace our calling in this life *now*, without hesitation—for it is but a vapor, a puff of wind, that soon vanishes."

"But what if we're wrong?" Kelila insisted in desperation. "That passage could mean any number of things, Philip. Perhaps it's symbolic."

"Then we must consider what else the Lord has to say about this matter, such as, '*There shall not be found among you anyone who makes his son or his daughter pass through the fire, or one who practices witchcraft, or a soothsayer, or one who interprets omens, or a sorcerer, or one who conjures spells, or a medium, or a spiritist, or one who calls up the dead. For all who do these things are an abomination to the Lord.*' How could one possibly misinterpret a passage as undeniably clear as this one?"

Crestfallen, Kelila turned away, wrapping her arms about her own slender frame and bowing her head as if attempting to shut out the cruel world.

"Oh, beloved," Philip whispered, turning Kelila around to face him. Wrestling against her doubts, Kelila looked away. "I think we must acknowledge a very real possibility here, one almost too frightening to comprehend."

Kelila lifted teary eyes to his, deeply unsettled by the urgency of his tone.

"Based on the information I have gathered about this sorcerer, I think it's highly likely he is far more than a skilled deceiver. I believe Simon has given himself to the evil one in exchange for the power and prestige he currently enjoys."

"What does that have to do with my father?" Kelila asked him, hating the battle raging in her soul.

"It's entirely possible that Simon has, indeed, communed with spirits—he may even believe it was your father. But as children of the Most High God, we know any such encounter is the deceptive ploy of evil spirits, agents of darkness."

"Are you saying *the devil* revealed this information to Simon?" Kelila asked incredulously.

"It's very likely, Kelila," Philip replied evenly. "The devil, or more likely his agents at work within the sorcerer. Having dabbled in forbidden arts for many years, Simon has opened himself to a host of frightful possibilities, including encounters with familiar spirits and demonic possession."

"But...but how? Only God knows the future, Philip."

"Remember the story about King Saul and the witch of En Dor?" Philip reminded her, his expression sober. "Assisted by demonic forces, she conjured up an image of the dead prophet, Samuel. And her prediction came true, even though her revelation was one of darkness, not of light." Allowing that information to sink in, Philip continued, "The devil is the great deceiver of men, Kelila. For thousands of years, he has studied the human heart and mind. He knows our weaknesses, and he knows exactly when to close in for the kill."

"Oh, Philip," Kelila wept, covering her face with her hands. "The Lord must be so disgusted with me. I'm supposed to be sharing the gospel, but here I am—doubting His Word and nearly giving in to temptation!"

"He knows your frame, Kelila," Philip said gently, stroking her lush black hair. "He knows your pain and uncertainty, your desperation to find peace in this hurtful situation. And He is here for you, to strengthen you in this moment of weakness. Cling to Him, don't resist His love."

"I want to cling to Him, Philip. I really do."

"Then trust Him. Trust His Word and choose to obey it."

Nodding slowly, Kelila cast a host of emergency prayers heavenward, begging the Lord for strength.

"I believe now is the time to stand firm, Kelila," Philip said, taking his wife in his arms and resting his chin upon her dark head. "We must see this situation for what it is: an attack from the pit of hell."

Shuddering, Kelila hid her tear-streaked face in her husband's broad shoulder.

"Satan hates our work here, hates to see so many Samaritans forsaking darkness to embrace the light of Christ," Philip said firmly. "If he can weaken our resolve, or worse, get us entrenched in unholy, godless pursuits—such as endorsing Simon's sorcery by communing with the dead, and thus deceiving these

Samaritan sheep to whom we are called—then the devil has won. We cannot allow him a foothold. Do you understand?"

Nodding her head in prayerful silence, Kelila closed her eyes. She could feel her husband's heart pounding beneath his tunic, almost in rhythm with the rushing blood pulsing through her throbbing temples. Taking a deep, steadying breath, she resolved to stand upon the promises of God, rather than falling prey to the deceptions of a wicked necromancer.

I will not be shaken, she told herself, lifting her head in resolve. Meeting her husband's gaze, she knew they were in agreement.

If Simon approached her again, she would be ready.

CHAPTER 42

Tabitha

Joppa

"Ahem…a word, please."

Glancing up in surprise, Tabitha saw Eli hovering in the simple stone doorway which the servants utilized to access the kitchen from the wide outer court behind the mansion. Lowering the heavy rod used to beat the dust from the enormous Persian rugs draped over wooden frames, Tabitha wondered what she had done wrong this time. Her uncle seemed to relish sending his overseer after her to check up on her, or worse, to question her work ethic. She almost felt sorry for the staid overseer, who seemed to appreciate Tabitha's sunny presence and Laurel's entertaining antics despite himself. She doubted he relished being sent to do Joram's dirty work.

"Yes, Eli?"

"Regrettably, you have a guest awaiting you, miss."

"A guest?" Tabitha blinked in surprise. It couldn't be Tirzah since she was already on the premises, occupying Laurel in Joram's lush, exotic gardens. Tabitha didn't like the idea of the little girl breathing in the resulting dust as she beat the rugs in this confining, walled-in stone court.

So who could it possibly be?

"Who is it, Eli?" she asked frankly, frowning slightly as she considered her untidy appearance. She must be quite a sight, with ruddy, dust-smeared cheeks, her long hair tied back in a plain head scarf, and her apron touting the stains of honest hard work. She was certainly not presentable for a guest!

"The master isn't going to like this," Eli fretted, nervously wringing his hands.

"Eli? Who is it?"

"A rather unpleasant old woman," Eli muttered, annoyed. "She has a tongue like a scorpion."

As Tabitha's eyes widened in disbelief, a surge of excitement coursed through her. She could scarcely believe it herself! Aflutter with anticipation, Tabitha dropped the heavy rod in her hand, hurrying past the puzzled overseer to welcome her guest.

"Thank you, Eli!"

"Don't be long," Eli called after her, clearly anxious, "or the master will have both our heads."

**

Having undoubtedly refused Eli's offer to be seated, Ruth stood awkwardly in the opulent reception hall, wringing her weathered hands and looking quite uncomfortable. The moment she spotted Tabitha hastening toward her, her eyes hardened in dismay.

"That took long enough," the old woman quipped in her gravelly tone.

"Ruth!" Tabitha exclaimed, delighted to see her. "What a pleasant surprise!"

"I was about ready to up and leave," Ruth huffed, ignoring Tabitha's obvious delight. Briefly looking the girl over, she arched a reddish gray brow in question. "Residing in a fine home like this, shouldn't you be sporting fancy robes and ordering the servants about?"

"Oh," Tabitha chuckled, tickled by the old woman's observation. "I am not a lady of leisure. I work for my uncle in exchange for room and board."

"Joram puts his own niece to work?"

"He's not entirely fond of me," Tabitha admitted with a rueful little smile.

"Well," Ruth harrumphed, a fist planted on her ample hip. "Joram always was a stubborn, greedy old fool."

Holding back a smile, Tabitha supposed perhaps, in a way, Ruth had just granted her a compliment.

"I'll get straight to the point," Ruth announced, dragging her threadbare shawl over her shoulders. "No point wasting your time and mine."

Tabitha simply waited, smiling patiently.

"That thing you said the other day about helping us widows of seafaring men," Ruth dared, and Tabitha saw it took a great deal of humbling herself to even voice the thought. "Did you mean it?"

"With all my heart," Tabitha replied, warmed to her core.

Ruth nodded slowly, clearly allowing that shocking bit of information to sink in.

"What can I do for you, Ruth?"

"Ain't for me," Ruth shot back, proudly lifting her chin. "I can take care of myself. But I know a few young widows with sickly little mites. They could do with some rations and a bit of warm clothing, if you can spare anything."

T*hank you, God,* Tabitha's heart cried in worship and thanksgiving.

"I wouldn't ask for myself," Ruth continued, her eyes shifting uncomfortably. "But them young'uns are barely grown themselves, and struggling to provide for their children."

"I am overjoyed to assist them in any way I can," Tabitha assured Ruth, taking the old woman's bony hands in hers. "I shall piece together some garments this evening and deliver them—along with some provisions—first thing in the morning."

"That would be most appreciated." Withdrawing her hands, Ruth stoutly maintained her crusty demeanor. "The children are wee toddlers and babes. I know of four or five in need of clothing."

Tabitha nodded her understanding, mentally piecing together the tiny garments she would soon design.

"I wasn't going to come here," Ruth confided, warily eyeing her surroundings. "But Adam thought you were sincere. Guess he was right."

It took Tabitha a moment to remember who Adam was—the kind young man at the vendor's booth. She'd have to remember to thank him, later.

"Shall I deliver the provisions to your home, or arrange a meeting with the widows?" Tabitha asked, eager to meet the young women to whom she would be ministering.

"You can leave everything with me," Ruth responded curtly, crushing her hopes of meeting them. "I'll see to it that the widows receive their share."

"All right, then," Tabitha agreed cheerfully, unwilling to allow disappointment to hinder this opportunity. "I shall see you tomorrow morning then."

"Good day," Ruth responded gruffly, turning to take her leave.

***

Tabitha was grateful Martha had been willing to lend her sewing needles and a few miscellaneous supplies she had been unable to bring with her from Jerusalem. Soon, she must visit the marketplace to make purchases of her own. Especially now that the widows and orphans of the region were receptive to her help!

Oh, if only I still had my mother's loom, Tabitha thought, though her joy overwhelmed her fleeting disappointment. She knew she could make do with the limited supplies she had, and the Lord would enable her to fulfill His purpose.

Just thinking about the cherished loom her former mistress, Mary, had taken such great pains to secure for her in Jerusalem sent a little pang through her heart. Smiling at the thought of her lady, she recounted the encouragement-filled letter she had recently received from her, brimming with practical but godly parenting advice and biblical exhortation. It had certainly proven a great comfort to her.

Now, having recently put Laurel to bed, Tabitha settled down on one of the plush chairs in the great reception hall with a lap full of soft wool, thankful for the steadily burning lamps lighting the large room. She would need to purchase some additional oil lamps to brighten her own small bedchamber—this way, she could sew each night without leaving Laurel alone. She didn't wish to continue sewing in this vast, empty hall each evening—especially since her daughter slumbered in their own room near the servant's quarters.

Slowly but surely, the tiny garments began taking shape in her skillful hands. Delighting in her task, Tabitha worked quickly and efficiently late into the night, even stitching some warm blankets for the babies and shawls for the widows. She hoped the young women would be pleased with her work! Though simple and unembellished, the pieces were sturdy and well-made.

"What do you think you're doing?"

Stiffening in dismay, Tabitha glanced up from her work, annoyed by the sight of her scowling uncle looming beneath one of the curtained entrances. What he was doing up at this late hour, anyway?

"Well?" Joram demanded, a silver brow arched imperiously. "You should be in your chambers at this hour."

"Typically, I would be," Tabitha answered honestly, forcing a sunny smile. "But a concerned widow has brought a matter to my attention, and I am trying to help."

"Help with what?" Joram ground out, peeved.

"The young widows residing in the tenements near the docks are in dire poverty," Tabitha explained, supposing her uncle wouldn't understand... or care. "I am piecing together some little garments for their children."

"You can scarcely clothe yourself, and yet you

bother yourself with the wretched brats belonging to filthy sea rats?"

"They aren't rats," Tabitha said, evenly meeting her uncle's gaze. "They are *people*. And the widows they have left behind need help."

"You are a foolish woman," Joram said coldly, closing the distance between them, his eyes resting upon her in disdain as he towered over her. "Why work yourself to the bone for ungrateful lowlife?"

Resisting the urge to point out that Joram didn't mind if she worked herself to the bone for him, Tabitha responded instead, "I don't do it for them, my lord."

"No?" Joram drawled, lowering himself into the chair across from his niece, much to her dismay. "Who is it for, then? You? Do you take pleasure in lording your self-righteousness over the rest of us?"

"I do it for Jesus," Tabitha explained, wrestling to maintain her composure. An angry outburst is exactly what Joram wished to extract from her, and she refused to give him what he wanted.

"Jesus?" Joram repeated blankly. "The rogue Rabbi you first mentioned by letter?"

Shocked her uncle even remembered that first letter in which she had so neatly outlined the message of salvation, Tabitha realized she had yet to expound upon the subject with her uncle. He'd scarcely given her the opportunity to speak one word, much less share the gospel in its entirety! And yet now, in these unexpected, late-night hours, God had graciously provided an opportunity to reach this lost sheep for whom she had forsaken everything. By God's grace, she might lead him to the Good Shepherd and streams of living water!

"Well?" Joram huffed, leaning forward in his chair. "Can't you answer a simple question?"

"Before Jesus returned to His Father in Heaven, He told us something very important about the last days and the Final Judgment," Tabitha explained, praying silently for guidance. "As a God-fearing Jew, you undoubtedly know that the time will come when the Messiah shall return to earth with the angels in all His glory. And all the nations will stand before Him to be judged. At that time, He will divide the people into two categories—the sheep and the goats—placing the sheep on His right hand, and the goats on His left."

"And you presume this Jesus—a dead Carpenter from Nazareth, mind you—is this glorified Messiah?"

"I *know* He is," Tabitha assured him, setting aside her sewing. "Now, to the sheep at His right hand, the King will say, '*Come, you blessed of My Father, inherit the kingdom prepared for you from the foundation of the world: for I was hungry and you gave Me food; I was thirsty and you gave Me drink; I was a stranger and you took Me in; I was naked and you clothed Me; I was sick and you visited Me; I was in prison and you came to Me.*'"

"How poetic," Joram observed with a sardonic curve of his mouth. "And how might mere mortals deign to assist the heavenly King?"

"How funny that you should ask," Tabitha smiled, catching her uncle off guard. "The sheep in this parable asked the very same question, and Jesus assured them, '*Assuredly, I say to you, inasmuch as you did it to one of the least of these My brethren, you did it to Me.*'"

Joram's closed expression indicated his glaring skepticism.

"But the story doesn't end there," Tabitha continued, carefully watching her uncle's flickering hazel-green eyes so similar to her own, "for He has a special word for the goats on His left hand, as well—'*Depart from Me, you cursed, into the everlasting fire prepared for the devil and his angels: for I was hungry and you gave Me no food; I was thirsty and you gave Me no drink; I was a stranger and you did not take Me in, naked and you did not clothe Me, sick and in prison and you did not visit Me.*' Confused, the goats will ask, '*Lord, when did we see You hungry or thirsty or a stranger or naked or sick or in prison, and did not minister to You?*' And He will answer their inquiry, saying, '*Assuredly, I say to you, inasmuch as you did not do it to one of the least of these, you did not do it to Me.*' At this point, those who refused to render aid in this life will be destroyed, and the righteous will enter unto eternal life."

"That's quite an imaginative tale." Grimly stroking his chin, Joram's sober expression indicated his disdain.

"It's more than a fanciful tale, my lord. It is the truth—a glimpse of what is to come."

Joram's lips tipped sardonically, reminded of another young woman of his distant past, so eager to serve those in need.

"So in answer to your initial question, my lord," Tabitha gently explained, "I sew these garments not only for the suffering widows and orphans of this region but also for Jesus, my Lord and Savior whom I love. How can I not serve Him gladly when He sacrificed everything for me?"

"I've known better women than you," Joram scoffed, his eyes hardening in his seething bitterness. "Their good works couldn't save them, either."

"You're right," Tabitha easily replied, surprising him. "No amount of good works can save me or anyone else. Even the most righteous soul among us cannot compare to a holy God."

"Then why, pray tell, do you stubbornly persist in this madness?"

"Followers of Jesus, also known as followers of the Way, strive to do good works because they love Jesus and long to serve Him, not to earn His love. We needn't earn His love because we already have it."

"All your good works are but an exercise in futility," Joram scoffed, irritated. "You yourself confess your works won't save you!"

"Of course, they won't," Tabitha smiled. "But faith in Jesus Christ and His shed blood upon the cross will."

"Your doctrine is bizarre and strange, bordering blasphemous."

"You must know the Scriptures point toward a Messiah who will rescue us from sin, restoring us to God," Tabitha pointed out. "Is it really too difficult to believe that the Messiah has finally come?"

"A dirt-poor, uneducated Carpenter hailing from a filthy, godforsaken town seems like an awfully poor candidate."

"God resists the proud, my lord," Tabitha carefully reminded him. "Jesus came in humility and meekness to save us from sin."

Ignoring her, Joram selected one of the tiny garments from the woolen pile Tabitha had placed on the gold-encrusted, marble-topped table between them. Holding it up for inspection, his eyes flickered slightly, betraying his surprise and admiration. "You are a decent seamstress."

D*ecent,* Tabitha thought, resisting the temptation to roll her eyes. Joram's fleeting expression had betrayed his obvious approval of her skill! Was there no end to his pride and condescension?

"I have some mending for you," he challenged, heedlessly tossing aside the tiny garment and rising imperiously. "I shall have Eli deliver the work to your private chamber. And you shall speak of it to no one, you hear? Not even that pesky potter woman of yours."

Though she was tempted to argue with him, Tabitha somehow held her tongue, strangely intrigued.

Intending to take his leave, Joram drew his elaborate silken robe closer about his frame. Pausing beneath a heavily curtained exit, he barked tersely, "What ailed your late husband?"

Tabitha's head came up in surprise, completely unprepared for her uncle's abrupt query. Wondering how much she should tell him, she answered quietly, "He was murdered."

"Murdered," he mused. Clearly, Joram hadn't been expecting that. "Was his killer brought to justice?"

Steeling herself against the familiar waves of debilitating grief, Tabitha sensed the Holy Spirit urging her to speak the truth. "Stephanos was stoned by an angry mob, instigated by a Pharisee named Saul of Tarsus and the religious leaders of Jerusalem."

Joram's brows lifted in surprise.

"Stephanos is in God's hands, my lord," Tabitha

said quietly, meeting his gaze with faith-filled certainty.

"And the man who plotted against him—Saul of Tarsus, yes? What happened to him?"

"He now rages against the followers in Jerusalem," Tabitha answered honestly. "His aim is to snuff out the light of the gospel, once and for all."

"You must crave vengeance upon this man."

"He is deceived by a cruel adversary," Tabitha told him, reminding herself as well as her uncle. "On the contrary, I pray for his salvation every day."

"You are a foolish, misguided woman."

"I am a child of God, a daughter of the King of kings, and safe in the everlasting arms," Tabitha responded with great conviction.

"Safe?" he sneered. "Your husband was *murdered* for spouting off the same bizarre doctrines!"

"No," Tabitha gently corrected him. "Stephanos laid down his life for the sake of Christ and the furtherance of the blessed gospel, the salvation of all mankind."

"Yes, indeed," Joram warned ominously, slipping into the gathering shadows. "And I imagine you'd do very well to remember that, too."

CHAPTER 43

Tabitha

Joppa

Tabitha arose even earlier than usual the following morning, eager to tackle as many chores as possible before sun-up in preparation for her impending trek to Ruth's tenement apartment to deliver provisions. Working like a whirlwind, she accomplished nearly half her list for the day before the sun had fully risen above the glittering Mediterranean.

Allowing herself a moment to remove her dusty apron, change into fresh garments, and freshen up, Tabitha decided to twist her long honey-gold tresses into a simple knot, pinning it at the nape of her slender neck. Recalling the aggressive sea breezes of the bustling harbor, she selected her sturdiest head covering, securing it in place with a tight band. After dressing a sleepy Laurel—who squirmed and writhed in protest—and braiding the girl's wispy brown curls, Tabitha decided it was time to be off.

The short trip to the docks was pleasant, for the sun's searing summer heat wouldn't reach its full strength for several hours yet. The cloudless sky was a pale blue, and as Tabitha approached the sprawling harbor, she noticed the sea remained the color of slate at this early hour, shortly after sunrise.

Hastening toward the long row of market stalls on the tenement's lower level, Tabitha steeled herself for the steep flights of stone stairs awaiting her. With a large basket balanced on one hip and her daughter clinging to the other, she carefully crossed the street, cautious of any oncoming traffic. It wasn't uncommon for rumbling ox or mule-drawn wagons to rattle down the cobbled way at a dangerously fast pace, the drivers paying little heed to harried pedestrians.

"Good morning to you!"

Relieved to have safely crossed the street, Tabitha saw Adam stationed behind the fruit vendor's stall, flashing that winning smile of his. "Hello," she smiled back, warmed by his friendly demeanor. His manner was painfully but sweetly reminiscent of her dear Stephanos and the beloved brethren she had left behind in Jerusalem. If it weren't a near impossibility, she would have assumed the man was a fellow believer!

"I see Ruth has accepted your kind offer," Adam grinned, noting the heavy basket she balanced carefully against her hip.

"And I hear you had a little something to do with that," Tabitha shot back with a knowing smile.

"Ah, Ruth's concern for the younger widows would have eventually outweighed her pride and she would have come to you of her own accord," Adam assured her a bit playfully. "I merely quickened the process a bit."

"I appreciate your help," Tabitha told him honestly. "Thank you, Adam."

"No, thank *you*," Adam shot back, his brown eyes betraying his appreciation. "It is remarkably kind of you and your husband to take an interest in the widows of this region."

Your husband? Taken aback, Tabitha almost corrected Adam's error but then thought better of it. Pointing out the fact that she was an unmarried woman might appear forward, possibly even inappropriate. Adam must have simply assumed she was married since she had a daughter, as well as the means to help ease the burden of the needy.

"Many of the widows here remain in desperate need, with no one to turn to," Adam was saying, drawing her attention back to their conversation.

"Does the local synagogue offer aid of any sort?" Tabitha inquired curiously.

"It's not a top priority of theirs, to say the least," Adam admitted ruefully.

"Do you attend services?" Tabitha asked. It was unlike her to forget a face, and she certainly didn't remember seeing Adam there.

"Unfortunately, my father is too ill to venture that far," Adam explained, his tone betraying deep concern. "As such, we worship together at home. It's uncustomary, I know," he added frankly, "but a friend of ours is a former Pharisee and very learned in the Scriptures. He often leads our little services in my father's house."

"It sounds lovely," Tabitha smiled. "Though I do wish your father was well."

"Your family is free to join us anytime you wish," Adam told her warmly. "Our door is always open to you."

"Thank you," Tabitha responded, sorely tempted to join him the following Sabbath simply to escape the suspicion and hostility of the local synagogue. "I shall keep that in mind."

"That's quite a hefty load you have there," Adam observed, changing the subject and offering little Laurel a genuine smile as Tabitha hoisted her a bit higher on her hip. "Do you need any assistance hoisting that heavy basket up the flights of steps?"

"I think I can manage," Tabitha assured him, gratified by his willingness to help. "But thank you, nonetheless."

"All right, then," Adam chuckled, aware of her eagerness to distribute the provisions she had brought. "Ruth is waiting for you upstairs."

Smiling her deepest gratitude, Tabitha prepared to take her leave.

"Have fun," Adam called after her, his tone laced with mischievous good humor.

Returning his smile, Tabitha took her leave, anxious to fulfill her promise to Ruth.

***

Surprised to find Ruth's door already open, Tabitha ventured cautiously inside, unsure about what kind of reception she might receive. Much to her amazement, she found the tiny tenement overcrowded with raggedly clothed women huddled around Ruth, their young children knocking noisily about in their active play.

"There she is," Ruth observed, the women pausing mid-conversation and turning to get a good view of Tabitha.

"*Shalom*," Tabitha greeted, a bit confused. "Good morning!"

"These here widows were nigh desperate to meet you," Ruth grumped, crossing the room to accept Tabitha's basket. "When I told them there was a new widow in town who wished to help them, they couldn't believe it. They wanted to see you for themselves."

Surprised, Tabitha glanced up at the young women, all of them poorly dressed, several in need of a decent bath. She recognized most of them from the synagogue and hoped perhaps they, too, remembered her. That fact alone might set them at ease.

"My," Ruth declared after placing the heavy basket on her low table and lifting one of the little garments for inspection. "You're a fine seamstress."

The widows' eyes filled with hope and admiration at the sight of the sweet little garments and the freshly baked bread, dried fruit and fish, nuts, and produce.

A desperately young woman cradling a sleeping baby stepped forward, her features gaunt, her dark-circled eyes glittering with tears. "How can we ever thank you?"

Before she could answer, Laurel squirmed from her arms, eager to join the other children in their play. Releasing the little one, Tabitha laughed as Laurel rushed the group of children, giggling in sheer delight.

"Your daughter is beautiful," another widow added timidly.

"But why would a perfect stranger do such a kindness for us?" another dared, receiving a look of exasperation from several others who feared Tabitha might take offense.

Actually, Tabitha welcomed the question, for the Lord had graciously provided the perfect opportunity to share the gospel with these dear women!

Eyes sparkling with joy, Tabitha dared, "How many of you have heard of the Man named Jesus?"

***

Returning home after a delightful morning of prayer and conversation, Tabitha thanked the Lord for the widows' eager reception of the gospel. Though none had yet confessed Jesus as Lord, they were eager to learn more about Him—except for Ruth, of course. The gravelly old woman was stubborn and independent as ever. More than that, Tabitha sensed she dealt with deep secret, hidden pain. How could she not, having lost both son and husband?

Offering a silent prayer for the stalwart widow, Tabitha returned her thoughts to the younger women she had met that morning. They had wept for joy when she promised to return the following week with more provisions. She also intended to share a bit more about Jesus. Perhaps His love in action through her would eventually win them for the truth.

Entering her uncle's vast reception hall, she was surprised to see Tirzah pacing about like a caged tigress.

"Tirzah!" she exclaimed. "I'm so sorry, friend. I've returned a bit later than I expected."

"How did it go?" Tirzah asked casually, though Tabitha sensed her friend's burning curiosity.

"Oh, Tirzah, it went so well!" she exclaimed, doing a little dance after releasing Laurel, who ran into "Aunt Tirzah's" arms with a squeal of delight.

"Old Ruth is finally lightening up, then?" Tirzah surmised, hoisting an excited Laurel onto her hip.

"Well, I wouldn't go that far," Tabitha chuckled, amused. "Tirzah, your mother-in-law is nothing like I expected!"

"*Former* mother-in-law," Tirzah amended somewhat tersely, clearly eager to change the subject. "Did you meet any of the widows?"

"Several," Tabitha informed her, excitement sparkling in her hazel-green eyes.

"Were they appreciative?"

"Oh, yes," Tabitha replied, warmed by the memory of time spent with them. They were such kind, timid souls, anxious to meet the needs of their children amidst extremely harsh circumstances.

"Tirzah," Tabitha said, watching with a smile as her friend produced Laurel's favorite doll, eliciting a squeal of delight from the bubbly toddler. "You know you can always make yourself at home in my private quarters? You needn't pace up and down the reception hall!"

"Not according to your uncle," Tirzah shot back.

"What do you mean?" Tabitha asked, her hackles rising. Had Joram forbidden Tirzah to do so?

"Apparently, I am not to set foot in your quarters until you have completed some *secret* project he left for you in there!"

"My uncle said this?"

"Of course not," Tirzah grumped. "He sent Eli,

his little minion, after me!"

"Hmm," Tabitha mused, her curiosity getting the best of her. "I'd best go see what he's left for me to do."

"You mean, you don't know?"

"I suppose I will soon," Tabitha grinned. "Will you be all right with Laurel until I return?"

"That's a silly question," Tirzah scoffed. "Go on, go on. We'll wait for you in your uncle's gardens."

CHAPTER 44

Tabitha

Joppa

Bursting into her bedchamber, Tabitha's observant eyes immediately fell upon the most stunning bridal gown she had ever seen, draped almost reverently across her narrow bed frame. Covering her mouth in awe, Tabitha approached her bed, gently dropping to her knees and fingering the soft folds of the breathtaking ivory gown.

She had never seen anything quite like it. The fabric was lush and soft, embroidered with delicate silver thread and laced with elegant, intricate beadwork. Though the gown was now stained with age, torn, and had likely seen a few hungry moths in its day, it was still ravishing. Tabitha could hardly fathom how stunning it must have appeared when new.

Tracing the lovely beads along the high neckline, Tabitha suddenly realized this must have been Pennie's wedding dress, the gown she had lovingly worn for Joram on their wedding day.

Instantly, her practical mind kicked into action. A gifted seamstress, she knew she could mend the dress as good as new. As for reviving its initial luster and shine, she would have to put in a good deal of creativity and effort for that.

Resolving to restore the gown to the very best of her ability, Tabitha set right to work. Joram wasn't even aware that she knew about Pennie, so she decided to refrain from asking him any questions about the bridal gown. That would only stoke his ire and incite his wrath. Perhaps, in time, he would trust her enough to tell her about the compassionate aunt she had never known. She would simply tackle the project head-on, a labor of love for the hardened man who hadn't dared to love another since the loss of his beloved bride.

Perhaps, if she persisted in faith and patience, Joram would someday understand the incomparable, unwavering love of Christ, the faithful Bridegroom.

***

Philip

Sychar

Returning home from the fields, Philip allowed himself a moment of prayer and respite alongside a quiet, trickling stream shaded by tall trees boasting verdant green canopies of leaves. Jesus had often found solitude in lonely places where He communed with His Father, and Philip had learned to follow suit very early in His walk with the Lord. How he savored the serenity of uninterrupted prayer, basking in the beauty of creation and knowing the masterful Creator heard him!

Lowering himself onto a large gray rock at the stream's marshy edge, Philip folded his hands in his lap, leaned his head back, and closed his eyes, contemplating the Scriptures he planned to share during the evening prayer service.

Nearly the entire village turned out for services now, all of them eager to learn more about the compassionate, gentle Savior who once visited their forgotten little city, turning the lives of many upside down. Most had embraced Him as their Lord and Savior, though some still flocked to Simon's sorcery booth, looking for an "easier" or more "expedient" way to solve their problems. And Simon was all too eager to accept them, along with their hard-earned coins.

The thing that most concerned Philip was Simon's seeming determination to win back his followers, no matter the cost. Just thinking about how the despicable man had preyed upon Kelila in her moment of weakness sent Philip's heart hammering into protective overdrive! Clearly, Simon—like his father, the devil—sought the slightest crack in the door of their hearts, eager to locate a foothold and in turn, establish a fearsome stronghold.

"You look tired, but it would seem you've found a lovely little place for respite."

Stiffening in dismay, Philip recognized the sound of the alluring voice directly behind him just as a pair of slender hands with bejeweled, manicured fingers landed on his broad shoulders.

Jerking away in surprise, Philip stood and turned

to find himself face-to-face with Helena, the sorcerer's muse.

"You didn't expect to see me here, did you?" Helena purred, coming around the large rock and closing the distance between them.

"Greetings," Philip said hesitantly, his every nerve ending alive and tingling with caution. His mind was flooded with ghastly images of Joseph and Potiphar's wife. All he knew was that he must escape—and fast. Lifting his gaze heavenward, he offered a silent prayer of desperation, asking the Lord to deliver him. To be alone in this quiet place with a seductive woman was a recipe for disaster, and undoubtedly, Helena was aware of that.

"Did Simon send you?" Philip dared, one sandaled foot sliding on the slippery bank as he neared the water's edge.

"Is it difficult to believe I have long sought a private audience with you?" Helena teased, sizing him up like a cat with a mouse.

"I do apologize, my lady," Philip said, turning to leave, "but I really must be going. I have a rather pressing matter at hand—"

"And is that why you sat here alone, whiling away the time and enjoying the sweet tranquility? Because you're in a hurry?"

"I really must go. But if you wish to discuss something with me, I shall be speaking tonight in the public square. Please feel free to join us—"

"Silly man," Helena chided, clicking her tongue and taking another bold step toward him. "How am I to have a moment alone with you all those people vying for your attention?"

Groaning inwardly, Philip skirted the riverbank, attempting to go around her. The woman appeared as a vision from Homer's Odyssey in her sheer, sleeveless white robe and glittering jewels. He imagined many men had fallen prey to her seductive wiles, and he certainly didn't wish to be counted among them.

God, get me out of here!

"You entice me." Taking his arm, Helena attempted to stop him. "Surely you see I am a powerful woman, drawn to mighty men."

"You belong to Simon," Philip pointed out, sweating in his distress. Her fingertips felt cool upon his flushed skin. "It isn't proper to seek my company."

"Do I look like a *proper* woman to you?" she teased, releasing his arm and striking a rather dramatic pose, her sleek figure emphasized by sheer, gauzy clothing and the thick golden belt strapped about her slender waist. "I want to know your secret," she whispered into his ear, her breath coming out in hot puffs against his neck. "I am willing to purchase this information in whatever method of payment you wish," she added, gazing up at him with clear blue eyes that glowed like dangerous fire.

Philip distanced himself from the sorceress with several purposeful steps, sickened by her suggestion. "Surely you must know I have no power in and of myself," he exclaimed, struggling to hold his anger in check. "The miracles you have witnessed are by the power of the Holy Spirit at work in me. I can do nothing in and of myself."

"But how does one obtain this great Spirit?"

"Only by true repentance and acceptance of Jesus Christ as the Son of God," Philip told her, certain she wouldn't appreciate his response. "Again, I will be addressing this very matter before sunset this evening. If you have any more questions, please join us."

"You look nervous," Helena observed, flashing her dazzling smile and closing the distance between them once again. "Are you afraid of me?"

Yes, actually, Philip thought, peeved. *Afraid of the great deal of trouble you could easily stir up!* Though he had tried to be polite, he realized he must now *flee.* Helena had dismissed his every effort to end the conversation civilly. With his marriage and his ministry at stake, he knew better than to prolong this dangerous encounter any further.

"Philip? What are you doing out here, brother?"

Thank God! Philip could have wept for joy when Ephraim emerged from the nearby path, his dark eyes betraying pointed questions as his gaze darted back and forth between the modest evangelist and the haughty seductress.

"Ephraim," Philip declared, raising a fist in greeting. "I am glad to see you, brother." *More than you'll ever know!*

"I was passing by and thought I heard voices," Ephraim explained, his eyes darting toward Helena and revealing his keen distrust.

"Helena stumbled upon me as I was taking a few moments to pray," Philip explained, his eyes communicating far more than his words.

"I see." Nodding his understanding, Ephraim looked toward the bold, painted woman. "Please excuse us, but our wives must be wondering what has happened to us. We must be going now."

Helena's eyes betrayed her intense chagrin. "Then you'd best be hurrying home to the anxious little wives," she purred, her tone dripping with condescension. "We wouldn't want them to worry now, would we?"

"Good day," Philip managed as he joined Ephraim on the path, all too eager to escape the dragon's lair.

Helena watched them depart, her eyes glowing with fury. If Simon wished to keep his power and position, he had better step up his game. His coveted prestige was fading fast in light of the maddening young evangelist.

She would speak to Simon, harshly if need be. She refused to relinquish their power. Only fate would tell if he was up to the challenge.

CHAPTER 45

Kelila

Sychar

Inwardly stewing, Kelila sat on a low wooden stool near the door, attempting to listen as Philip addressed the large group of faithful Samaritans assembled in the town square. Mulling over the shocking story about the sorceress which Philip had nervously recounted after returning home, she couldn't believe the nerve of some women. To think—that the wicked seductress had gone after a married man, *her* married man! She was sorely tempted to bang down the door of Simon's nasty little booth to give his kept woman a piece of her mind!

O*h, but that wouldn't be very Christlike, would it?* she reminded herself, annoyed. As an evangelist's wife, she knew she should pity the sorceress and pray for her, not loathe her. The woman was drowning in darkness and depravity. She certainly couldn't expect Helena to behave like a modest woman of purity and character, given the circumstances! With a bit of effort, she returned her attention to Philip's sermon once again.

Night was swiftly falling, and Kelila realized that Philip was making his closing remarks. Relieved, she decided she would like nothing better than to fall into bed beside her husband, succumbing to sweet, dreamless sleep. She was exhausted—mind, body, and spirit. How desperately she longed for respite!

"Are you well?"

Shaken from her deep reverie, Kelila glanced over her shoulder to find a worried Adorina standing behind her. "I'm fine," she whispered back, wondering if the perceptive woman sensed her inner struggle. Though she had done everything in her power to mask her pain, Kelila knew she hadn't been acting like herself lately. It was as if her strength had been sapped, her zest for life stolen, her hope utterly dimmed.

Oh, Lord, I feel so weak, so useless to You right now, she prayed listlessly, her gaze sweeping over the sea of people to whom she had been called. Their faces shone with eager expectation, their countenances alight with joy. Overhead, the first evening stars began to wink and twinkle almost playfully, set in a velvety pastel canopy of swirling sunset hues. The entire square was washed in the breathtaking colors cast by the setting sun, the bright canopies casting slanted shadows along the broad street.

Nothing about this calling has proven easy, Kelila thought, seriously questioning her own endurance. First, she had been required to relinquish her dream of putting down roots and building a permanent home with Philip. After that, she had experienced constant discontent, and only by the grace of God had she battled against it and overcome. And finally, the sudden death of her father had nearly paralyzed her with guilt, grief, and fear. Now she moved woodenly about, feeling overcome with exhaustion most days. Perhaps it was the grueling toll of stress and anxiety that had so efficiently sapped her strength.

B*ut Philip is right,* she reminded herself, straightening her drooping shoulders with firm resolve. *The devil hates our work here. The fact that he has come against us in every possible way is evidence that God is at work. I cannot give up. I must press on.*

Suddenly realizing that Philip was offering the closing prayer, Kelila quickly bowed her head, hoping no one had noticed her embarrassing blunder. Anxiously folding her hands in her lap, she tried to focus on her husband's earnest prayer. She felt Adorina's slender hand come to rest upon her shoulder and almost wept, touched by the stoic woman's silent compassion.

Philip had scarcely uttered the last *amen* when the sorcerer arose from the midst of the crowd, almost appearing to materialize like an apparition rising from the grave. "Before this lovely little gathering disperses for the night, I'd like to share an important word with you," he said, his dark eyes glittering like fiery coals, his lips twisting in an enigmatic smile.

Kelila's gaze snapped toward Philip, instantly wary. Adorina, too, exchanged concerned looks with her husband, who stood near Philip with legs splayed and hands clasped behind his broad back.

Without bothering to obtain Philip's permission, Simon floated through the crowd toward the front of the gathering, his smoldering presence warning those nearest him to make way. Drawing alongside Philip beneath the stall's gently flapping canopy, Simon clasped his hands together, his every movement calculated and presented with dramatic flair.

"Greetings, my brothers and sisters," the sorcerer pronounced, his tone deceptively gracious and welcoming.

Writhing inwardly, Kelila shot a pointed look at Philip. Surely he didn't intend to let this man address the people from their very own threshold. To permit such would seemingly condone his profession and speech!

Clearing his throat in discomfort, Philip turned to the sorcerer. "It is getting late, and these people should return to their homes before darkness closes in."

"This will take but a moment."

"Simon, the meeting has ended."

"You heard him, Simon," Ephraim put in, drawing protectively alongside his comrade. "Go home."

Glancing over her shoulder, Kelila exchanged looks of concern with Adorina. The Samaritan woman stood still as stone, her dark eyes flashing in indignation, her fists clenched at her sides. Kelila couldn't help but wonder if she was considering going after the sorcerer herself! Turning to survey the crowd, Kelila saw the confusion on their faces. Several stood, poised, as if considering fleeing for their lives. She couldn't help but consider the prospect herself!

And then she saw Helena, standing on the farthest fringe of the crowd. Her cold blue eyes, kindling with hatred, were pinned upon Philip.

Heart pounding, Kelila suddenly realized who had instigated this uncomfortable situation. Helena had failed to obtain Philip's secret through seduction; thus, she had arranged a showdown.

Casting a desperate look toward Philip, Kelila prayed God would grant him wisdom to overcome.

"I must say, I am surprised by your lack of hospitality," Simon drawled, his mesmerizing eyes falling first upon Ephraim, then Philip. "I thought you preached love and kindness toward all. Are you afraid for me to speak? Afraid I might have more power than you?"

Tension crackled heavily in the air, so thick Kelila thought she could easily slice it with a knife. Closing her eyes, she prayed fervently, sensing that Adorina was praying, as well.

"We've been over this, Simon," Philip responded readily. "I have no power in and of myself. The signs and wonders you see are proof of the Holy Spirit at work."

Ignoring him, Simon turned to the people, his majestic robes fluttering in the cool evening breeze, his features eerily illuminated by burning torchlight. "My people," he addressed the breathless crowd, his tone resonating with confidence and authority, "the sheep of my pasture," he continued, turning Kelila's stomach, "I have been patient. I have waited for you with open arms, even as this clever charlatan snatched you, one by one, from the safety of my pasture."

Clenching her fists, Kelila considered calling down fire from heaven to consume the dreadful man.

"Now, I shall prove once for all that I am the great

396 | RACHAEL C. DUNCAN

power of God, and this man—a liar and a deceiver," Simon cried out, lifting his arms heavenward. "I possess the power of God, the knowledge of good and evil. I possess the power of life and death, and by this mighty display I shall prove once for all my prowess. Even the spirits of the underworld must perform my bidding. Can this simple Jew profess the same? Watch therefore and be amazed."

Stomach turning, Kelila rose upon shaky legs, clasping Adorina's arm as Simon closed his eyes, chanting in a manner that caused the hairs on the back of her neck to stand on end. The crowd exchanged nervous looks, apprehensive about Simon's intent.

"Enough of this!" Philip shouted, approaching the sorcerer with Ephraim hot on his heels.

"By the powers that move mightily within me," Simon shouted, his eyes rolling back in his head, "I command you, spirit, come forth!"

Putting out his arm, Ephraim halted Philip in his course as an ethereal mist arose from the earth, encompassing the sorcerer and seemingly materializing into the wavering form of a somber African man, his stance proud, his dress and ornamentation exceedingly elaborate.

Gasping in very real fear, Kelila swayed as if she would faint. Steadying her friend by the shoulders, Adorina's dark eyes flashed in anger. "What *is* that?" she hissed into Kelila's ear, referencing the bizarre apparition before Simon.

"My father?" Kelila whispered hoarsely, her heart pounding in her throat like ancient war drums. Gazing upon the face of what *appeared* to be the departed, her former resolve to stand against Simon's devious schemes nearly evaporated. She was shaken—utterly shaken to her core—as spiritual forces raged in her heart and mind.

The crowd cried out in fear and dismay as Simon released a string of laughter from deep within his throat, the bizarre hues of the steely-eyed apparition reflected upon the sorcerer's cruel features.

Eyes hardening in uncharacteristic fury, Philip approached the sorcerer head-on, utterly ignoring the demonic vision he had conjured up. "Simon, I command you to stop this madness!" he shouted.

"And who are you to command me, Jew?" Simon sneered, turning wild eyes upon the apparition. "Have *you* power over the spirits of the dead?"

"Only our God possesses the power of life and death!" Philip declared forcefully. "When Jesus Christ rose from the dead, He snatched the keys of Death and Hades from the evil one, once and for all! You have no power here, Simon!"

"I imagine your audience might disagree," Simon quipped with a wicked grin, his eyes sweeping ominously over the frightened, cowering crowd. "Now you have seen who wields the most power here," he informed them coldly. "Now you can return to me!"

On the heels of Simon's bold invitation, the shimmering image of the powerful-looking African man turned his head as if in slow motion, undulating like the flora at the bottom of the sea.

Kelila's knees nearly buckled under her weight when the apparition turned and looked directly at her, as the Holy Spirit within her battled against the doubt and confusion rearing its ugly head. Grinning like a wicked fiend, Simon clasped his hands together, gleefully approaching a trembling Kelila.

"You, my dear girl, know who this is, do you not?" he declared as Philip and Ephraim cut him off, standing like two powerful sentries between Kelila and her opponent. "Pray, tell us!" Simon mocked, shouting around the two strong men. "Who is this man, Kelila? Humor us—do tell!"

Oh, God! Oh, God, help!

Glancing at the frightened crowd, Kelila's terrified gaze fell upon Helena. The woman's features were twisted with laughter and contempt, relishing Kelila's torment.

And then the Spirit of the Living God coursed through her, strengthening her faith and bolstering her resolve. By the grace of God, she recognized the apparition for what it truly was—*a deception from the pit of hell.* Simon thought he had found his foothold, a chance to kick the door of her heart wide open. The chance to disprove her faith once and for all, and before the entire village, no less.

Turning her determined gaze upon the sorcerer, Kelila straightened, her entire being resonating with the fearless confidence known only by children of God. "I rebuke you, Simon, in the name of Jesus Christ, the Son of God, who loved me and gave Himself for me!"

Philip and Ephraim turned to look at Kelila in shock at the mighty shout that escaped her lips, for it was the cry of a warrior in battle with victory in sight.

Stepping around Philip and Ephraim, Kelila addressed the people for the first time since her arrival in Sychar, her eyes blazing with confidence, her faith fully restored. "My husband speaks the truth, for only God possesses the power of life and death. The

Scriptures are clear—communion with spirits of the dead is strictly forbidden."

Marveling at her courage, the crowd exchanged anxious glances, nearly paralyzed with fear, their eyes reflecting the disturbing image of the apparition before them.

"This 'spirit' that Simon has conjured up is nothing but a clever deception," she cried out, throwing her arm in the direction of the fierce image resembling her dead father. "It is nothing but a spirit of darkness masquerading as an angel of light. Simon hoped I would believe it was my father, but I know the Word of God, and I stand against this deception from the devil and his fallen angels!"

Turning to face the apparition head-on, Kelila declared in a loud voice that nearly shook the entire square, "In the name of Jesus Christ, I rebuke you! Depart from us, you spirit of deception, and never return!"

Face contorting in grotesque rage, the eerie, rippling image evaporated in an instant, drawing a shout of triumph from the crowd and a cry of fury from the sorcerer. Turning to address the people once more, Kelila said boldly, "Now, I challenge you to decide for yourselves—who possesses the most power here? Simon, the sorcerer, or Jesus Christ, the Son of God?"

CHAPTER 46

Mary

Jerusalem

It was late, too late to be strolling about.

Approaching a gently splashing fountain illuminated by flaming torchlight, Mary pondered the cryptic message she had received earlier that evening. A sealed parchment scroll had been flung over the high wall of her outer court, and one of her guards had stumbled upon it during his evening round. Exasperatingly enough, the scroll bore no signature and the seal was not inscribed.

Even so, the message had sounded urgent, desperate even.

Pausing before the elegant, landmark fountain in the heart of the Upper City just a few short paces from her own villa, Mary contemplated the letter's mysterious plea, requesting her presence under cover of darkness at this very fountain, this very night. *I have questions about Jesus. Questions only you can answer,* the letter had insisted.

Daniel, the captain of her guard, insisted it was nothing but a ruse and a deadly trap, nearly forbidding her to acquiesce. But after a vigilant hour of earnest prayer, Mary realized the Holy Spirit was, indeed, guiding this mission. She would go, unafraid. Her safety was in God's hands.

It was a perfect night, the kind of evening one might find depicted in romantic literature or in a whimsical child's tale. Glancing up at the full silver moon rising high overhead, Mary judged the lateness of the hour. Allowing her gaze to sweep over the ethereal, moonlit scene, she noted graceful marble benches cast in silver light, set upon a stone pavement of swirling mosaic patterns. The fountain was a massive affair, boasting shimmering cascades of clear water which accumulated in a marble-rimmed pool below its lovely stone pedestal. The large recreational area was sectioned off by a semi-circular, colonnaded wall boasting impressive stone arches with steadily burning torches mounted symmetrically between each arch. Towering palms dotted the way, their verdant green fronds casting writhing shadows on the pavement as evening breezes whispered through broad leaves. Overhead, a canopy of brilliant stars glistened and gleamed, appearing rather like the vast multitude of heavenly hosts.

Approaching the fountain, Mary put forth her slender hand, delighting in the delicious feeling of cold, tiny water droplets upon her warm skin. A gentle breeze whispered its way through the palm fronds overhead and tickled the plain head covering she had discreetly selected before setting out. It simply wouldn't do to don expensive, conspicuous robes, thus making herself a far more appealing target for robbers or brigands undoubtedly patrolling the vacant streets.

Shivering in the chill breeze, Mary drew her shawl closer about her shoulders, briefly considering taking a seat upon one of the inviting marble benches before the fountain. But she quickly dismissed the idea, deciding it was far more important to remain alert, vigilant. She had no desire to become a sitting duck.

Perhaps I should have accepted Daniel's counsel by stationing my guards around the perimeter here, she thought. And yet, whoever had left the urgent message for her had gone to great lengths to remain anonymous. If they even suspected her guards were nearby, they would surely abandon the mission rather than compromising their identity, vanishing into the night. Thankfully, Daniel and the other guards knew her location. If she failed to return home within the hour, they would descend upon the scene like hungry birds after seed. Besides that, she had a sneaking suspicion about who was going to show up for this meeting. And if her instincts could be trusted, that particular "someone" was far from dangerous, posing little to no threat to her.

Crash! The sound of shattering glass sent her heart slamming into overdrive. Poised to flee, if necessary, Mary's sharp eyes scanned the broad, darkened avenue before her from whence the heart-stopping explosion of sound had erupted, her ears pricked.

Wait... Too late, she recognized the decoy for what it was. Certain she heard quiet footfalls directly behind her, Mary spun on her heel just as a rough feed sack was crammed over her head. Crying out, her voice was muffled as a firm hand clamped over her mouth and a strong arm encircled her waist. Exploding into action, Mary swung at the air like a madwoman, determined to overcome her assailant. The grip about her midsection tightened painfully as strong fingers dug into her face, sealing her mouth shut. Battling against her assailant with all her might, she landed a solid elbow blow to his ribcage, eliciting a groan of shock and pain. Gasping for air beneath the heavy feed sack and her assailant's firm grasp, she landed another firm kick against his shin, receiving yet another grunt of agony. And then the terrifying sensation of cold, sharpened steel against her throat instantly halted her struggle. Wondering if she was about to die, Mary went utterly still, committing her soul—and her son—into the hands of her Creator.

"Stop moving," a male's gruff voice commanded her, wrought with frustration and impatience.

Heart pounding wildly, Mary considered her odds against at least two armed, male assailants.

"You're coming with us."

***

Kelila

Sychar

Gathered around the table in Ephraim and Adorina's cozy little home, Kelila clutched a mug of warm, soothing tea in both hands, overwhelmingly grateful for the Holy Spirit's intervention that night. Though she'd felt dead on her feet just a few short hours ago, she now felt alive and energized with passion and purpose—despite the exceedingly late hour. The enemy had sought to deceive and entice her with the greatest of temptations, and yet God, in His mercy, had proven faithful, revealing the sorcerer's schemes for what they were—cruel, demonic deceptions intended to trap and utterly destroy.

"Your boldness before Simon was thrilling, Kelila," Adorina was saying, leaning over the table and covering her friend's hand with her own. "Your courage was a beautiful testimony to my people."

"Frankly," Ephraim added, "I didn't even recognize you."

"As Philip says so often," Kelila quickly spoke up, glancing fondly at her husband beside her, "I can take no credit for what happened tonight. It was the Holy Spirit in me, enabling me to stand firm."

"Praise God," Philip breathed, drawing her a bit closer.

"I told you that man was trouble!" Adorina put in forcefully, slamming her mug down on the table and receiving a look of fond amusement from her husband, who was cozied up beside her. "Still, I can't believe you resisted that temptation, Kelila. Had he conjured up such a convincing mirage of my mother, I'm not sure I would have possessed the strength to resist."

"By God's grace, you would," Kelila assured her. "Besides, you are learning the Scriptures just as I am. You, too, understand that the image Simon conjured up tonight was *not* my father."

"I shudder to think what it *really* was," Adorina

declared, accepting her husband's proffered hand.

"Demonic forces are undoubtedly at work," Philip said with a firm shake of his head. "The Scriptures make it perfectly clear that the dead do not commune with the living, and yet Satan continues in his deceptions. In his unspeakable cruelty, he sends dark agents to target grieving, hurting people. Just imagine the power evil spirits could wield against us masquerading as departed loved ones."

The four pondered that dreadful possibility in somber silence, sobered by the devil's hateful ploys.

"You should have told us about your father, Kelila," Adorina finally spoke, her tone serious. "Had we known about his death, we could have borne your burden with you. That's what the body of Christ is called to do."

"I see that now," Kelila admitted. "I just didn't want to burden the new believers with my own troubles."

"First, Ephraim and I hardly count as new believers," Adorina pointed out with a wry smile. "After all, we accepted Christ long before you did."

"Well, that's true," Kelila laughed. "I was still in Cyrene when Jesus visited this place, met you at the well, and changed your life—and your village!"

"And, second, *your* burdens are *our* burdens," Adorina persisted in her serious, straightforward way. "In Christ, we are one body. How can one of us suffer without the rest of us feeling it, too? We were made to support and encourage each other through difficult times, not to suffer in silence."

"Don't worry, I've learned my lesson," Kelila assured her with a rueful smile, receiving a playful tweak on the shoulder from Philip. "The only thought that continues to plague me is the matter of my father's salvation. I will never know—at least, not in this life—if he accepted Christ."

"But remember what Candace wrote in her letter," Philip gently reminded her. "The night that he passed away, he'd spent the evening asking your sister dogged questions about our faith. Candace said he went to bed upset. So upset, in fact, that they thought he had made himself sick."

"And if I knew my father at all," Kelila agreed with tears shimmering in her eyes, "the only reason he became so upset is because his heart was convicted by the truth. That's how my father has always responded when crossed—by instantly lashing out in frustration. But oftentimes, my father would deeply ponder the options presented to him. Despite his pride, he was a logical man."

"In that case, it is entirely possible he accepted the Lord before his death, Kelila," Ephraim told her, his eyes betraying his conviction.

"I certainly hope so," Kelila nodded. "That remains the fervent prayer of my heart."

"Well, it's late," Philip finally said, pushing back from the comfortable table. "I suppose we should be on our way—"

"Absolutely not," Adorina interrupted stoutly, crossing her arms over her chest. "Lodge with us tonight. In the morning, you can return home."

"We certainly wouldn't wish to impose—"

"It's no imposition," Adorina interrupted again. "In fact, I insist."

"Thank you, my dear friend," Kelila declared, relieved. She certainly hadn't relished the idea of traveling home in the dark, especially after turning a dangerous sorcerer completely against them!

Rap, rap, rap!

Both couples started at the completely unexpected knock at the door, exchanging looks of puzzlement and concern. Warily, Ephraim rose slowly, approaching the front door with Philip close behind him. The women also rose from their chairs and waited a reasonable distance from the door, their avid curiosity nearly overcoming their concern.

Swinging open the door, Ephraim's eyes hardened fiercely at the shocking sight of Simon, the sorcerer, standing anxiously upon the threshold.

Somehow, Kelila managed to suppress the sharp intake of breath threatening to escape her lips. Glancing at Adorina, she saw that her friend's features reflected the same stunned disbelief she was experiencing.

"I hoped to find you here, Philip." Appearing unsure of himself for the first time since the evangelist's arrival, Simon cleared his throat, clearly attempting to ignore Ephraim's kindling gaze. Shuffling his feet and glancing nervously about, he inquired nervously, "May I have a word with you?"

CHAPTER 47

Mary

Jerusalem

Thrust onto a surprisingly comfortable, straight-backed chair, Mary waited, her hands bound at the wrists and resting calmly in her lap. Despite the smelly feed sack covering her head, she believed she still possessed a decent grasp of her surroundings. After being loaded onto a small cart, undoubtedly mule-drawn, for the consistent *clippety-clop* of little hooves betrayed the animal's identity, her capturers had driven the wagon a considerably short distance before stopping, securing the animal to a fence or post of some sort, and assisting her from the rough wooden bed. Having paid close attention to the distance and the direction in which they had traveled, Mary knew they hadn't left the Upper City. Rather, she was certain they were now in the priestly precinct near the graceful, colonnaded bridge which adjoined the magnificent Temple Complex.

The house into which she had been led was not nearly as palatial as many of the presiding religious leaders like Caiaphas, the high priest, or Annas, his prestigious father-in-law. Gauging by the reasonably sized outer court she was forced to travel before being thrust through a seemingly wide doorway, she decided the home must belong to someone of somewhat high status. The lack of servants or household staff also affirmed her suspicions—that the owner was wealthy, but not exceedingly so.

"I have questions," a familiar voice said, far gentler and kinder than the voice of an attacker should be. "All I require from you is honesty. Then we shall return you to our meeting place. From there, you may return home."

Lips tipping in a knowing smile, Mary straightened in her chair, amused, her sneaking suspicions confirmed. "Good evening, Gamaliel."

The breathless pause lingering heavily in the air was more than enough to validate Mary's assumption.

"I certainly wouldn't have expected you to be the kind of man who goes about the city armed with a knife," Mary continued, her tone betraying amusement rather than condemnation. "Will your kitchen staff notice its absence? If so, you might consider returning it before we proceed. After all, your home is but a stone's throw away from here. It wouldn't take long."

Her quip was met by a long-suffering sigh, followed by Gamaliel's terse command, "Remove the feed sack."

"But, my lord—" the second voice, also vaguely familiar, protested.

"Remove it!" Gamaliel's tone boded no argument. "I should have known better than to try fooling this perceptive young woman."

Mary could sense the hesitation of Gamaliel's accomplice as he grudgingly removed the sack from her head. Squinting against the steadily burning lamplight, Mary swiftly assessed her surroundings. It would seem she was sequestered in a rather impressive office boasting a large desk facing two plush, gilded chairs—one of which she currently occupied. Rather like her own study, the back wall was lined with wooden shelves boasting numerous cubby holes housing important scrolls and ledgers. Though Gamaliel, the highly respected president of the Great Sanhedrin, sat behind the desk with hands clasped before him, she knew this was not, in fact, his home office. Chancing a daring glance toward his accomplice still standing nervously at her elbow, the feed sack clutched in anxious hands, she arched a slender brow in recognition.

Meeting her gaze with a hint of exasperation, Agabus' wide eyes begged her not to give away his secret. Clearly, the young Pharisee didn't wish for his superior to know he was already investigating the Way for himself.

Honoring his silent plea, Mary couldn't help but be amused by his inner chagrin. *This must be his house,* she decided, surprised the young man boasted such a fine home. She realized Gamaliel must have been concerned she would recognize the familiar route to his own palatial estate, which she had frequented many times before embracing the Way. *Besides that,* she thought, *it would prove nearly impossible to smuggle me into his home, unnoticed, with dozens of priests, scribes, Pharisees, and Sadducees buzzing about.*

"You could have simply requested an appointment, you know," Mary informed the stoic leader across the desk, her gray eyes flashing with hidden merriment. "You needn't have gone to all this trouble, though I must admit, I'm flattered by all the attention," she added, lifting her bound wrists for inspection.

"Agabus, remove her bonds."

Bending nervously over her chair, Agabus did so, tossing the thin rope into a nearby basket used for collecting old scraps and waste.

"I do apologize for the manner in which this meeting has been conducted," old Gamaliel confessed, rubbing the back of his neck as if deeply troubled, "but I'm sure you can see why anonymity was preferable in this instance."

"And why is that?" Mary pressed, her curiosity piqued.

"I suppose that's of little consequence now," Gamaliel sighed, looking far older than she remembered. Clearly, the strain of leadership within squabbling, divisive ranks was taking its cruel toll. "You are a difficult woman to fool, which makes this matter all the more confounding, I'm afraid."

"Meaning?" Mary asked plainly, folding her hands in her lap and glad to be rid of those nasty ropes.

"Meaning, you have embraced the controversial doctrine of the Rabbi Jesus with reckless abandon, without thought for yourself, your family, your business, or your well-being," Gamaliel expounded, stroking his gray beard in his endearing, familiar way.

"On the contrary," Mary responded, sensing the eyes of Agabus upon her, "I have embraced the Way with all those things in mind, especially since Jesus is the only Way to life and the source of all true wisdom."

"And this you believe," Gamaliel observed, marveling at her unwavering conviction, "with all your heart and soul."

"I do."

"I shall get straight to the point, Mary," Gamaliel said tiredly, exchanging a brief look of trepidation with the anxious Agabus. "I do not wish to alarm your guards with a long absence."

Mary nodded her regal head, crossing her legs and draping one slender arm casually over the back of her chair. Gamaliel couldn't help but think she appeared rather like a queen in her own court, despite her unnerving circumstances.

"Perhaps you—better than most—understand the turmoil and upheaval rocking our blessed city to its core," Gamaliel sighed, deeply, inexplicably troubled. "It pains my heart to witness my fellow Jews—brothers and sisters, neighbors, relatives, and friends—arrested, tortured, even put to death."

Mary nodded once more, comprehending and sympathizing with his secret pain.

"Though I have not yet reached a satisfying conclusion regarding this Jesus of Nazareth, I do not condone the Sanhedrin's response to this movement," Gamaliel admitted, shaking his head in a tired manner that betrayed his weariness. "Even so, a religious and political ball has been set in motion, and I am but one, lone man standing against a living, breathing monster intent upon destruction."

"Your description of the Great Sanhedrin is impeccable, my lord," Mary remarked, cocking her head to observe his reaction. "With the exception of but a few good men."

Leaning back in his chair, Gamaliel stroked his long gray beard, watching Mary closely. "You believe I can put a stop to this?"

"You are the great Nasi, my lord, the most revered and highly esteemed teacher in Judea and beyond," Mary patiently reminded him. "If anyone can put an end to this madness, you can."

"You must understand there will be bloody consequences regardless of my actions," Gamaliel told her, almost as if attempting to convince himself, as well. "The desired end is peace and harmony within our blessed nation. If I cast my vote against your sect, bloodshed and strife will undoubtedly continue. And if I stand in favor of your religious faction, I face even higher odds of violence and revolt. As you can see, neither outcome is favorable."

"I would think obedience to God the most favorable outcome, my lord, regardless of what is at risk."

"Obedience," Gamaliel muttered, his tone tinged with bitterness. "And how is one to know what that is? Yet again, our nation is torn, divided. Very few agree."

Mary refrained from speaking, sensing the Holy Spirit at work in the heart of this great man. He had everything to lose —from an earthly perspective, that is. She understood his hesitation to condone the Way before the Great Sanhedrin. Despite his lofty position, he might very well share the same bloody fate as Stephanos, their beloved evangelist, should he choose to take a stand.

"It all comes down to this, Mary," Gamaliel solemnly stated, folding his hands over the desk and meeting her gaze with burning intensity. "I cannot dissuade the Sanhedrin from hunting down your people, one by one. I can, however, guarantee that the persecution will cease—*if* the followers of the Way will keep their faith to themselves. Cease from preaching, cease from proselytizing, cease from antagonizing our religious leaders, and I can guarantee that your loved ones will abide in peace and safety."

Mary met his gaze with an air of quiet strength and firm resolve.

"I'm sure you understand that I am not asking you to relinquish your faith," Gamaliel persisted, his aging features shadowed beneath his hooded prayer shawl. "I am only asking the followers to be discreet. Your very lives depend upon it, and it pains me to watch my people suffer. Surely, it must pain your heart, as well."

"Indeed," Mary responded, her gray eyes flickering in challenge. "Even so, I cannot honor your request."

"And why ever not?" Gamaliel beseeched her, his eyes betraying his hopelessness and frustration. "Surely this is not the world in which you wish to raise your son, Mary. I fear for my grandchildren and my great-grandchildren, day after day. Surely you wish to stop this utter madness, to intervene."

"I certainly do," Mary responded without missing a beat. "But not at the cost of my salvation, the salvation of my loved ones, or the salvation of the world. Jesus was unmistakably clear when He said, "*Whoever denies Me before men, him I will also deny before My Father in heaven.'"*

"And I am not asking you to *deny* Him, Mary," Gamaliel persisted in exasperation. "I am simply asking you to be *quiet*, discreet."

Mary held his gaze, her own burning with conviction. She could almost feel the respected Pharisee's anxiety like a tangible force in the room, tainting the entire atmosphere. Agabus, too, shifted in obvious discomfort, his dark eyes flitting from the regal woman seated in the elegant chair to the humble, most respected teacher in the Jewish nation seated behind his desk.

"Your concern for us is indeed noble," Mary finally spoke, her luminous gray eyes conveying her gratitude. "And perhaps there may come a time when the Lord advises a bit more discretion on the part of believers. However, today, the command is this: *Go therefore and make disciples of all the nations.* Today, the call is to stand firmly against opposition, proclaiming the gospel to all men. The Holy Spirit has strengthened and emboldened us to do the will of God, and we cannot forsake it."

Sighing deeply, Gamaliel exchanged another telling look with the troubled young Pharisee standing at Mary's elbow.

"Then I suppose there is nothing more I can do for you," Gamaliel sighed, his tone inexplicably grieved. "I am afraid your fate is sealed."

"My fate is in God's hands," Mary told him quietly, her eyes gleaming with steadfast trust. "As is the future of all His people."

Looking away, Gamaliel ran a troubled hand over his covered head, releasing another deep sigh. "Agabus, please escort Mary back to our meeting place. It is late. A woman shouldn't travel alone at this hour."

Exchanging a long-suffering look with his superior, Agabus' dark eyes betrayed his distaste for the mission. "Yes, my lord."

Gripping the gilded arms of her chair, Mary tilted her head, studying Gamaliel with a question in her eyes. "Your message said you had questions about Jesus, my lord. Questions only I could answer."

"My questions pertained to the followers' willingness to serve Him in secret," Gamaliel replied, folding his weathered hands. "You answered that question for me, did you not?"

"I suppose I did," Mary replied, saddened that Gamaliel's cryptic message had proven to be nothing more than a clever ruse. He had known she would refuse no one the opportunity to meet her Savior, even at risk to her own life. "Good night, my brother," Mary said warmly, rising from the chair. Leaning over Agabus' desk, she covered Gamaliel's folded hands with her own. "May my Lord and Savior Jesus Christ grant you the peace you seek."

Turning away, Mary followed Agabus from his office, her heart breaking for her dear, old family friend. She couldn't be certain, but she thought she had detected a faint sheen of tears reflected in the eyes of the gentle teacher.

CHAPTER 48

Mary

Jerusalem

"Thank you," Agabus said under his breath as he and Mary reached their original meeting place near the central fountain. "For not betraying my secret."

"Gamaliel does not know you are seeking the truth?" Mary asked him pointedly, looking him squarely in the face.

"*Seeking* is a rather strong word," Agabus amended, holding up a hand as if in protest. "I have questions about your Rabbi. That is all."

"Then come to our gathering tomorrow night," Mary beseeched him, her bright eyes daring him to take courage. "The apostles will answer any questions you may have."

"If I showed my face at your forbidden gathering, word would be out before the night's end," Agabus said bitterly, his severe black garments fluttering in the evening breeze. "Unlike you, I prefer to remain discreet."

"But at what cost?" Mary asked him earnestly.

"Your soul?"

"Only if you are correct in your way of thinking."

"I am," Mary asserted boldly. "Jesus is Lord, Agabus. Surely you know this."

"I must be certain before doing anything… anything foolish," the Pharisee muttered under his breath, clearly agitated. "Should I embrace this way of life—"

"The *only* Way of life," Mary interrupted him with an enigmatic smile.

"Should I embrace it," Agabus continued, his expression betraying his annoyance, "I could—I *will*—lose everything."

"And thus we have come full circle," Mary stated calmly. "We've had this discussion before, Agabus."

Looking away in shame, Agabus released a troubled sigh.

"I have been praying for you," Mary confessed, surprising him by placing a firm hand upon his shoulder. "May God work mightily in your life, Agabus, displaying beyond any shadow of doubt that Jesus Christ is indeed the Son of God."

Lifting solemn eyes to hers, Agabus' pained expression betrayed his surprise and inner turmoil.

"I believe that God will reveal this to you, Agabus," Mary declared, her lips tipping in a knowing little smile. "It is only a matter of time."

***

Kelila

Sychar

The summer month of Av swept in rather like the arid breezes overtaking the region, ushering in not only the sweltering heat, but delightful surprises, as well.

Having spent recent weeks investing heavily in the residents of Sychar, Kelila felt she now knew and understood her Samaritan neighbors far better than before. Feeling led by the Holy Spirit to do so, Kelila intentionally took notice of the needs of those around her, offering assistance whenever possible. Just in the last week alone, she had sat patiently with a sick child, aided a middle-aged couple in the care of an elderly relative, and delivered several warm meals to a young mother who was feeling particularly under the weather. Now, she wondered why it had taken her so long to realize her role as a minister's wife by reaching out to her community with joyful abandon. It wasn't that she had chafed or rebelled at the idea; she simply hadn't thought of it until recently.

It's almost as if the dreadful face-off in the village square with Simon bolstered my faith and courage, reminding me of the importance of this mission, the sanctity of this blessed calling, Kelila thought. True, she still deeply grieved the loss of her father, aching over the reconciliation she so desperately desired, the reconciliation that never came. But, by God's grace, she had learned to entrust her hurts and fears to the Lord, focusing instead on the tasks He had placed in front of her. She could scarcely believe how much had transpired in the few short weeks since then.

Now, traveling the worn, familiar path to the village well alongside Adorina, Kelila decided that Sychar was truly becoming a thriving community of believers, eager to serve God and love their fellow men. It was lovely to behold!

With the shocking conversion of Simon, the sorcerer, the village had experienced a far greater measure of peace. Apparently, the unexpected show-down in the village square had finally convinced the former sorcerer that God's power far surpassed the enemy's. To everyone's great shock and amazement, Simon now met with Philip at every available opportunity, plying the patient evangelist with endless questions and etching everything he learned onto his writing tablet with an elegant golden stylus.

"It still staggers me," Adorina confessed once they reached Jacob's famous well, "watching a sorcerer seated at the table with an evangelist, desperate to learn all he can about the Word of God."

"It is certainly beyond anything I could have imagined," Kelila agreed, placing her empty stone jar upon the well's wide brim.

"How does Simon seem to be faring?" Adorina asked frankly, expertly attaching her vessel to the line above the well and lowering it into the deep, darkened cavern. "Is he an able student?"

"Philip says so," Kelila replied, watching as Adorina hoisted her heavy jar, now brimming with fresh water, from the depths of the well.

"You don't sound sure," Adorina pointed out, propping her jar on one hip and studying the young woman with a practiced eye.

"Well…" Kelila stammered, uncertain about how much she should say. Though Philip had tried to emphasize the importance of forsaking one's old ways to embrace the new and living Way, Simon seemed markedly hesitant to do so. Though he studied with Philip often, taking fastidious notes and plying him with difficult questions, he had not yet discarded the tools of his former trade, nor had he remedied the questionable circumstances regarding his promiscuous consort. Instead, they continued living together, even as Simon stoutly insisted there was no longer any physical activity between them. Even so, the situation was uncomfortable, reeking of dishonesty and perversion. That aside, Helena made it abundantly clear she detested the followers of the Way with every breath she drew. Even if Simon truly abstained from indulging in a physical relationship with her, it was highly likely the former prostitute would soon persuade him to abandon his newfound faith.

"Well...*what*?" Adorina persisted, aware of Kelila's distraction. She hadn't even attempted to draw water yet.

"It's a bit complicated, that's all," Kelila responded hesitantly. "Simon has much to learn, many changes to make. It won't be easy. Philip says we must pray for him without ceasing." Receiving no response after what felt like a particularly long pause, Kelila turned to look at her friend.

Adorina stood still as stone, her mouth open, her dark eyes wide. The stone jar slipped from her grasp, punching into the soft green earth with an unpleasant *thud*, the water gushing out like a rapid fountain. Clasping her hands over her mouth, Adorina shook her head in wonder, her eyes filling with tears.

"Adorina?" Kelila drew alongside her friend, following her gaze.

And then she saw it. A small envoy of believers from Jerusalem traversing the faded path Kelila herself had taken with Philip to reach Sychar! Blinking in stark surprise, Kelila studied the distant but familiar figures, her heart fluttering in frantic excitement. *Surely my eyes deceive me!* But no, there was the Apostle John, Simon Peter with his wife, Anaia, and—wonder of wonders—*Mary*, leading the way!

"Mary!" Kelila cried, abandoning her jar on the stone ledge and running toward the approaching entourage, arms outstretched. "Simon Peter! John! Anaia!"

Within moments, Kelila and Mary were in each other's arms, laughing and crying as the rest drew up to them, grinning broadly. Adorina, too, hesitantly joined them, her serious features conveying the deepest awe.

"Adorina, this is Mary of Jerusalem," Kelila explained, pulling away to introduce the two believing women. "She led me to Christ in the Upper Room."

"I had nothing to do with that whatsoever," Mary chuckled, taking Adorina's hand in greeting. "It was the Spirit who drew you, Kelila. And, Adorina, I am overjoyed to finally meet you."

"And this here is Simon Pet—"

"Simon Peter and John," Adorina finished for her, her dark eyes widening in amazement. "I remember them well."

"And we remember you," John spoke up, his boyish features alight with joy and recognition. "Greetings, Adorina. I see you have not forsaken the Lord."

"Never," Adorina said vehemently, blinking back tears.

"And this lovely creature is my wife, Anaia," Simon Peter added, drawing his petite young wife further into the joyous circle. "Anaia, this is Adorina."

"The woman whom Jesus met at the well," Anaia

finished softly, her warm eyes reflecting wonder. "Adorina, you have become a legend in Jerusalem. I believe your faith will be passed down throughout the generations until the end of time."

"That is unlikely," Adorina chuckled in her frank manner. "But thank you, Anaia, nonetheless."

"We received word that Peter and John were coming," Kelila explained, thrilling at the prospect of worshiping and studying with these dear brethren once again. "And I hoped that perhaps you would travel with your husband, Anaia. But, Mary, I hadn't the slightest idea you would be joining them! I am nearly overcome!"

"I couldn't let my niece have all the fun now, could I?" Mary teased, exchanging mischievous smiles with Anaia. "And we didn't send word about my joining them because I wished to surprise you, Kelila."

"You certainly did!"

"Candace had also hoped to accompany us, Kelila," Mary told her gently. "But little Rufus has taken ill, and as you can imagine, she was reluctant to leave him."

"Oh, no," Kelila breathed, her eyes conveying her concern for her beloved nephew. "Is he all right?"

"It is nothing more than a summer cold, but we mothers are prone to worrying, are we not?" Mary smiled, squeezing Kelila's arm in gentle assurance. Changing the subject, she said warmly, "Kelila, you are positively glowing, sister. This place must certainly agree with you."

Funny, Philip said that very thing this morning, Kelila thought, blushing prettily. "Thank you, Mary," she smiled. "I do love it here!"

"It shows," Mary nodded, looking lovely and regal despite her arduous trek and simple traveling garments.

"Now, you will all need a place to stay," Adorina spoke up, always ready to get down to business. "There is plenty of room available in my home for guests—"

"Oh, but Mary, you must stay with us," Kelila interrupted. "I insist!"

"All right, then," Adorina decided. "Mary, you can stay with Kelila and Philip. The rest can lodge with Ephraim and me. Is that arrangement satisfactory to each of you?"

"Oh, yes!" The typically shy Anaia answered for all of them, excitedly clutching her husband's muscular arm. "We cannot wait to meet the believers here!"

"And the villagers will be beside themselves with joy when they learn of your arrival," Adorina assured them.

"Well, then, what are we waiting for?" Simon Peter demanded, his exuberant tone etched with mischief and a hint of his old impatience. "If we're all in agreement, let's be on our way!"

CHAPTER 49

Rhoda

Jerusalem

It was a positively lovely morning to be sent to the market!

Unaware of the chipper spring to her step, young Rhoda balanced a small basket brimming with aromatic packets of exotic eastern spices on one arm, swinging it happily back and forth as she strolled through the Upper Market. The lively square bustled and hummed with noise and activity, for which the maidservant was secretly grateful. Shy and somewhat timid by nature, she always appreciated being able to blend in with a large crowd. The attention of others often made her nervous and uncomfortable. She far preferred the safety of solitude, entrusting her heart to a mere handful of people whom she dearly loved.

Pausing near a perfumer's booth to enjoy the delightful fragrances filling the air, she closed her eyes, breathing deeply of the wonderful, mingling scents.

The strident voice of a young woman met her ears, disturbing her tranquil moment of enjoyment. "It's really not so very expensive," the young woman was insisting, her tone petulant. "It's only right to buy gifts for your lover, John Mark. But you never buy me anything!"

John Mark. Rhoda froze, her heart beating so wildly in her chest she wondered if it would come crashing out. Opening her eyes, she spotted John Mark standing dangerously close to a breathtakingly beautiful Roman girl, her lush, abundant golden curls piled atop her proud head and trailing about her bare shoulders in an elaborate Greco-Roman hairstyle. Blushing at the young lady's blatant lack of modest attire, Rhoda's entire being filled with indignation.

Your lover, the spoiled young woman had whined. And suddenly, everything made sense—the way John Mark had begun sneaking around, dousing himself in overpowering fragrances, and seemingly obsessing over his appearance and apparel. Now she understood why he had become jumpy and rebellious, discontented, and often distracted. John Mark had taken a secret lover—and not just any lover, but a *Roman* girl, at that!

Feeling sick to her stomach, Rhoda wondered about her chances of slipping, unnoticed, past the pair standing at the jeweler's booth next door. She decided it might be best not to pass directly in front of them. Instead, she would go the opposite direction, taking the long way around the square and circling back behind the row of expensive market stalls catering to the upper class.

Yes, that's what I shall do, Rhoda decided. Anxiously, she wondered if she should tell her mistress about what she had witnessed at the jeweler's booth. But Mary was currently many miles away, having recently departed for Samaria.

At least I shall have time to pray about this troubling matter before deciding whether or not I should bring it to Mary's attention, she thought, deeply disturbed. Turning quietly on her heel, Rhoda prepared to flee as silently and inconspicuously as possible.

"Rhoda?"

Stiffening at the sound of John Mark's surprised address, Rhoda froze, utterly mortified.

"What are you doing here?"

Wishing she could sink through the broad stone tiles and disappear through the floor, Rhoda turned ever so slowly, reluctant to meet her young master's gaze. Cheeks aflame with embarrassment, she desperately attempted to mask her shock and displeasure, though she supposed she was failing miserably.

"Hello, John Mark," she managed weakly, certain all the color had drained from her face.

"Come, join us," John Mark invited, looking incredibly uncomfortable and even a bit sheepish, as if he had just been caught red-handed. "I didn't realize you had been sent to the market today."

Clearly not, Rhoda thought, peeved. *Next time, I shall be sure to alert you so you can carry on your flagrant immorality in secret!* Though she preferred to flee the dreadfully uncomfortable situation, Rhoda did as she was asked, crossing in front of the perfumer's booth and pausing before the jeweler's sprawling tables laden with heavy, shining gems.

"Why, John Mark," the Roman girl cooed, taking

his arm and nestling her golden head quite comfortably on his broad shoulder. "What a darling little child! Your little sister, perhaps?"

A darling little child? Why, I know young ladies my age betrothed to be married! Rhoda thought, miffed. *I am not a child!* Instantly indignant, Rhoda realized she was experiencing a brand-new sensation, something completely foreign to her in the past. Could it be jealousy, she wondered, deeply unsettled. Surely not!

"This is Rhoda," John Mark clarified, placing a brotherly hand upon the maidservant's shoulder. "She has served my mother faithfully many years."

"Ah, a house slave," the Roman girl observed airily, turning Rhoda's stomach with her condescension.

"My mother doesn't own slaves," John Mark quickly amended.

"Why ever not?"

"She doesn't believe men should own other men," John Mark explained simply, flashing Rhoda an embarrassed smile.

"How odd," Aurelia observed, reaching for a gaudy crystal pendant on the jeweler's table. "Slaves are far more economical."

"Slavery is a cruel practice, and it renders free men unable to find work," John Mark dared, clearly expecting a reprimand. "What is economical about that? It's hard for a working man to compete with free labor, is it not?"

"Jews say the strangest things." Turning her attention back to the heavy pendant in her hand, she lifted it for inspection, having already dismissed the humble maidservant. "What about this one, John Mark? Even *you* could afford this one. It is merely an imitation diamond, though it does resemble the real thing."

"I should walk Rhoda home," John Mark decided, eliciting a look of surprise and dismay from the haughty Roman aristocrat.

"Why?" Aurelia demanded, her lips forming a girlish pout. "She can find her own way."

"I shall see you tomorrow," John Mark informed her, and Rhoda looked away, repulsed, when he leaned in to kiss her gently. "Until tomorrow."

The walk home felt strained and unnatural, and Rhoda wondered how such a lovely day could so quickly turn sour. Surprised, hurt, and angry, she refrained from asking John Mark any questions, though she could tell her young master was mulling over excuses in his mind, determined to explain himself and justify his actions.

"What do you think of Aurelia?" he finally asked, flashing her that boyish smile that had instantly won her heart. Now, it hurt to even look at him.

Grip tightening upon her basket, she pretended to study the towering green palms dotting the stately paved avenue which they traveled, battling the raw emotions threatening to sharpen to her tongue. *What do I think of her?* She thought, peeved. *I think she is spoiled, petty, manipulative, mean, and immodest.*

"Come on," John Mark teased, giving her arm a playful swat. "I want to know what you think!"

No, Rhoda thought, *I don't think you do.*

"So?" John Mark prodded playfully. "Tell me."

"She is very pretty," Rhoda finally answered safely, wishing the young woman's character rivaled her outer beauty. John Mark deserved more, so much more than just a pretty face!

"That, she is," John Mark mused. "She is the daughter of a retired Roman commander, now a powerful official. They are currently staying in the Jerusalem palace of Herod Antipas, the tetrarch."

Rhoda wondered if she was supposed to be impressed. It saddened her that John Mark had been so easily lured by superficial beauty and the promise of fame and fortune. Why, his mother had taught him better than that! He knew to seek a young lady of character and sustenance and most importantly, a fellow believer—not a shallow Gentile woman seeking nothing but her own pleasures!

"Does your mother know?" Rhoda finally asked, certain she already knew the answer.

John Mark grew very quiet, the confidence in his step waning slightly

"I see," Rhoda sighed, having received answer enough.

"Rhoda, it's not like that," John Mark tried to explain. "You know Mother would disapprove of Aurelia. I cannot introduce them until I can find a way to convince Mother to accept her."

"Why do you think your mother would disapprove of her, John Mark?" Rhoda dared, curious about his response.

"Mother has her own ideas about what my future should look like," John Mark finally answered, his dark eyes flashing with hidden resentment. "Already, she has decided where I will live, what I will do for a living, and what kind of girl I should marry. Aurelia doesn't quite fit her aspirations."

"And why not?"

"You know why not," John Mark told her a bit

snidely. "She's far too beautiful for Mother's liking."

"And that's why you believe your mother would dislike her? Because she is beautiful?"

"You know what I mean," John Mark said a bit impatiently.

I know exactly what you mean, Rhoda thought, deeply saddened. The two strolled along in thoughtful silence for a time, contemplating the bind in which John Mark had somehow placed himself. Surprisingly, Rhoda was the first to speak.

"Is Aurelia a believer?"

"Not yet," John Mark confessed, his eyes scanning the quiet street ahead of them, deep in thought.

"And have you shared the gospel with her?" Rhoda pressed.

"Not yet," John Mark responded with a rueful smile.

"But why not?"

"She is a Roman, Rhoda," John Mark sighed, exasperated. "Our way of life is completely contradictory to everything she has ever known."

"And that does not concern you?"

"Why should it? We Jews are mired in centuries of age-old traditions! It certainly couldn't hurt us to shake things up a bit, to experience new, exciting things."

"We *have* experienced something new," Rhoda gently reminded him. "We have embraced the new and living Way, John Mark."

"You sound like Mother," he observed wanly.

"Do you intend to forsake this way of life, this faith, once you win Aurelia?" Rhoda asked quietly, her heart aching.

"Of course not," John Mark shot back, annoyed.

"I'm simply saying, it's not impossible for two people of different religions, heritages, and backgrounds to fall in love and live in peace. Besides, in time, it's entirely possible that Aurelia will come around."

"And it is just as possible that she will win you over to her side," Rhoda said softly. "Please, John Mark, be careful."

"Win me to *her* side? For Heaven's sake, Rhoda, this isn't a war!" John Mark declared in frustration. "Lighten up."

"But it is," Rhoda reminded him gently. "Your soul is at stake, John Mark. I am just asking you to be careful."

After an awkward moment of lingering silence, John Mark finally spoke again, his tone begging Rhoda to understand. "Rhoda, I am asking you not to say anything about this to Mother—or to anyone else, for that matter—until I can get everything figured out."

Biting her lower lip, Rhoda trembled inside. She loved John Mark and desperately wished to please him, but making such a promise might actually harm him in the long run.

Halting mid-stride, John Mark turned and took Rhoda by the shoulders, gazing directly into her eyes. "Rhoda, you have always been like a sister to me. I know I can trust you. Please, just give me some time. It will all work out in the end."

Heart throbbing in her chest, Rhoda gazed into the only face she had ever loved and wondered why it had to hurt so much. It wasn't supposed to be this way.

Though John Mark resumed his stroll with ease, Rhoda lagged anxiously behind, her heart aching, her mind conflicted.

Heart sinking, she realized the laughing, teasing, daring young man who had stolen her girlish heart the moment she set foot in Jerusalem would never see her as anything more than his darling little sister.

CHAPTER 50

Kelila

Sychar

"That was positively lovely, sharing a meal together again," Mary stated in her calm, elegant manner. "How kind of Ephraim and Adorina to open their home to us. They seem like a wonderful couple."

"Oh, they are," Kelila assured her, strolling alongside the regal widow as they passed through the central square, fast approaching Kelila's own dwelling. She was rather excited to show it off to Mary, as she had invested quite a bit of time and attention making it feel more like home. "I must admit, I am relieved Adorina insisted upon cooking for everyone. She is a far more talented cook than I am!"

"Ah, but I imagine you are learning well," Mary smiled knowingly.

"It was rather necessary to learn," Kelila chuckled, nodding warmly toward each merchant as they passed their respective market stalls. "Poor Philip was quite patient with me throughout the learning process."

"Philip has always been a patient man," Mary smiled, her eyes twinkling with fun. "If I recall, he waited quite some time for you to come around before claiming you as his bride."

Blushing, Kelila chuckled along with her dear friend.

"It was good to see Philip again, Kelila," Mary told her, her eyes reflecting her sincerity. "It's obvious the people here greatly respect him. And he and Ephraim seem to have built a solid friendship quite reminiscent of the companionship he once shared with our Stephanos."

"The Lord has provided wonderful friends here," Kelila agreed brightly. "I'm just so thrilled you are here to meet them, Mary! I can't imagine a better time than we had today, talking and laughing and praying and sharing around the table! Oh, how I miss our church family in Jerusalem!"

"You would hardly recognize it," Mary said, her gray eyes tinged with sorrow. "There are so few of us left in Jerusalem."

"But why?"

"Saul of Tarsus has wreaked his havoc in the city. He's caused quite a stir. Many have fled out of sheer necessity; others, to carry the gospel to other lands. Your sister and brother-in-law are among the faithful few remaining."

"How is my family, Mary?" Kelila asked, her dark eyes betraying her intense longing for them. "How are they *really* doing?"

"They are well, despite the circumstances," Mary assured her, acknowledging a group of nearby merchants with a gracious smile. "Your sister is a strong woman, and her husband, a godly man. I have no doubt they shall continue to thrive, fully rooted in the will of God."

"Amen, may it be so," Kelila whispered. "And my mother—have you met her, Mary?"

"She has been attending church meetings faithfully," Mary divulged, bolstering Kelila's spirits. "I think she is fascinated by the Way. She listens with avid interest, though reluctant to voice her questions aloud. She is a quiet, compassionate woman with a sensitive spirit."

"I couldn't have described her better myself," Kelila laughed, thrilling at the prospect of her mother joining the Way. "We plan to visit Jerusalem for the Feast of Tabernacles, and I can hardly wait! It has been such a long time since I have seen my mother, though I must confess, I'm a bit nervous about it given the circumstances."

"You needn't be," Mary assured her. "It is nearly impossible to squelch a mother's love. She will be overjoyed to see you again."

"I do hope so," Kelila mused, her delicate brows knitting together in concern. "But after losing Father so unexpectedly, I can't risk losing my mother without reconciliation. I would be on my way to Jerusalem this very moment if Philip wasn't needed here."

"Have you written to her?"

"She cannot read."

"But Candace can," Mary reminded her, her eyes sparkling. "She would gladly read a letter to your mother. Write her an earnest letter from the heart, Kelila. I shall deliver it to her myself when I return to Jerusalem."

"Oh, Mary!" Kelila cried, releasing a girlish squeal and throwing her arms around Mary's neck, thoroughly surprising her. "That would be wonderful! I can't thank you enough!"

"Your mother will be delighted to hear from you," Mary smiled when Kelila finally released her. Smoothing her flowing robes, she resumed their stroll.

Kelila couldn't help but notice the way every eye in the square seemed to track Mary's graceful movements. Her presence was queenly and enigmatic, and somehow, she seemed to draw everyone's attention without trying. Kelila admired her effortless poise.

"You look like you belong here, Mary," Kelila decided, finally approaching her humble abode. "Sychar is worlds apart from Jerusalem, and yet you seem right at home."

"I have always loved to travel," Mary admitted as Kelila opened the door for her. "Before my husband passed away, we traveled many times each year— mostly reviewing his business holdings. Now, I send workers to evaluate such things, though I must confess, I miss it."

"I guess I shouldn't be surprised," Kelila laughed. "Is there anything you *can't* do, Mary?"

"My, what a lovely abode!" Mary exclaimed, stepping over the threshold, her gray eyes sweeping over the tidy living space. "Kelila, you have done a fine job converting this simple storage space into a worthy home!"

Honored by her praise, Kelila smiled broadly.

"And Philip addresses the people just outside the door, under the canopy?"

"He does," Kelila nodded. "I wasn't too happy about this arrangement at first, but the Lord knew the perfect location for Philip's ministry. It has worked very well."

"I can see why."

"What is this?" Wrinkling her brow, Kelila bent to retrieve a writing tablet from the low table. Completely covered from top to bottom in hastily scratched markings, Kelila suddenly realized what it was.

"Someone has been very busy working on that," Mary observed with a knowing smile.

"A new student of Philip's," Kelila muttered, wondering if she should deliver the tablet to Simon or simply wait for him to come looking for it. "He must have left it here when they met this morning."

"Shall we return it to him?"

Kelila took a good look at the tablet—she couldn't help herself—and felt strangely unsettled by its contents: *Philip bowed head and closed eyes. Uttered silent prayer, formula unknown. When he lifted his head, he spoke...*

"It looks as if Simon is taking careful notes about everything Philip says and does," Kelila murmured, scanning the contents with a practiced eye: *During prayer meeting, Philip laid hands on blind woman. Touched her forehead, then her eyes. Gazed heavenward, uttered silent prayer, and pronounced, "Be healed!" The woman's sight was restored. What did his silent utterance entail? Learn this.*

Sensing Kelila's discomfiture, Mary joined her, studying the suspicious tablet over the young woman's shoulder.

A sharp knock on the door surprised both women, and Kelila was quite sure she jumped at least a foot. "I'll get that," she said a bit sheepishly. "I think I know who it is."

Swinging open the door, Kelila's stomach dropped in dismay when her suspicions were confirmed. Forcing a sociable smile, she was about to greet her guest when he brusquely addressed her.

"I see you have found my tablet," Simon quipped sardonically, his dark eyes glittering in hidden challenge.

"Mary and I just returned home and stumbled upon it," Kelila informed him, attempting to sound casual and at ease.

"Mary?" Simon questioned, glancing over Kelila's shoulder.

"Hello, Simon," Mary said coolly, surprising both Kelila and the former sorcerer. Drawing alongside the startled young woman on the threshold, Mary boldly met his gaze. "We meet again."

"So it would seem," Simon drawled, looking the widow over with a strange combination of admiration and disgust. "You look lovely as ever."

"Ah, and I see flattery is still a useful weapon hidden in your vast arsenal."

"Have you not spoken with this delightful young woman here, my lady?" Simon challenged, his gaze flickering toward Kelila. "I am *changed*. A brand-new man."

"I certainly hope that is the case."

Kelila watched, mystified, as Simon's lips twisted in a cold smirk. "I suppose only time will tell," he drawled, boldly looking her over as if assessing his prey.

Holding his gaze without flinching, Mary took

the tablet from Kelila's shaking hands, offering it to him without explanation. "Good day, Simon," she said curtly, preparing to close the door.

"My lady," Simon said, accepting the tablet with an overly dramatic bow.

Mary shut the door firmly and without ceremony.

Staring at Mary with wide eyes, Kelila realized her mouth was open. Promptly closing it, she attempted to gather her thoughts. Shaking her head to clear the confusion, she exclaimed, "You know him?"

"I've had the honor—or should I say, dishonor—of encountering him before," Mary sighed, her eyes kindling with indignation.

"But...but *how*?" Kelila stammered, amazed.

"He practiced his black arts in Cypress, my homeland, many years ago," she explained, crossing the small room and pausing beside the window. Looking out onto the street, she appeared relieved the sorcerer had departed. "He practiced unspeakable blasphemies there."

"That sounds like him," Kelila nodded. "Miraculously, he recently accepted Jesus Christ as Lord."

"I can scarcely believe it," Mary said, shaking her head. "I'm not entirely sure I *do* believe it."

Looking at Mary in surprise, Kelila realized she, too, wrestled with the same doubts about the former sorcerer. She certainly didn't wish to be critical or harbor a judgmental spirit. She truly believed that no one was beyond the Lord's redemptive hand, not even Simon. Even so, there was something about Simon's "conversion" that seemed...lacking, insincere.

"I would advise Philip to keep a close eye on him," Mary advised, her gaze fixed upon the main thoroughfare beyond the window. "I'm not convinced that Simon can be trusted."

"In all honesty, Philip was a bit hesitant to baptize Simon," Kelila admitted, joining her at the window and wondering how much she should say. Mary was a wise, godly woman, and she desperately longed for her counsel. She knew Mary could be trusted to impart godly advice. "After meeting on many occasions to study the Word and the Way of salvation, Philip consented to baptize him. He didn't want to bar Simon from repentance if he was sincere."

"I understand Philip's reservations," Mary nodded, turning to meet Kelila's gaze. "Of course, we hope and pray that Simon is sincere in his conversion. Even so, Kelila, I would counsel you to remain vigilant, on guard."

Nodding slowly, Kelila resolved to do that very thing. After all, Simon had come after her once. She certainly wouldn't put it past him to try it again.

CHAPTER 51

Tabitha

Joppa

As promised, Tabitha returned to Ruth's tenement to deliver food and supplies, but most importantly, to instruct the eager young widows about the Way of salvation. In recent visits, more and more widows had begun gathering to learn about Jesus, His great love for them, His compassion for widows and orphans, and His desire to give them abundant life. Many had even embraced Jesus as their Lord and Savior, to Tabitha's sheer and utter delight! What a privilege it was to lead these dear women to Jesus! What a blessing to build a brand-new family of earnest believers in Christ!

Standing near the door in Ruth's crowded living space, Tabitha told the widows and their young children about Jesus' most famous sermon, which the believers had fondly begun to reference as the Sermon on the Mount. Watching the shining, eager faces before her, Tabitha realized she would soon need to find a larger meeting place. Only so many women and children could squeeze into Ruth's tiny, one-room tenement apartment. Even now, women and children crowded on the narrow balcony and trailed out the door, listening from the threshold and the narrow hall. A few had taken advantage of the comfortable cushions Tabitha had supplied for the old widow to scatter about her low kitchen table, providing more comfortable seating.

Lord, we are going to need a new place to meet, and though Joram's estate would be perfect for such a thing, I already know better than to ask him for that, Tabitha prayed. *Please, Lord, provide a place for us to meet, to study Your Word.*

Eventually reaching a reasonable stopping point, Tabitha announced that she would continue recounting Jesus' sermon the following week. Many of the women smiled and nodded their enthusiasm, and Tabitha marveled at their utter transformation. Formerly gaunt, hopeless faces now shone with joy and faith. The change was lovely to behold.

If only Ruth shared their willing belief, Tabitha thought, saddened. Week after week, the old woman stood in the corner with her arms crossed, her expression just as closed as her loud, clear body language. Clearly, she appreciated Tabitha's willingness to invest in her fellow widows but remained skeptical of her message.

Perhaps, in time, that will change, Tabitha thought for the umpteenth time.

After exchanging a bit of laughter, playful banter, warm embraces, and farewell pleasantries with the happy widows, Tabitha thanked Ruth for opening her home to them, scooped up her excited little daughter, and took her leave.

***

"Your audience grows larger by the week!"

Pausing just before reaching the cobbled street, Tabitha glanced over her shoulder to see Adam at his vendor's booth. "I didn't see you there when I came down the stairs," she apologized, turning to join him at his stall. "Good day, Adam."

"And good day to you, my lady," he smiled broadly, offering Laurel a bunch of plump purple grapes from his stand. "Compliments of your favorite merchant," he teased the little one, who accepted the grapes with a delighted squeal before shyly burrowing her face in her mother's shoulder.

Shifting the girl's weight—which seemed to increase steadily by the day—on her hip, Tabitha smiled her gratitude. "Thank you, Adam. That's very kind."

"I was helping a vendor a few booths down when you came down the stairs," Adam explained. "But I'm glad I caught you before you left. I must speak with you about something."

"Oh?" Tabitha asked, surprised.

"Ruth has told me a bit about your 'outrageous, hare-brained religious ideas,'" he confessed.

Laughing heartily, Tabitha shook her head fondly. "As you can see, I haven't made much headway with Ruth yet."

"You are affecting her more than you realize," Adam told her honestly, his eyes flickering with genuine concern. "Which brings me to my next point,

Tabitha. I've heard enough to know what you are teaching these widows. It's dangerous, and it's risky. The widows here have endured trouble enough, and yet the danger brewing in larger cities like Jerusalem will eventually touch the outer regions, like this one."

Holding her breath, Tabitha's heart began to pound in anxious rhythm. What was Adam saying? Was he going to chastise her for sharing the gospel? Attempt to put an end to her flourishing ministry?

"Are you prepared to face that kind of hardship, Tabitha?" Adam asked genuinely, his hazel-flecked brown eyes betraying his concern for her.

"I have faced hardship far worse than that, and yet God delivered me," Tabitha told him, drawing courage from the Holy Spirit within. Trembling inside, she wondered if this seemingly kind young man was about to come against her. Drawing her daughter closer, she braced herself and stood her ground, her luminous eyes fixed upon him.

Nodding slowly, Adam came around the market stall and did something entirely unexpected. Taking a knee on the dusty, grit-covered pavement, he drew a curved line in the sand, looping his finger back up to form another curved line that intersected the first.

Watching his strange movements with a pounding heart, Tabitha instantly recognized a symbol she had only heard about. The sign of a fish etched in the sandy grit, a secret sign between believers to confirm their faith.

Rising to his full height, Adam met her gaze, his own burning with intensity. "Jesus Christ, Son of God, Savior."

Flabbergasted, Tabitha stared at him with wide, hazel-green eyes, utterly speechless.

Amused by her reaction, Adam tossed her a playful wink. "All I'm saying is, you have an ally here in Joppa, Tabitha, if ever you need one."

"But how…" Tabitha stammered, shaking her head in confusion. "How…how do you know about Jesus?"

"Last year, I met a man unlike any I'd ever known," he said, his eyes flickering with passionate inner strength. "His ship docked in the harbor here amidst one of his many travels. This man was bold for the gospel, and I believed his testimony. Though it's highly unlikely, perhaps—just perhaps—you have heard of a man named Barnabas?"

Shaking her head in awe, Tabitha marveled at the mysterious, hidden ways of her great God!

***

Kelila

Sychar

Kelila watched in amazement as nearly the entire square filled with eager Samaritans, all of them thrilling at the prospect of hearing Peter and John address the crowd. Nearly beside themselves with excitement, some even remembered the apostles' first visit to Sychar with the beloved Savior.

Clustered near the threshold and overlooking the immense sea of expectant faces nearly filling the entire square, Kelila, Philip, Mary, Adorina, Ephraim, and Anaia waited in eager anticipation as Peter and

John drew before the crowd, their confident yet humbly clad figures resonating with the power of God.

Standing closest to Mary, Kelila grasped her hand and gave it an excited little squeeze. She could sense the Spirit's presence here, filling the entire square, drawing sinners unto Himself. What a privilege to participate in this calling, this mission! She had learned many important lessons here—lessons she knew she would carry with her for the rest of her life.

Returning Mary's encouraging smile, Kelila turned and surveyed the crowd, blown away by the shocking turnout. Many of the shining faces were now familiar and even dear to her heart. She saw the baker and his large family, as well as the middle-aged couple she had recently begun to assist, the former demoniac with his mother, and a slew of his smiling relatives. With a hint of dismay, she noted Simon the sorcerer at the very front of the crowd. *Well, naturally,* she thought, a bit peeved. *Nothing but the very best seat for Simon, of course.* Sighing, she inwardly repented of her critical attitude, choosing instead to pray that his conversion was sincere. Even Helena, his muse, watched from a distance, propped indolently in her doorway, her arms crossed, her blue eyes glowing with malice.

"Greetings," Simon Peter suddenly announced, drawing Kelila's attention and eliciting a welcoming roar from the crowd that seemed to shake the ground beneath their sandals. "It is an honor and a privilege to speak with you this afternoon."

Another deafening roar, followed by shouts of welcome and ecstatic applause.

"You are all too kind." Peter smiled, holding up a hand to silence the crowd.

"Brothers and sister," John fervently declared, his eyes flitting warmly over his audience, "when we received word that the Samaritans had embraced the Way of life, we couldn't wait to see the truth for ourselves. And now, your faith has surpassed even our greatest expectations! Praise be to God!"

Clapping along with the rest, Kelila shook her head in awe, remembering tales which the apostles had recounted about their first trip to Samaria. At that time, they had thought Jesus was out of His mind to even consider stopping in Sychar! But what priceless fruit had been borne of that unlikely journey, still flourishing years later! And what bittersweet memories this trip must stir for Peter and John, who had last visited Sychar with their beloved Savior walking beside them. How they must ache for His presence now!

Focusing her attention on the apostles' sermon, she listened intently as they described the arrest, crucifixion, and resurrection of their Lord. Then, they explained what had happened on that sacred Pentecost following Christ's miraculous resurrection when the Holy Spirit fell upon the church.

"Just before His ascension, Jesus promised He would send the Holy Spirit to lead and to guide," John explained. "He said, '*You shall receive power when the Holy Spirit has come upon you; and you shall be witnesses to Me in Jerusalem, and in all Judea and...*'" Eyes sparkling with fun, John paused and exchanged a knowing look with Peter. "'...*in Samaria!*" he declared, pumping a fist in the air.

In response, the crowd shouted their joy and triumph, clapping their hands and raising their arms heavenward.

"'...*and to the end of the earth*,'" Simon Peter finished for John once the joyous shouting and mad applause finally tapered off. "Brothers and sisters, you were part of God's plan all along. You, too, are called to be His witnesses, to participate in the furtherance of His gospel unto the ends of the earth! Which means you, too, will need the gift of the Holy Spirit!"

A reverent awe fell over the crowd as they contemplated the wonder of Peter's announcement. The Holy Spirit of God imparted to *Samaritans*? It was simply unthinkable, far too good to be true!

Exchanging a knowing look with Mary, Kelila somehow managed to silence the squeal of delight arising in her throat. She had a sneaking suspicion she knew what was coming next!

"My brethren," John continued, his boyish features earnest in the warm afternoon sunlight, "I traveled with Jesus the day He arrived here in Sychar. If you will recall, He met a woman at the well upon our arrival. This woman here, in fact." Turning slowly, John smiled at Adorina, who responded with an emphatic nod of her own, tears streaming down her face. "That day, Jesus gave Adorina a special promise. He said the day would dawn when we would worship Him *in spirit and truth.*"

"Brothers and sisters," Peter declared, his entire being resonating with scarcely harnessed energy and enthusiasm, "we are pleased to announce that the promised day has come! My fellow worker, John, and I can't think of a better place to start than by imparting the Holy Spirit to this faithful woman and her husband! Both have followed Jesus without wavering, even amidst His seemingly long absence."

Gasping, Adorina covered her mouth with both hands.

"Ephraim, Adorina," John prodded gently with an encouraging, outstretched hand. "Please, come."

Nodding his encouragement to his trembling wife, Ephraim gently guided her toward the powerful apostles, his strong countenance alight with humility, wonder, and thanksgiving.

Grasping Mary's hand on one side and Philip's on the other, Kelila watched, spellbound with joy, as Simon Peter and John laid hands upon the faithful Samaritan woman and her husband.

"Ephraim and Adorina," Peter declared, his eyes alive with passionate fire. "Receive the gift of the Holy Spirit!"

Standing at the front of the vast crowd, the sorcerer's dark eyes widened as an undeniable power like a mighty breath of wind descended upon the village square, seemingly coming to rest upon the humble servants standing with Peter and John.

CHAPTER 52

Kelila

Sychar

Gathered around the table near the glowing hearth in Ephraim and Adorina's modest house, the believers shared another delightful supper, laughing, talking, and enjoying the easy camaraderie they had once shared in Jerusalem.

Nestled contentedly close to her husband, Kelila observed the believers' cheerful, good-natured interactions, realizing that Ephraim and Adorina fit right in with the followers from Jerusalem.

It's rather amazing, she thought, *how God knits His church together regardless of race, heritage, or background. Why, this small group alone represents multiple people groups, and yet we are one in Christ!* Here, there were staunch Judeans like Mary and Philip, rugged Galileans like Peter and John, and now even Samaritans had joined their ranks! Why, she herself hailed from an entirely different continent, and yet she, too, had become a beloved member of God's blessed family of faith!

An unexpected knock at the door silenced Kelila's thoughts and the lively conversation, eliciting looks of curiosity from the women and concern from the men. Rising with caution, Ephraim went to the door, with Philip close behind him. Peter and John also rose, their countenances thoughtful in the soft evening firelight.

"Greetings."

Stiffening in dismay, Kelila glanced over at Mary. The widow's gray eyes flickered in recognition at the sound of the sorcerer's smooth voice. Adorina, too, appeared displeased, while Anaia's brown eyes conveyed her confusion. She hadn't yet encountered the questionable convert.

Ushering him inside, Ephraim graciously permitted Simon to enter his home. Pressing his hands together, the sorcerer drew boldly before Peter and John, his features sharpened rather than softened by the lamplight. Kelila couldn't help but note the lack of humility in his posture and presentation. Sporting exquisite robes intricately embroidered with gold and silver thread, his fingers, wrists, and throat glittered with jewelry boasting an impressive array of costly gems, standing in stark contrast with the humbly dressed, unadorned men standing before him.

Acknowledging the women with a faint bow and a special smile of condescension reserved just for Mary, Simon bowed low before the apostles, his robes swishing dramatically as he straightened. Kelila knew Peter and John would have ordered him to rise, had he prostrated himself or even hinted at any form of worship, as that was reserved for God alone.

"I am Simon," he said enigmatically, standing before Peter and John. "Perhaps you have heard of me."

"Philip briefed us about your past, as well as your recent conversion," Peter answered as the evangelist and Ephraim joined them near the roaring hearth.

"Excellent," Simon murmured, his eyes gleaming with avarice. "I could not rest until I had spoken with you both in person. You are indeed mighty men."

"We are lowly men, former fishermen," John put in firmly. "The power you sense is the Holy Spirit at work."

"That is exactly what I wish to discuss with you," Simon said quickly. "The way you laid hands upon the people today, bequeathing this mighty Spirit upon them…I have never seen anything like it."

"I noticed you failed to join us when we laid hands upon your brethren, bestowing the Holy Spirit upon them," Peter pointed out, his dark eyes assessing Simon's every practiced movement.

"Only because I wished to speak with you about this gift privately, in person," Simon assured him.

Peter and John exchanged looks of concern, wary about where this conversation was headed.

The women, too, listened with bated breath. Heart pounding, Kelila sensed dark undercurrents at work, like the smothering darkness that had encompassed the square the night Simon attempted to ensnare her. Clenching her hands in her lap, she began to pray in earnest.

"As you know," Simon addressed the apostles, seeming to ignore the presence of Ephraim and Philip, as well as the women seated quietly around the table, "I was once the mightiest man among these parts. I traveled throughout Samaria and abroad, employing my great power for the betterment of mankind."

For the betterment of mankind? Resisting the urge to roll her eyes, Kelila noted that both Mary and Adorina also appeared to be biting their tongues, while Anaia looked rather perplexed.

"Soon after this young man's arrival," Simon said, acknowledging Philip for the first time, "it became evident that *his* God possessed the greater power. As such, I was ready to change sides. Why employ a lesser force when a far higher power is at your disposal, yes?"

Sickened by Simon's opportunistic viewpoint regarding her faith, Kelila looked to Mary and shook her head in dismay. She had a feeling the apostles wouldn't take too kindly to Simon's greed-soaked perspective, either.

"Gentlemen," Simon announced with a sardonic smile, the firelight casting writhing shadows which danced eerily across his hardened features, "I have seen what you can do, and I am ready to join your ranks."

Kelila almost laughed aloud at the expression that crossed Peter's face, and the confusion etched all over John's. Even Philip and Ephraim, standing guard close behind them, looked puzzled.

"Who is better suited than I, a natural born leader of this stubborn, headstrong people, to possess this great power and lead in your ranks?" Simon persisted, reaching for the intricate money belt strapped to his waist. "Gentlemen, I am ready to resume that role."

"Simon," Peter said slowly, exchanging a sorrowful look with John, "it is the Holy Spirit who bestows leadership upon His chosen vessels. Leadership in the church of God is a sacred calling, not to be lightly dispensed on a whim."

"Ah, but surely there are ways around that," Simon pointed out, reaching into his money belt and drawing out several gleaming gold coins. Holding them up for inspection, the coins glittered in the firelight, almost as if reflecting the avarice in Simon's glowing eyes. "It is no secret that men of my profession exchange their well-guarded secrets for a tidy sum. I shall pay whatever you ask in exchange for the power you possess."

The room grew deathly silent. So still, in fact, Kelila could hear the wood crackling in the hearth and her own rapidly beating heart.

"Come now," Simon drawled in his most persuasive tone. "Give me this power also, that anyone on whom I lay hands may receive the Holy Spirit." Convincingly, he placed a firm hand upon Peter's broad shoulder.

Shaking off Simon's hand like a venomous snake, Peter drew back, his countenance fierce. "Your money perish with you," he declared, his eyes flashing fire, "because you thought that the gift of God could be purchased with *money*! You have neither part nor portion in this matter, for your heart is not right in the sight of God."

"Please," Simon stammered, swiftly pocketing the coins, "I meant no disrespect. I only desire to serve as you do. Could you not use my 'donation' to further your sacred work—"

"You haven't the slightest desire to serve Christ,"

Peter shot back, angrily shaking his head. "Your desire is for fame, fortune, and power, Simon. In your burning greed, you have failed to see that the Way is not the way to wealth, power, and fame, though Christ has allowed some to achieve such things for His glory. No, the Way of Christ is the way of life, salvation, self-sacrifice, and service. You, Simon, are no more equipped to lead God's people than to sprout wings and fly!"

Sensing Peter's righteous anger and the power of God coursing through him, Simon's swarthy features grew deathly pale as he drew back from the apostle's honest rebuke.

"There is still hope for you, Simon." Seeing the sorcerer's fear, Peter softened ever so slightly, offering the merciful compassion of Christ. "Repent therefore of this your wickedness, and pray God if perhaps the thought of your heart may be forgiven you."

"But how?" Simon almost groaned, his eyes glazed over with fear at the power resonating from the apostles' unyielding forms.

"You are poisoned with bitterness, Simon," Peter told him frankly, "and bound by iniquity. Confess your sins before God, and He will forgive you. Truly relinquish your heart to Christ, and He will enable you to walk in victory."

Taking Peter by the shoulders, Simon begged him, "Pray to the Lord for me, that none of the things which you have spoken may come upon me! Please, please pray for me!"

Looking toward Mary, Kelila saw her gray eyes brimming with sorrow, even as Adorina's flashed with indignation. The cautious Anaia's gaze was fixed upon her husband, clearly concerned for him.

"Even now, you ask another to intercede on your behalf," Peter told Simon, gently putting him away. "Only *you* can present yourself before the throne of grace. Only *you* can make the decision to repent of your sins and follow Christ—I cannot do that for you."

Straightening to his full height, Simon's firm jawline hardened as his dark eyes kindled with anger, his reverential fear having vanished in his humiliation. "I see you are utterly useless to me." Turning toward the door, he shot a final look of condescension over his shoulder, reserving a special one just for Mary, who returned it with a clear, unperturbed gaze. Without another word, Simon pushed open the door, slamming it angrily behind him, and vanished into the night.

CHAPTER 53

Rhoda

Jerusalem

Troubled in spirit, Rhoda paced the lamplit upper corridors of her lady's opulent villa. Since sleep refused to come, she decided to make herself useful. Rather than tossing and turning for several unproductive hours, she would travel the tranquil halls and pray, instead.

Pausing outside the closed door of John Mark's private quarters, her heart constricted painfully inside her chest. What a heavy burden she bore for her young master tonight! It had taken but one golden-haired temptress to lure him from the safety of his family, his faith, his heritage. Couldn't he see that the shiny new object would tarnish over time, while his God remained ever steadfast? Couldn't he see that he and Aurelia had nothing in common, least of all their religion? Couldn't he see how much he would one day regret his decision to betray his godly upbringing to pursue fleeting, carnal passions?

Placing a trembling hand upon his closed door, Rhoda bowed her head in fervent prayer for him. Lips moving in silent petition, she poured out her heart to God, anxious and unsettled.

Bump, bump. Creak!

Startled, Rhoda raised her head, heart pounding. John Mark must be moving about in his room! But at this hour? It must be past midnight! What was her young master doing up and about?

Concerned for him, Rhoda wondered what she should do. Should she check on him? Summon a male servant to do so? Or simply ignore the suspicious circumstances and mind her own business?

Eventually, her concern and curiosity overtook her hesitation. "John Mark?" she whispered, her voice trembling in her timidness. "John Mark?"

No response.

"John Mark? Are you well?"

Her anxious query was answered by resounding silence.

Glancing nervously both ways, Rhoda gathered her courage and pushed open the heavy door, praying fervently that her young master was decently attired.

Her senses were immediately overpowered by the lingering fragrance of sweet-smelling incense—the strong scent John Mark had begun to douse himself in every time he left the house. Crinkling her nose, Rhoda gingerly stepped inside the dimly lit chamber. Nervously allowing her gaze to sweep about the perimeter, her heart began to pound even more rapidly when she assessed an empty bed with plush, rumpled blankets cast hastily aside. Apparently,

John Mark hadn't yet readied himself for bed, as his sleeping robe remained strewn over an elegant chair beside his bed. But it was the open window with scarlet curtains fluttering in the midnight breezes that turned Rhoda's heart inside her chest.

Hastily crossing the room, Rhoda drew before the open window, placing trembling hands upon the cool stone ledge. A sturdy rope tied to a nearby pillar hung out the open window, dangling just before it hit the gray flagstones below.

Covering her mouth in dismay, Rhoda saw John Mark's retreating back far below as he headed for a gate within the large stone walls encircling the entire villa.

Heart pounding frantically, Rhoda lifted the sturdy rope in shaking hands, contemplating what she was about to do.

***

Following John Mark had proven easier than Rhoda had expected. So eager was he to reach his destination that he scarcely paid any heed to his surroundings. He certainly hadn't expected to be followed, least of all by a timid servant girl.

Surprised by the amount of distance John Mark had covered, Rhoda found herself panting to keep up. His long, eager strides far outdistanced her own. It was eerie—traversing the somber, sleeping city drenched in silver moonlight. Passing the entire length of the enormous Upper Market, Rhoda hugged the pillared colonnades framing the massive court rather than following him straight through the center. The pillars cast strange, sloping shadows across the pavement, which appeared like ghostly sentries in the eerily still market.

Eventually, John Mark appeared to reach his destination dangerously near the tetrarch's palace, which perched like a menacing bird of prey at the Upper City's highest point, cloaked in darkness and glowering torchlight. Heart swelling with apprehension, Rhoda followed him into a deserted, flowering garden dotted with disturbing marble statues glistening stark white in the silver moonlight. Mortified by the Romans' lack of modesty, Rhoda flushed, quickly averting her gaze from the less-than-attired likenesses of pagan heroes and deities.

This place must be frequented by Romans, Rhoda realized, instantly nervous. No devout Jew would dare set foot in this place! Why on earth would John Mark venture here? The fact that he appeared perfectly at ease in a garden permeated with idols only quickened her apprehension.

"My love!" Emerging from a nearby grove, Aurelia threw herself into John Mark's eager arms, taking his neck and kissing him in a manner reserved for husband and wife. Utterly sickened, Rhoda dodged behind a gnarled, flowering tree, wondering if her pounding heart would give her away.

"I thought you would never arrive," Aurelia said breathlessly, caressing the curve of John Mark's firm jawline. "I must speak with you, love. It is urgent."

"Has something happened?" John Mark's posture betrayed his unease.

"I'm afraid so," she said, though her glowing eyes revealed her glee. Taking him by the hand, she led him to a gracefully curved marble bench a mere stone's throw away from Rhoda's hiding place. "Come. Sit with me."

John Mark did so, his apprehension mounting steadily.

Settling cozily onto the bench with John Mark, Aurelia took both his hands in her own, boldly meeting his gaze. "My father and I must return to Rome."

Closing her eyes, Rhoda felt relief wash over her entire being like a welcome tide. Aurelia was leaving! *Praise God for His abundant mercy!* But even as her heart swelled with gratitude at the girl's welcome announcement, she recognized that *Aurelia* was not the root cause of John Mark's defection. His was a heart concern, a fluctuating faith, a serious matter that only *he* could address.

Opening her eyes, Rhoda's gaze fell upon John Mark's stricken face, and her heart went out to him despite her irritation toward his recent behavior.

"You're leaving?" he asked brokenly, softly caressing her cheek.

"I must return with Father," she told him, her blue eyes kindling with something that turned Rhoda's stomach upside down. Taking his wrist, she met his gaze with fierce determination. "Come with us."

W*hat?* Rhoda thought, her heart springing into her throat.

"What?" John Mark repeated, as if echoing Rhoda's own silent sentiment. "You mean, to *Rome?*"

"Yes!" Aurelia declared emphatically, her entire face lighting up. "This doesn't have to be the end of us, John Mark. In fact, it is only just the beginning."

Stunned, John Mark appeared lost for words. It took every ounce of willpower Rhoda possessed to resist the urge to emerge from her hiding place, take John Mark by the arm, and drag him from the pagan garden despite the wicked Roman girl's protests!

"You cannot possibly fathom the life we could have together in Rome," Aurelia persisted, leaning in to give him a convincing kiss. "Just imagine a life of ease, pleasure, and luxury in the most important city on earth! I can promise you the world, John Mark."

Squeezing her eyes shut, Rhoda recalled a story shared by the Apostle Matthew. Just before Jesus launched His public ministry, the devil visited Him, bombarding Him with temptations. And Aurelia's deceptive words reeked of the enemy's empty promise to the Savior when he took Him to an exceedingly high mountain, showing Him the kingdoms of the world and all their glory. *All these things I will give you,* the devil had sworn, *if You will fall down and worship me...*

Throat closing in fear, Rhoda realized that the enemy was closing in, once again. As her wise mistress once said, the devil didn't make a habit of wasting his fiery darts. There was obviously a reason he had come against John Mark with hateful fury. God must have a plan for the young man, a plan the enemy was now targeting with single-minded determination.

Oh, God, Rhoda's heart cried in distress, *help John Mark to stand firm!*

"My father has powerful connections in Rome," Aurelia continued, interrupting Rhoda's desperate plea. "With his help, you can become anything you wish, John Mark. Soon, you shall become someone of value in the greatest city on earth!"

Someone of value? Annoyed, Rhoda wondered if John Mark realized what Aurelia was implying. In her opinion, he was a nobody, one unimportant Jewish boy in a dusty, forgotten province.

Tearing her gaze from Aurelia's mesmerizing blue eyes, Rhoda looked to John Mark, her beloved. His intense inner struggle was betrayed in the bleakness in his eyes. On the one hand, he loved his mother, his church, his brethren, and his homeland. And yet, on the other hand, he had fallen hard for this girl. The thought of losing her might prove sufficient to cloud his thinking and mar his better judgment.

Merciful God, Rhoda prayed, clinging to the gnarled trunk of an ancient tree. *Help him!*

Suddenly, John Mark's countenance brightened, though his features were barely discernible in the waning moonlight. "Aurelia," he said, his voice laced with excitement, "I have an idea."

"An idea?" she asked, lifting a skeptical brow.

Sliding off the bench, John Mark knelt at her elegantly sandaled feet, trembling with emotion as he grasped her hands.

"What are you doing?" Aurelia protested, annoyed their conversation had taken an unexpected turn. "Get up. You look ridiculous."

The words John Mark uttered next struck Rhoda like a dagger in her heart. "Marry me, Aurelia," he said, his eyes shining with young love. "Marry me and make me the happiest man alive!"

"Marry you?" Aurelia repeated dumbly, perturbed.

"Yes," John Mark declared in a rush, squeezing her delicate hands. "If you marry me, you needn't set sail for Rome with your father. You can abide with me, and we can establish a life together. I am qualified to build a house and provide for a wife, Aurelia. I have been trained to operate—"

"Wait," Aurelia sputtered, withdrawing her hands. "Why on earth would you want to stay in this dull, stuffy old province when we could go to *Rome*?"

"Because this is where I belong," John Mark told her gently, caressing her cheek. "And you belong with me, Aurelia. You will learn to love it here. I know you will."

"I *hate* it here," Aurelia vehemently declared, pushing aside his hand. "And you will, too, once you get a taste of everything Rome has to offer! There is an entire world out there you have yet to experience, John Mark. It's not your fault that your mother hovered over you like a fussy old hen, sheltering you from the world. But now I can show you what you're missing! I can give you a life unlike anything you've ever experienced!"

No! Heart crashing frantically in her chest, Rhoda shook her head in vehement disagreement. She knew exactly what Rome—and Aurelia—had to offer, and none of it would please the Lord. She knew John Mark was aware of that, too, deep in his heart. But, like Aurelia, Rome was breathtaking and alluring, brimming with grand but empty promises. Its golden façade was but a shallow mask concealing the lewdness, drunkenness, and debauchery which threatened to destroy the Imperial City and its citizens from the inside out.

"Don't you want to marry me?" John Mark asked, confused. Clearly, her less-than-desirable reaction to his proposal surprised him.

"Why marry when we can enjoy love's pleasures without the constraint of marriage?" Aurelia chided him, arms crossed. "You love me, and I love you. Isn't that enough?"

"Of course it's enough," John Mark managed, stunned. "But why wouldn't two people who love each other choose to marry? Isn't that the point?"

"Oh, John Mark, I love you. But you are so naïve."

"Naïve?" John Mark repeated, appearing nettled for the first time. "How?"

"Marriage is terribly unfair to women," Aurelia argued, and Rhoda noticed that her delivery was both polished and refined. It was highly likely this wasn't the first time she had delivered this speech. "In Roman society, a woman relinquishes her freedom, her money, and her assets—not to mention her *rights*—the moment she gets married. Everything she owns automatically transfers over to the husband. Does that sound fair to you, John Mark?"

"It doesn't have to be like that. If a man truly loves a woman—"

"Not only that, but what if one of us eventually tires of the other?" she persisted. "It's highly likely, you know. Divorce is so messy, so stressful. Wouldn't you prefer to simply avoid all that and play it safe?"

"Divorce?" John Mark repeated, astonished. "Aurelia, divorce is not an option. God hates divorce."

"See!" Aurelia pouted, petulant. "This is exactly what I'm talking about! We aren't even married yet, and already you have begun restricting my freedoms."

John Mark stared at her, dumbfounded. "Are you saying we should enter into marriage *planning* to fail? *Planning* to end in divorce?"

"I'm saying we shouldn't enter into marriage at all! This is exactly why it's such a confounded institution," Aurelia said vehemently. "Marriage sets us up to fail! Can't you see it? Why place such an enormous amount of pressure—such unreasonable expectations—on a young couple with their entire lives ahead of them? Very few people remain madly in love for a lifetime, John Mark. It's just a fact of life. But unreasonable traditionalists forbid divorce, criminalizing people who simply fall out of love—as if it's their fault!"

"Love is a choice," John Mark said quietly.

"So if you truly love me," Aurelia shot back, her kindling gaze pinning him in place, "don't force me to relinquish my rights as a woman, nor pressure me to accept an ancient institution which is destined to fail."

Rising from his knees, John Mark straightened to his full height, running an anxious hand over the back of his neck.

Sensing his subtle withdrawal, Aurelia rose from the bench, going to him. Taking his neck, she kissed him deeply, disturbed that he now seemed reluctant to return her ardor. "You have a lot to learn, John Mark," she told him, tenderly caressing his cheek. "Let me show you how the real world works. Come to Rome with me. Share my home, my life, my bed. Throw off the constraints of religion and society, and truly *live*!"

"What you ask would displease the Lord," John Mark said, his brown eyes begging her to understand.

"The *Lord?*" Aurelia asked, shrinking back slightly. "What does the Lord have to do with *us*, John

Mark?"

"Everything."

"You're only saying that because it's what you have been taught. It's all you know."

John Mark gazed into her eyes, hurt and conflicted.

"You think the entire world revolves around this God of yours," Aurelia purred, tracing his jawline with her manicured finger. "But it doesn't. He is but one deity a vast pantheon of heroes, gods, and men. Stop denying yourself life's simplest pleasures as if *He's* all that mattered."

Clenching her fists, Rhoda prayed unlike she ever had before, desperately trying to calm her racing heart. Despite the tranquility of this quiet garden respite, she sensed dark forces at work, intent upon the destruction of a beloved child of God. With a pounding heart, she watched as Aurelia reached upward with slender fingers, plucking a ripe piece of fruit from the flowering branches overhead. "Your future is ripe for the plucking, John Mark," she whispered, her eyes glowing with dark promises as she offered him the glistening piece of fruit. "Now all you have to do is reach out and take it. Don't be afraid to open your eyes and see the world for what it truly is."

It was too much, simply too much! Reminded of a deadly serpent in yet another tranquil garden of ages past, Rhoda cried out in trepidation, emerging from behind the gnarled trunk and marching bravely toward her confused young master.

"Rhoda?"

"*Her* again?" Aurelia threw up her hands, annoyed. "For heaven's sake, John Mark! Send your little serving wench back home where she belongs!"

"Don't do it, John Mark," Rhoda cried, tears streaming down her pale cheeks. "Don't listen to her. Please, don't make the biggest mistake of your life. God loves you. He doesn't want this for you."

"This is unbelievable!" Crossing her arms, Aurelia shot a look of disdain toward the trembling maidservant. "If you belonged to my father, you would be beaten within an inch of your miserable life!"

"Aurelia," Rhoda said, turning soulful eyes upon the fuming young woman, "God loves you, too. Just as he desires the best for John Mark, He wants nothing but the best for you, as well."

"And by 'the best,' I assume you are referring to a life of submission and drudgery in this barren wasteland?" the haughty young woman snapped, shaking her head in disdain. "If your God is so powerful, then answer me this: Why are you a lowly serving wench without a shekel to her name, and why do I—a pagan, by your God's standards—reside in kings' palaces, feasting upon everything life has to offer?"

"You are deceived," Rhoda said softly. "God has blessed me beyond measure. I am privileged to serve a kind, godly woman in a beautiful home. What more could I possibly ask for?"

"Well, that just shows how low your standards are," Aurelia laughed contemptuously, tossing a cascade of golden curls over her shoulder. "But what more should I expect from a mere child one lowly step above a common slave?"

"Aurelia, stop," John Mark cut in, torn between his desire for the beautiful Roman seductress and his loyalty to Rhoda, the girl he adored and cherished like a sister. "Rhoda has done nothing wrong."

"You can't be serious!" Aurelia exclaimed. "She followed you here like a foul little snitch, and now you're *defending* her?"

"I should take her home," John Mark sighed, soul weary. "We can finish this discussion tomorrow."

"We can finish it *now*," Aurelia snapped, flinging the glistening piece of fruit into a nearby bush. "Father and I must depart within the week. So are you coming, or not?"

Rhoda turned large brown eyes upon him, her troubled expression conveying her fear for him.

Feeling utterly defeated, John Mark released an impatient sigh. "There must be another way," he groaned, running his hand through dark brown hair. "Must you leave so soon?"

"As I said, within the week," Aurelia told him, her tone uncompromising. "If you wish to accompany me, John Mark, then meet me here at dawn in three days' time. And if not, well then, I suppose this is goodbye."

Turning sharply on her heel, Aurelia stalked down a flowering garden path, her lengthy blonde curls bouncing in time with her angry steps, leaving Rhoda and John Mark to stand, dazed, in the silver moonlight, wondering about what had just happened.

CHAPTER 54

Rhoda

Jerusalem

"Rhoda! Rhoda, wait!"

Pausing amid a blossoming garden path, Rhoda turned sorrowful eyes upon her young master as he hurried after her, dismayed.

"Where are you going?" John Mark asked, catching up to her.

"I'm going home," she whispered, feeling spiritually and emotionally drained.

"Rhoda," John Mark stammered, looking worse than she'd ever seen him. "About tonight...I don't know what to say..."

Rhoda simply gazed up at him, her brown eyes clouded with tears.

"I must ask you not to say anything about this to anyone," he sighed in frustration. "Not until..." Looking away, his voice trailed off in defeat.

"What do you plan to do, John Mark?" Rhoda

certainly hadn't intended to voice the question. But, somehow, the query had flown past her lips before she could stop it.

"I…" Shaking his head, John Mark's misery was apparent. "I just don't know."

"Aurelia said she would be leaving within the week," Rhoda said quietly. "It is doubtful your mother will return from Samaria before that."

"I know," John Mark nodded miserably.

"Would you truly leave Jerusalem, setting sail for Rome, without consulting your mother, without even saying goodbye?" Rhoda asked in shock, anxious for her lady. Should John Mark choose to do such a thing, it would surely break Mary's heart.

"There are no easy answers, Rhoda," John Mark protested, his features appearing especially tragic in the melancholy light of a silver moon. "You know how I feel about Aurelia."

Eyes filling with tears, Rhoda turned and resumed her walk down the path, utterly grieved.

"Rhoda!" John Mark groaned, hurrying after her. "Rhoda, come on. Don't be that way."

Swinging around to face him, Rhoda shook her head in consternation, her soft eyes brimming with anguished tears. "Do you really *love* Aurelia, John Mark, or do you simply love the *idea* of being with a beautiful, forbidden woman?"

"I want to marry her," John Mark said, surprised by the shy maidservant's frank question.

"But does *she* want to marry *you*?" Rhoda implored him. "She hasn't the slightest intention of marriage!"

"In time, that will change."

"Oh, John Mark, you are so deceived."

Eyes flashing in anger, he met her gaze. "That's not true!"

"Don't you see?" Rhoda beseeched him, in tears. "Aurelia is no better than that serpent in the garden, tempting Eve to forsake the ways of God in pursuit of carnal pleasures."

John Mark stared at her, blinking in surprise. "Are you calling her the devil?"

"Well, if the sandal fits!" Unaccustomed to the anger welling up inside her, Rhoda turned and stormed from the garden, weeping softly. It would seem no amount of reason or logic would sway the stubborn young man in his reckless plunge toward destruction. Perhaps he was further gone than she had thought. Perhaps there was little hope for him.

The thought was enough to shatter her heart.

Standing alone in the moonlit garden, John Mark lifted the golden chain from beneath his tunic. Cradling the heavy pendant in his palm, he gazed into the ruby eyes of the serpent, feeling as if his soul was being ripped to bitter shreds.

***

Tabitha

Joppa

"Perfect!" Stepping back to survey her work, Tabitha decided her difficult task was finally complete. It certainly hadn't been easy, but she had somehow succeeded in restoring her aunt's wedding gown to its original luster, mending the tears, replacing missing beads, and coaxing its ivory shine back to

474 | RACHAEL C. DUNCAN

life.

She could hardly wait to show her uncle! She was convinced that even *he* would be impressed with her handiwork!

Glancing over at her daughter sleeping peacefully in the corner, Tabitha wondered if perhaps her uncle hadn't yet retired for the evening. She knew it must be late—exactly *how* late remained uncertain.

Lovingly draping the elegant gown across her flimsy straw mattress, she knelt to kiss her daughter's forehead before slipping quietly from the room. Perhaps, just perhaps, her uncle was still up and about!

Wandering about the slumbering mansion, Tabitha decided it must be even later than she first suspected. Not a single servant remained in sight—not even Eli, who was always the last to retire for the evening. Sighing, she realized her announcement about the dress would have to wait until morning.

Passing through an elegant, frescoed upper corridor, Tabitha decided to return to her own quarters on the first level. It certainly wouldn't do for Eli to awaken and stumble upon her wandering aimlessly about the house. He reported back to her uncle with the faithfulness of an old dog.

Turning on her heel, Tabitha was about to depart when the sound of quiet weeping met her ears. Instantly on alert, her penetrating gaze swept about the dim, lamplit corridor.

There! At the very end of the vast hall, an impressive door overlaid in gold and silver remained slightly ajar. Not once since her arrival had she seen that particular door open. In fact, the servants always hastened past it, intentionally averting their gazes.

Intrigued, Tabitha cautiously approached. The sound of brokenhearted weeping increased as she drew nearer the mysterious door. Gingerly, she pushed it open, stepping cautiously inside—

And instantly felt as if she had been transported to another house! Mesmerized, she found herself standing an enormous bedchamber, brimming with feminine grace and soft, elegant touches. Unlike the garish décor of Joram's mansion, this room was tastefully decorated and expertly arranged. Gently burning lamps stood like graceful sentries, illuminating marble-topped tables, upholstered chairs, and pearly tiles underfoot. A large canopy bed draped with elegant curtains reposed on one wall, covered in a smattering of plush, inviting pillows. Tabitha was most delighted by the charming vanity set complete with a gilded mirror and matching chair gracing another wall, noting several elegant bottles of sweet perfume still neatly arranged on the table.

"What, pray tell, are you doing here?"

Stiffening, Tabitha groaned inwardly at the sound of her uncle's gruff voice. Bracing herself for the lecture of the century, she came reluctantly around the side of the large bed from whence the voice had come.

Dressed in an elegant, silken bed robe, Joram was seated on the floor with his back pressed against the bed, a flask in his hand. Shocked to her core, Tabitha saw that his eyes glistened with a sheen of angry tears.

"You shouldn't be here," Joram growled, his hazel-green eyes narrowing in fury. "You have no right to be here."

"My lord, forgive me," Tabitha apologized humbly, wondering if she had unwittingly sealed her own fate by stumbling upon him in his present state. Joram's incorrigible pride would surely cry out against her unwanted intrusion.

Sighing, she supposed she would soon be packing her bags.

"Leave," Joram commanded tersely, ignoring her heartfelt apology.

"Are you hurt?" Slowly, Tabitha lowered herself to the floor, seating herself across from him.

"I said, leave!" Joram growled, his expression fierce. Taking another long swig from his flask, he swiped his mouth with the back of his hand, his eyes resting upon her in challenge.

"This must be the chamber you shared with Pennie."

"How do you know about Pennie?" Joram demanded fiercely.

"You have left it just as it was the day she died, haven't you?" Tabitha prodded gently, her gaze sweeping over the lovely room. "This is your shrine to her."

"Who told you about Pennie?" Joram demanded again. "It was my cursed staff, wasn't it?"

"No one on your staff said a word," Tabitha assured him, concerned for their well-being in Joram's present state.

"That big-mouthed potter woman," Joram realized, his silver brows drawing together in consternation.

Hiding a smile, Tabitha folded her hands in her lap, waiting patiently.

"Why on God's green earth do you sit there staring at me when I clearly ordered you to leave?" Joram hissed, taking another swig from his flask.

"Because you are hurting," Tabitha said gently, praying silently as she spoke. "Because you needn't suffer alone, my lord."

"I have suffered alone for decades."

"But you needn't do so now."

"You don't know me," Joram told her, his cold eyes forming two narrow slits. "The fact that the same blood flows through our veins is inconsequential."

"But the fact that God brought us together is not," Tabitha reminded him patiently. "My lord, I understand your pain, your secret burden. But you can lay it down. In faith, place it at the foot of the cross. There, *Jesus* bore your burdens and your griefs so you wouldn't have to."

"You are a naïve young woman," Joram lashed out, loathe to relinquish his bitterness. "You know nothing of what it is to truly suffer."

"On the contrary," Tabitha readily answered, "I know a great deal about suffering. My parents were murdered when I was child. I lost both of them on the same day. Several years later, a kindly man named Mark with his wife, Mary, took me in. When he passed away suddenly, it was like a dagger to my heart, for he had become like a father to me. And after that, I married the most wonderful man on earth. He, too, was killed."

Joram simply studied her with glittering eyes, clearly contemplating what she had revealed.

"So you see," Tabitha said quietly, "I, too, have faced my fair share of pain and suffering. It could have destroyed me. But God, in His mercy, kept me from destruction."

"Should it concern me that everyone who happens to get close to you dies of unnatural causes?" Joram quipped in condescension, clearly aiming to nettle her.

"No," Tabitha smiled graciously. "But it should encourage you that God has the power to prevent me from falling apart despite the tragedies I have experienced. Truly, His grace is sufficient."

Joram shook his head vehemently, taking another long drink. Tabitha wondered why he bothered with the dangerous tonic. Clearly, it had failed to numb his pain and frustration.

"When I lost my husband, I nearly lost my faith, as well," Tabitha confessed to him, silently beseeching the Lord to speak through her. Though she hadn't known it when God called her here, she and her uncle had experienced similar pain and loss. Perhaps the Lord could use her testimony to reach this stony-hearted man!

"After his death, I felt robbed of the years I was supposed to share with Stephanos," she continued honestly, watching as a series of expressions passed over her uncle's face —annoyance, misery, regret. "I became angry and embittered for a time, but God was merciful to me. He refused to let me perish in my iniquity, setting me free from my own self-inflicted prison."

"How?" Joram demanded gruffly, skeptical.

"First, He wooed me with a still small voice," Tabitha smiled in remembrance. "He simply wouldn't leave me alone! Despite my brooding and my bitterness, He kept calling me, reaching for me. He also sent fellow believers to speak frankly with me, helping me through the pain and suffering. Having endured the loss of her own husband, my former mistress was incredibly helpful during that time."

"And I suppose you think God has sent *you* here to free *me* from my self-inflicted prison?" Joram drawled, a sardonic edge to his tone.

"Yes," Tabitha answered frankly, surprising him. "Yes, I do."

"And just how do you intend to do that?"

"By loving you unconditionally," Tabitha answered without hesitation. "By sharing the love of Christ any way I can. By uplifting you in prayer and interceding on your behalf."

"My, my," Joram mused, his tone tinged with mockery. "I hadn't realized there was a saint in my employ."

"As I'm sure you've noticed, I'm far from a saint," Tabitha sighed. "But I don't believe it's a coincidence that you and I have both experienced the loss of a beloved spouse. I know from experience that God can heal your heart, my lord. I know because He is healing mine."

"You are ignorant and careless in speech," Joram growled, catching her off guard. "We have nothing—I repeat, *nothing*—in common. Did your husband suffer for days on end, writhing in pain and agony as his spirit struggled to depart from his body? Did you lose your own child in a pool of blood?"

"I haven't lost a child," Tabitha conceded quietly. "But I have lost many loved ones. I understand that your wife's death was traumatic, my lord. Stephanos' death was dreadful, as well. Surely you know what execution by stoning entails? The victim is bound, both hands and feet, then flung over a high precipice or tied to a tree or post, totally immobilized as stones pummel them to death. The torture is agonizing and prolonged. This is the kind of death my husband suffered. For weeks, my sleep was haunted by ghastly nightmares as I agonized over the cruelty my beloved experienced at the hands of wicked men. But in the end, Stephanos triumphed over his foes. He is safe in the arms of his heavenly Father, just as your beloved Pennie is safe in the arms of Christ."

"Stop," Joram ground out, looking away.

"This life is temporal, my lord," Tabitha persisted, her eyes beseeching him to understand. "If we hadn't eternity ahead of us, then I would understand your refusal to accept peace, to find solace in Christ. But this life is not the end. In fact, it's only the portal by which we obtain everlasting life through Christ! Please, my lord, I beg you, cast your cares on Jesus! He will comfort your heart."

The silence that followed was heavy, crackling with tension and foreboding. When Joram finally spoke, his bloodshot eyes conveyed his dangerous wrath.

"Your husband was a foolish man," he spat out, casting aside his empty flask. "If he hadn't sense enough to keep his mouth shut, then he deserved every ounce of what he got."

Tightly clenching her jaw, Tabitha resisted the urge to verbally dismember her uncle for his glaring insolence and hateful pride. Indeed, she knew he would like nothing better than to nettle her to the point of losing all control, and she was determined not to grant him the satisfaction.

"I can see why you married him," Joram continued coldly, carefully gauging her reaction. "After all, you're very much like him. You, too, seem entirely incapable of keeping your mouth shut, even at the expense of your better judgment."

"If you think I am anything like my dear Stephanos," Tabitha said earnestly, "I shall take that as the highest of all compliments."

"Take it however you wish," Joram shot back, perturbed. "But know this: your husband *asked* for trouble, walking into it with eyes wide open. But my beloved Pennie? *She* didn't deserve to die, nor to suffer the way that she did."

The two sat looking at each other for a lingering moment, each measuring the other's response.

"Now *go*!" Joram demanded, his eyes flashing angry fire. "Or I shall command my guards to forcefully remove you from this room!"

Heart pounding like angry war drums, Tabitha rose with grace and dignity despite the ire tearing at her soul. Departing without a word, she left her uncle alone to brood and wallow in his own misery.

And to add yet another stinging regret to the lengthy list he harbored deep within his heart.

CHAPTER 55

Kelila

Sychar

"How I shall miss you!" Kelila mourned, drawing back from Mary's warm embrace. The lovely widow held Kelila at arm's length, her luminescent eyes upon the vibrant young woman.

"It was a pleasure lodging with you and Philip," Mary assured her kindly. "I couldn't have asked for a better hostess."

"The pleasure was entirely ours," Kelila insisted, wishing Mary could stay forever. Even so, she knew that would be entirely unfair to the believers in Jerusalem who depended on her in so many ways. Mary was truly an inspiration, brimming with courage and calm conviction.

"Adorina," Mary acknowledged warmly, taking the Samaritan woman in a sisterly embrace. "What an honor to meet you. Thank you for your hospitality."

"The honor was truly mine," Adorina replied. "I hope we meet again soon."

"And I, as well."

Stepping back a pace, Kelila watched as Philip, Ephraim, Peter, and John exchanged manly embraces, slapping each other on the back and ribbing one another with good-natured humor. It had been such a blessing to share their little town with believers from Jerusalem! How desperately she would miss their sweet fellowship and cheerful camaraderie!

"Will you journey directly to Jerusalem?" Adorina asked Mary and Anaia. "Or do you plan to visit other towns along the way?"

"Peter and John plan to travel throughout Samaria preaching the gospel," Mary explained. "But before we left Jerusalem, the men made arrangements for Anaia and me to return directly to Jerusalem with a traveling caravan."

"Is that safe?" Adorina asked frankly, her brows drawing together in concern.

"The caravan is owned by a wealthy neighbor and fellow believer named Simon," Mary assured her. "His son-in-law is a worthy guard. We shall be safe in his care."

"Excellent." Adorina nodded, satisfied.

"Even so, it will be rather interesting bedding down with smelly camels each evening," Anaia giggled, eliciting smiles of amusement from the women.

"May God go before you, paving the way for safe travels," Kelila said with great feeling.

Taking Kelila's hands in her own, Mary smiled knowingly. "You have blossomed into a powerful young woman of God," she observed. "I am proud of you."

"You wouldn't have been a few short weeks ago," Kelila confessed. "But God is patient. He continues to convict and guide me."

"Amen."

"And if the Lord wills it," Kelila continued, her large brown eyes sparkling with fun, "Philip and I shall see you in Jerusalem at the Feast of Tabernacles!"

After a prolonged farewell, Kelila, Philip, Ephraim, and Adorina watched as Mary, John, Peter, and Anaia stepped onto the main thoroughfare.

Clinging to a post upholding the market stall's colorful canopy, Kelila smiled through her tears. "Oh, how I shall miss them!"

"We all will," Adorina agreed, drawing alongside her and placing a consoling hand on her shoulder. "I think our husbands would gladly sit at the apostles' feet for weeks on end, learning all they could," she added, nodding toward Philip and Ephraim a short distance away. Both men stood in the street, shading their eyes from the glaring sun as they watched the believers' departure.

"Perhaps it's wrong to feel this way," Kelila admitted ruefully, "but I can't say I feel the same about Simon and Helena's recent departure. I must confess, I was relieved when they left."

"Do you suppose they will return?"

"Only the Lord knows," Kelila sighed. Regardless, she was grateful for the welcome reprieve from the sorcerer's smoldering presence.

***

Rhoda

Jerusalem

Trembling from head to foot, Rhoda wondered if she was making a terrible mistake.

Standing anxiously alone in an enormous, unfamiliar reception hall, the young maidservant waited, her hands folded before her, her large brown eyes downcast.

"The master will see you now."

Glancing up in surprise, Rhoda was both relieved and frightened that her request to meet with the master of this grand house had been granted. Would he understand her concerns and lend her aid, or would he simply assume she was a meddlesome servant and hastily dismiss her?

"This way," the manservant instructed abruptly, leading her down a labyrinth of frescoed halls. Taking a sharp turn, the servant ushered her into his master's office with a hasty bow. "My lord," he said in a mechanical fashion. "I present to you Rhoda, the maidservant of—"

"Of the famed Mary of Jerusalem," the broad-shouldered man seated behind the desk responded with a mischievous grin. "Yes, indeed."

With another hasty bow, the manservant departed by the wide corridor from whence he had come.

Folding large hands atop a stack of parchment paperwork, the tall man seated behind the desk flashed the maidservant the friendliest of smiles, his light brown eyes reflecting his fondness. "Greetings, my dear Rhoda," he said, instantly setting her at ease. "What a pleasant surprise! How, pray tell, is that courageous sister of mine?"

"Greetings, Master Barnabas," Rhoda managed a bit shakily. "Your sister has been well. She has not yet returned from Samaria, but the entire household eagerly awaits her imminent arrival."

"I imagine so," Barnabas nodded, sensing the

girl's unease. "Please, be seated," he invited, gesturing toward the pair of upholstered, straight-backed chairs facing his desk.

Surprised by the invitation, Rhoda hesitated. Was it proper for a maid of her low status to be seated before this great man? Rather like his stalwart sister, Barnabas had become legendary in Jerusalem—both in the church and in the world of business. It seemed as if God had granted him success at whatever he set out to do, rousing the jealousy of some and the admiration of others.

Rhoda, too, greatly respected the compassionate church leader. Barnabas had been present that fateful day when her mistress had rescued her from ruthless slavers in Cyprus. She would never forget his kind manner and gentle encouragement aboard the ship bound for Judea after her last-minute rescue. At the time, she'd been quite certain his was the kindest face she had ever seen!

"You needn't fear, dear one," Barnabas spoke up, his warm eyes conveying his understanding. "I imagine something must be heavy on your heart to prompt this unexpected visit."

"Yes," Rhoda nodded timidly, her eyes downcast. "With my mistress away, I wasn't quite sure who to turn to."

"It took great courage to come here, child," Barnabas reassured her. "I'd like to hear all about it. But first, do be seated. It's a bit of a trek from your lady's house, and the weather is rather stifling. Did my staff offer refreshments upon your arrival?"

"Yes, my lord," Rhoda nodded again, though she didn't bother telling him that she had graciously declined the offer. The thought of eating or drinking anything in her nervous state was nauseating.

"Very good, very good." Barnabas smiled, pleased, when Rhoda hesitantly selected the nearest chair. "Now tell me what troubles you. I shall do everything in my power to help you, Rhoda."

Reluctantly meeting his gaze, she saw that he meant it and thanked God for him. "It's not me, my lord," she managed, desperately praying she was doing the right thing. "It's...it's John Mark."

"My nephew?" Barnabas' eyes sobered along with his expression.

"My lord, I'm afraid he is about to make a terrible mistake," Rhoda whispered, her pounding heart racing ahead of her explanation. "And there is very little time to reach him."

***

Tabitha

Joppa

"Tirzah, this is too kind," Tabitha declared, joyfully accepting the heavy crate of beautifully crafted pottery. "I'm sure these will come in handy for the widows."

"I do hope so," Tirzah responded, her eyes sparkling. "I thought about donating food instead, but you have already rallied many well-to-do women of the town to contribute sustenance. Even so, everyone has use for sturdy jars and cookware."

"I wouldn't have even thought to donate such things," Tabitha confessed, her eyes bright. She couldn't help but wonder when Tirzah would accept the truth about Jesus for herself. The spunky but compassionate young widow already behaved so much like a believer! To embrace Jesus as Lord was the natural next step for Tirzah, and Tabitha prayed for this without ceasing.

"Are you still having trouble squeezing everyone into Ruth's small apartment?" Tirzah asked, turning to stoke the fire in her large kiln.

Glancing over at her daughter playing happily on the floor near Tirzah's low table, Tabitha shook her head in perplexity. "I continue to pray for guidance about that," she sighed. "Last week, I suggested meeting in shifts."

"That sounds rather complicated," Tirzah said in her forthright manner. "It would require much more of your time, and Joram won't appreciate that one bit."

"I'd thought of that," Tabitha confessed. "I also considered reaching out to the local synagogue to request the use of one of the rooms in which they instruct students during the week."

"I imagine the religious leaders won't be too eager to swing their doors wide open for someone who teaches doctrine contradictory to their own!"

"I'd thought of that, too."

"It's a downright shame your uncle hoards that big old mansion all for himself," Tirzah huffed, carefully retrieving a hot pot of stew from the glowing coals kindling in the kiln. "It would be the perfect meeting place for your widows and orphans!"

Tabitha simply nodded her agreement, having agonized over the same thought herself. Multiple times. On many occasions.

Her uncle was a mean old lout.

Inwardly repenting of her less-than-godly sentiments toward her uncle, Tabitha resolved to leave the matter in God's hands. He would provide a solution in His own time and way.

"Why don't you instruct the widows here?" Tirzah piped up, catching Tabitha completely off guard.

"Here?" Tabitha repeated, wondering if she had understood correctly. "In your house?"

"Why not?" Tirzah shrugged, lifting the lid from her stew pot with a thick cloth and inspecting the sizzling contents. "I may not have a mansion like Joram, but you could certainly fit more people in *here* than in Ruth's minuscule tenement. We could even leave the door and the windows open so people could gather in the courtyard to hear, as well."

"Oh, Tirzah, how can I possibly thank you?" Tabitha exclaimed, nearly beside herself with excitement.

"Don't be silly," Tirzah replied in her typically forward manner. "It will be good for me, too. I'd like to hear a bit more instruction about your Rabbi, as well."

Heart soaring, Tabitha hugged the crate of pottery close to her chest, nearly overcome. *The widows will be so excited to learn we now have a permanent place to study!*

Well, most of them would be excited...all but one...

"Tirzah," Tabitha began slowly, wondering if she was about to ruin the perfect plan. "You do realize it's quite likely your mother-in-law will attend these meetings?"

With her back facing Tabitha, Tirzah's spine stiffened as she slowly replaced the lid on her cookpot.

"*Former* mother-in-law," she amended brusquely. Releasing a stubborn sigh, she turned to face her friend. "I thought you said Ruth despised your teachings?"

"She hasn't seemed interested thus far," Tabitha conceded. "But she does seem to care deeply for the widows of the region in her own gruff way. It's highly likely she will attend just to keep an eye on them."

"She cares for the widows around here, eh?" Tirzah repeated, a sardonic edge to her tone. "All of them but one, that is."

Cringing inwardly, Tabitha realized her careless comment had merely fanned the flames of Tirzah's hidden animosity. Biting her lower lip, she watched as Tirzah crossed back over to the kiln, poking at the coals rather aggressively with a long rod. Turning once more to face her friend, Tirzah folded stubborn arms across her chest, leaning indolently against the stone counter. "If Ruth wishes to attend meetings here, then by all means, let her attend," she said carelessly, though her eyes betrayed her secret chagrin. "But proud as she is, I can't imagine she'd have the nerve to show her face here."

"May I ask why not?" Tabitha prodded gently, wondering at her friend's unusual hostility. She was terribly curious about the bad blood between her feisty friend and the terse older widow.

"Never mind that," Tirzah replied, setting back to work in her kitchen. "We'll see if she shows up. If so, I guess we'll find out how much brass the old crone has left in her."

CHAPTER 56

John Mark

Jerusalem

Slamming aside his stylus, John Mark pushed back his chair and rose with such force he nearly sent it reeling behind him. Pacing his mother's resplendent office library, he gripped his head in his hands, wishing he could simply squeeze the stress and anguish from his mind.

The woman he loved was leaving, returning to Rome. Should he let her go, he would never see her again. He had no doubt the sensual beauty would have a slew of young admirers chasing after her the moment her elegantly sandaled feet set foot upon Italian soil.

God, why aren't you helping me? John Mark demanded, frustrated beyond belief. *Is this Your way of punishing me because I fell in love with a Gentile? Would You rather pair me with a dull, drab, religious girl?*

I **want the best for you, My son.**

Halting mid-stride, the troubled young man felt chills prickling up and down his spine. Though he'd heard his mother and fellow believers refer to a still small voice on countless occasions, this was the first time he had experienced it.

Composing himself with a bit of effort, John Mark placed a trembling hand upon a magnificent, painted pillar, attempting to steady himself. Deep in his heart, he had no doubt that God wanted the best for him. Even so, he feared what "the best" might turn out to be. He wanted to marry a beautiful girl who set his blood on fire, igniting his passions and fulfilling his deepest longings—not a dowdy Jewish girl who dressed in drab garments and mechanically did everything she was told.

G*od, help!* his heart cried out in desperation. *I want to marry Aurelia! What's so bad about that?*

Do not be unequally yoked together with unbelievers. Can two walk together, unless they are agreed?

You can speak the universe into existence, Lord, John Mark argued adamantly, wondering if he was going mad. *Would it really be so difficult to turn one heart toward You? It was Your idea to reach the Gentiles, not mine! Why can't You help me fix this?*

Silence. Maddening, raging silence.

G*od, I can't let her go,* he groaned inwardly, resuming his anxious pacing. *She makes me feel alive. With her, I see the world in vibrant colors. I can't go back to the way things were before. I can't bear the drudgery of life without her!*

Another lingering silence.

Releasing an impatient sigh, John Mark turned

back toward the desk. He'd like nothing better than to dash the paperwork and office supplies off the polished desk with one angry sweep of his arm. And why shouldn't he? He felt as if the Lord had done that very thing to his life, dashing his hopes and dreams in one fell swoop.

God, grant me a sign, he prayed forlornly, fearful he already knew what the Lord's answer would be. *If I'm not supposed to go to Rome, then stop me dead in my tracks. Otherwise, I shall board ship and begin the life I've always dreamed of.*

"Greetings, my boy!"

Heart nearly stopping, John Mark glanced up bleakly at the sound of his uncle's cheerful voice. Taking one look into Barnabas' warm brown eyes, he knew the reason for his unexpected visit.

It would seem the Lord had given him an answer.

"I thought you were setting sail for Cyprus," John Mark grumped, feeling slightly guilty about his lack of enthusiasm regarding his relative's sudden appearance.

"Next week," Barnabas supplied, closing the distance between them and studying his nephew with a practiced eye.

Wrestling against bitterness and defeat, John Mark simply waited, his insides churning in the most unpleasant way. He already knew what his uncle would have to say. He didn't wish to hear it, but supposed he had no choice.

Dropping a heavy hand upon his nephew's shoulder, Barnabas smiled his encouragement. "May I trouble you for a moment of your time?"

Clenching his fists at his sides, John Mark wondered how on earth Barnabas had learned of his secret romance. No one—absolutely no one—knew of his relationship with the sultry Roman girl.

No one, that is, except a quiet, unassuming maid-servant whom he'd thought he could trust.

***

Aurelia

Jerusalem

Pacing the flowering Roman garden, Aurelia wished there was a sundial handy. John Mark should have arrived long before now! But she had no doubt he *would* arrive. He would be mad—utterly mad—to relinquish a splendid opportunity like this.

Peeved, she resolved to make him pay for forcing her to wait around like a common handmaiden! Perhaps she would flirt with her father's young men once the journey commenced, reminding John Mark that his position was tenuous at best. Should he fail to meet her expectations, she had a vast array of desirable options from which to choose. And he had best keep that in mind.

Caught off guard, Aurelia started when a kindly looking Jewish man entered her domain, the golden chain which she had gifted to John Mark dangling casually in his hand. She detected traces of her lover in his features, despite his abundant sea of light brown curls and a matching beard. Disgusted, she realized a relative must have come in John Mark's stead.

"Hello, Aurelia."

Confused by the stranger's familiar address, the

girl drew slender brows together in challenge. "Who are you, Jew?"

"Ah." Lifting his brows in amusement, the tall, bearded man smiled knowingly. "I am Barnabas, John Mark's uncle."

Peeved, the girl studied him with unveiled hostility. "Have you tried to stop your nephew from coming with me?"

"There was no need," Barnabas said with a knowing little smile. "He made the decision himself."

"I don't believe you."

"I wouldn't lie to you." Returning her pendant with an outstretched hand, Barnabas could see why his nephew had quickly become smitten with the beautiful young woman despite her condescending nature. She was truly a vision, enough to make even the most logical young man lose his head...and very likely, his soul, as well.

Snatching the pendant with little ceremony, Aurelia glared at Barnabas with flashing eyes. "Your nephew is going to regret this."

"On the contrary, he has saved himself a great deal of pain."

Aurelia stared at him in openmouthed shock, her blue eyes filling with venom.

"Should you ever change your mind," Barnabas graciously advised, "you are welcome to join us in study at the house of Mary, John Mark's mother. We would be happy to share the Good News about the blessed gospel of Christ—"

"Save it," Aurelia shot back, seething. "I detest pious Jewish morality."

"Then I suppose you made a rather strange decision chasing after a pious and moral Jewish boy,"

Barnabas observed, a playful twinkle in his kind eyes.

Aurelia simply glared at him, her true colors on full display.

"Good day, Miss Aurelia," Barnabas said with a slight bow and a knowing little smile. "Despite your open hostility against my God, my nation, my heritage, and my people—not to mention my dear nephew—I shall pray earnestly for your salvation and the knowledge of the one true God."

***

Tabitha

Joppa

Descending the stone steps two at a time despite her daughter's added weight upon her hip, Tabitha smiled broadly, hardly able to bear the wait until the following week when the widows would meet in Tirzah's home for the first time! The women had received the welcome news with joy and gladness—all, that is, except Ruth. Tabitha had closely watched her expression while disclosing where the next meeting would be held. The old widow's lips had pursed into a thin, grim line, but she hadn't questioned Tabitha's announcement.

Nor had she promised to attend.

Emerging at the base of the tenement's stone stairs, Tabitha rounded the corner and nearly collided with Adam.

"Whoa, easy there," Adam chuckled, grinning broadly. His muscular arms stretched forth to steady her, but seeming to think better of it, he quickly dropped his hands. "I was just headed up to Ruth's place to see if the women needed any assistance on their way out."

Smiling deeply, Tabitha nodded her appreciation. Recently, Adam had begun assisting the older widows down the flights of steps and carrying their baskets for them. Tabitha greatly appreciated his assistance, as did the elderly widows. The younger women also seemed to appreciate his cheerful presence, though Tabitha suspected it was for an entirely different reason than the aging widows!

"Adam," Tabitha said slowly, flushing slightly when his hazel-flecked eyes met hers. "Last week, you mentioned your willingness to be an ally, if needed."

"And I meant it," Adam assured her wholeheartedly.

"I have a special request," she dared. "It's regarding our next meeting, and I'm hoping you can help."

"At your service, miss," Adam grinned with an exaggerated but chivalrous bow. "How may I be of assistance?"

Biting her lower lip, Tabitha wondered if he would prove so amicable after she confided her daring plan.

CHAPTER 57

Rhoda

Jerusalem

"Rhoda."

Heart leaping into her throat, the pretty maidservant lowered her dust cloth and swallowed hard. She needn't turn around to know who addressed her. She would know the sound of her beloved's voice anywhere.

Today, however, his tone was tinged with anger, even deep resentment.

Trembling inside, Rhoda turned from the tall lampstand she had been dusting in the Upper Room. John Mark stood at the mouth of the wide stone staircase by which believers accessed the large chamber filled with wooden benches, brightly burning lamps, and a humble platform for speakers. Judging by the tight expression on John Mark's handsome face, Rhoda realized that Barnabas must have already paid him a visit.

How had John Mark responded to his uncle's earnest entreaties?

"A word, please," John Mark said tersely, his subtle nod indicating that she was to approach him.

Setting aside her dust cloth, Rhoda gracefully picked her way around the vast sea of benches, pausing anxiously before her young master. Clasping her hands nervously before her, she waited, head bowed in a posture of respect.

"You went to my uncle behind my back."

Rhoda's head came up in surprise at the harshness of John Mark's rebuke.

"I trusted you, and you betrayed me," he continued, his strained voice conveying the intensity of his emotions. "How could you do that?"

Heart fluttering in her chest like a caged bird, Rhoda prayed for guidance.

"Well?" John Mark demanded, uncharacteristically severe.

"I feared for you, John Mark," Rhoda confessed, her gaze and expression downcast. "I was afraid you might be deceived."

"Deceived?" John Mark shot back. "Thanks to you, the woman I love is now on her way to Rome without me!"

"Did your uncle force you to stay behind?" Rhoda asked, deeply saddened. She had hoped and prayed that John Mark would come to his senses on his own.

"I wouldn't say *forced*," John Mark admitted, though anger still clung to his tone. "But he made it quite clear he thought I was making a mistake. He sounded very much like you, actually," he added, his gaze coming to rest accusingly upon her. "I'm curious, did you feed Barnabas his neat little speech word for word, or did he come up with it all on his own?"

Rhoda raised wide eyes toward John Mark, stunned by his blatant disrespect. It was so unlike him.

What had that dreadful girl done to him?

"My uncle convinced me to stay in Jerusalem for now, though he cannot keep me from corresponding with Aurelia," John Mark continued bitterly, running his hand through his hair. "As I'm sure you know, he is setting sail for Cyprus and won't be here to speak with my mother about all that's happened, but I imagine you'll tell her everything the moment she arrives home."

"It isn't my place to tell her," Rhoda said softly, deeply hurt.

"Well, that certainly didn't stop you from running to my uncle," John Mark accused her bitterly.

"That was a special circumstance," Rhoda tried to explain, trembling. "Aurelia gave you an ultimatum, John Mark. I was afraid you might depart for Rome without your mother's knowledge or consent. That would break her heart."

"Ah, so you've broken mine instead. Is that it?"

"Please," Rhoda implored, stretching out her hand. "I never meant to hurt you. I only wished to help you."

"*Help* me? I don't need or want your help," he declared harshly. "Next time, stay out of it." With that, John Mark spun on his heel, clearly planning to take the curved staircase two at a time. It would seem he couldn't escape her presence fast enough.

"John Mark," Rhoda called after him, her voice

catching poignantly.

The angry young man paused on the steps, casting a careless look over his shoulder at her heartfelt entreaty.

"You may not understand what I had to do. But someday, you will," she whispered, her large brown eyes wet with tears.

Shaking his head in frustration, John Mark jogged down the stairs without another word or even a second glance.

Covering her face with trembling hands, Rhoda wept as only the brokenhearted can, feeling utterly alone.

***

Tabitha

Joppa

The widows converged upon Tirzah's house chattering happily, clustering in large groups in the outer court and greeting each other with merry exuberance as their children laughed and played, scampering about the courtyard like jovial little rabbits. Standing in the doorway with Tirzah, Tabitha watched them with sparkling eyes. The widows' and orphans' utter transformation of recent weeks was uplifting and profound. As more and more accepted Christ's message, their joy and contentment grew by leaps and bounds.

Lifting a hand to shade her eyes from the zealous rays of the morning sun, Tabitha scanned the flower-studded lane. Though it was past time to begin the instruction, Ruth had not arrived—to Tirzah's apparent relief. In addition to that, another special guest remained glaringly absent. Heart sinking, Tabitha realized her hopeful invitation must have been declined.

Despite her keen disappointment, Tabitha smiled brightly as she prepared to address the chattering women. Once she announced it was time to begin, as many as possible crowded into Tirzah's cozy home, their countenances bright as they waited to hear more of Jesus' most famous sermon. Tabitha was excited to resume the Sermon on the Mount, for through it, she had obtained many wise words to live by. She knew the message by heart, having heard the apostles expound upon it repeatedly in Jerusalem. And no matter how many times she heard or contemplated the life-changing words of her Savior, she never tired of them. Instead, she gleaned something new each time.

"Thank you so much for coming," Tabitha announced, standing near the front door so those gathered in the outer court and leaning through the open windows could also hear. "It is such a privilege to study with each of you! Let's pick up where we left off last week, shall we?"

A flutter of excitement rippled through the gathering, indicating their eagerness for the lesson to commence.

Suddenly, a dreadful, unexpected stench floated upon the air, causing several to wrinkle their noses or cover their mouths with their shawls. The widows and children exchanged looks of alarm, clearly caught off guard.

"What's that awful smell?" a little boy seated beside Laurel asked frankly, pinching his nose with chubby fingers. Embarrassed, his mother scooped him up and placed him firmly in her lap, casting a look of apology toward the others.

"Don't be alarmed," Tabitha said quickly, holding up her hands in calm assurance. "I am expecting a guest who has a rather smelly, hands-on job. Though he cleanses himself thoroughly before leaving his home, the smell lingers a bit. Even so, I'd like to ask each of you to welcome him warmly. He, too, desires to learn about Jesus."

Exchanging knowing looks with Tirzah, who had positioned herself in the kitchen near the glowing kiln, Tabitha couldn't resist indulging in a broad smile. Apparently, Adam had succeeded in the unlikely mission upon which she had sent him!

***

Simon the tanner insisted upon listening from Tirzah's gate at the edge of the outer court, despite the women's friendly entreaties to join them inside the house. Looking somewhat daunted, it was apparent the big man was completely unaccustomed to receiving a warm welcome. Fleetingly, Tabitha hoped the proud craftsman wouldn't be indignant or offended that she had invited him! Thankfully, Adam had already agreed to stay and participate, hoping the presence of another man would ease the tanner's initial discomfort. Dutifully, a smiling Adam remained rooted by Simon's side near the gate, eager to see him accept the truth. Taking Adam's cue, Tabitha ceased fussing over the big man and the widows followed her lead, which seemed to finally set the gruff tanner at ease.

Resuming her place near the front door, Tabitha offered a silent petition heavenward before beginning.

"Excuse me. Pardon me. I said, *excuse me*!"

Tabitha's heart sprang into her throat at the sound of a familiar, gravelly voice making its way through the outer court.

Ruth. It would seem the gutsy old woman had decided to attend after all! Pushing past the throng gathered near the front door, Ruth emerged, her flashing eyes daring anyone—especially Tirzah—to defy her.

Several widows whispered cheerful greetings to the matronly woman as she pushed through the gathering, heavily seating herself behind the potter's wheel.

Feeling apprehensive for her friend, Tabitha shot an anxious glance toward Tirzah. Her typically friendly features had stiffened along with her spine as her large brown eyes narrowed in contempt. Briefly, Ruth glanced her direction, appearing unsure of herself for the first time since Tabitha had known her. Then she promptly looked away, ignoring the attractive younger widow entirely.

Tabitha wasn't the only one who sensed the tension crackling in the air. The widows and children exchanged nervous glances, as well, clearly wondering about the unusual undercurrents circulating in the room. Hoping to distract from the uncomfortable situation, Tabitha decided it would be best to plunge straight into the lesson. After opening the session with an earnest prayer for wisdom and guidance from the Holy Spirit, Tabitha began.

"Last week, we learned about the special prayer Jesus taught us," she said, steadying her voice with a bit of effort. "If you can, please recite it with me."

A chorus of voices arose, joining hers with passionate sincerity and filling the small house like sweet-smelling incense: "*Our Father in heaven, hallowed be Your name. Your kingdom come. Your will be done on earth as it is in heaven. Give us this day our daily bread. And forgive us our debts, as we forgive our debtors. And do not lead us into temptation, but deliver us from the evil one. For Yours is the kingdom and the power and the glory forever. Amen.*"

"Beautiful! Thank you, friends. I can see you have all been studying!" Smiling at the enthusiastic little body of believers, Tabitha clasped her hands in delight. "I hope our Savior's prayer has proven a comfort to each of you throughout the week!"

Earnest *amens* rippled through the gathering, accompanied by smiles and nods of confirmation, even among some of the little ones.

"Now, this leads us to Jesus' next words," Tabitha explained, inwardly concerned about the deep discomfiture marring Tirzah's typically bright features. "After teaching us how to pray, Jesus taught us yet another difficult but important lesson by saying, '*If you forgive men their trespasses, your heavenly Father will also forgive you. But if you do not forgive men their trespasses, neither will your Father forgive your trespasses.*'"

The room resounded with thunderous silence as each listener contemplated the gravity of their Savior's profound instruction. Undoubtedly, this lesson was a tough one to swallow for many of the widows, most of whom faced severe oppression on numerous fronts.

Oh dear. Heart dropping into her stomach, Tabitha watched as Tirzah reached for her worn gray shawl and slipped out a narrow back door. Had she said something to offend her hospitable hostess? Or perhaps Ruth's glowering presence was simply too troubling for Tirzah to endure. Tabitha couldn't be sure. But she was deeply troubled for her friend.

Glancing anxiously at her audience, Tabitha realized the women and children were so enthralled with this new teaching of Jesus that they hadn't even noticed their hostess's odd behavior. Silently entrusting her dear friend into the hands of God, Tabitha resolved to find Tirzah as soon as the meeting was over.

CHAPTER 58

Mary

Jerusalem

Though she had thoroughly enjoyed her stay with Kelila and Philip in Sychar, Mary was delighted to return home. The journey by caravan had proven dusty but exciting. She had savored the adventurous new experience, while Peter's quiet wife, Anaia, had kept a suspicious eye on the lowing camels. Barabbas, the sturdy and reliable caravan guard, had kindly taken every possible precaution to ensure that the women's journey was pleasant, safe, and swift.

Mary's homecoming had proven both joyous and sweet. The servants had carefully strung garlands of fresh flowers, hanging them throughout the courtyard and reception hall as a warm welcome. In the kitchen, her chefs had busily prepared her favorite cuisine. And Rhoda, bless her kind heart, had been waiting at the door, eager to usher her inside, relieve her of her traveling bags, and gently wash her soiled, aching feet. There was no doubt in Mary's mind that it was the thoughtful young maidservant who had organized the entire household in preparation for her arrival. Being practical, efficient, and quick to notice the needs of others, Rhoda was fast assuming the role of her former mentor, Tabitha. And Mary couldn't have been prouder of the lovely young Cypriot.

Preparing to retire early, Mary pulled back the plush blankets of her canopy bed, mulling over the heartwarming events which had transpired that morning. She hadn't planned to rest so early in the afternoon, but Rhoda had insisted she replenish her strength after her arduous trek from Samaria. Slipping gracefully beneath the blankets, she remained seated upright in bed, deep in thought as she twisted her long, dark brown tresses into a simple braid. While her staff had seemed overjoyed at her arrival, her son had held himself strangely aloof. His uncharacteristic behavior was beginning to concern her deeply, though she wasn't entirely sure how to address it. His lack of enthusiasm about anything pertaining to his faith, his work, or the church deeply disturbed her. He often seemed bored, listless, or lost in brooding thought.

Perhaps I shall reach out to one of the apostles or deacons, she thought. She had no doubt they would willingly speak with her son, and perhaps they would be better suited to the task of comprehending the strange inner workings of a young man's mind, being men themselves! *Simon Peter might be the wisest one to seek,* she decided. *He's had a special place in his heart for John Mark since the death of the boy's father.* But she hadn't the slightest idea how long Peter planned to remain in Samaria with John. Though she assumed the apostles would return to observe the Feast of Tabernacles, their homecoming could be weeks away, and she wasn't entirely sure she should wait that long to act on behalf of her straying son.

Even more perplexing than John Mark's behavior was the odd strain clearly existing between him and Rhoda. And though she couldn't be certain, her maidservant's typically clear brown eyes had revealed traces of weeping when she had met her at the door. What could have possibly transpired between the two of them during her brief absence to sour their innocent friendship?

Tucking away this troubling bit of information, Mary settled comfortably beneath her blanket, both physically and mentally drained. For now, she would keep a close eye on the situation, seeking the Lord's guidance about the best way to move forward.

***

Tabitha

Joppa

"I thought perhaps I would find you here." Drawing alongside the troubled widow, Tabitha gazed over the sheer drop of a plunging precipice overlooking the crashing waves of the Great Sea battering the jagged black rocks below. Dizzied by the fearsome sight, Tabitha swiftly lifted her gaze, looking instead upon the face of her friend.

"Where is Laurel?"

"I stopped by my uncle's on the way here," Tabitha explained, touched by Tirzah's concern for her daughter. "She is safe with Martha."

"Did Simon the tanner enjoy the meeting?" Tirzah asked dully, her eyes fixed upon the crashing waves below.

"I do hope so," Tabitha answered honestly. Much to her dismay, he had vanished amidst her closing prayer, leaving her to wonder about his response. Adam had said the tanner listened grimly throughout her recitation of the Sermon on the Mount, appearing both thoughtful and troubled.

"And how did you find me?" Tirzah demanded, her tone betraying a hint of annoyance. "I haven't brought you here before."

"No, but you've mentioned this place many times," Tabitha reminded her. "This is where you come to think."

Looking away, Tirzah's clouded features betrayed her deep inner turmoil.

"If I didn't know better, Tirzah, I might fear you were considering taking a flying leap off this edge," Tabitha teased, hoping to lighten the mood a bit.

"I considered it once," Tirzah said soberly, drawing a look of wide-eyed surprise from her friend.

"What happened?" she asked softly. Since the spunky widow had proven somewhat evasive about her past, Tabitha hadn't dared to ask many questions. On the rare occasions Tirzah had opened up to her, her manner had been factual rather than emotional, as if relaying the details about a random person off the street rather than sharing the painful realities of her own life.

"It was many years ago. At the time, I thought I

had lost everything," Tirzah sighed, her gaze traveling the vast expanse of the blue horizon rising above crashing, slate-colored waves. "First, my father died when I was a child. I began working at five or six years old to help support my mother and me. I didn't mind the grueling labor, but the abuse I suffered at the hands of various masters was deplorable. Some of those men make your uncle seem like an angel."

Resisting the urge to smile at the unlikely comparison, Tabitha simply nodded, encouraging her friend to go on.

"Without a father to arrange a suitable marriage, I fell prey to a slew of young men eager for an easy conquest," she continued, her tone tinged with self-loathing. "Though I refuted the advances of most, I was dazzled by the attentions of an unbelievably handsome sailor. My mother harbored great reservations about him, but I was impetuous and headstrong. I married him anyway, leaving my mother to live alone in the house that is now mine."

"Was your mother right about him?" Tabitha asked, sensing she already knew the answer.

"That man proved far more cruel than my mother could have possibly predicted," Tirzah said, a muscle in her jaw jerking in barely suppressed anger. "He turned out to be a drunk, a gambler, and a womanizer, becoming abusive and dangerous if I dared to confront him about his behavior. Before long, I loathed that man with my entire being, praying that God would wipe him off the face of the earth just as He did Nabal, the wicked husband of Abigail who later married King David."

Welling with sympathy for her, Tabitha nodded her understanding. She couldn't imagine the nightmare the anxious young bride must have endured at the hand of a broken, abusive young sailor.

"A few years after we wed, my mother became deathly ill," Tirzah continued, her brown eyes brimming with pain and regret. "I will always wonder if perhaps my selfishness and rebellion brought the wasting illness upon her. I know she was worried sick about me, for she suspected I was suffering at my husband's hand. When the sickness became debilitating, I moved into my mother's house to care for her, which was a huge point of contention in my marriage. My husband threatened to accuse me of infidelity if I moved into her home to care for her, which could have led to my condemnation and eventual execution. But I couldn't let my mother suffer and die alone. I went to her anyway, regardless of his threats." Lowering her gaze, she said quietly, "Intoxicated, he fell overboard and drowned a few days later, perishing at sea."

Sensing the roiling combination of emotions tearing at her friend's heart, Tabitha said nothing, praying silently for the Lord's wisdom.

"You know," Tirzah said, her eyes flickering with a slew of confusing emotions as she spoke, "when I learned of my husband's death, I was *relieved*. I felt quite certain God had delivered me from the hand of my oppressor. But then my mother died a week later."

"Oh, Tirzah," Tabitha whispered. "I'm so, so sorry."

Eyes filling with angry tears, Tirzah shook her head fiercely as if attempting to scatter emotions she had buried for over a decade. "I must confess, I was utterly appalled when Ruth dared to set foot in my house this morning. She knew about the abuse, Tabitha! She *knew* what her son was doing to me. I went to her, begging her for help, seeking relief. And do you know what she did?"

"What did she do?" Tabitha asked softly, aching for her.

"*Nothing*," Tirzah spat out in harsh derision. "Absolutely *nothing*. She was so afraid of losing her boy's affections that she willingly allowed me to suffer at his hand! I blamed her, too, for raising such a wicked, dreadful son. Surely she was at least partially at fault for the way he turned out. And when her son died at sea, I could only hope that vile woman would suffer as desperately as I did all those years she refused to help me, refused to intercede."

"I can't imagine what that must have been like for you," Tabitha said softly, feeling at a loss for words. How was she to comfort her friend? She had never experienced abuse at the hand of her own husband, nor the harsh indifference of selfish relatives who did nothing to ease the pain.

"But now you say *forgive*," Tirzah said bitterly, her gaze fixed upon the billowing waves below. "*If you forgive men their trespasses, your heavenly Father will also forgive you. But if you do not forgive men their trespasses, neither will your Father forgive your trespasses.*"

Tabitha's heart leaped in her chest. Was Tirzah saying she sought the Father's forgiveness for her sins and the salvation of His Son?

"Years ago, I stood right here in this very spot," Tirzah confessed, her features softening slightly. "I had lost father, mother, and the hope of a loving marriage. I was a widowed orphan, and the future seemed insurmountable."

"But something changed your mind," Tabitha said gently, her hazel-green eyes filled with empathy.

"I heard a voice," Tirzah explained, her eyes glistening with tears. "A still small voice, as if carried along by the wind upon the waves. Perhaps it merely spoke to my heart, but I heard words reminiscent of the great prophet Isaiah: *I am your Father. You are the clay, and I, the Potter. You, beloved, are the work of My hands. Be still, and I will show you the way.*"

Clenching her eyes tightly shut, Tirzah said brokenly, "Chills claimed my entire being in that moment, for I knew the Lord had spoken to me. He had a plan for my life, which didn't include my ending it by diving headlong off a rocky cliff. From that point forward, I resolved to make the most of my circumstances, and I did. I returned to my father's old potter's wheel, and by the grace of God, was able to scratch out a living. But the bitterness against my husband and my mother-in-law lodged within my heart somehow and remains to this day." Glancing sideways at Tabitha, she whispered softly, "And then *you* showed up, Tabitha, years later. And lo and behold, you came bearing Good News about forgiveness and salvation and the Son of God who is *the Way*. I suppose I knew the moment you first spoke of it, but I cannot argue against it any longer. Jesus is the Way, isn't He? The Way God promised to reveal to me. Jesus is the Way to the Father, the Way to overcome my bitterness, the Way to forgive and, in turn, be forgiven."

Tears streaming down her cheeks, Tabitha nodded earnestly, overcome with relief, gladness, and gratitude toward her merciful God!

"In that case," Tirzah said, releasing a tremorous sigh, "I know what I must do. But first, Tabitha, will you pray with me? I want to receive Jesus as my Savior. I cannot forgive, I cannot move forward, without His help."

CHAPTER 59

Tabitha

Joppa

Returning from the seaside cliff and approaching Tirzah's lovely little cottage, Tabitha wasn't the least bit surprised to see crotchety old Ruth seated patiently in the outer court, her leathery hands folded resignedly in her lap. After all, it was just like her tender, merciful God to arrange this sacred meeting right on the heels of Tirzah's sweet conversion! Exchanging a knowing look with Tirzah, whose features now shone with newfound peace and assurance, the two widows entered the court through the narrow iron gate.

Rising a bit hesitantly, Ruth stood with hands clasped before her as the two young women closed the distance between them. Anxiously twisting her hands, Ruth lowered her gaze, daring a peek at Tabitha and then Tirzah.

"Greetings, Ruth," Tirzah said, her tone devoid

of the former malice. "Believe it or not, I am glad to see you."

"Shalom, my dear friend," Tabitha added sincerely, feeling especially blessed to witness the unlikely reunion.

Ruth lifted heavy, red-tinged brows in surprise, looking back and forth between the two of them with mounting apprehension. "I'm right glad to see the two of you together," she finally admitted. "Tabitha, I'm thinking it's high time I swallowed my pride and received some forgiveness. Perhaps you can assist me in that prayer, if you don't mind."

"I would be honored to pray with you, Ruth," Tabitha said with great feeling, nearly overwhelmed with joy.

"And from you, Tirzah," Ruth dared, her tone a bit unsteady, "I come seeking your...well, your..." Voice trailing off, the old widow wrung her hands in an anxious manner, struggling to maintain her daughter-in-law's clear gaze. Taking another shaky breath, she finally raised her head, speaking with deep conviction, "I come seeking your forgiveness."

***

Mary

Jerusalem

The entire house was aflutter with preparations for the three monumental events of the sacred month of Tishri. Soon, the first day of the seventh month would usher in the Feast of Trumpets with a mighty blast, which in turn readied religious Judeans for the Day of Atonement. Knowing the high priest was powerless to provide atonement for sins through animal sacrifice, the believers had taken to gathering in the Upper Room on that sacred day, rejoicing and celebrating the blessed salvation they had obtained through the shed blood of Jesus Christ. Swiftly following on the heels of the Day of Atonement, the Feast of Tabernacles would then commence with great feasting and rejoicing.

Expertly overseeing the various preparations, Mary wondered where the time had flown. It had been nearly a month since her return from Samaria, and yet the Lord had remained strangely silent regarding her persistent prayers about her troubled son. It seemed odd to her, sensing the Spirit's urging to be still and *wait* when everything in her longed to take the stubborn young man aside and conduct a thorough interrogation regarding his odd and uncharacteristic behavior. She had to admit, she was puzzled by it but unable to detect any underlying reason for his silent withdrawal and sudden lackluster for life. And if she was perfectly honest with herself, it perturbed her greatly to see him moping and trudging about the house as if he carried the weight of the world upon his shoulders! Couldn't John Mark see how exceedingly blessed he was? There was certainly no need to conduct himself like a martyr!

If only my brother was here in Jerusalem, she thought, aching for Barnabas' sound counsel. Inwardly, she resolved to pay him a visit the moment he arrived in the holy city to observe the Feast of Tabernacles! And she had already spoken with Simon Peter, as he and John had recently returned to

Jerusalem for the feast. Grimly, Peter had asked her if she would like him to speak with her son. Though she had greatly desired to say yes, she shared with him the Spirit's surprising admonition to *wait*. Nodding his understanding, Peter had promised to pray for John Mark and pay special attention to his unusual behavior. Perhaps he could glean some useful information about the situation with a bit of careful observation. Mary certainly hoped so. As a woman of action accustomed to tackling problems head-on, it nearly drove her to distraction to simply wait and do *nothing*. Nothing, that is, but pray.

In addition to that trying dilemma, Mary was also becoming exceedingly aware of yet another unwelcome situation. The mounting tension between her favored maidservant and her glowering son was unmistakable. At first, she had wondered if she was merely imagining it. But now, the great lengths to which both Rhoda and John Mark went simply to avoid each other would have almost proven comical had she not been so concerned about it.

If I didn't know better, I would think the two of them shared a lovers' quarrel in my absence, she thought, pausing on a balcony overlooking the outer court to survey materials gathered to construct a sukkah on the appointed day. But no, the thought of a lovers' quarrel was utterly preposterous. Though Rhoda adored her son, John Mark wasn't the least bit interested in the quiet maiden.

Resting her hands on the elegant ledge, Mary decided to turn her thoughts upon happier subjects. She certainly wasn't solving any problems brooding and stewing over the matter. In time, the Lord would reveal the best course of action or provide a worthy solution. But until then, she must simply watch, wait, and trust Him.

With a bit of effort, Mary maneuvered her thoughts back to her lengthy to-do list, mentally checking off the tasks she had accomplished and reviewing what remained undone.

I should check with Candace to see if she has food enough for guests, she decided, smiling at the thought of Philip and Kelila's impending arrival for the third of the upcoming holidays. Though she would have loved to host the young couple at her own large estate, she understood Candace and Simon's desire to accommodate their own family. Turning from the balcony to see to her remaining tasks, Mary continued to pray that Kelila would be fully restored to her mother during her stay in Jerusalem. She had dutifully delivered Kelila's letter to Candace, who in turn had read it to the sedate older woman.

According to Candace, her mother's reaction to the letter was reserved, at best.

***

Kelila

Sychar

Lying still in the gathering darkness, Kelila gazed up at a ceiling she couldn't see. She could hear the comforting sound of Philip's soft breathing beside her, the steady pattern indicating that he was deep in sleep.

Tomorrow, they would depart for Jerusalem. It

felt strange, leaving Sychar for even a brief trip. She felt obligated, somehow, to remain, to oversee the believers' growth and development, and to ward off opportunistic deceivers like Simon and his wicked enchantress, Helena. Though she knew she and Philip would soon return to Sychar, she felt rather like a mother hen leaving her chicks susceptible to ravenous wolves.

The thought was deeply concerning.

Even so, she reminded herself that God would watch over the Samaritans in her absence. In addition to that, Ephraim had promised to oversee church gatherings and keep his eyes open for any possible threats while Philip and Kelila were away. Knowing this helped set her troubled mind at ease. Ephraim, along with his wife, Adorina, was a capable, godly believer. She had no doubt he was qualified for the task of shepherding the church in their brief absence.

How strange it is, she thought, smiling to herself as she drew the covers to her chin. *To think that God has established a church here in the heart of Samaria! His wonders never cease!*

Releasing a tremorous sigh, Kelila touched her forehead, wondering if she was slightly fevered. She hadn't felt well at all lately, and the thought of hard travel only increased her trepidation. It certainly wouldn't do to come down with a dreadful sickness in some remote region between Judea and Samaria!

Perhaps it's simply nerves, she thought, considering how anxious she was about seeing her mother again. She desperately longed to mend the broken relationship, but it was quite likely her mother would want nothing to do with her.

Closing her eyes, Kelila decided to pray rather than waste any more time in worry. Perhaps she would soon feel better in the presence of her beloved family and fellow believers of Jerusalem.

***

John Mark

Jerusalem

The Feast of Trumpets came and went, ushering in the Day of Atonement, and with it, a tense solemnity that seemed to hover over the entire city like a brewing storm cloud. Despite the spirit of heaviness that had settled upon Jerusalem's inhabitants, the Upper Room maintained its cheerful glow as faithful believers gathered together for prayer and worship.

Pacing the inner garden court later that evening, John Mark mulled over the sermon that had been presented by the Apostle Matthew, a former tax collector. Somehow, Matthew's testimony had shaken him to the core, despite the fact that he'd heard it many times before.

"Before I met Jesus," Matthew had explained, *"I lived for myself and my own pleasures. Betraying my people, I became 'Roman' in every sense of the word. I lived like the Romans. I dressed like the Romans. I feasted and reveled and caroused like the Romans."* Matthew had gone on to explain that, despite his desperate aspirations to achieve pleasure, happiness, wealth, and success, he had remained utterly miserable. *"A life without morals, without boundaries, without Jesus, is no life at all,"* he'd confessed, his soft brown eyes coming to rest upon

John Mark in the most unsettling way. *"During that godless season of my life, I was constantly waiting for someone to betray me, to stab me in the back, to end my thriving career in one fell swoop. I never knew who I could trust, and frankly, none of the people whom I surrounded myself with could be trusted. It was a miserable way to live, and I'll never regret leaving it all behind. Never."*

Hours later, as he paced his mother's tranquil garden courtyard in the waning light of early dusk, John Mark's heart and mind remained utterly conflicted, as if his soul was being torn to shreds in a battle waged between opposing forces.

On the one hand, he couldn't stop thinking about Aurelia. At this point, she was probably aboard the most luxurious ship money could buy or residing in an opulent palace in an exotic Roman outpost along the way. Considering the time that had elapsed since her departure, John Mark supposed she might have even reached Rome by now. Groaning inwardly, his heart throbbed at the mere thought of her, filling him with indignation against those who loved him most. After all, *they* stood between him, the woman he loved, and the exciting future he desired.

On the other hand, despite his raging indignation, he *loved* his mother. He *loved* his uncle, his church family, his city, his heritage. And even more importantly, he loved his God, despite the fact that He seemed determined to keep him from the future he craved. John Mark knew salvation was through Christ alone, and the possibility of turning against the Lord frightened him. Jesus made it abundantly clear that a believer must walk by faith, in obedience. To disregard a clear command of God, choosing to yoke himself to a flagrant unbeliever, might very well endanger his soul.

Pausing amidst his mad pacing, John Mark placed a steadying hand upon a graceful pillar, leaning in until his forehead touched the cool marble. Remembering his final conversation with Aurelia, he wondered why he was still so crazy about a girl who had made it perfectly clear she had no intentions of remaining faithful to him and possessed absolutely no desire to marry him. And then he recalled her alluring blue eyes, arresting features, graceful curves, and soft, sensual kisses, and he was swept away once again.

Annoyed by his own lack of resolve, John Mark balled his hands into fists and resumed his anxious pacing. Was he really such a weak-willed young man? Could his fleshly passions truly dominate his common sense and better judgment, even his faith?

Apparently, yes. Yes, they could.

Why, oh why, couldn't Aurelia be both beautiful and noble? he thought, peeved. *Why must the most gorgeous of women lack strength of character?* It just wasn't fair, not fair at all!

Running his hands through dark brown hair, John Mark would have groaned aloud if he wasn't worried about alerting the entire household as to his whereabouts. Right now, he needed to be alone. He needed time to think, time to pray, time to let the Holy Spirit get ahold of his rebellious, stubborn heart!

Drawing a calming breath, John Mark lowered himself onto a marble bench, attempting to sort through his raging thoughts. The evening's pleasant song filled his senses with the sound of chirping crickets, the crackling of burning torches, and the wind whispering its way through low hanging branches. The night seemed perfect for contemplations, and he couldn't help but wonder if the Spirit had lovingly drawn him to this time, this place, this moment.

For the first time in many months, he was ready to evaluate his own heart, his past, present, and future choices.

Matthew's timely sermon remained fresh on his mind, reminding him that he was, indeed, being pulled in two entirely different directions. And now it was time to make a *choice*. What kind of life did he truly desire, and even more importantly, what kind of life did *God* desire for him? Whom did he wish to serve? Himself? His own fleshly passions? Did he truly wish to forsake the path of everlasting life to pursue a shallow young woman who had made it perfectly clear she would leave him the moment issues arose or their attraction for each other waned?

Grasping his head in his hands, John Mark knew what must be done. He needed to speak with his mother—not because his uncle, Barnabas, had made it perfectly clear he was expected to do so—but because he desired true restoration. He must confess his deception and his sins, seeking first God's forgiveness, then hers.

Rising hesitantly from the bench, he glanced up at the silver moon rising steadily in the evening sky. Its light filtered through the graceful canopies draped about the garden court, washing the tiles underfoot with a bright, heavenly glow. And suddenly it occurred to him that, in his rebellion and selfish pride, he had unwittingly hurt another innocent victim to whom he owed a fervent and sincere apology.

Squaring his shoulders in firm resolve, John Mark beseeched the Lord for forgiveness, help, and guidance. He certainly didn't relish the humbling task ahead of him.

***

Mary

Jerusalem

Kneeling in earnest prayer, Mary rested trembling hands upon the stone ledge of an open bedroom window as delicate curtains fluttered in the soft evening breezes. Her son remained heavy on her heart tonight, heavier and heavier by the day.

His was such a difficult age. She remembered wallowing through that season of life herself, desperately longing for love, for acceptance. Seeking a place to belong. Wondering what the future held for her. If one wasn't firmly rooted in the love of God, determined to live by obedience rather than one's own fleeting, fickle feelings, he or she could easily be swept away by a wicked world's relentless tide.

Righteous Father, Mary prayed, seeking to calm her anxious heart, *I feel as if John Mark is slipping away. He seems uninterested in spiritual things and discontent with the blessings You have lavished upon him. I sense he is seeking more, little knowing the excitement he craves will likely destroy him. Please, Father, draw him close to You. Fill his heart with a desire and longing to know You, to love You, to please You.*

Resting her head upon the window's cool ledge, a tear slipped down Mary's slender cheek. *I have raised him in Your Word, Father. I have surrounded him with godly witnesses and sought to instill the*

Scriptures in his heart and mind. I have tried to live by example, though Heaven knows I often fail. What more can I do, Father? What more can I do?

B*e still.*

Releasing a tremorous sigh, Mary lifted solemn eyes toward Heaven.

P*recious Lord, I was afraid You might say that.*

I ***AM working. I AM here. Trust Me.***

Y*es, Lord.* Clasping her hands tightly, Mary nodded in tearful submission. *I trust You.*

Mary wasn't sure how long she remained in a posture of prayer, her heart and mind wide open for the Spirit's gentle leading. All she knew was that she needed this time alone with her Savior, this time to cast her cares upon Him and to accept the strength He so freely gave.

"Mother?"

Mary lifted her head in surprise, her heart pounding in her chest.

John Mark stood in the doorway, his handsome features clouded with regret.

And Mary knew her prayers of many sleepless nights had been answered. Rising slowly, her perceptive eyes met his. The look upon his young face warned her she'd best steel herself for whatever confession he was about to make.

"John Mark," she said with great feeling, stretching forth her hand.

Hesitating slightly, her son looked more vulnerable than she had ever seen him. After what felt like a very long pause, John Mark finally managed to speak.

"May we talk?"

CHAPTER 60

Kelila

Jerusalem

The journey to Jerusalem proved far more challenging than Kelila had anticipated. With each mile traveled, she felt weaker and weaker. Pounding headaches and bouts of nausea only furthered her intense discomfort. On multiple occasions, she had considered asking Philip to turn back, fearful she had become seriously ill. But then, just as suddenly, the symptoms would vanish, leaving her feeling famished, frustrated, and ill-tempered.

Despite her misery, she had somehow refrained from voicing her discomfort to Philip. He was so excited about returning to the brethren in Jerusalem, and she couldn't bear to mar his joy by worrying him.

Now, as she and Philip approached the familiar little house dotting a bustling avenue in the Lower City, Kelila's heart began to pound in time with her throbbing temples. It had been less than a year since this cherished little home had filled her vision, and yet, it seemed like an eternity. Dark eyes welling with tears, she gripped Philip's strong hand, her own trembling with joy...and apprehension.

"Well, it looks like we made it." Sensing his wife's unease, Philip smiled down at her, offering her hand an encouraging squeeze.

"We did," Kelila breathed, wondering what to expect. Had her loved ones changed in the months of their absence? Would her friendship with Candace feel natural or stilted? Would her nephews still remember her?

Drawing up to the gate she had passed through so many times before, Kelila no longer resisted the tears streaming down her cheeks.

I'm home, she thought, her heart constricting in her chest. *Oh, Jerusalem, beloved Jerusalem, how I've missed you!* For here, in the holy city, God had revealed Himself to her in a powerful way. Here, she had been restored to her beloved sister, her brother-in-law, and her precious nephews. Here, she had fallen in love with the most wonderful man in the world and married him, surrounded by family and friends. Here, she had learned what love truly is. And here, she was freed from the guilt and shame of her past.

Well, *almost* freed...for now she faced yet another hurdle to overcome, and she hadn't the slightest reason to believe she would be successful.

Suddenly, the front door of the house flung open, interrupting her anxious thoughts. And then she saw Candace, her arms outstretched as she closed the distance between them, weeping tears of joy.

"Kelila! Oh, my sister, is it really you?"

Within mere seconds, the sisters were in each other's arms, laughing and crying all at once as Simon, three and a half-year-old Rufus, and nine-year-old Alexander flooded out of the house, closing in on them with broad smiles and warm embraces.

Simon went straight to Philip, clapping him firmly on the back and welcoming him home. And everyone laughed as the rambunctious Rufus and even the typically quiet Alexander clamored for their aunt's attention, coming between the two sisters to tug on Kelila's garments and wrapping their arms around her. Laughing merrily, Kelila knelt and swept them both up in eager arms.

What was I worried about, anyway? Kelila thought, blinking back tears of joy. *It's as if we never left. Truly, God knits families together forever.*

"Kelila, you look positively radiant!" Candace declared as her sister arose with Rufus clinging to her leg and Alexander, her opposite arm.

"And you look beautiful, as always!" Kelila laughed, warmed to the core by the presence of her dear family. "I can't even begin to describe how happy I am to see you! How desperately I have missed all of you!"

"And we've missed you both, as well," Candace assured her, her soft features aglow with warmth. "We pray for your ministry in Samaria without ceasing."

"Your prayers are deeply felt," Philip told her, exchanging a knowing look with his beaming wife. "You wouldn't believe how mightily God is working there."

"Peter and John gave us a full report when they returned," Simon informed them, shaking his head in disbelief. "Truly, God is with you in this mission."

"We can't wait to hear all about the new church in Samaria," Candace said in her calm, tranquil way. "I hope neither of you were planning to get any sleep tonight!"

Both couples shared in the hearty laughter that followed, reveling in the joy of being together once again.

And then the lively chatter ceased when a lovely but somber African woman emerged from the door-way, her serious features clouded with concern.

"Mother," Kelila breathed, her hand fluttering to her heart.

Sensing Kelila's mounting tension, the boys reluctantly released her, looking back and forth between their beautiful young aunt and their stately grandmother. The outer court grew deathly still as the striking older woman drew before Kelila, her dark eyes betraying a flicker of sadness...and something else. Was it anger? Resentment? Indifference?

And then, entirely unexpectedly, the sedate older woman held out her arms to her youngest as tears trickled down both cheeks.

"Oh, Mother," Kelila wept, going to her without hesitation.

The entire gathering released a collective breath as the mother held her estranged daughter, strok-ing her quivering back and whispering words of comfort. Taking her sons by the hand, Candace exchanged a knowing look with Simon and Philip, her own brown eyes filled with tears.

"Oh, Mother, I'm sorry," Kelila gasped when her mother finally drew back, holding her at arm's length. "I'm so sorry I hurt you and Father. It was wicked, and it was wrong, and I—"

"Hush, child," her mother said firmly, placing a slender finger upon her lips. "All is forgiven."

"But I—"

"All is forgiven," she repeated, her tone boding no argument. "How could I withhold my forgiveness from you when Jesus has forgiven me a lifetime of sin?"

"Wait," Kelila gasped, looking at her mother with wide eyes. Casting a brief look of utter shock toward Philip, who appeared equally surprised, Kelila pulled her attention back to the woman standing before her. "You accepted Jesus, Mother?"

The rest of the family broke into knowing smiles, nodding heartily to confirm Philip and Kelila's suspicions.

"Oh, Mother!" Kelila cried, throwing her arms around her mother's neck. "Just when I thought I couldn't possibly get any happier!"

"Praise God," Philip breathed, thrilled for his wife and newfound mother-in-law.

"God is good," Simon agreed with a small smile.

"Indeed," Kelila's mother answered, taking her daughter's hands in her own and gazing warmly into her eyes. "Now we are knit together in Christ. And nothing shall ever separate us again."

***

Mary

Jerusalem

Seated on a bench in the Upper Room between a beaming Kelila and her fully restored son, Mary closed her eyes, savoring this precious moment, a gift from God, as Philip addressed the church gathering from the humble speaker's platform. The moment the believers had learned of their beloved deacon's arrival, they had insisted that he deliver the sermon that evening. And Philip had graciously acquiesced, clearly excited to share about all that God was doing in Samaria.

Thanking God, Mary rejoiced at the sight of her previously straying son as he leaned forward on the bench, thirstily absorbing Philip's teachings. And he wasn't the only one seemingly entranced, for the entire room of believers appeared to hang upon Philip's every word, thrilling about the fulfillment of Jesus' great commission and the Holy Spirit at work.

Turning to offer Kelila an encouraging smile, Mary's slender brows drew together in concern at the sight of the younger woman. Seated slightly hunched over with arms encircling her own waist, Kelila's typically rich complexion had suddenly grown deathly pale.

"Kelila?" Mary whispered, worried for her. "Are you all right?"

Looking utterly miserable, Kelila turned her head almost painstakingly to meet Mary's gaze. But before she could respond to Mary's question, her brown eyes grew wide with alarm. Springing to her feet, she turned and fled the room, one hand clamped firmly over her mouth.

Having witnessed his wife's shocking behavior, Philip appeared frozen on the platform, shocked and openmouthed. Appearing to compose himself with a bit of effort, he exchanged an imploring look with Mary seated on the front row. Nodding in response to the evangelist's silent petition, Mary's eyes conveyed a clear message: *You needn't worry, Philip. I will check on her.*

Hesitantly, Philip resumed his teaching, although it was obvious his thoughts remained with his wife.

Rising slowly so as not to cause any further disturbance, Mary whispered her intentions to a worried Candace, who in turn relayed the message to her mother.

Hiding a knowing smile, Mary hastened after Kelila, descending the steps of the gracefully curved stairway two at a time.

It would seem her dear friend, Kelila, was in for a rather unexpected surprise.

***

Kelila

Sychar

Kelila was quite certain she had never been more humiliated in her entire life!

Sequestered with Mary in a dim, quiet washroom typically utilized by the servants, Kelila sat on a simple chair while leaning heavily on a wooden table, her rich cascades of ebony tendrils draped over one shoulder. At her feet, a convenient little bucket had been supplied by a kindly servant at Mary's request, for which she was quite grateful. Though she certainly hoped she wouldn't need it.

"How are you feeling?" Mary, seated beside her, asked as she dipped a wash rag in a basin of cool water on the table. Wringing it out, she dabbed at Kelila's face and forehead in a motherly fashion.

"I should be up there with Philip," Kelila moaned in response, clutching her own churning belly. "Not hiding down here in this washroom feeling sorry for myself. He must be worried sick about me."

"Philip is just fine," Mary assured her, wringing out the cloth in a separate basin on the table, which was utilized for storing used water. "He knows I'm with you. Your family knows, as well."

"I interrupted the first sermon he has been privileged to deliver here in Jerusalem since we left! How could I do that, Mary?"

"You certainly didn't do it on purpose," Mary reminded her with a rueful smile, feeling Kelila's forehead with the back of her hand.

"I'm positively mortified," Kelila groaned, covering her face with her hands. "I can't believe I got sick at the bottom of your lovely staircase!"

"There is no need to apologize," Mary assured her, graciously waving aside her concerns. "It's happened to all of us, at one time or another."

"It's never happened to *me*!" Kelila declared emphatically. "Not until this evening. Quite frankly, I don't know what's gotten into me lately. I'm beginning to worry."

"Have you shared this with Philip?" Mary asked, suspecting she had not.

"Not yet," Kelila supplied a bit sheepishly. "You know how he worries about me. I didn't wish to trouble him."

"I think he would want to know," Mary told her gently. "He would want to take care of you."

"He has far more important things to worry

about," Kelila insisted, battling fresh waves of nausea. Reaching for the convenient little bucket, she clutched it close to her heart, closing her eyes in misery. "Oh, Mary. I just haven't felt at all like myself lately."

"How so?" Mary asked, hoping to confirm her secret suspicions.

"It's the strangest thing," Kelila murmured, her brows drawing together in perplexity. "One moment, I'm so hungry I feel as if I could eat every ounce of bread in the village. But the next, I'm so nauseous I simply want to die!"

"What else?"

"Well, I've been dealing with headaches," Kelila ventured, recalling her most recent symptoms. "And I feel so tired, Mary, so unbelievably tired. Even after a full night's rest, I feel as if I can't even lift myself out of bed."

"I see."

"And worst of all," Kelila confided, dropping her tone lest a passing servant overhear her secret angst, "I'm gaining weight! Can you believe it? Oh, I'm positively mortified!"

"Kelila," Mary chimed in, tickled by the young woman's reaction.

"I have always had a slender waistline, Mary," Kelila plunged ahead, clutching her bucket like a lifeline. "Sooner or later, Philip is bound to notice! I will be so humiliated if he says anything—"

"Kelila!"

Kelila froze mid-sentence, surprised and somewhat miffed by Mary's abrupt interruption.

Chuckling softly, Mary reached across the table, covering Kelila's hand with her own. "There is nothing wrong with you, beloved," she assured her, her luminous gray eyes alight with joy.

"There's not?" Kelila repeated dumbly, perplexed.

"No, there's not."

"If there's nothing wrong with me," Kelila ventured in confusion, "then why do I feel like I'm dying?"

"Because the Lord has greatly blessed you," Mary replied, resisting the urge to burst out laughing at the look Kelila gave her. "Kelila, you feel this way not because you are dying, but because you are nurturing a brand-new life within."

"A brand-new life…" Halting mid-sentence, Kelila stared at Mary, her brown eyes growing wide as saucers.

Laughing musically, Mary simply nodded in joyous confirmation. "Congratulations, my dear sister. It would seem you are expecting a baby!"

CHAPTER 61

Kelila

Jerusalem

If Philip thought it was strange his wife had requested an evening stroll after a day's worth of rigorous
travel, he somehow refrained from voicing his
opinion.

"I wish I hadn't missed your sermon this afternoon, Philip," Kelila said, taking her husband's arm
as they traveled a quiet lane. It had been rather difficult to locate this lonely street, as every family in
Jerusalem was busily welcoming swarms of relatives
and guests arriving for the pilgrimage feast and constructing impressive tabernacles on their rooftops,
in their courtyards, or lining the bustling streets.

"And you're sure you're all right?" Philip asked
her, giving her hand a playful squeeze. "I've never
seen you run so fast!"

"I'm fine," Kelila shot back, rolling her eyes in
mock exasperation. "But there *is* something I wish

to speak with you about."

"Oh?" Philip asked as they approached a quiet nook situated by an ancient stone fountain. Though the trickle of water produced by the old structure was less than impressive, the couple appreciated the solitude. Lowering himself onto a bench cut directly into the aging stone wall encircling the fountain and surrounding court, Philip glanced both ways to ensure they were alone before pulling his wife onto his lap.

Giggling, Kelila draped her arms over his broad shoulders, clasping her hands behind his neck.

"This is nice," Philip teased, encircling her waist with his arms.

"Though I am thrilled to be staying with my sister's family, I coveted a quiet moment alone with you," Kelila admitted, biting her lower lip as her nervousness mounted. "I considered waiting to tell you until we returned home, but I just couldn't! I couldn't wait!"

"To *tell* me?" Philip repeated, a mischievous glint in his eye. "Tell me what? Should I be worried?"

"Perhaps," Kelila laughed, wondering what his reaction would be.

"And how long do you intend to keep me in suspense?"

"That depends," Kelila grinned, enjoying their little game. "I saw this lovely little jeweler's stall when we were passing through the market square. I'm sure I could be persuaded to reveal my secret if you were willing to make a few paltry purchases—"

"Nice try," Philip grinned, nuzzling her slender throat. "I know you're not after gold and jewels."

"Not anymore," Kelila confessed. "Once, I was."

"In another lifetime."

"It certainly *felt* like another lifetime," Kelila mused, marveling at all the Lord had accomplished in such a brief period of time. And to think, soon, they would be welcoming a *baby*! What a gift from God!

"Philip," Kelila said slowly, her brown eyes fixed upon the kind face she adored. "What if I told you I plan to bring someone back home with us?"

"You do?" Philip's features betrayed his confusion. "Your mother, perhaps? She might enjoy a trip to Sychar—"

"It's not my mother."

"Your sister, then?"

"No, not my sister."

"Mary?" Philip asked, running out of ideas.

"No, it isn't Mary."

"Then who?" Philip asked her, his eyes betraying his puzzlement.

Taking Philip's strong hands, Kelila fitted them around the barely discernible bump forming on her abdomen, lifting teary, joy-filled eyes to meet his.

"No!" Philip exclaimed, nearly beside himself. "Kelila, are you saying…are you…?"

Kelila could only nod, so overcome with tears of joy.

"No, I can hardly believe it!" Philip cried, his hands tightening on her abdomen. "Kelila, my love! Is it true? Are we really expecting a baby?"

"Yes," Kelila laughed, nodding through her tears. "Yes, Philip. God has blessed us with a child!"

"Oh, my love! I'm so happy, so happy!" Cupping

her shining face in his hands, Philip kissed her firmly, pulling her close.

***

Kelila

Sychar

Kelila decided she'd never had more fun in her life than the moment she and Philip gathered the family together and announced their happy secret!

"Praise Adonai!" Kelila's mother breathed, her eyes filling with tears. "Another grandchild!"

Rushing from her chair beside the hearth, Candace grasped her sister in a warm embrace. "I am so happy for you, Kelila! So happy!"

Even the typically staid Simon's eyes sparkled with joy as his young sons pranced about the small house, squealing and thrilling about the brand-new cousin soon to enter the world.

"How far along are you?" Candace asked, clearly eager to welcome the little one.

"Mary thinks I'm about four or five months along," Kelila supplied, her eyes sparkling with excitement as a beaming Philip draped his arm about her shoulders, pulling her close.

"Perhaps you should remain with us until the child is born," Candace suggested hopefully, always protective of her little sister.

"I'm afraid we must return to Sychar after the feast," Kelila explained gently, sensing her sister's—and mother's—keen disappointment. Though she would have loved to remain with her family in

Jerusalem, she knew they must fulfill the Lord's calling in Samaria.

"But will the journey home be safe for the little one?" Candace dared as her husband drew alongside her, placing a comforting hand on her shoulder.

"Jesus' mother traveled in her final month of pregnancy!" Kelila laughed merrily. "I think I can manage it being just four or five months along."

"Jesus' mother, Mary, did indeed travel in her final month," Philip agreed with a playful twinkle in his eye. "Though I'd prefer not to repeat her story!"

"Why? You don't relish the idea of your wife giving birth in a stable with all the animals?" Candace teased him.

"Not particularly," Philip admitted with a chuckle, and everyone in the room shared a laugh with him.

Gazing around the lamplit home that had become so dear to her heart and observing the sea of beloved, shining faces before her, Kelila decided she had never been more blessed in all her life.

Truly, truly, God was good.

***

John Mark

Jerusalem

Night had fallen upon Jerusalem, casting the ancient city in shadows and flaming torchlight.

Emerging at the top of a steep stone staircase, John Mark stepped onto the flat, sprawling rooftop of his mother's villa, allowing his gaze to sweep across the slumbering city below. Thousands upon thousands of makeshift booths called tabernacles filled his vision and the holy city, representing the dry desert years in which the Israelites had wandered through the wilderness. Yet even in their imperfect, discontented state, God had preserved His people.

Shaking his head in awe, John Mark sent a prayer of thanks heavenward. For in His unfailing love and faithfulness, God had preserved *him*, too. Falling prey to his own carnal passions, John Mark had wandered through a wilderness of his own making, nearly losing his head in the perilous quest to follow his heart.

Tearing his gaze away from the mesmerizing cityscape beyond, John Mark drew closer to the elaborate sukkah the servants had busily constructed in preparation for the Feast of Tabernacles, which would commence at sunset the following day. The temporary structure was truly stunning, boasting sturdy canvas walls, plush Persian rugs underfoot, flickering hanging lanterns overhead, a low table at which to recline, and garlands of fresh, fragrant flowers.

Coming around the side of the lovely tent, John Mark peered through the wide opening where two massive flaps had been tied back to reveal the sukkah's cozy interior.

And his heart sprang into his throat at the unexpected sight of his mother's favored maidservant standing inside the tent, her slender back facing him as she reached high overhead to secure another thick garland of flowers. Deeply absorbed in her work, Rhoda remained completely unaware of his presence as she adjusted the fresh garland, stepping back slightly to survey her work. Fingering another lovely garland draped around her slim shoulders, she appeared to be searching for the perfect spot to place it.

Watching her intently, John Mark was struck by the girl's quiet strength and graceful dignity. She was fast becoming a lovely young woman, her deep inner beauty mirrored upon her gentle features. Someday, possibly quite soon, she would grow up and marry a godly man, leaving his mother's estate—and him—behind.

To his great surprise, the thought disturbed him.

At that moment, Rhoda must have sensed his eyes upon her. Turning slowly, her large brown eyes scanned the tent's plush interior...and landed unexpectedly upon her handsome young master standing on the threshold, his dark eyes fixed upon her.

"My lord," she nearly whispered, startled by his sudden appearance and clearly unsettled by his company.

Wincing inwardly, John Mark could not blame her for her unease. After all, he had been harsh, demanding, and condescending in his treatment of her. With a slight pang to his heart, he wondered if she would ever trust him again. As Rhoda met his gaze with anxious brown eyes, a garland of pastel flowers draped over her shoulders and framing her sweet face, his heart constricted at the harsh way he had spoken to her.

In that moment, a realization hit him like a ton of bricks: Rhoda had always had his best interest at heart. Always, from the very beginning.

"Rhoda," John Mark said, his tone sounding

hoarse in his own ears. "I owe you an apology."

Looking surprised and slightly cautious, Rhoda waited with hands clasped before her, her dark eyes glimmering with hope.

"I shouldn't have spoken to you that way," John Mark confessed, taking several steps inside the sukkah to close a bit of distance between them. Even so, she still felt far away. Had she distanced herself emotionally, as well?

"I was wrong about Aurelia," John Mark continued, causing her head to come up in surprise. "In fact, I was wrong about so many things. And yet, you stood firm. You spoke the truth, even when you knew I wouldn't like it."

Bowing her head, Rhoda blinked back tears, rousing a new protectiveness within John Mark. In that moment, he vowed to do everything in his power never to hurt her again.

Composing herself with a bit of effort, Rhoda raised her modestly covered head, her clear brown eyes seeking his. "You needn't apologize, my lord," she whispered softly.

"Oh, but I must," John Mark amended, taking yet another step closer. "And, please, call me by my given name. 'My lord' sounds far too…lordly," he added, rousing a knowing smile from the maidservant. "Especially between close friends."

Rhoda nodded warmly in response.

"That being said, do you forgive me?" John Mark dared, watching her reaction closely. For some reason unbeknownst to him, he couldn't stand the thought of remaining at odds with her.

"Of course, I forgive you," Rhoda promised, shyly meeting his gaze.

"Praise God," John Mark declared, enjoying the relief flickering across her gentle features. "In that case, all is well in the world again." Turning to depart, John Mark paused before slipping from the tent, casting a gentle smile over his shoulder for the girl who hadn't given up on him.

Watching him go, Rhoda stood rooted in place, her heart pounding at the look in his eyes and the tenderness of his smile.

CHAPTER 62

Joram

Joppa

Slipping unobtrusively into Pennie's bedchamber, Joram swiftly closed the door, careful to secure the bolt behind him. This time, he didn't need any self-righteous intruders invading his personal space and private reflections. With his back against the door, Joram's cold eyes scanned the perimeter of the familiar room, almost expecting his niece to pop out from some unexpected location behind the bed or a large piece of furniture.

Relieved, he saw that he was, indeed, alone.

As morning sunlight angled in from the balcony's open double doors, an unusual glimmer caught his eye, drawing his attention. Crossing the room, he paused before the elegant canopy bed, grimly lifting the ivory bridal gown his beloved had worn for him on the day of their vows. The intricate silver beadwork glimmered and shone in the light of the morning sun.

Closing his eyes, Joram battled against memories he simultaneously cherished but also longed to forget. Pennie had looked like an angel in this gown. At the time, he'd thought he was the luckiest man alive.

What a joke, indeed.

Surveying the gown with a critical eye, Joram sought any flaws or imperfections he might bring to his niece's attention but could find nothing. She had done an impeccable job, and he couldn't argue with that annoying fact.

Fully restored, the bridal gown looked even better than the day his wife had worn it.

Reverently draping it over the bed, Joram stood back, chin in hand, noting the flawless skill with which his niece had repaired the lovely gown. She must have invested a great deal of time, effort, and yes, even *love,* into the task he had imperiously assigned to her. Joram's silver brows drew together as an unwelcome thought flitted through his mind, rousing an unfamiliar sensation of unwanted guilt.

He hadn't even offered to pay Tabitha for her time and services, and yet she had poured her heart and soul into that gown.

Just as she had done for him.

Strangely unsettled, Joram stood rooted in place, deep in troubled thought.

It was uncanny, the similarities between the exasperating young woman who had shown up, completely unwanted, upon his doorstep, and the beautiful bride he had cherished with all his heart.

***

Philip

Sychar

It felt good to be home.

Funny that he would ever consider this place "home." Jews had detested the land of Samaria and her people for centuries, and yet, Philip couldn't imagine having been sent anywhere else. God had worked mightily in Sychar.

Strolling alongside the bubbling crystal stream which had become his secret refuge for both prayer and reflection, Philip marveled at all that God had done since his and Kelila's arrival.

Suddenly, a gentle puff of wind whispered its way through swaying branches overhead and fresh blades of grass below, giving Philip pause. He sensed God's power at work, filling the air and the space around him.

Lowering himself to his knees, Philip knelt in the dewy grass, clasping his hands in awe and the deepest kind of reverence. The Spirit was moving. He could feel it in the air, in every fiber of his being.

Instantly, with the magnificence and speed of a lightning bolt, a blinding light exploded overhead, filling his entire field of vision and shaking him to his very core. Trembling in fear and awe, Philip pushed himself up on one elbow, shading his eyes from the piercing, otherworldly light, his eyes widening in inconceivable wonder as he was granted a fleeting glimpse of the power of the heavenly realm.

***

Kelila

Sychar

Placing a warm bowl of gruel on the low table, Kelila straightened, one hand resting upon the small of her back, the other cradling her baby bump which was growing steadily by the day. Philip should be returning from his hour of prayer any moment now, and he would surely be looking for his breakfast! Crossing the small room, she reached for the tray of fresh bread she had purchased from the local baker and carried it to the table, as well.

Praying silently as she went about her morning chores, Kelila sensed the Holy Spirit was preparing her for...*something.* For *what*, exactly, she couldn't be certain. She could only hope and pray that whatever that *something* happened to be, it would be welcome news!

Kelila started and nearly jumped a foot when the door slammed open entirely unexpectedly and her husband barreled into the house, his countenance shining like the rising sun.

"Philip!" Kelila chided, whirling around to face him. "You gave me and the baby a terrible fright!"

"Kelila!" Philip exclaimed, nearly sprinting across the room and grasping her firmly by the shoulders. "You'll never believe this! Never!"

"Um, Philip..." Kelila's voice trailed off as she studied her husband's shining face, deeply perplexed. "You're...you're *glowing!*"

"Of course, I am! I was just visited by an *angel!*"

"*What?*" she gasped, her mouth agape. "An angel! You're sure?"

"Unmistakably so," Philip nearly panted, his features ruddy, his eyes and countenance brighter than she'd ever seen them. "And he has given me very specific instructions. Instructions I must follow."

"Instructions?" Kelila repeated, her apprehension rising steadily. "But we have only just returned from Jerusalem—"

"It doesn't matter," Philip told her, his bearded face stretching into a broad smile. "God knows what He's doing, Kelila."

Indeed, He does, Kelila thought, purposefully allowing the Holy Spirit to settle over her, strengthening her for whatever might lie ahead. Cradling the unborn child nestled safely within her womb, Kelila realized that she, too, was nestled safely in the hands of a faithful God.

Her future was safe in His hands.

"Kelila, my darling, my love." Gazing into his wife's bright eyes now mirroring his own excitement, Philip's entire countenance reflected his determined purpose. "God has shown me what is next."

***

Tabitha

Joppa

Strolling barefoot along the sandy beach with her daughter, Tabitha smiled deeply as Laurel's chubby little legs chased after sluggish white gulls, squealing her delight when they spread their snowy wings and took flight.

"Look, Mama! Look!" Pointing a sand-caked finger heavenward, Laurel squealed her enthusiasm as the gulls soared high into the deep blue sky, their majestic silhouettes casting swiftly moving shadows upon the pearly white sand below.

"I see, sweetheart," Tabitha smiled, warmed by her daughter's innocence and appreciation for the unrivaled beauty of God's creation.

Rushing toward the shoreline, Laurel giggled excitedly as swift-moving waves tickled her toes and swirled about her ankles. Utterly delighted, the child splashed happily in the lapping waves.

Pausing a few short paces from her enthusiastic toddler, Tabitha crossed her arms, shaking her head in fond amusement as she watched her daughter play. She couldn't imagine a more beautiful scene than this, with the golden sun, in all its glory and brilliance, rising steadily in a cloudless sky and reflecting off the shimmering turquoise waters of the boundless Mediterranean.

For the earth will be filled with the knowledge of the glory of the Lord, as the waters cover the sea, Tabitha thought, marveling at the truth of the unchanging Word of God. Truly, the knowledge of God's great love for the world as demonstrated in the selfless sacrifice of His beloved Son was now taking the world by storm, touching hearts and transforming lives. And by the mercy of God, she, too, was privileged to participate in the great commission.

Lips tipping in a whimsical smile, Tabitha considered all that Stephanos' incredible sacrifice had set into motion. If only he could see the thousands upon thousands who had already received Christ as a result! And there was no doubt in her mind that there remained many more to come. As Jesus Himself had predicted, the fields were, indeed, ripe for harvest.

Joining her daughter in the gently lapping waves, Tabitha scooped the little girl up, lifting her high overhead. Squealing in merriment, Laurel spread her chubby arms, mimicking the majestic gulls in flight.

True, Tabitha thought, gently lowering her daughter and chuckling as the little one scampered off, sending little splashes of cold water high into the air. *My life has unfolded far differently than I expected.* Considering her dear friends scattered all over the province, she realized that they, too, had experienced the same bittersweet phenomenon. Surely Mary, her former mistress, had not expected to lose her seemingly healthy husband and to raise their adventurous son alone, standing firm while battling against forces of darkness in the holy city. Nor had Kelila and Philip planned to leave their home and family behind to plant a church in the unlikeliest—and possibly most dangerous—of regions. And she, Tabitha, certainly had not expected to surrender her beloved Stephanos into the arms of God so soon after their sacred union, nor could she have possibly imagined how his martyrdom would influence the salvation of the entire world for all eternity. And she certainly couldn't have guessed that she would be called to the seaport town of Joppa to reach the lost, the destitute, and the brokenhearted.

No, this wasn't the life she had planned, nor was it the life she would have chosen. But it *was* a beautiful life, a sacred calling. Rather like the intricate patterns upon a breathtaking tapestry, every thread of her life had been purposefully and skillfully woven together by the loving hand of the Master Weaver, intent upon the very best for His children, orchestrating the salvation of the world.

Casting aside her head covering, Tabitha lifted her face heavenward, relishing the sun's warmth upon her skin and the foamy waves swirling about her bare feet. Reveling in the glory of the moment, her senses were filled with the salty air, the soothing sound of ocean waves lapping upon the beach, and her daughter's childish giggles. Opening her eyes, she marveled at the breathless majesty of her surroundings mirroring the incomparable beauty of a life fully submitted to God.

What an unspeakable comfort to know that her future was safe in God's hands! Now and forever, she was eager to embrace the life He had in store for her, thrilling at the unimaginable victories that might be just around the corner. For Jesus had entrusted His people with a sacred task, a holy calling, and she could scarcely believe that she was part of it!

Soon, perhaps very soon, the entire world would know the name of Jesus, and His grace and glory would indeed fill the earth just as the mighty waters covered the sea!

A LOOK AT BOOK SEVEN: GRACE PREVAILING

Experience the captivating portrayal of an epic battle between good and evil in this compelling tale of faith and triumph.

The saving gospel of Jesus Christ has exploded in Jerusalem, Samaria, and beyond—transforming thousands of lives. As faithful believers continue carrying out the Great Commission, Saul of Tarsus seethes and resolves to hunt down every last one of them.

Warned of Saul's murderous plans, the noble Mary rallies her fellow believers to pray for the hate-crazed Pharisee. And despite the great odds against them, she senses spiritual forces at work. In Joppa, Tabitha ministers to her unbelieving uncle. Sensing his declining health and determined to stop at nothing, her faithful witness touches many lives along the way, even that of a handsome young merchant named Adam.

In Sychar, Kelila braces herself as her husband, Philip, is called to traveling evangelism. Though she supports his mission, she can't help but fear that his ministry will keep him away and unable to welcome their first child into the world.

Grace Prevailing *is a powerful re-telling of one of the most destiny-altering moments in Christian history, showcasing the resilience of the human spirit in the face of persecution and the transformative power of unwavering faith.*

AVAILABLE NOW ON AMAZON

ABOUT THE AUTHOR

Rachael C. Duncan is a passionate follower of Christ. Her goal is to reach as many people as possible for the sake of Christ and His kingdom. She believes that God has gifted each of His children with different gifts to be used to strengthen the body of Christ and fulfill the Great Commission. (Matt. 28:19-20; 1 Cor. 12)

Rachael was blessed to be raised in a strong Christian home, and she accepted Jesus Christ as her Lord and Savior at a very early age. Since then, she has determined to live her life in accordance to His Word and to share the love of Christ through the gift of writing.

Rachael has been passionate about writing since she was a small child. She especially loved writing plays and short stories. At the age of fourteen, she wrote her first play, which was performed as a dinner theatre production by a local school.

She has been actively involved in both women's and children's ministries for over a decade. Currently, she enjoys teaching a weekly girls' Bible study, writing plays for a local homeschool group, and participating in local ministry outreaches for women and children.

Rachael currently resides in Texas with her husband and their first "child"—a playful rescue puppy named Riley! In addition to her writing, she is an enthusiastic "keeper of the home" and "helpmeet" as well as being actively involved in ministering to the women and children God has placed in her life. (Titus 2:3-5; Gen. 2:20-23)

www.ingramcontent.com/pod-product-compliance
Lightning Source LLC
Chambersburg PA
CBHW011649010726
47496CB00012B/3003